GRAVEDIGGER

Michael-Israel Jarvis

Booktrope Editions
Seattle WA 2015

Copyright 2012, 2015 Michael-Israel Jarvis

This work is licensed under a Creative Commons Attribution-Noncommercial-No Derivative Works 3.0 Unported License.

Attribution — You must attribute the work in the manner specified by the author or licensor (but not in any way that suggests that they endorse you or your use of the work).
Noncommercial — You may not use this work for commercial purposes.
No Derivative Works — You may not alter, transform, or build upon this work.

Inquiries about additional permissions should be directed to: info@booktrope.com

Cover Design by Amalia Chitulescu
Edited by Josie Cruz

Previously self-published as *Gravedigger*, 2012

This is a work of fiction. Names, characters, places, brands, media, and incidents are either the product of the author's imagination or are used fictitiously. Any resemblance to similarly named places or to persons living or deceased is unintentional.

Print ISBN 978-1-5137-0310-7
EPUB ISBN 978-1-5137-0361-9
Library of Congress Control Number: 2015915773

ACKNOWLEDGMENTS

Thank you, Katie, my beloved wife. Your common sense and endless patience, not to mention your love, have kept me sane.

Thank you to my family.

Thank you to the deviantArt community! Without you, I would not have begun *Gravedigger*. I certainly would not have completed this book without the continued support and friendship of many of you.

A massive thanks to my editor, Josie Cruz, who has not only polished and honed *Gravedigger* into the book it was meant to be, but improved my writing itself.

Additional thanks to Amalia Chitulescu, for her beautiful cover art, and to Cheri Norwood, our proofreader.

Gratuitously immense thanks go to Dane Cobain, my Book Manager at Booktrope, fellow author, friend and much of the reason that I am now a published author.

Jay Knioum / Memnalar, thank you for the attention you brought *Gravedigger* when it was just a few chapters long.

Daniel Stamp, thank you so much for your support; you remain a true friend.

To the McNerney clan, Bryan, Cate, Flora and Jamie:

You are much loved. Thank you for your hospitality, past, present and future.

This book is about brotherhood and is dedicated to my brothers, Simon Jarvis and Joseph Jarvis.

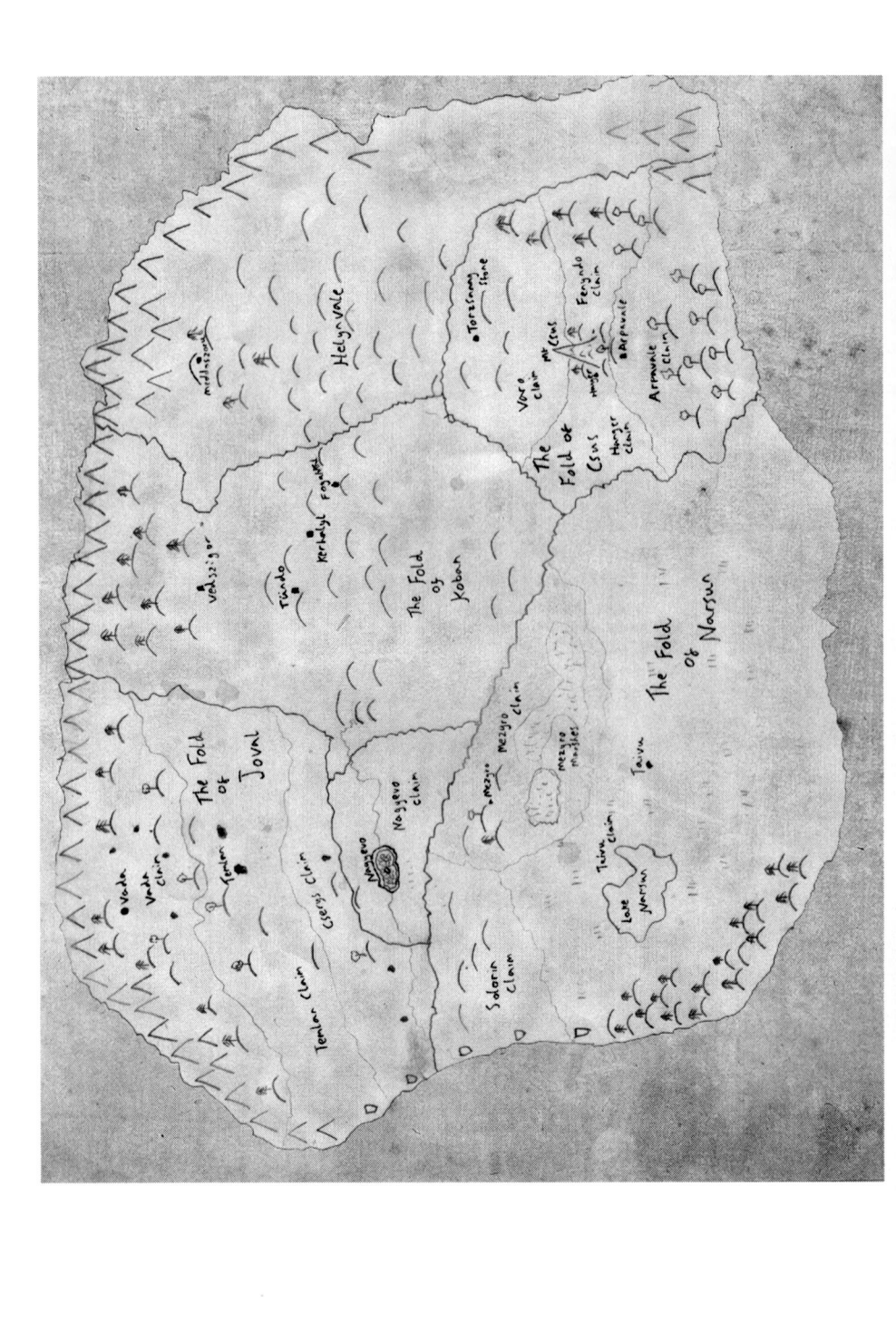

PROLOGUE

SHOW ME THE WAY.
No light shone in the passage to the surface. The wall of rock was black. Keresur could only sense it with his hands, running his fingers across the rough stone with feverish desperation. He had no time for caution anymore. His quarry had escaped, and gods knew where he had gone.

Behind Keresur came the sounds of combat, distant shouts. Figures moved in the dense emptiness back the way he had come, seeing without their eyes, fighting with spear, with sword, with bare hands. Keresur muttered to himself and increased his pace, listening to the voice in his head.

The voice that some of the fighters obeyed.

The voice in his head was the only reason they hadn't torn him apart days before. As for the others, it was the reason they wanted him dead. Perhaps worse.

The cooling of the air around him suggested that he neared the opening to the rest of the world. The things he had discovered deep beneath the mountainside were amazing, but he still thirsted for fresh air. It had been too long. The part of him that wasn't the voice couldn't bear the stifling warmth down there, nor the blue light that glowed everywhere, coming through his eyelids when he tried to sleep, while the bodies moved around him in the gloom.

"Best work you've ever done," he muttered to himself. Or was that the voice speaking? It was true in any case. What he'd discovered had the potential to change Valo forever.

When he stumbled onto the open slope, the moonlight gleamed so brightly it hurt his eyes. Rags of cloud flew black and silver above. Below, more clouds formed an argent sea over the rumpled landscape. The thin air was nearly as bad to breathe as the air under the mountain, but sweeter, so much sweeter.

A group of five men stood blocking his path down the slope. They all looked very thin in the moonlight, their bodies strung with rags of cloth and mail. Their spears gave Keresur pause, though. The voice had given him power, but a spear in his chest would still kill him.

Or worse.

"Get them away." He narrowed his eyes at them, crooking his fingers into claws and raising his hands. "Get them gone. Leave me alone! Out of the way!"

"No, trueborn." Their leader spoke in a deep, hoarse voice. "Our king has gone. You will not be permitted to follow him. You've done your damage to us. It ends here."

Their clothing was not the only thing that hung from them in ribbons. They had missing or torn flesh, bare in places to the breastbone, some with flensed shins, white bone showing through in the moonlight. Some of the wounds appeared fresh. But blood did not flow from the tears and gashes, did not pump through their bony limbs. As Keresur looked, he realised that the voice gave him a sense of superiority he had never felt before. Uttermost confidence swelled in his chest where his heart beat steadily.

What do you have to fear from them? They're already dead. Already dead. Grinning widely, the man extended his arms toward the five corpses.

They spread themselves out, wary of his crooked hands.

"Hah! You were born dead!" the man raged, and the energy flowing in his living blood began to translate into usable power. The moon shone down on his bald head, reflecting from his crazed eyes. The wind, unhindered on the broad hillside, played with his dirty robes, whipping them around him in a promise of conflict.

The leader of the dead men said nothing. As one, they levelled their spears and charged.

Force and thunder shook the mountainside. Keresur's hands twisted and pulled at the air, as if ripping the fabric of the world. Around him, the dead warriors were thrown about like dolls. Some smashed to the ground, as if crushed by an invisible hand; others were thrown from the mountainside, tumbling over the rocks. After the destruction ended, only the wind remained. Keresur went on his way, barely delayed by their intervention.

One survivor from among the dead sat in twisted ruin, legs broken beneath him. He was aware that his spine was broken. Much of the flesh on his thin frame had been flayed from him. He could not feel the pain of the wounds, only the ache in his chest, a sense of loss, of sorrow. The survivor's leader was dead, body broken in two, void of the unnatural life that had once made it animate. The survivor cradled his leader's head in his lap. If it had been possible for him to cry, he would have.

Looking up the slope, the survivor could see figures coming out of the mouth of the mountain, creeping between the shadows of the moonlit clouds. He recognised them with a resigned acceptance. They were the ones who had helped the trueborn man escape.

The dead man squeezed his leader's skeletal shoulder and gently lay the body down at his side. The Damned were coming closer. He knew that they were coming to destroy him.

The survivor closed his one remaining eye and turned his face upward toward the moon. As the enemy dead descended on him, blades in hand, he managed to calmly hum the fragment of a tune through his cracked lips. It was the last thing he heard before he left his battered body behind and empty, fleeing back beneath the mountainside, nothing more than a shred of consciousness.

Keresur walked south, practically insensate, muttering to himself and the voice in his head. He focused on returning to where his discoveries would be appreciated for what they were. And then he would find a way to track down the escaped king.

He would put what he had learned to use.

ONE

THE BODY OF MAGISTRATE RAFELL lay beside the hole it would soon inhabit. The family, of which there were few, and the friends, of which there were fewer, had already deserted the graveside. They left Graves and his apprentice to nail down the lid and lower the magistrate into the earth.

Rain fell. Graves glanced up at the weeping sky. "Rain's puddling. Good wood, that. Going to spoil fast, mind."

Perin, his fifteen-year-old apprentice gravedigger, nodded simply to acknowledge that he had heard.

Graves shook his head, looking down the slight incline of the hill toward the iron cemetery gates through which Magistrate Rafell's nearest and dearest had hurriedly left.

"'Tain't right, Perin, my boy. Family should wait 'til the body is proper interred. 'Tain't right, leavin' like that."

Perin said nothing. He didn't consider himself an intelligent boy, but he knew well enough about Erdhanger, a little nowhere town sitting with its graveyard tucked in against the forested hills. Like all the other towns and villages nearby, Csus, the great mountain, overshadowed it. Small towns were quick to lose their secrets, and Perin knew that the most disliked man in the settlement had been Magistrate Rafell.

The lawman had persecuted all manner of smugglers and vagrants. The smugglers provided cheap luxuries from the bazaars of far-off Nagyevo, the fortified city across the plains to the West. The vagrants had provided diversion as entertainers, storytellers, mystics.

Rafell had taken his duties as a magistrate of the Tacnimag very seriously. The Tacnimag mages were the centralised government of the Claimfold, but rarely did they involve themselves with the details of provincial life. Rafell had chosen to ignore this convention, had waged his personal war and won.

The result was a settlement lacking in both luxuries and culture. Perin had little interest in this, not being able to afford the first, and not seeing the necessity of the second. His life consisted of digging graves for Graves until Graves died, and then he would take Graves's name. That was all there was. He had no high ambition in him.

Graves shook his head as he shovelled earth. "He'd be up and living if he 'adn't closed the brothel, I reckon. That was the last crack in the ice. Towns like Erdhanger can't keep without one."

Perin had heard that a client of the condemned brothel had decided that the best thing to do, all things considered, was introduce the magistrate to the sharp end of a log-wedge. He had fled the town the night after. No one had felt inclined to hunt him down.

The brothel had officially opened again, and a company of actors had appeared, as if from nowhere, to resume their crude but much-liked performances. The townspeople loved tragedies. In their reckoning, Rafell's death seemed more of a comedy. Family aside, only two people in Erdhanger felt able to show respect to the lawman's last remains. Respect, as Graves would often say, is part of the gravedigger's work.

Perin knew that Graves was in no state to take advantage of brothels, nor was he in any way a patron of the arts. The change in the town had completely passed Graves by, and in any case, he disliked and feared people who still had a pulse.

The old man made the finishing touches to Rafell's grave.

By tomorrow, the faces of the clients—Rafell's wealthy widow and a disinterested cousin—would have faded from Graves's memory. But he would never forget the name of the man buried in plot number eleven, for that name was inscribed on a cheap tablet of stone, and written in the enormous graveyard tome. Clients were forgotten. But "guests" were marked down and remembered forever.

Perin felt a measure of contained sorrow for the unloved man now buried six feet beneath the topsoil. It was an emotion he felt for any body that came through the iron gates, destined for a wooden bed and a quiet resting place.

The sorrow was somehow inappropriate for someone in his work, he knew. He'd tried to suppress all feelings while working a job like this, but the emotion was a poetry that would not leave him and he could not escape. Perin couldn't write, and he could only read enough to tell who was buried where.

He sighed deeply. He didn't understand the people in the town any more than Graves did. Their politics and infighting were beyond him. He cared nothing for the theatrical troupes, nor for the whores. He found the plays unrealistic, and he did not get the jokes. And as for women, although Perin was the perfect age to have an interest, they were, to him, very much like theatre. They did not hold his interest any longer than it took for him to note that they were attractive.

And they thought little of him.

The boy picked up his shovel and his edging spade and carried them to Graves's hut, walking in the footsteps of the old man.

The rainfall pattered persistently on the sodden earth heap, making the overgrown grass around the cemetery dance. In Graves's cabin, Perin lit the oil lamp, casting golden light out into the wind and rain through the single-shuttered window. It was just light enough outside to see the dirty brown clouds drag themselves across the grey sky. Perin couldn't see any signs of the sun, but it was surely low now.

For a while, he stood at the window and peered out into the growing dark. The firs shook and swayed in the heavy weather. They loomed over the crowded little graveyard from the high banks on which they stood, seeming to Perin like a gathering of darkly caped giants in the failing light. He shivered and closed the shutters.

Perin walked directly to the butcher's shop. He kept his head down, knowing that if other apprentices or children saw him, he would be easy game. He was no one's friend. Those that kept house with the dead were strange to start with, and nobody was as strange in Erdhanger as Perin Foundling—except perhaps Graves.

The butcher silently cut and wrapped the meat that was Graves's weekly order while his wife attempted to make conversation with Perin.

"You know, we can have our boy make delivery each week, seeing as how Master Graves always wants the same thing. It's only a little walk up the hill, after all."

The butcher gave his spouse a dark look, but Perin was already shaking his head.

"That's all right. Thank you, Mistress Hoer. Graves... Master Graves says I should get the walk into town for my health and wellbeing, Mistress Hoer. I'm happy to come for it."

Mistress Hoer watched him. Perin tried to meet her gaze without looking directly in her eyes, disconcerted by her interest. She was unusually kind and always looked at him like that, as if trying to imagine what he'd look like without the dried mud on his clothes.

He said goodbye politely and left with the cloth bundle under his arm. The order was always the same. Chopped mutton and some pig's liver. The meat was in small portions, but the parsimonious gravedigger would make them last the week, with nothing else to eat in between midday meals, save for hard bread that he got cheap from the baker and maybe thin cabbage soup to go with it.

Perin closed the iron gate of the graveyard behind him and stepped up the poorly kept path of stones cut into the bank. He followed the path to the cabin, walking through the plots. The gravestones passed by on either side. Autumn's first fallen leaves had been blown in from the lower hillside, and the air smelled fresh and clean. The firs on the higher bank hardly stirred today.

Perin found himself humming a melody. It had slipped into his head, and he had not noticed the beguiling notes passing his lips until he heard a loud, incredibly deep voice boom out from in front of Graves's cabin, "Where did he hear that tune?"

Graves stood in a nervous posture that he always adopted when dealing with those that still breathed. It was not he that had spoken, but the enormous stranger that stood next to him. Perin was so surprised that he did not register what the voice said. He almost dropped the meat.

The stranger was very broad across the shoulders, with legs like the trunks of young trees. His clothing was a rumpled canvas, vividly dyed dark red and blue, seemingly without a fixed pattern. His hood was up. Nothing of his face could be seen beneath its red covering.

The stranger strode forward, two strides to three or four of Perin's, removing his hood and leaning in with urgency, looking down at the apprentice from a height of nearly nine feet. Perin fumbled with the package of meat out of shock but managed to catch it before it could hit the cracked paving at his feet.

Beneath the hood, the stranger's face was dark-skinned and monstrous, almost bull-like. There was an eagle-like wisdom in his large eyes. A broad, strong-lipped mouth—the lips themselves a dark, black-red—concealed large teeth, clean and white but frightening to Perin. The bull-like effect was caused by the large gold ring in the stranger's flared nostrils, and the pale horns that pushed through his thicket of black hair curved outward slightly from just above his temples. They were some seven or eight inches long.

"I said, where did you hear that tune?" The voice had an almost melodious quality itself, now that Perin heard it up close. The creature looked down at him impatiently, but without aggression.

"Come now, boy, haven't you ever seen a prigon before?"

Perin shook his head dumbly, aware that his hat had fallen off, clutching the meat bundle to his chest. The prigon chuckled like thunder and crouched down to retrieve Perin's hat from the ground. He settled it on the apprentice's head with a large, dark-nailed hand consisting of four broad fingers and a thumb. Perin noticed the nearly ordinary hands and fixated on them, as if to pretend that he couldn't see the person's strange face and pale horns.

"I am Kesairl. From Helynvale. I am conducting business with your…" He looked back at Graves with a question in his tone.

"He's 'prenticed to me," Graves supplied gruffly.

"Indeed." The prigon tribesman fixed Perin with a smile, which, although terrifying, forced Perin to remember his well-learned manners.

"It's nice to meet you, Kesairl Prigon from Helynvale. I'm Perin Foundling, apprentice to Master Graves. At…at your service."

The prigon raised his heavy brows, still smiling.

"Indeed! Well said, boy. Though be careful. Putting yourself at someone's service is a heavy risk and far more than a figure of speech. And 'prigon' is not the name of my family, nor my tribe, but the name of all my people."

Kesairl bowed deeply, seeming to have forgotten the tune that had caused such a reaction moments before. Then, with a smile, he returned quickly to Graves's side and began to talk to him once more.

With a faltering bow, Perin quickly carried the meat into Graves's cabin where he placed it in the stone chamber at the back. The space had been quarried out of the bank against which the cabin stood, with shelves going some way back into the earth. Those on the right were sparsely occupied by Graves's treasures and money, as well as his perishable food supplies. The shelves on the left were much more crowded by the collected and catalogued bones of former inhabitants of the graveyard. Each bone within had been buried long before Graves had finished his own apprenticeship. The plots where they had once lain were filled now with new "guests."

Perin had never been bothered by bones. In fact, the familiarity of the clean, white, scrupulously tagged femurs on his immediate left served to calm the fright put in him by the appearance of the prigon. He knew little about their people, save that they were considered a respectable race, allied to the men of the Claimfold. Technically, they were also allied with the ruling Tacnimag.

Perin knew more than a little history, as Graves was an amateur student of the discipline. It pleased the gravedigger deep down because very few of the people in it were alive.

The Claimfold had been founded a long time before even Graves's grandfather was born. The farmsteads and settlements that had been planted by mankind in the unspoiled hills and forests of Valo had come under attack by hordes of wire-furred creatures known as drizen. They were wild-eyed, broad-snouted, and, according to legend, ate the men, women and children that they killed.

It had seemed certain that mankind would be wiped from the face of Valo. But another monstrous looking people had emerged, Perin had learned from Graves, dressed not in crude plates of armour like the drizen, but in thick, studded leather, caped and hooded. Noble. Fearless. The famous human warrior, Hanger, had fought alongside them, and returned to the city that would one day become Nagyevo, accompanied by an envoy. The message was received, and the two races entered into alliance.

Man gave the prigon people trade and metalwork, and prigon gave mankind education in magic. Each race had proved adept at mastering the gifts of the other.

In a way, the alliance between man and prigon was responsible for the creation of the Tacnimag. Magic, for those that mastered it, made men who could rule unchallenged.

Perin made his way back into the one-roomed cabin, closing the oaken door to the crypt. He sat in his chair by the door, hoping to catch some of his master's conversation with Kesairl.

"...Foundling is an unusual name. What kind of family are called that in your culture?" Any guilt Perin might have had at eavesdropping on his master vanished. They were talking about him.

Graves coughed, seemingly surprised at the turn in the conversation. "It's the name given to any lad, or lass, that's born from the house of pleasure in town. If a girl there gets taken with child, then she'll have it, and leave it where she will, if she wants to work still..."

"You mean the place where females...women mate with men for money?" A slightly disapproving tone. Graves did not reply but must have nodded, for Kesairl continued, "I see. So he never knew his sire or his dam. Hard for a child to find his way with such a beginning."

"Well, his way now is digging graves, if you'll pardon me bluntness, Master Kesairl."

"No. Pardon me. You must be anxious to return to business. Now, I know you do not normally serve people of my race here, but size will not be an issue. It is not a prigon that needs burial. The plot need be no larger than for any man. All that I require is secrecy on your part, and naturally on the boy's."

"That won't be a problem. He don't talk all that much; he's got no friends. Nor 'ave I, for that matter. Not many wants to make friendly with a keeper of the dead!"

"All people, be they man or prigon, or something else entirely, should know friendship," the prigon intoned solemnly.

A stab of regret hit Perin hard. It was an emotion he had not known before. Friendship. Perin had known loneliness all his life, but never had he felt it as keenly. It made a harsh, bittersweet song in his chest.

"Well, as you say, Master Kesairl," the gravedigger muttered gruffly outside the door. "Bring the departed through the woods and down the bank then, if you don't want watching eyes. I'll 'ave locked the gates already."

"Very good, Master Graves. I shall return then, at nightfall on Seconday of this coming week. Until then?"

"Aye, until then. It…it has to be the full moon, does it? Only I don't normally do burials under a full moon…"

"Meaningless superstition, my friend. I am afraid no other night will do. Goodbye."

"Fare thee well then, Master Kesairl."

Perin listened to Kesairl's heavy footfalls die away, not in the direction of the path into town, but toward the bank and the fir trees. Graves's feet stamped at the doorstep to kick off mud, and then he entered, grumbling under his breath.

"We'll have the liver tonight then, lad. All of it. We'll be getting paid very well come next Seconday so we can afford to feast for once. C'mon now, up with you and get it! That's right, the sooner we cook, the sooner we eat…" He tailed off for a moment, rubbing the cold out of his hands.

"Funny fellow, that prigon. Not that they aren't all funny in their way. Wanted to talk 'bout you. Odd. You must 'ave got 'is attention with that tune you was humming, lad. Heard it in town did you? Come on now, find the pan, and there's an onion there. Look lively, I want to eat…"

Perin set to work at once, on his knees, turning over the fire in the little stove. Soon, the cabin filled with warmth and the smell of frying. Graves went to close the door and the shutters, hiding the night sky from view.

After they'd eaten, Perin went and opened the shutters while Graves dozed. He leaned on the sill, thinking about Kesairl's promised return and wondering, perhaps for the first time, what strange and distant places the moonlight might also be shining on, beyond the bulk of Csus and its wooded hills.

And the moon was nearly full…

TWO

THE WEEK PROGRESSED, eerily quiet.

No one in Erdhanger died, no landscaping had been appointed and no one commissioned any work for Graves's chisel. This would normally have been cause for worry, for quiet periods meant poor eating. However, the mysterious business offered them by the prigon Kesairl allowed them both some leisure.

At last, the time came. The day was nearly spent. The forest birds came in to roost, rooks filling the air with their harsh cawing. Perin could taste smoke on the air as families throughout Erdhanger began to light fires against the autumnal chill.

As Perin walked up the slope to the black iron gates of the graveyard, the grass crunched beneath his feet, the dying greenery already crisp with an early frost. The iron of the gate chilled his fingers as he closed it behind him, remembering to bring the chain across and close the lock. Only Graves kept the key to open it.

Graves had been into town earlier in the day to buy onions and a little butter. He grumbled contentedly when Perin entered the cabin, stamping his cold feet and rubbing his hands together in the sudden warmth. The tiny fireplace crackled with blazing wood.

After they had each eaten — hot, savoury mutton with fried onions, accompanied by a piece of buttered, fire-warmed bread — the two gravediggers put on their heavy coats and hats and stamped out into the cold. They each held a pewter mug of boiled water, which sent steam rushing up past their cold faces to vanish in the dark.

They didn't have to wait long. Fully visible under the abundantly full moon, the bulky figure of Kesairl emerged from the trees. He strode toward them, jumping down the sandy bank into the graveyard. A figure followed him slowly, moving with awkward heistancy. He was swathed in a great deal of loose cloth.

Kesairl halted beside the grave that Graves had dug unaided earlier that day, much to the concern of Perin, who had not been there to meticulously edge the hole with his sharp new edging spade.

"Greetings by moonlight, Master Graves, young Master Perin. I hope you are both well." Kesairl's voice rolled out above the subtle noises of the night.

"Oh, aye, and yourselves, too, we 'ope," said Graves, peering at the cloaked stranger beside the prigon, "I imagine you two've got the recently departed in the woods. Well, if it wants burying, we may as well get started, as you don't want peepers."

Kesairl hesitated for a moment, brow furrowed. "Well, I'm afraid the one that wants burying, as you accurately put it, is not so recently departed."

"Ah. Fine. S'to be expected I suppose, if you've travelled far. S'all right, Master Kesairl. Me and the boy aren't unaccustomed to a bit of decay."

"You misunderstand me, good man Graves. The one I speak of has been dead for a very long time, indeed. He was born that way—if birth is the right way to put it. Allow me to introduce—nay—to present my companion."

The prigon smiled, white teeth gleaming in the dark to match the moon. His arm gestured to the shrouded figure beside him. With a strange, jerking motion, the figure unwrapped the main cloak from his body, revealing himself to be exceedingly thin. He was, in fact, skeletal. Skin clung to his frame, close as a glove, undamaged but as pale as the prigon's teeth.

As pale as the full moon.

His wan, skull-like face stared mournfully at them. His head was devoid of hair of any sort, though it was crowned with a circlet of silver. His eyes were pale, but not empty or decayed, and Graves and Perin both knew the eyes were the first thing to go. Soulful meaning radiated behind the orbs, proof somehow of the creature's being. Aside from that, and the wonderful preservation of the body, he was quite dead.

"I am aware that I am quite troublesome to look upon." The creature spoke in a voice that made Perin think of the way fallen leaves whispered across the ground underfoot. He watched the dry mouth speak, in shocked fascination. It moved very little, yet produced the words distinctly. "I am not…conventionally alive; but please, I am not to be feared."

Graves seemed to think otherwise. "Undead!" He growled, hands gripping the handle of his spade, knuckles almost as white as the dead man's.

Perin stared.

The undead man nodded uncertainly and then bowed. Graves considered for a moment, fear and amazement clashing.

Kesairl watched, not speaking a word.

"All right. So. What's you wanting on your stone, then?" Graves muttered at last, shifting his stance.

Kesairl smiled, seeming to appreciate the human's return to composure.

The undead man spoke. "A marker stone? How thoughtful! I am Medrivar, if you need a name to engrave."

"King Medrivar," Kesairl corrected his companion in a soft tone.

"Just because that is who I am, it does not mean I need always to announce it," the undead man returned with a sharp reprimand.

Graves coughed. "What do you want under the name, Your Majesty?"

"I would very much enjoy the phrase, 'At rest', as it will be no falsehood."

"Sort of, 'Back in a little while', then?"

Both the undead king and the prigon chuckled at Graves's joke. The old gravedigger smiled. Here was a person who had qualities Perin knew Graves admired, in particular the complete lack of a heartbeat. In some ways, this was familiar ground. Graves often talked to the dead. They'd never spoken back.

"I will need the plot for a year. It is, of course, important that I am interred and raised at full moon. Kesairl will serve me very well in performing the rites, I am sure."

"They are not difficult," the prigon said. He winked at Perin, who found he could no longer keep his silence.

"This is...amazing! Where did you come from?"

The undead king gave a crooked smile. "I am from the North. But I get the sense that your question meant more than that. You have an inquiring mind. Very good. You would know the secrets of the undead, young man of breath and blood?"

"I would." Perin said, still trying to grasp the reality of the situation.

The emaciated king folded into a sitting position and closed his blank eyes for a moment. His eyelids were thin and papery.

Perin leaned on his edging spade, feeling it sink into the frost-hardened earth.

Medrivar smiled again. "I will be brief, but this is an important story, so listen closely."

"I was once a thought. Existence, merely a fragment of being, borne on currents of magic through the North, so long ago. There is a great range of mountains up there, each as large as the mount you call Csus. They are armoured with ice and cloaked with snow, snow deeper than a man stands tall.

"The plains below these mountains were the haunts and territories of the first men of Valo, ancients long since lost, buried in great quantity, with wealth and finery arranged around them. They are buried beneath the hills there, and all their descendants that remain have forgotten their gravesite.

"Many enchantments were placed on the burial places of that land. Magic runs strong in the rocks there, and by whatever power, the catacombs are more than just tombs. I was drawn there, and others like me, by the power in the rock and the call of the thrones under the earth…"

Medrivar tailed off, looking at his audience to ensure they understood the significance of the thrones.

"One night, there was a full moon, as now. The powers in the earth and air were at their strongest. So I…became. My essence gathered to itself the dust of an ancient king, lying as he was amongst the belongings that he had sought to take with him to the next world. Whether he reached there or not, I do not know. I am not he. He is gone. But his body was mine to use." The king raised his bony hands, as if in emphasis.

"As soon as I had a body, I slept. When I awoke, perhaps a year, perhaps a hundred years later, I had generated the form which had once been worn by that dead king. He no longer needed it. I was complete, a strong man, knit together by magic. Gold hair, I have when I'm fresh. Strong arms, fast legs. Yet my heart never beat, my blood never flowed. I do not need to breathe. Look! No mist in this cold air, not from my mouth. See how it gushes from yours?"

Perin blew out and watched the vapour vanish.

"Out of respect to the long-passed king, I chose to guard the strange ruin. Once, maybe it was a temple, or a tomb for kings. Perhaps a prison. It was a rich and wonderful place beneath the mountainside. I frightened off many, killed others, became a terror to looters and excavators. They came at me with sword, spear and magic, even sorcery, which is worse. Where I was pierced or cut, my flesh was damaged, but I did not feel pain or tire under blows. And in one sacred chamber, my throne room, I was able to regenerate my wounds.

"Others like me came out of the hills. Soon I had an army. Looters learned to stay away. But the living were not a lasting foe. They forgot us and passed on. From my own kind came the new foes. They fight for their own throne, for the right to conquer the living. I led my Bright Dead against the damned in those mist-ridden hills for many, many years."

Perin stared, the images of the tale running through his mind like lightning. Medrivar leaned forward and grinned, seeing that he had the boy entranced.

"The Damned, I call them—if there are any gods to damn them, as I believe there must be. They fight my Bright Dead even now, far beyond where most men or prigon travel. The only living beings to dare those slopes," he said, pointing a gnarly finger, "are the drizen, and raveners, and wolves. Until this year."

Here the king paused, examining his skeletal hands. Silver rings shone in the moonlight. Although they should have slipped off with ease, they did not, as much part of the undead warrior king as his skin.

"Are your dead winning?" Perin asked breathlessly. Medrivar bowed his head.

"I know not. I can no longer lay to rest in the throne room where we go to heal. The ground there has been sullied. Sorcery. A man, a living man has been...experimenting."

"Who?"

"I don't know his name. I did not know it was possible. Spirits are involved now. Not the dead, mind you. They depart and do not return. I mean instead what I once was, a creature without physical frame. And powerful ones at that. I don't know who called on them. But sorcerers need their sources. And it seems my army is without such powerful friends."

Medrivar sighed. "The world is changed. I must rest and return renewed. So, I befriended one of the living—Kesairl. He has been preparing my way to a safe burial. Mankind and his own people must not know of my existence. The dead are feared, irrationally, viscerally. Desperately. You must know of this fear. You are keepers of the dead yourselves."

Graves and Perin glanced at each other and nodded.

Kesairl shifted at the graveside.

"It grows late. Medrivar, Your Highness, let us inter you soon. I fear to tarry."

"Yes, yes, you are right, faithful Kesairl, right as ever. It is time for me to rest. When I am woken, I will be whole again. I will at least look young and alive. I will go and talk with the magi that sit on the council of the Tacnimag. I may be able to gain their support. Mages who can defeat the sorcery. I believe that what happens under the northern hills is important. The Meddoszoru is a place of balance. Without balance, Valo suffers." He winked at Perin. "There. Now you know all about me, young Perin. I know you will keep your word. Secrecy! Kesairl trusts you."

With a sigh, the king rose to his knees, swung his legs out over the edge of his grave, and let himself down into it. He looked up, smiling with thin lips. "I have no need of a coffin, and this is a well-dug grave. Kesairl?"

The prigon nodded. He crouched beside the hole, the moonlight catching his horns. A faint, colourless glow rose from his upraised palms and flickered on his forehead. His nose ring seemed to catch the glow as well, and now Perin saw that it was engraved with tiny sigils. Kesairl spoke.

"Dead, yet valiant, dead that serves the light. Sleep beneath the full bright moon, sleep this night. Cast away worries; cast off fear. Embrace the quiet oblivion; let none come near."

Medrivar raised a bare brow at the prigon. "There was no need to make it rhyme."

Kesairl frowned. "Hush. You're interrupting. I speak as a friend, this blessing, over he that now takes this rest. Let him rise to take up the fight once more. Until then, let him sleep now in this sanctified ground. Loved comrade, take your rest now." Kesairl's hand trembled and closed.

King Medrivar closed his eyes. As the rite took effect, he murmured, "Goodnight." He stiffened, falling back in an almost languid motion, landing softly as a leaf in the bottom of his temporary grave.

"So it is done." The prigon straightened, a softness of his tri-coloured eyes betraying the strength of his emotion. He handed a pair of leather purses to Graves.

"Here is your pay, Master Graves. Use it well. I will see you again in a year's time. Goodbye to you both. May the powers of light watch over you."

The prigon mage bowed his bull-like head, the nose ring catching the moonlight. He glanced back at where Medrivar lay, blissfully still. "Goodnight, Medrivar."

Giving a final nod to them both, Kesairl walked away. With a quick, easy movement, he hauled himself up the steep bank into the fir woods and soon melted away into the dark between the trees. Perin couldn't help but watch him go.

"Well." Graves shook his head in wonderment. Then, with a look that seemed to indicate a return of the real world, he set about shovelling earth into Medrivar's grave. Very soon, the king's form disappeared beneath a layer of dark soil.

After they had finished with the grave, Graves examined the two leather pouches Kesairl had left them. He pocketed the larger one without opening it and with a magnanimous smile, handed Perin his own pay.

The gravedigger's apprentice gaped, as gold and silver coins tumbled into his shaking palm. They were Claimic coins, menel and ranar, but unlike the common coinage, which imitated gold and silver, they were real. The bag bulged with more. Perin rushed to stow the money in safety. The worth of it frightened him more than the conversation with the undead king.

Medrivar lay beneath six feet of soil, lost to the strange rest granted only to the dead that yet walked.

THREE

THE WINTER TREATED Perin and Graves very well. Their little cabin stayed stocked with wood and charcoal throughout the dark months, keeping the fire going. A single gold menel from Graves pouch paid for all the food they needed, and they did not need to draw any more on the funds now kept safe in the crypt, as winter was a good season for business.

Perin helped Graves complete four burials during the cold months. Two of them were for individuals of fairly high status and were relatively lucrative. The cold made the earth hard, so they took more pay for their hours than in the summer. Graves raised a block of stone over one grave as a memorial. Stonework paid very well, and Perin and Graves were contentedly fed through the winter without having to draw on their saved money.

Five months later, in the following summer, when business had slowed down—after a death in the spring due to pneumonia—Graves became ill.

Perin worried about his master so much that he felt ill himself, withdrawn and quiet even by his standards. The summer was by no means a quiet season. Disease and logging accidents normally provided unexpected work at this time of year. Thankfully, Perin was not required in his mentor's stead. This allowed him to nurse Graves as best he could.

The Erdhanger physician made a brief visit, clearly unimpressed by Graves's state. "He's well on in years," he said, as he left. "Perhaps this is his appointed time."

Perin glared at the man's back as the physician hurried away down the path. It was almost as if the town wanted the old gravedigger to die.

Perin went about Erdhanger doing various landscaping jobs, gardening for the wealthier townspeople and digging ditches with the logging crews when such work was needed. The effect of this was that he spent more time with other people. As Graves weakened from the effects of the illness,

Perin's confidence grew and his knowledge increased. Always, he hurried to return to the graveyard when the work was over. He hated leaving Graves wheezing and feverous. The man's temperature changed sporadically, and he talked nonsense in the night when Perin feared sleep.

When he was not working, Perin sat beside Graves's bed and cooked the old man's meals. Perin found those months terrifying, but he continued to work with stalwart determination. He stood straighter and talked more assertively. Mistress Hoer's friendliness no longer disturbed him, and he was able to smile back at her when at the butcher's.

The stress put fight in his muscles. When the carpenter's apprentice tried to ambush him, Perin responded by breaking the boy's nose. Though it did not give the townspeople a better opinion of him, his harassers backed off.

Perin noticed when Mistress Hoer started making sure her daughter was in the shop when Perin came in. He wasn't sure why, but the girl's father grew more foul-tempered and intimidating than before, sometimes pushing her out of the room when Perin came in, shooting black looks at his wife.

At the new moon of mid-autumn, almost a year since Medrivar's burial, Perin sat beside Graves. The old man seemed weaker than ever. Perin gripped a damp cloth in his hand, feeling useless. The rag had brought Graves no relief.

"Will you make me a promise, lad?" Graves stared up at Perin with bright, feverous eyes.

"Of course, Master Graves…"

"You can know my name, boy. You may need it." Perin swallowed, understanding the unspoken message in that sentence. Would he be carving that name in stone so soon? The thought strangled him, and he had to take a deep breath.

"It's Jesik. Jesik Graves. Did his job with dignity. Joined now with…those he served. Got that? You got it, lad?"

"I won't forget, Jesik."

"Ahh. Is good to hear my name spoken. Now, that promise…" He broke off into body-wracking coughs. "You have to…you have to take the money I'm leavin'. Buy yourself some good clothes: hat, coat, gloves, all of it. Hear me?"

"Y-yes."

"Right. And don't hang around here no more. Stay long enough to dig up old Medrivar, give him my compliments…"

"I live here, Jesik!"

"No! This is where the Erdhanger gravedigger lives. I don't want my life fer — fer you, all right? It's no good — no one loves you — no one cares about a keeper of the dead! You're young, you're a good lad, and since Medrivar came, I saw that there could be more…more than this. This isn't…any sorta life."

The intensity of Jesik's emotions burned in his eyes behind the fever.

Perin had tears coming. "I'm proud of who I am, Jesik. You're a gravedigger…"

"And well I know it. It's not for you! I don't...you can't... I don't want it for you!" he shouted.

"Don't...don't get up... Stay down, rest. I hear you, Master Jesik." The young man held back sobs, fighting the tightness in his throat, the heaviness between his shoulders.

"I see you go for walks when you're free. Walking for hours. That's what you really want. You want travel, lad. You want to find your own way. Gravedigging ain't fer you. When Kesairl comes back...you go with him, if he'll take you. Find your own way!"

Perin felt a certainty come to him. He put his hand around Jesik's, straightening the man's fingers as they contorted with pain.

"I don't want you to die, Jesik. Since Kesairl came, everything's been different for us. We've been moving toward some...something. I've never had purpose before. I don't think either of us have. Right now we do: to protect Medrivar 'til he wakes. That's a job only a gravedigger could do.

"If you die, Jesik, I'll do as you say. I'll give you the best grave the Claimfold has ever seen, then I'll help Kesairl and Medrivar. I'll go off adventuring even, but listen to me, Jesik... You are my family, my example, like it or not. People hate you, fear you, all for no good reason, and you don't much like them, but you never let that spoil the way you work. You've always done great service, you never shirk... You could bear grudges, but you don't. And you give the ones nobody cares about—the dead—the dignity even their relatives don't sometimes give them."

Perin sighed and hung his head. "I'll do as you say. But I won't ever stop being a gravedigger."

A week later, the fever broke and Jesik Graves did not die. Perin hurried into Erdhanger and bought as much good food as he could carry back. He fed Graves the best meals he could provide, every day, until the old gravedigger regained his strength. The day that Jesik Graves took up his shovel once more, Perin bought a bottle of apple brandy and shared it with his mentor when the man returned—dirty and aching, but healthy.

The moon grew fuller in the night sky, obscured occasionally by rainfall and cloud, but ever there.

Perin was digging a border one gloomy, overcast day when the impressive figure of Kesairl stepped down from amongst the drooping firs, into the soaked grass at the edge of the graveyard. As if greeting an old friend, Perin threw down his spade and ran over to him.

"Whoa! Easy, boy-man! You will fall in the wet grass. It is good to see you again! I trust all is well?"

Perin nodded enthusiastically. The prigon looked tired but genuinely pleased to see him. "Everything is well. Graves got ill, but he came through. He's fine now. Come on, come inside the house…"

"No, thank you, Perin."

Perin smiled when the prigon remembered his name, and it pleased him to see Kesairl's expression pass through concern to relief at hearing about Jesik's illness.

"I will not fit comfortably in your home, so I will stay out here, if that is well with you."

"It is. Make yourself at home."

The prigon chuckled at this.

Perin shrugged, cheeks colouring. "As at home as you can be in a graveyard, I mean."

"Very well." Kesairl removed his hooded cloak, draping the red and blue garment over a nearby gravestone. His forearms were now visible, as was his leather-covered torso. The purplish brown skin of his forearms was decorated with gold armbands. Gold shone at his wrists, too. The jewelry was plain but for the symbols etched in its surface.

"You're a mage," Perin said. All he knew of magi was that they wore gold devices to aid in their magic.

Kesairl nodded. "Yes. A skirmisher by magistry. That's why I wear the red and blue. And these—" he indicated his arm ornamentations, "—are designed to draw magic from the air into my being. To a certain extent, of course, there is already magic in me, but it is important to augment it with power borrowed from nature."

"Do you use magic much?" Perin asked curiously.

Kesairl looked thoughtful, tugging absent-mindedly at the little beard he had grown on his chin since the last time he had been there. "I suppose so. Often enough. I am only a skirmisher though. My strengths are small-scale combat, and I've some minor healing talent. I am no battlemage. Not yet. But I grow more adept every day!"

Perin gaped, trying to think of something to say. The prigon simply smiled peaceably down at him, apparently not feeling the awkwardness of silence. Perhaps, Perin mused, awkward silences were a strictly human thing.

"Oi! Get that cloak off Valheim Nyer!" Graves stamped toward them up the path from town, a smile spreading on his face as Kesairl immediately snatched up his cloak. The words VALHEIM NYER—DIED YOUNG AND WILL GROW NO OLDER became visible.

"That there's one of my favourite guests, you know. Family paid very well, as I remember, an' he had a sense of humour! He'd not mind, thinking about it. You can put the cloak back if you want. How has the year treated you, Master Kesairl?"

"Please, Kesairl will do. The year has been...eventful. I heard you recovered from illness?"

"Yes, I did, and thank you for caring." Graves grinned up at the massive prigon. "Nearly took me, as well, but old Gravesy ain't ready for planting just yet. The worms will have to wait."

Kesairl raised his eyebrows in amusement, a smile flickering on his broad lips. For the first time, he looked over to the corner of the graveyard where Medrivar was buried still.

"I see His Majesty is happily resting, then."

"Quiet as the dead, Kesairl. Not a peep." Graves joined in with Kesairl's rumbling laughter.

Perin looked from one to another, smiling. Any pangs of loneliness that had lain hidden, faded under the glow of friendship he felt for the prigon. It didn't matter that Kesairl was still mostly unknown to him.

Perin and Graves shared stories with Kesairl about the year since they had parted. Perin felt that his own stories were far less interesting than Kesairl's, though the prigon never seemed bored. Graves went into the cabin to prepare some food.

Kesairl proved his strength by helping Perin to construct a table outside the cabin underneath the slight overhang under which the tools of the trade were kept. The prigon lifted the round wooden covering from the old well, balancing it on a roughly hewn cube of stone that would one day be a memorial marker. Perin got chairs from inside for himself and Graves, while the prigon seated himself on a stack of yet to be used timber. The old well gaped up at the sky behind them.

The world grew dark as they talked and ate. The air was still and warm for autumn, and they did not notice the night as Graves passed the brandy across to Kesairl. The prigon sniffed the liquid, took a sip, then, with a wide grin, he pulled a bottle of something orange from his studded jerkin.

"This is what my people drink. I am afraid I would have to drain most of your bottle to fully enjoy its effect. To Medrivar!" He raised the bottle skyward and took a large gulp. Graves did the same with the brandy, passing it immediately to Perin.

They drank to the sleeping king.

Finally, Kesairl rose from the table. "I will take my leave now. Thank you for eating with me on your territo—at your home. I have enjoyed your companionship more than I can say... Where I have been in the last year, I have been afforded no friendship. I bless your table, your draught and your beds." He bowed low.

Graves rose and did likewise. In the lamplight, following Kesairl's speech, the action became ennobled in Perin's eyes, as if Graves were a lord of great dignity, parting with an equal. Perin did not bow, privately awed as he was, but raised a hand in farewell. Kesairl did likewise, meeting Perin's gaze. He raised his forefinger, ring finger and middle finger to his forehead, between his horns, then pressed the palm of the same hand against his chest, over his heart.

With that gesture, Kesairl left, his cloak swirling as he turned, brightly coloured in the lamplight. When he reached the bank and was barely visible, he called back, "I will camp in the woods a half league up the hill. You can come find me when Medrivar is ready to rise. He will let you know when it is time. Goodbye!"

Graves and Perin sat in contentment for a while after Kesairl's departure, both lost in their thoughts.

Perin broke the silence. "It will be sad when Medrivar and Kesairl are gone."

"I'll miss that prigon, for sure. He's pleasanter company than any from the village has ever been, and I've been here a long time. Having Medrivar buried here is good as well. Working near where he rests is pleasant, like 'is nobility's rubbed off on the place…you know?"

Perin nodded. The threat of loss lurked at the edges of his mind. Friendship had come in the form of Kesairl and formed so quickly. He had seen the prigon only once the year before, and yet it seemed they had known one another for a long time. It had been easy to feel accepted. And Medrivar inspired wonder. There was no better word for him. Without them, life would return to a mundane slog.

How would Perin find friendship of that kind in Erdhanger? For the first time, Perin resented his life digging graves, resented the long, mud-splattered coat and wide-brimmed hat that were the uniform of the gravedigger. They were good for keeping out the rain, but poor garb for making social connections.

Graves seemed to know what Perin was thinking. "You could…maybe you should…if Kesairl doesn't mind, once Medrivar's up…"

"I won't go off with Kesairl. If you'd died, I would have done, but you didn't die, so I'm sticking here. All right?" Perin stared fiercely across at his mentor. He would not be ashamed of his duty, for that would be the same as being ashamed of Graves. "I'm not going anywhere, Jesik."

Graves regarded him thoughtfully across the table, lips tight, eyes slightly narrowed. Finally, he spoke in dark tones. "No. Right now we aren't going nowhere. Neither of us. Stuck in the mud, we'll be, unless something unsticks us. Stuck in the mud 'til we're lying in the stuff, and then it'll be too late. What if we lets it pass us by, Perin, my lad? You don't get many chances at life. Don't make a decision that'll mean one day you end up wishing you'd done different. You got to know when you're done digging!"

FOUR

THE FOLLOWING DAY, a message came up from the town informing Graves that Heimia, Roofer Plaff's daughter, was dead.

Perin immediately went outside to knock the mud off Graves's spade. While he was out, he cleaned his own edger. Aware that Graves wasn't watching, Perin indulged in a moment of play-acting, whirling the thing around his head like a sword, making bold thrusts at invisible enemies. When he spun it into the air and fumbled the catch, he cut his finger on the keen blade. Feeling foolish, he looked around to see if he'd been seen. It was his own fault for over-sharpening the tool.

Perin sucked on his cut finger for a moment, sobered by the memory of little Heimia Plaff playing games with other children in front of Erdhanger's tavern. When the bleeding stopped, he walked across the graveyard to the part used for burials of the poor. They were no worse than the other plots, but were farther away from the gate and the town. The headstones and memorials made for the richer dead of the graveyard were more seemly, and their presence at the front of the graveyard was as close as Graves got to advertising his skills. But these shaded back plots were the ones that Perin and Graves loved to work on most.

Perin used the sharp edger to break the soil, knowing that Graves would chastise him for not using the string and nails to keep it straight.

Graves crossed the cool graveyard, his shovel on his shoulder. Halfway across, he noticed something that made him stop and stare. Perin had missed it because of his spade whirling, but it had Jesik Graves's full attention.

"Hey, Perin. Come'n look at this!"

Perin came running, hearing the surprise and excitement in Graves's voice. It became obvious what had commanded Graves's amazement halfway to the grave where Medrivar lay.

A profusion of colourful spring flowers, many quite foreign to both gravediggers, seemed to explode from the soil of Medrivar's grave. Grass grew there as well. The rest of the graveyard was drab with brown leaves and faded, pale grass, but this…this had grown into a patch of lush paradise.

Perin stared. "Well, I'll be…"

Graves leaned on his shovel, shaking his head admiringly. "Kesairl did say Medrivar'd let us know. Style, he's got. Well, I s'pose you should run and get Kesairl. Dig a foot or so of Heimia Plaff's last resting place first, though. Medrivar might as well stay comfy for a little while. I gotta go into town and collect our money for the gardening we've been doing in that miser Dryagof's park of a place. Should be back after I've argued with 'im for a couple'a hours."

"All right. Foot of the new grave, then fetch Kesairl. I've got it. Will you lock the gate?"

"Aye, I will. See you after." Graves moved off, leaving his shovel leaning against the well cover that was still serving as a tabletop.

Four hours later, Graves hadn't yet returned. The sky had darkened once again. The full, pale disk of the moon had appeared in the afternoon sky earlier, and it now grew brighter as the sky around it turned a deeper blue. Perin delayed entering the woods, having done the promised digging. To pass the time, knowing that nothing could be done for Medrivar until nightfall, Perin played a game he had taught himself while Graves had slept fitfully through his fever.

He spent a cold half hour flinging coffin nails a short distance into the side of Graves's cabin. The target marked there was difficult to see in the gathering dusk. Kesairl jumped down the bank into the graveyard.

"Hail, Perin, my friend!" Kesairl performed the gesture he had used last night, and Perin returned it almost automatically. He had been practicing it throughout the morning in his idle moments.

"Thus, we greet as brothers, Perin. Ah, he is ready to awaken!" Kesairl exclaimed, striding toward where the flowers stood proud on Medrivar's grave.

Perin nodded. "We have to wait until dark?"

"Not at all, not at all. As long as the full moon is in the sky, it does not matter… I would awaken His Majesty now, only something has happened."

Worry sparked in Perin's stomach. "What?"

"A hunter came upon my little camp. He'd been looking for other hunters and was very relieved to find me."

"He was?"

Kesairl blinked at the surprise in Perin's voice. Then he smiled as he apparently realised the reason. "Oh, this Claim's hunters have knowledge of my people, Perin, and we are renowned for our enmity with drizen."

"Why should—"

"I didn't get that far, did I? It appears that one or more drizen are abroad on the higher paths. I promised the man I would join him in hunting for them. If it's not a false rumour, then Erdhanger is in real danger. There haven't been any drizen in the Claimfold for a long time. I said I would join him as soon as I'd made contact with my friends."

"Your friends?"

"Yourself, Graves and Medrivar, of course."

"Oh. Be careful!"

"I will. Where is Graves, anyway?"

"In town. He should be back by now…"

"I see." Kesairl looked distracted, evidently anxious to get hunting. Suddenly, he smiled down at Perin. "Perin, come to my camp for a moment, I want to give you something. Don't worry, it will not delay me, and I cannot raise Medrivar until I've helped the hunters."

Perin paused, wondering if he should abandon the graveyard. But Graves had been gone for ages now, so he could hardly blame him for taking a short break, could he? He threw down his edging spade at the side of Medrivar's grave.

Kesairl had to heave Perin up the bank, but after that, it was easy going between the trees to where a canvas tent stood beside the ashes of a fire.

Kesairl rummaged in his pack for a moment.

Perin found himself anxious to get back to the graveyard. He looked up through the thickly clothed branches to the deep-blue sky, which grew darker with every passing minute.

"Here." Kesairl returned from his pack, holding a golden pendant shaped like an eye. It had sigils etched across its surface and the design was stylised and only just recognisable for what it was. Kesairl draped the cord of the pendant around Perin's neck. This close to the prigon, Perin could see the cord of an identical pendant hanging beneath the neckline of Kesairl's clothes.

"This is the symbol that Medrivar chose for himself and his Bright Dead. I felt that I should give it to you. Ever since I heard you humming that tune…"

But then a cry rang through the woods, and the prigon hurriedly stood, rolling back the sleeves of his blue and red cloak. His magical arm rings glinted in the half-light. "It sounds as though I am needed… Go back to the graveyard!" And then he was gone, running away from Perin through the trees.

Perin hurried back through the firs to the graveyard. He had just slidden down the bank when he heard voices.

Graves was having an argument with a tall, bald-headed man. Crimson tattoos swirled up the neck of this stranger; the designs dancing wildly on his pate. A tattered black robe enveloped him, drawn tight about his waist by a gilded belt. From where Perin now sat, frozen still against the sandy bank, he could see the man, imposing and tall, gesturing with one hand, insistent, controlled. His back was straight, his head bowed slightly. It was not a deferential manner. It reminded Perin of the downturned head of a wolf circling its prey. A falcon in the killing stoop.

Graves was clearly audible and his arms were waving about, gesticulating his anger. "No! You get outta my graveyard, you power-crazed crat! Mad is what you are! There's nothin', *nothin'*...untoward 'bout my graveyard, you hear me?"

Not a bloody inspection, not today, Perin thought, groaning inwardly as he began to creep forward between the graves, keeping himself hidden. Without knowing it on a conscious level, he worked his way toward Medrivar's grave.

The cold, assertive tones of the stranger were now audible. "I have been told of an unauthorised burial. Something to do with magic. You would not lie to me, now, would you old man?"

"Get. Out! You've no right to come snooping here."

"I am Mage Keresur," the man replied, head high, voice full of arrogant certainty. "Besides, power gives rights to those that wield it, old man. There is something buried here... Ah! Your eyes give you away. Over...here?"

Perin froze. He'd made it to Medrivar's flowering grave. His right hand curled in the loose topsoil.

The man sauntered in his direction. He would surely see the grave with its unnatural flowers, and it would be over...

If you can hear me, Medrivar...hide the signs of your presence...

Perin put his forehead to the cold ground. His new pendant rested against the grass at the graveside. Suddenly, footfalls sounded beside him. A hand grabbed his shoulder and dragged him to his feet.

"What's this? A lurker...an apprentice, it seems." The mage's iron-grey eyes bore into Perin's own hazel eyes. He kicked the edging spade Perin had left earlier, his voice dripping with disdain. "Doing a little edging, were we? But this grave is already perfectly maintained. And flowers as well!"

Perin turned his gaze fearfully to the mound but it was not as bad as he had expected. The flowers there were all rotted, faded against the soil. Medrivar must have heard him...

"They're…they're just something we thought would make the grave nice but they went bad because winter's coming…" Perin babbled, trying to struggle free of Mage Keresur's grip on his shoulder.

"Liar," the man said coldly, his lip curling. He pointed at the stone that rested flat, heading the grave. "It was most foolish to name the occupant. Medrivar is not a common name. It is an old name. A northern name."

"Let go of my apprentice! Unhand him, or I'll belt you one with my old faithful, you bald son of a whore!" Graves walked steadily toward the two of them, holding his shovel like a club.

The mage ignored him, staring hungrily at the name carved in the stone. Now Perin could see the dark silver bracelets on the man's wrists. The hand that held his shoulder was traced in a faint, colourless glow. Perin recognised it, remembering the luminescence of magic from Kesairl's rite. This though, appeared different. A reverse version, a faint shadow in the air.

"I warned you!" Graves raised the shovel threateningly.

A flicker of irritation passed across Keresur's face and his other hand closed into a fist.

The old gravedigger was thrown backward by invisible hands, tossed against a headstone some feet away, the breath knocked out of him.

"Medrivar, Medrivar, Medrivar. The king, at last." A force, irresistible and cruel, gripped both of Perin's shoulders and forced him to his knees. The mage began to slowly circle the dead king's grave.

"You shouldn't lie to me, boy. I knew my mission here too well to believe your falsehoods. And you have not hidden him well. Ha! His name on a headstone, flowers marking his grave…and of course, you wear his pendant, boy. I've seen it before, around uglier necks. No matter. I have found him."

"Stay away from him!" Perin yelled, struggling against the force that bound him.

Keresur snarled, as if holding back sudden violence. He kicked Perin's edging spade at him so that it glanced off his thigh. Pain exploded in Perin's leg. Then Keresur completed his circle of the grave, standing in front of Perin with his back to Graves.

"Do you hear me, dead king? I wonder…perhaps he will see us coming." He knelt. "Know the truth, dead man. You're no king. There are spirits far, far greater than you. When we've torn you from your body, you'll be no more than a mouse among wolves."

Anger and frustration surged in Perin, mixed with some measure of fear. The eye pendant around his neck seemed to be growing warm.

"Silent as the grave, Medrivar? Hah!" The mage spat onto the earth.

Graves got to his feet, his voice fierce. "Rot-membered scum. Magic an' old man would you? You'll pay, you maggot-brained, slime-sucking rat filth! You—"

The tattooed man swept his arm back, anger at Graves's interruption pushing him too far. With a terrible cry, Graves was swept into the air and thrown earthward again, sent tumbling against another headstone some paces away.

"No! Bastard!" Perin, who had never sworn at a person before, now did so with extreme vehemence, actually falling forward across his edging spade as he challenged Keresur's spell on him.

However, the man was himself pre-occupied, muttering fast under his breath in a language Perin had not heard before.

"Leave him alone! Medrivar... He's...he's a friend to the Tacnimag..." Perin moaned desperately. The pendant around his neck raged with an anger that was not his. The man laughed suddenly, breaking off his spell.

"Friend of the Tacnimag? Do you not know? I am from the Tacnimag! Why would we sully ourselves with some northern undead? I'm the only one with the interest, the aptitude. The voice spoke only to me."

The mage muttered further phrases under his breath. The spell must have been difficult because the magical hold on Perin lessened in strength. The pendant around his neck grew hot. Perin closed his hand about the handle of his edging spade.

Raising his hands, weaving shapes, Keresur raved, "At last. At last, we'll never be the same. I'll have you, use you... Never have to fear the dark again... Such power, wasted on dead bones—I'll have it in me. Never again..."

Fear on Medrivar's behalf, and rage at the trespasser's attack on Graves, liberated Perin. Tacnimag magic was not strong enough. With a desperate cry, Perin rose up to his knees and swung out with his edging spade.

The keen blade caught the man across his right shin and the blow made him stumble.

In that moment, his hold over Perin failed and the gravedigger's apprentice rose up, bringing his spade around. The keen edge glinted in the day's last light. Keresur threw out a hand, but before the glow of magic could swell about his silver manacle, Perin struck.

The wild swing proved lucky. The very edge and tip of the tool slashed across Keresur's throat. Blood spilled and an airless shriek tore from the man's lips. He staggered backward, gore reddening the front of his robes, gurgled curses becoming lost in his ragged throat.

Determined to prevent him from releasing a word of magic, Perin followed him, driving him back with frantic blows designed not to make contact but to prevent further spell-casting. The hurried, desperate, weakening footsteps of the Tacnimag mage took him past the great wooden well cover that served as a table, past the corner of Graves's hut, to where the well itself gaped, inviting and black-mouthed.

Perin stood stock-still. Keresur was gone, bloody hands flailing, swallowed down by the old well. Perin had never believed the nonsense the townsfolk said, that ghosts from the graveyard hid from the sun down there, but it seemed a good myth to send the mage down to.

Perin turned, dropping the bloodied spade to the grass as speedy footfalls hammered across the graveyard toward him, signalling Kesairl's arrival.

A thought entered his mind from deep down. *Well done, Perin.* He had done well.

Then Kesairl's massive prigon hands were holding his shoulders, shaking him, asking him what had happened. Then Perin was released. The moon's light had become the strongest colour in the sky; night had arrived with the passing of Keresur into the well. Kesairl let out a cry of horror from Medrivar's grave. Somehow, he could tell that the undead king no longer occupied his burial place.

Perin walked numbly to where Graves lay against the gravestone of someone called Reger Myrvo. The details stood out in high focus in Perin's mind. He knelt down, knowing what he would find. His hand gently turned his mentor so that the old man stared up into the moonlight.

Wordlessly, Perin closed Jesik Graves's eyes for their last time. The heat in the pendant had faded to a dull warmth. It rested below where a great pain rose in Perin, and now another one joined the sweet agony in his throat that came from holding back sobs. This, in turn, flooded his chest with a heavy stirring of emotion. Another beautiful, terrible song. Trapped. Perin knew that the only way its melody would break free was if he let it out. But the wail of grief would not come. He was not ready for that kind of honesty. Silent tears spilled instead.

The colour of the flowers on Medrivar's grave had vanished. All true brightness, save for the unfeeling moon, was absent.

The Pendant of the Bright Dead rested cool and secret against Perin's collarbone.

FIVE

KESAIRL WATCHED IN tense silence as Perin slid the lid of Jesik's coffin into place. The young gravedigger paused for a moment, staring down at the dark wood. It was the best quality coffin he could have found, and he had placed his mentor in its confines with great gentleness. The gravedigger would rest in honour. Graves would lie in the earth where Perin had dug the grave for Heimia Plaff because he knew that had been the old man's favourite part of the graveyard.

Perin picked up one of the long, heavy coffin nails he had recently been playing with. They had no heads. They were just simple spikes of iron, because people did not generally want to pull nails from coffins once they'd been hammered in. The aim was not to open them but to close them in permanence.

"Place the nail as if to hammer it in." Kesairl's deep voice spoke quietly.

Perin did as he was told.

The prigon raised his right hand. A moment later, the spike shot home into the wood. The two repeated the process with the other nails.

"I can lift him with magic..." Kesairl offered.

Perin shook his head, teeth clenched. His eyes were prickling again.

"I want to carry him there. I'll need your help, though."

"Of course."

They lifted the coffin between them and carried it across the dark graveyard to the pit where they were to lay Graves's body. The prigon jumped down into the grave and accepted the coffin from there, lowering it carefully. Then he scrambled back out, dusting earth from his leather breeches.

"I'll do what you said, J-Jesik," Perin stammered out as the prigon turned to regard the coffin's new position, hands folded in front of him. "I'll do it all. You wait, I'll go all across Valo, do all the things you might have done if… if…" He crushed a sob.

"I killed him you know. The Tacnimag mage. He's dead. Down the old well. Funny really. The town children always said that well was evil. Haunted. Now it's taken his evil away."

Kesairl had stiffened at the word "Tacnimag," and now he watched Perin closely as the boy continued his last goodbye.

"I did it with my spade, Jesik. See, that's gravedigger's work." Perin laughed a little at this through his quiet tears, and Kesairl reached out and put a massive hand on his shoulder. "I meant it all, Jesik. I'll honour what you told me to do. But I'll be a gravedigger forever, too, 'cos that's what you were. Goodbye, Jesik. Thank you for everything."

Perin stepped back from the grave and took a deep, shuddering breath. It was a relief.

Kesairl moved his arms as if he were attempting to draw two magnetically attracted objects apart. The earth pile responded and spilled submissively into the grave, covering the coffin instantly. Moments later, the grave was filled and the earth on top compressed by Kesairl's art.

His deep voice rumbled out. "I did not know you well, Master Jesik Graves, but I could see that you were a good man. I cannot affect your state now through magic, but I do pray that you rest well. You've earned it. This is a beautiful graveyard."

Perin did not think that anyone could have spoken better words than that.

The headstone, now rising from the earth against the bank of the graveyard read: *Gravedigger and mentor Jesik Graves rests here*, and below that, *He did his job with dignity and now sleeps with those he served so well*, and beneath that, *Slain in service to the King*.

The benevolent eye symbol of Medrivar was carved at the very bottom of the stone, where it would one day be obscured by grass, weathered beyond recognition. But it was there. Looking down at it, bleary-eyed in the cold autumn dawn, Perin experienced a slight sensation of energy from the pendant again. At the same time, a sense of ratification and approval rose in him. The boy blinked, looking around as if he might find some external cause for this.

"Medrivar is not lost." Kesairl walked across the dewy grass to where Perin stood. The prigon had carved Graves's headstone an hour ago and had then seen to the cabin, removing all items of use before locking its battered door.

Perin stared up at the prigon, not understanding. A strange expression haunted his friend's face. "You were at the graveside when he was torn from his body. And you were wearing his symbol. That talisman is powerfully wrought, and its potential for storing magic is known. But that is exactly what Medrivar is, what all spirit is: sentient magic."

"He…he's in the pendant?"

"He is transferred and transported by the thing, yes. But if he is anywhere, he is within you. Spirits are designed for inhabiting bodies, even his kind. That they were capable of symbiosis with the living, I did not know."

"That's why I've been feeling things…almost hearing things that are not my own mind?"

"I believe so. This renews my hope. The news that the Tacnimag are corrupted was a great blow, but I feel that we shall overcome, despite them. Medrivar has chosen you. I very much doubt that he would do so without providing you with certain gifts. He has many skills, after all—healer, soothsayer, warrior, scholar… discernment and strength, both physical and mental, great confidence."

"I thought you said you knew nothing of this sort of symbio…symbio…"

"Symbiosis. And I don't. We are in unmapped lands now. But I do know Medrivar, and that is enough."

"Oh." Perin's mind raced with the ideas now rising there. Would he really be changed? Did he want that?

Kesairl looked across the graveyard. The trees moved a little. The rising sun was already hidden by grey cloud. Perin could not read the prigon's fears and doubts on his face.

"We will have to leave. The Tacnimag will investigate the disappearance of their man. I am astonished that they are in enmity with our aim…that they know of Medrivar's people at all is surprising. All very ominous, as well, for the only humans that we thought might know of the dead were known to be sorcerers. If this mage was here to drain Medrivar of his power, then he is surely consorting with enemy spirits."

Perin listened to this speech in silence, his eyes on Graves's headstone. At last he spoke. "All right, Kesairl. Where will we go?"

"Through the forest and out onto the hillside beneath Csus. There are prigon on the slopes there. We should be allowed shelter. Then…I do not know. Medrivar always had all the answers. Damn those drizen! If they had not… I could have been here. Ugh! His doing, do you think, as a distraction?" He gestured toward the well. Perin did not have an answer.

"My pack is with my tent," Kesairl continued, "But I have no spare pack for you to use."

Perin walked to where his hat rested in the damp grass. There was a tear in the heavy, battered leather. He looked on it now with fondness; it had been Graves's before the old man had passed it on to him. He picked up the hat and walked past Kesairl to place it on the peak of Graves's headstone.

"I'll go into Erdhanger. I'll get provisions for myself so that we don't run low on food. I'll buy a pack in town as well." Perin smiled a little, remembering his promise to the fever-wracked Graves. There would be a few other things for him to buy as well.

Perin went to Master Eledserzam's tool and equipment shop first, entering with an expression of such determination, he might've been about to rob it. Instead, he placed three silver coins on the counter and pointed out a large external-frame haversack made of fine waterproofed leather and oiled wood. Master Eledserzam was so surprised at the appearance of Perin in his shop that he brought down the pack from the wall and handed it to him in silence. His expression of shock steadily became one of glee as Perin continued to buy equipment from him.

He bought a large, steel spade with a lengthened head and the slightest point to the blade. It was surely the finest tool in Eledserzam's shop, with an oiled, gleaming handle, smooth and with worked grips on the wood itself. The blade shone. It was a spade the tradesman had not expected to sell. Only a rich customer seriously into their gardening or landscaping would have been able to afford it, but here was strange, reclusive Perin paying good silver ranars for it.

"You…you came into some money then? It's a nice spade. I suppose you and Graves will be using it for poor little Heimia Plaff's grave, will you?"

Perin felt a pang of regret and guilt go through him. There would be no one around to bury the girl that afternoon, and Graves now occupied the place that had been chosen for her.

"Don't know what you want with a haversack, though," Eledserzam continued. "Is this all for Graves, or for yourself?"

"Graves…Master Graves is dead." Perin emphasised the word, 'Master'.

Eledserzam's smile faded. "Oh. I…I heard he was ill. That's a shame. A right shame. You, er, that isn't his saved fortune you're spending, is it?"

Perin fixed the man with a gaze that caused him to step backward.

"I only meant…he left it to you, I'm sure… No offence meant, lad." As if to placate the boy, he took a step forward and gestured toward a box full of four-inch-long iron spikes.

"Coffin nails? I'll throw 'em in free, lad. How about it?" Perin nodded. He stared back at the shopkeeper without nervousness, leaving Eledserzam shaken. Then he left the shop.

He walked back through the town to the tailor's place. It was cool and quiet, the air rich with the scent of wool and leather. With some urgency to his pace now, Perin picked out a long coat of heavy, waxed leather, very similar to the old coat he was wearing, but of much higher quality. It was dark tan in colour, with a semi-rigid collar that could be lifted to protect his cheeks from the wind. It reached down to just below Perin's knees, buttoning down the front with brass bars.

When Perin arrived at the Hoers' shop he made Mistress Hoer start with surprise.

He removed his new wide-brimmed hat, barely aware of Master Hoer, who gaped at him in surprise.

"You've bought yourself some nice things!" Mistress Hoer blurted out delightedly, making Perin smile and look down at himself. Beneath his new coat, which he wore open, was a jacket of fine, soft leather. If Mistress Hoer had known that the jacket was padded with folded silk, she would have been all the more astonished. Perin had asked for something 'resistant'.

Perin's breeches were different, and he wore a cream-coloured belt. Everything had changed, even his boots, which were sturdy and expensive looking. Perin could see Mistress Hoer taking it all in, but for once it didn't make him uncomfortable.

"I need as much cured beef as I can carry, please." Recovered from his shock, Master Hoer threw Perin a dark look and went out into the back of the shop.

Perin moved over to the counter. Mistress Hoer continued to look him up and down appraisingly. Perin felt an urge to talk, so that he wouldn't leave Erdhanger without some kind of farewell.

"Mistress Hoer. You've always been unusually friendly towards me. I don't feel as though I owe an explanation to anyone here, as they've always ignored me and Master Graves, but I want to talk to you."

She beamed. "Please, call me Yana, Perin. And thank you! I'm glad to see you've dressed yourself up. You look a fine figure of a man…you know, my daughter, she…"

"I'm sorry, Mistress Hoer, I don't have much time. Your daughter is a lovely girl, but this is very important."

"All right, Master Perin, you have my attention." She leaned on the counter.

"First, you should know that Master Graves is dead. They're going to think he died of illness. When they read what's written on his stone, they're not going to believe it, but I need someone, even if they never tell anyone, to believe it."

"All right. You can tell me." Her voice lowered to a hush.

"He was killed by a Tacnimag mage who was trying to… desecrate one of the graves."

"Gods of Valo!"

"You believe me?"

"I...yes. I believe you."

"I...I killed the mage with my...well, with my spade."

Mistress Hoer covered her mouth, shocked.

"He fell into the well. I have to leave Erdhanger. The Tacnimag may try to hunt me down."

For a moment, Mistress Hoer said nothing. Everything about Perin's story was unbelievable, and yet, she seemed to believe him.

"How will you live like that? Do you have money? Do you need...?"

Master Hoer re-entered the room, carrying a stack of cured, seasoned beef strips. He wrapped them up on the counter.

"No, no," Perin said calmly, glancing at Master Hoer. "All I will need is the beef, thank you, Mistress. Just...just remember what I said."

"Always. Good luck, Perin."

Perin paid, took the meat from Master Hoer and turned to go, putting his hat back on. In the doorway, he waved goodbye to Mistress Hoer. He felt a sense of regret that he had found a friend in her, at the moment of his leaving Erdhanger, perhaps forever.

Kesairl pulled Perin up the bank into the shadow of the fir trees. He looked the boy up and down in much the same way as Yana Hoer had.

"A new spade?" he asked incredulously.

"I may need it," Perin said simply, hoping to keep his face bland, assuring he gave nothing away. He tucked something into his coat's inner pocket. Four coffin nails were threaded in the band of his hat. The prigon stared at them.

"What are those for?"

"They're something I can't leave behind. I won't be forgetting my job."

"I see. No, actually, I don't..."

"I may need them." Perin walked past the astonished prigon into the trees, a small smile briefly on his lips. On his shoulders he bore his pack, his new edging spade strapped loosely to it, glinting in the morning light.

And the talisman eye of Medrivar's Bright Dead hung about his neck.

SIX

FOUR HOURS LATER, Kesairl called a halt. Perin still felt fresh, though sweat dampened his dark fringe. His coat swirled about him as he turned back to Kesairl.

They sat on the edge of a clearing among the pines, Kesairl's broad back against a tree, Perin on a nearby stump. The prigon took a deep breath and began to draw energy down into his gold bracelets and armbands, storing it as a measure against the exhaustion of his natural reserves.

The colourless glow of magic made a haze about the prigon as he meditated. There was no breeze, but the prickle of magic moved in his thick, spiky hair. As his adornments reached overflow, he began the harder task of refocusing the energy into his core.

Perin watched Kesairl as he meditated, finding it almost unsettlingly beautiful. Kesairl's alien looks and sense of calm seemed at odds with his great size and obvious physical power.

Copying Kesairl, Perin relaxed, closing his eyes. He emptied his mind, surprised at how easy it was...

He was in an audience chamber. It was plainly that, for the shadowy room in which he now stood had only one chair. A great seat of gilded wood. And now, as if he had always been there, seated regally, enthroned...

Medrivar. But this was Medrivar as Perin had never seen him, fully restored in the body of the long-dead northern king. The body that Medrivar would never be able to return to. The hair on Medrivar's head was fair, as golden as Kesairl's nose ring. The king's arms were powerfully muscled, tattooed with swirling green and gold designs the like of which Perin had never seen. Blue eyes pierced Perin, but with a warmth that could not be missed.

"You are with me!" Perin exclaimed. He felt as if he should bow. After a moment's hesitation, he did.

Medrivar smiled. "Yes. As much a part of you, now, as I was part of this body you see here. Though my time in that form has passed. But a mind's expectation of a body's shape is hard to shake."

"I'm sorry…Majesty, we tried to stop him…"

"Do not apologise! You did me great service in risking your lives to protect me. Your mentor died for me, for you. A man of great worth. I will remember him."

At this, Perin's eyes filled with tears. It seemed ridiculous to him that such a thing could happen to him inside his own mind.

The king rose and walked quickly to Perin, placing his hands on the boy's shoulders. This close, there was a stillness about Medrivar. Perin realised the undead king was still not breathing, not even here as an image in his mind. But tears were in Medrivar's eyes as well, so perhaps the dead were not so different from the living, after all.

"Grieve for him, son. Your strength brings you honour. Your resolve gives me pride. Though it was forced, I could not be happier that I reside with you. From here, I will help you if I can. Trust Kesairl. He always served me well. Flee my enemies until other plans become possible. For now, follow Kesairl." The king embraced Perin and stepped back from him.

A loud voice became audible, made indistinct by the walls of Medrivar's throne room. Medrivar's voice came as a whisper as the room faded, the natural light of the forest rising. *"You are wanted."*

Perin opened his eyes and sprang to his feet. Kesairl was already up. The newcomer was a hunter. His reddish brown hair had receded with age and his face was lined and weathered. Fear made his eyes wide, although he looked relieved to see Perin and Kesairl.

"A mage! A prigon mage! Such great luck… Sorry for startling you. Naith — is my name, I mean. There are drizen loose in these woods!"

Kesairl's eyes narrowed and he flexed his large fingers. He shrugged back the sleeved cloak, the blue and red harlequin pattern rippling. The prigon's great, deep voice rumbled out in the still forest. "Again? How many?"

"Nine, I think. I ran soon as I counted them. I think one of them is a captain of some sort. Larger than the others and they listen to him. I thought they had all died out!"

"Obviously not. Where are they?"

"That 'ways about half a league."

Kesairl turned to Perin. "They are in our path. I do not think we should go around."

"Then come with me," the hunter urged. "My kith are just down the slope in the deeper forest, not far. If we group together, we'll have the edge on them."

"It is the best plan," Kesairl agreed. He set off at once, led by the hunter. Perin hurried along behind them.

They emerged in a smaller clearing in the endless pine. A well-made log cabin dominated the space. Smoke rose from a chimney, and the door stood open, letting out the sound of talking and laughter.

The hunter they were with burst in ahead of them. By the time Perin and Kesairl had entered the cabin, the prigon ducking under the doorjamb, all the hunters were on their feet and reaching for weapons.

"Ah, Dellyr." Kesairl nodded to a hunter who was pulling a fearsome boar-spear free of the wall. The cross-hilt behind the spearhead gave the weapon a formidable look.

The hunter nodded back. "Kesairl. We got the one yesterday easily enough. Let us be as successful today." The prigon introduced Perin to the hunter hurriedly.

Dellyr nodded. "Gravedigger, eh? Let's hope none of us will need your talents. Can you use a bow?"

Perin shook his head, feeling useless. Then, prompted by a surge of confidence he assumed to be from Medrivar, he pulled his spade free from his pack. "I can use this. It's quite sharp."

Dellyr looked at him with a little doubt. "Aye, it might do the trick. But keep back behind us spearmen. Use it if you really have to. Now. Are we going, or not? Quarry to hunt!"

His battle cry elicited a clamour of similar ones from his comrades. With Dellyr and Kesairl leading them, they all piled out into the bright sunlight.

Naith led them through the pine forest up the slope. They went in silence, the hunters treading with practised stealth across the carpet of pine needles. The tension was becoming unbearable. Perin had put his spade back, so that it hung again strapped to the side of his pack. It made him feel more vulnerable, but he could at least move with ease.

Suddenly, with a jolt of horror, Perin could see what Naith and Dellyr had already made out. In the same sunlit clearing that he and Kesairl had just left, nine incredibly ugly creatures were gathered. They were all talking rapidly in a language thick with monosyllabic words.

Perin swallowed, removing his pack as quietly as he was able. Kesairl did the same.

The drizen were tall—nearly as tall as Kesairl—though they had a hunched look about them. A snout, raw and damp, sat in the centre of each dreadful face. Their mouths were flanked by a pair of dark tusks. A third tusk jutted from the chin of each monster. Sparse, bristly hair covered the creatures' bared arms and faces. The skin beneath was like toughened leather. They were wearing ugly plates of heavy blackened metal jointed poorly together with chain links. Bowed legs were covered only by a kilt-like extension of the creatures' loincloths.

Dellyr signalled to the archers to draw closer. They were all set, ignoring their fear as they nocked arrows to their bowstrings. The archers began to inch closer, passing into the clearing with bows at the ready.

"Wait for them to see us," Kesairl whispered to Naith. "I would not shoot unknowing enemies in the back."

Naith grimaced. Clearly, he had no problem with doing just that, but he obeyed Kesairl and did not loose his arrow. Dellyr came to stand between Kesairl and Perin, angling his spear toward the nearest drizen as it turned to look over its shoulder...

With a harsh, guttural cry, it drew the hooked sword from its belt and charged, its fellows joining it. The archers loosed at close range, but to Perin's shock, only one of the drizen fell, although many stumbled under the blows.

The archers backed off hurriedly, hunters bearing boar spears stepping up to block the drizen from passing. One of the monsters made a choking bellow as Dellyr ran his spear into its throat. Blood spattered onto the pine needles.

The chieftain of the drizen group was not armed with a jagged sword like his comrades. He stood head and shoulders above his inferiors, wearing a pair of unpleasant-looking gauntlets. He made straight for Kesairl.

The prigon stood his ground, black hair moving in a secret breeze, as magic gathered about his wrists. The strange, arcane light danced off his horns and spiralled across his golden arm rings. An explosion of shape leaped out from the prigon, knocking three of the drizen backward off their feet. The drizen captain roared out his frustration as he began to rise again.

Naith put an arrow in another drizen, sending it tumbling to the forest floor. But now another stormed in, and its hooked, jagged blade struck with finality. Naith crumpled, blood rushing in bursts from his belly. His insides spilled as he fell on his face. The drizen that had killed him roared its victory, but it was short-lived.

With controlled vengeance, Kesairl clenched his left hand tight and swept his arm across to point at the drizen with his forefinger and middle finger. A beam of white heat jumped across the space between them, lancing into the side of the drizen's skull. With a shriek it died, sprawling on the pine needles.

Four of the creatures were now dead from arrows. The fifth had felt Kesairl's fury, and another had ended its life on the end of Dellyr's spear. The hunter roared his anger at Naith's death, challenging the final three to come closer. The chieftain made once more for Kesairl, the drizen on his left accompanying him. But the drizen to the right began to zigzag, dodging arrows and spear thrusts.

It broke through the line and headed straight for Perin.

Perin's memory and Medrivar's inspiration fused together and pushed past his fear. He reached up to his hatband and drew a coffin nail, holding the four inches of spiked iron loosely.

As the drizen charged forward, Perin brought his arm around with a whipping motion, launching the nail. To his surprise, it actually hit the charging monster, tearing its face but falling away. The creature came on, bellowing its rage.

Dellyr forced back the chieftain's helper, his boar spear buried in its stomach. With a screaming bellow, the chieftain itself fell on Kesairl. Moving with blinding speed, the prigon roared out a word unknown to the humans around him. His broad, dark hands grasped the creature's throat. Smoke issued from the monster's gasping mouth as Kesairl forced it to its knees. Then he cast it away, magic sending the creature tumbling some feet away. A terrible burn marked where Kesairl's hands had touched its neck.

Perin's second throw buried a coffin nail in his attacker's eye. An arrow hit it from behind in the shoulder at the same moment, and the creature blundered forward, shrieking pain and fury. Its flailing blade would have found Perin had another arrow not struck it in the reverse joint of its knee. It stumbled.

Perin let out a terrified scream, high-pitched and terrible. He swung at the thing's neck with his spade, suddenly appalled at what he was doing and had done, appalled at Naith's death, appalled at Naith's ruptured corpse.

Perin never knew afterward how many times he'd struck the drizen in the neck. The hunters stood in quiet shock, checking bruises and grazes, or making sure their enemies were truly dead. All the while, the creature kneeling in front of Perin, now dead, rocked under repeated blows. Blood spattered as the spade bit deeper each time, making a sickening, satisfying sound.

Perin roared his lungs empty and his throat hoarse, and it was only when his grip slipped and the spade tumbled from his grasp that he ceased. He had reduced one side of its neck to pulp. Blood dripped off its chin tusk, falling to the pine needles. It was quite dead, although its hoary hands twitched spasmodically.

Perin's blood thundered in his ears. He stepped away, feeling curiously empty. He knew this was an illusion, temporary, for he could feel Medrivar supporting him. He began to shake, his mouth dry. His eyes stared widely across the clearing at Kesairl who stared back, astounded by Perin's violence and strength.

Perin reached out and touched the rough bark. For a moment, he frowned at the pure detail of the trunk and the feel of its texture beneath his hand.

Then he threw up at the tree's base, coughing and sweating until he was dry-retching, his body heaving painfully.

Kesairl rubbed his back as he vomited, and Dellyr put a hand on his shoulder.

"Did well, gravedigger. Never seen a spade used like that, I must say. Were those nails you threw? That's right, cough it up. Get it all gone. You done brilliantly."

Kesairl said nothing, but his hand on Perin's back had much the same effect as Medrivar's silent comfort. Perin straightened up and managed a weak smile.

"See, I told you I might need it."

A hunter handed him his bloodied spade. Perin took a deep breath.

Kesairl still looked concerned. "If you want to rest a while…"

Perin pushed the edging spade's blade into the needle-strewn forest floor. It came free, cleaned a little by the earth beneath.

"No. Naith needs burying. And I'm the only gravedigger here."

SEVEN

PERIN AND KESAIRL left the forest's edge, walking onto open hillside under a heavy grey sky.

The hunters had parted ways some time ago. Since then, the two travellers had not spoken. Perin began to feel uncomfortable, though Kesairl seemed to enjoy periods of silence as much as conversation. Not speaking meant that Perin's mind lingered on the slaughter from earlier. Much of what had happened blurred in his mind, but now the memories were slowly resolving themselves into a horror that seemed less than real.

The great hillside gently sloped in a canvas of brown heather, fronds nodding damply in the chill wind. Here and there, Perin saw gorse and thorny trees breaking the drab underbrush. Even the colour of Kesairl's blue and red cloak was muted. The prigon's hood was up, raised in bumps by his horns.

It was night when Kesairl slowed down, finally matching Perin's smaller strides. Perin had said nothing, but his legs were burning from the exertion and the unrelenting hours of their journey. He gasped with relief as he saw the reason for Kesairl's slower pace.

A fire burned brightly in the growing gloom. The heaped blaze cast flickering light and shadow against the sides of high, colourful tents. Shapes moved in the spaces between the tents, and from their height and build, Perin could see that they were prigon.

Perin had expected Kesairl to break into a run, eager to meet fellows of his kind. In fact, Kesairl walked so slowly and deliberately that Perin overtook him for the first time.

Perin arrived at the fireside, nervous and smiling apologetically, a full five paces ahead of Kesairl.

A prigon woman stared down at Perin as if she'd never seen a human before. She murmured something in her own language. The other prigon gathered around. One of them saw the gold of Medrivar's eye-symbol reflect the firelight. His expression darkened a little. It darkened still further when he saw Kesairl walk stiffly into the firelight.

"King's men," the prigon murmured with derision, in Claimic, so that Perin understood. The prigon turned from the fire as if to walk away to one of the tents. The female prigon snarled at him in the same language she had used previously, and for the first time, Perin could see something predatory and aggressive about the prigon race. Yes, there was something reminiscent of a bull about Kesairl's features, but that did not mean that there was anything cow-like about this female.

"Hospitality, Jiyagor! Civility at all times. Do not disgrace this torzsa!" She spoke Claimic too. The male turned at once, placed his palm across his mouth and bowed his head, his eyes closing momentarily to mark the apology. His expression became less contrite, though, as soon as the female had turned her attention back to Kesairl.

"You are known to us, Kesairl uto Abrun. You and your companion are freely given the gift of our friendship, our food, and our fireside." The prigon woman paused. She looked from Perin's throat to Kesairl's, where Medrivar's symbol shone as well.

Kesairl answered any questions she might have had before she could ask. "Medrivar is not with me. You need not worry on that account. At least... he is not with us physically. He is not manifested here." The prigon took a deep breath, seating himself at the fireside, avoiding the gaze of his peers by staring into the dancing flames.

"A dark mage separated Medrivar from his body in the Erdhanger graveyard."

There were gasps. Clearly, while the undead king's company was not wanted, their animosity only went so far. Kesairl's tri-coloured eyes filled up as he went on, his booming, deep tones becoming rougher from emotion.

"When he was here, he slept outside your tents, he ate none of your food that was not offered him, he carried wood, tended the fire... He was—is!—a king, and he allowed himself to be treated like a pauper. His humility shamed your fear, and it does so now."

The expressions around the fire were now difficult to read. Many did twist in shame. Others were carefully inscrutable, although a few looked angry and defensive.

Perin pulled his arms to his side, trying to look as friendly as possible.

"Where is he now, Kesairl uto Abrun?" The female at least seemed sympathetic. She crouched beside Kesairl and raised her palm. Perin saw that her wrist was wound about with a silver band. Another kind of mage, then.

Kesairl did not answer her but averted his stare.

"I am taking your weariness. It is here, in your thoughts, for the most part." She looked over her shoulder at Perin. "I will help you in the same way, in a moment. Where is Medrivar now, Kesairl?" She repeated her question.

Kesairl pointed to where Perin still stood, looking uncomfortable. "Medrivar co-inhabits Perin's body. His Majesty had no choice. Do not judge the action."

The female raised her eyebrows at this. "He controls the youth's body?"

"No!" Perin blurted out.

The female prigon looked directly at him, her green, blue, and grey eyes piercing him. Her gaze was not unfriendly and she waited patiently for Perin to continue.

"He...he's in the back of my mind. I can feel what he feels...when he wants me to. I don't mind. Really. It's not uncomfortable."

"Very well. You must understand, we did not hate Medrivar. Fear and distrust, yes. No hate. Perhaps we were wrong in our distrust, but our fear has been justified in the past." The female rose from beside Kesairl and strode to Perin. In an instant, the weariness began to drain from his muscles; her hand now haloed again with magic.

"You speak amazing Claimic," Perin said, seeking to repay the gift with a compliment.

The female prigon smiled. This close, Perin could see that she was quite old. It was difficult to see, as her skin had not wrinkled as a human's would have, but had paled over time. The basic colour of prigon skin seemed to be some shade of purple, with males often having a brown edge to the colouring, while females retained a stronger blue tint.

"Thank you, young man. I studied Claimic tradition in Nagyevo many years ago. I was among the last prigon of the Torzsi to do so." Seeing the slight frown on Perin's face, she went on. "Torzsa is the prigon word for family. You would say clan, I think? Torzsi is more than one clan. There are six Torzsi in Valo. The language we speak is Priga. Any questions you have while you stay with us, please address them to me whenever you please."

"I speak good Claimic, too," Kesairl muttered indistinctly. Perin looked up to see his companion break into an uneasy smile. The tension around the fire had eased. Prigon all around the little camp were beginning to attend to their duties, albeit with a ready ear.

"I never imagined you as a sulky child," Perin murmured, sitting beside his friend and accepting a bowl of something from a nervously smiling prigon adolescent. A thrill went through him at teasing Kesairl, who surveyed him with a haughty expression.

"I am uncomfortable here. I have not always got on well with my kith. Besides, I am not so many years older than you."

Perin nodded, relieved that Kesairl had not taken offence at the jibe. For a moment he concentrated on the scalding-hot soup. A column of richly aromatic steam rose from the clay bowl, blasting the night's cold from his face. The contents of the thin stew were not easily identifiable, but it tasted like its aroma, rich and subtle, fragrant and earthy, salt and sweet tang, in equal measure.

"Mmmm. Best thing I've tasted since…since I don't know when," Kesairl murmured, lifting the bowl to his lips and disregarding the liquid's fierce heat. The cook chattered away in Priga to Kesairl as they ate. He was an elderly prigon, but Perin could see the corded muscles in his neck and shoulders, suggesting the strength of his youth. Kesairl passed on information to Perin between sups.

"It's full of good Helynvale vegetables. They carry dried supplies down from the hills. And a lot of the flavour comes from a kind of mushroom that grows on or around rocks on the higher moors. *Fuszgomba*. I think. I was never much of a cook."

"'S delicious," Perin replied, panting to cool his scorched tongue. He blinked rapidly to clear his eyes of the tears that had sprung there from the scalding.

Kesairl nodded enthusiastically, making his hood fall away from his head as he continued, oblivious to Perin's condition.

"This is Torzsa Kelish. That woman who took our tiredness, she's the matriarch. Call her Kelish when you speak to her. The others are all named as you were, from birth, though if you want to be formal you should add *uto* or *uta* Kelish to their name. *Uto* for males, *uta* for females. Means offspring, daughter or son, you see?

"I'm from the Abrun family," Kesairl continued. "Used to be in line to become patriarch of the whole torzsa but I threw that away when I chose to follow Medrivar. Sire Abrun was not that happy with me. He's even older than Kelish, and far more old-fashioned." Kesairl's expression darkened significantly.

"He taught me to speak Claimic. Along with half our torzsa. He was at Nagyevo before Kelish was. None of the new generation have ever been into the central Claim. Any Claimic they have will have been learned from elders.

"Won't be glad to see them again. Bad blood between me and my kin runs far deeper than it does with kith like the Kelish, though there are torzsi that treat me much worse. For a moment I feared we had run into the Lyen, or worse, the Darmir. They hate Medrivar's kind, fear the dead as much as they fear their own elders. The Darmir have a history of destroying the dead-that-walk, be they of the Bright Dead or the Damned."

Perin felt Medrivar's anger swell and fade. He swallowed, used now to the heat of the stew.

"Are we going to see your torzsa?"

"Yes. This news—an evil mage existing on the Tacnimag, possibly with their knowledge—forces Kelish to call a Torzsanag. A meeting. A council of the clans. We have a need now to discuss the old alliance."

"The alliance between man and prigon?" Perin asked breathlessly.

Kesairl nodded. "Especially regarding the Tacnimag. We were always wary of their goals and purpose. Many of us feared that giving humans knowledge of the Art would result in some kind of power-corruption. If we break the alliance, then the tribute of magic armoury and vestments will cease. That will put them under pressure. It may force any plan of theirs into the open.

"Then there's the matter of the drizen. They were thought to be extinct in the south and central Claims. Their presence is worrying. A council will be entirely necessary."

Perin spent the next four days listening to the Kelish torzsa discussions, with Kesairl quietly translating. As the week turned, Perin began to realise that the more basic Priga phrases were sinking in somehow, and he was able to form a simple sentence, congratulating one of the Kelish prigon on the standard of the food. The cook laughed freely and said something to Kesairl that the mage refused to translate, though he assured Perin that he had done nothing wrong.

The whole torzsa packed up their round tents into surprisingly compact rolls that the adults carried on their backs. Torzsa Kelish marched for a place called *talalkazohel*. Kesairl's slightly unsatisfying translation was "meeting place." Perin didn't know how they'd made contact with the other prigon but assumed some kind of magecraft.

The young of Torzsa Kelish travelled close to Perin, as fascinated by him as he was by them. To his growing bewilderment, listening to them speak, along with the diligent translation of Kesairl, caused his comprehension of Priga to grow steadily. He had never been much of a talker—even among humans—and now he found that he was good at something. His memory was uncanny. In fact, it was so strange that he began to wonder if this new lingual talent was more Medrivar than him.

When they stopped in the early evening to rest—they had been walking since midnight—Perin slipped away into Medrivar's throne room.

Medrivar was eating an apple.

Perin stared.

The king swallowed and released the apple from his hand. The half-eaten fruit vanished. Medrivar smiled as he rose, stepping down from his throne to greet Perin.

"It won't be long before you become very capable in the Priga tongue."

"Have you been helping me?" Perin's eyes focused on the space where the apple had been.

"In a way." Medrivar pulled up a chair from nowhere, still smiling at Perin's expression.

"You look as if you've seen a ghost. And I don't intend that as humour."

"I'm sorry... I just only got used to you being in my head, and now there are apples and chairs..."

"They were always in your head. Only they have never been used. You have more memory for fruit than meat, worst luck, so I tend to stick to apples. Do you want one?"

Perin swallowed, afraid of what might happen if he tried to eat an apple that existed only in his mind. He shook his head and focused on his reason for entering the throne room. "Um, Medrivar, sir, how is it that I can remember all the Priga words so easily?"

"I'm remembering them for you. I think you'll find that if you concentrate really hard at something, I'll be doing half the work. Make the most of it! Was that all you came to talk about?"

Perin nodded. A thought occurred. "You can see all my memories?"

"When you're not here with me, I can stroll through them at will. Don't worry; there are certain places that you've... I suppose you could say locked. Yes, some memories are locked, and I do not enter them. You realise that I can read you when you are in the physical realm? So, for instance, if you wish to relieve yourself, I close all the shutters in this room."

Perin went red. He had not thought about that. He had assumed that Medrivar could not see things as they happened.

"So you don't...? I mean, when I need to piss..."

Medrivar laughed, rose from his chair, which vanished, and clapped Perin on the shoulder. "Don't worry. If you wish to be private, then it is so. You are still in control. I sense every emotion. I spend most of my time in that orchard from your early childhood anyway, although when you are awake I watch carefully. You may have need of my memories of your memories sometime."

Perin blinked, making sure he understood what the king had just said.

Medrivar's expression became more thoughtful, and he sat once more. "I can be very useful to you, Perin. When there is something I feel I should draw your attention to, I will call you from here. Soon you will be able to speak with me from without. Just direct your thoughts. Perin, I have decided that I shall make you my champion."

Perin felt overawed. He knelt, bowing his head. Medrivar's joy at this gesture surrounded him like air, a hilltop breeze, refreshing and empowering.

The king's hand pressed lightly on Perin's shoulder. "Rise. You are a good servant, Perin, but with your love, I would have friendship."

Perin stood. Medrivar seemed more powerful than before, lit from within, stern and happy. The rings on his strong hands no longer looked out of place. Perin stared at the circlet resting in the gold of Medrivar's hair, and the shining torc that adorned the man's neck. The benevolent eye gazed up from the brooch that fastened his cloak. How this paragon of strength and virtue could have been banished and forgotten, on the fringes of Valo, forced to wither away… Medrivar had been fighting to keep others safe, unselfishly. And most people knew nothing of his existence. The word "undead" was off-putting, certainly, but there was something unmistakeably alive about Medrivar. The fact that he did not breathe was suddenly irrelevant.

"Valo should have such a king as you," Perin declared.

Medrivar smiled softly. "Thank you, Perin Foundling. But I do not think Valo will take a king like me."

"Then it does not deserve you!"

Medrivar did not reply, and his expression gave away nothing. Finally, he did speak, although he looked away into the night sky of the throne room. "I've dreamt of higher kings than me. So do living men; they build temples to the Nameless ones in Nagyevo, but they lead themselves. They will not have me lead them either.

"Go, Perin. You will need to have real sleep soon. You will not tire in here, but your mind needs time to work when you are not in the way. Come back when you are able, and I will teach you."

Perin nodded. The throne room melted away, but Medrivar remained, even when Perin had opened his eyes to stare up at the tent material.

Kesairl muttered something in his sleep. Outside, the stars were coming out. On the border between the Fold of Csus and the Fold of Helynvale, the prigon camp slept.

Eventually, Perin closed his eyes and slept as well, sharing his dreams with Medrivar.

EIGHT

THE MEETING STONE was a large, upright boulder, cracked with age and furred with lichen. It was twice the height of Kesairl, towering over Perin. The slopes had been devoid of bare rock for some time, but now the northern horizon was blocked from view by the rugged moors of Helynvale fold.

Prigon torzsi had been marching down out of the rocks throughout the day. Many of the arrivals stared at Perin, openly amazed at his presence. Others made a point of ignoring him completely, especially if Kesairl was nearby.

The torzsi gathered in a great circle according to their clans. Each torzsa raised a flag above them, representing their clan, and tents were pitched at their backs to keep the wind out. Preparations for a fire were being made in the centre.

Kelish nudged Kesairl as she passed him, bearing the flag of her torzsa; a green circle on pale yellow cloth with a Priga letter in the centre. "You cannot sit here, Kesairl uto Abrun. Join your torzsa." She flashed a smile Perin's way. "You may join him or stay as you wish, Perin Foundling. Our fireside is always open to you." When Kesairl grunted, rising to his feet, she frowned at him and said "Both of you."

Kesairl acknowledged this with the prigon gesture of brotherhood, his hand going from his forehead to cover his heart as he bowed, shamefaced.

"Relax some little," Perin murmured in Priga to his friend, who smiled at the young human's effort.

Kesairl nodded vaguely, walking reluctantly toward the Abrun flag.

The Abrun camp welcomed them solemnly, taking pride in the fact that the human visitor had come to them. Perin exchanged many gestures with the prigon around him, once again fascinated at the extent to which the prigon people preferred to communicate through wordless signs. He came to a halt alongside Kesairl at the feet of an enormously tall and very old prigon. His features were fearsome and warlike, but there was kindness of a sort in his red, yellow, and orange eyes.

"Kesairl."

"Sire." Kesairl touched his forehead between his horns and raised his palm toward his father. The old prigon responded with a small smile, repeating the gesture and pressing his palm against his son's. Then he intimated brotherhood to Perin, smiling wider than before.

"Welcome, visitor. It is our honour that you choose the Abrun to attend this council with. Forgive my poor Claimic, it is a long time since I studied."

Perin returned the gesture with familiarity now. "It is very good, Abrun."

They sat, Kesairl seeming more comfortable. His father leant across to speak to his son in Priga; the only word Perin caught was the Priga for dead, *hilylilana*. He assumed the prigon leader was asking after Medrivar. The father and son finished their conversation, both with slightly darker expressions than before. Abrun glanced along at Perin with a slightly changed look in his eye. It was not antagonistic, but it no longer held the unconditional welcome of moments before.

Kelish stood and walked into the centre, carrying a clay pitcher. She approached an ornate, shallow bowl of great breadth, which was filled with what looked like golden coal. Perin stared in amazement as Kelish emptied what he at first thought to be clear oil into the basin. The instant the liquid touched the rocks, light flared from out of nowhere. The heat blazed steady, but not as fierce as fire.

Kesairl leaned toward Perin. "They're *kotuzska*. Fire-rocks. On the Helynvale high moors, it is difficult to get lost at night, provided there is rain. The exposed seams of *kotuzska* burn brightly enough to show the land for leagues around."

"That...that's water?" Perin asked, incredulous.

Kesairl nodded. "The rocks will now give off heat and light for a long time. Eventually, they will dissolve away—unless they are taken out of the water, one by one, and dried off. One at a time they are not so hot. This is the opening ceremony; Kelish must perform the lighting, as she called the council."

Kelish proceeded to walk around the fire-bowl, addressing all the torzsi as she did so. Perin assumed she was detailing the story Kesairl and Perin had brought from Erdhanger. At last, she came to a halt and called out in Claimic, "Are all the torzsi translators ready, so that we may begin?"

Kesairl smiled as the various clans called out affirmatives. "This is in honour of your presence, Perin. She wants the elders to speak Claimic in translation, so that you understand what is happening."

Perin ducked his head self-consciously, feeling very out of place. A few of the prigon away on the other side of the circle were now eyeing him with expressions of annoyance.

Kelish began:

"The reason I called this council together is because we may be under threat. The Alliance needs to be considered. Drizen wander the hills again."

Sounds of disbelief were silenced as Kelish raised her hands in a swift gesture. "It is true! Kesairl uto Abrun and the young human fought some of their kind not long ago. When the drizen walked the lands of Valo in the past, a young prigon would become of age when he killed his first in battle. For many generations now, our youth have been unblooded. We need to know if our world has changed.

"Many here hold Kesairl uto Abrun's association with the northern undead to be a betrayal of his torzsa. He has chosen to follow a dead king, and it aggrieves many of our elders that it is so. However! It is clear to me that he fights for Valo and good Order. He joined with hunters of the Claimfold to kill drizen, an action that echoes our hallowed past when the Alliance was new. He bears his magistry well and has been a fine guest. The company he keeps, we value highly—a young human of great bravery. This young man is not a warrior. Nay, his trade is one considered poor by his own people. He is a gravedigger."

There was a pause. Prigon nodded their heads. Clearly, grave digging was a vocation that held no stigma among the prigon.

"We do not bury our dead, Perin, but burn them in a tradition no less sacred," Kelish explained. "My point, of course, is that you were not raised a warrior, but you still survived battle with drizen."

There was a little delay as the translators repeated her words in Priga. Kesairl rose. "Perin Gravedigger killed a Drizen himself using only his spade," he said proudly. He sat down again, amid the gasps and approving murmurs of prigon in the circle.

"I had help!" Perin muttered at his friend, face burning from the attention he was getting.

Kesairl merely grinned at him.

Kelish waited for the chatter to subside. "Perin Gravedigger wears the mark of Medrivar, a name many here dislike. Some here even hate the ones who call themselves the Bright Dead. This should be irrelevant to us! Perin and Kesairl are kith. They have been fully blooded in combat, fighting under the terms of our sacred alliance against ones we know as agents of chaos. This speaks of their service to all Valo. All will accept their presence among us now, or carry shame!"

Kelish drew herself up to her full height, her colourful eyes blazing around the circle.

Torzsa Darmir looked angrily back at her, stung by this attack on their honour. They did not speak though, and their neighbours, the Lyen, also held their silence.

"Now. The drizen are an old foe, apparently arising anew. We know how to deal with them. But there is a new threat to us now, which we know little of. Our suspicion of the Bright Dead comes out of the truth that we prigon do not trust rogue spirits—and what are the dead but dust re-gathered to house spirits? We have been told of sorcerers, magi who seek power drawn from the energies of spirits, and they are a new thing. A new fear. Medrivar, when he stayed briefly with my torzsa, spoke of them himself.

"We believed that the Tacnimag, although not formally allied to us, were policing the Claimfold so that such individuals did not make progress." Kelish paced, stopping now and then to lock her gaze with one torzsa leader or another. "We even tribute them frequently with fashioned amulets and ornamentation designed to store magic. People of the Torzsi! The Tacnimag had within their number a sorcerer!"

There was silence. Everyone paid full attention now as the translators hurriedly reeled off this information to their fellows.

"Perin's trust-sire was killed by a Tacnimag mage who drew on power from a spirit or spirits, intruders in this realm. We believe he used this power to destroy Medrivar's body. Medrivar lives on, I am told, in the body of Perin Gravedigger. They share it, and one benefits from the presence of the other.

"Prigon! The fact that such true evil raises an attack against Medrivar should show us that he has been misunderstood. The fact that one of the Tacnimag is so corrupted shows us that we can no longer tolerate alliance with the Claimfold if it means alliance with its ruling council. We should cease our tributes. Of course, we should certainly be wary not to cause conflict as we plan what to do. If any have thoughts on this, rise and give voice now!"

She sat down at the front of Torzsa Kelish.

There was muttered conversation. Abrun stood suddenly, raising his hands high above his head. The action quietened the others. He had been the first to rise and would now speak.

"Sorcery is not to be tolerated! Withdraw tribute and declare ourselves enemy to the Tacnimag!"

A great deal of argument followed, much of it carried out through gesture. The leader of Torzsa Etzsar rose, lifted her arms high and declared, "Worthy Abrun expresses a noble and forthright sentiment. However, my torzsa is not the only one bordering the Claimfold. We do not want hostilities with the

Claimfolk themselves, and enmity with the Tacnimag may be taken to mean enmity with the Claimfold in general."

The argument continued, with Perin hanging on to every word of Kesairl's rapid translation; the prigon torzsanag had abandoned Claimic for Priga.

After some time, the noise lessened and more attention by all was being paid to four particular speakers. Abrun was one—Kesairl's father. He kept up a steady, belligerent line of thought, while Kelish agreed in more reasonable terms. The other two were Kimr, who seemed to have become unofficial spokesperson for all the Torzsi settled on land near the Claimfold. The fourth was Darmir.

Darmir had a broad-shouldered build, even for a prigon, and his face had a long look, almost horse-like in comparison to Kesairl's strong but pleasant taurine features. But Darmir's eyes were not horse-like at all. His cunning gaze swept the rows of prigon as he spoke, often lingering over Kesairl and Perin.

"I believe we should find out more. Send the human boy as a scout. He knows their talk better than we do." Derision met this comment even before Kesairl had fully translated it.

Kelish rose and angrily responded in Claimic. "Perin has already done much for Valo! This problem is all of ours, Darmir, not his alone!"

Abrun caught his son's eye and spoke quickly to him. Perin understood very little of it. He could feel a vague sense of irritation that he assumed was Medrivar's reaction to the proceedings. For a moment, he contemplated entering Medrivar's throne room, but he thought better of it, not knowing what he looked like to those surrounding him when inside his own mind.

Abrun nodded to Kesairl and stood again. "I propose envoys be sent. We need to know how far this corruption goes. We need people who will be trusted, or at least ignored by hostile folk. They need to be able to speak Claimic. I believe that Perin Gravedigger and my son Kesairl should go."

Kelish frowned. "Such a task may become very dangerous if the Tacnimag has indeed fallen, Abrun."

"My son and his companion have both killed drizen. They are, as you pointed out, blood-proved! I would give the task to no other." Abrun sat with a look of satisfaction as Kelish nodded to concede the point.

"Abrun is right. However, we must be careful. They must go partly as envoys and partly as spies." There was dark muttering around the circle of the Torzsanag at this. "Wait until I have finished before judging the idea!" Kelish performed a sharp, sideways cutting gesture that Perin was unfamiliar with as she cut across the murmurings. "They will go as envoys to the City of Nagyevo, not the Tacnimag. Their purpose will be to find out the relationship between the two, and thus, tell us what we need to know."

There was a pause. The Torzsi seemed to be waiting for some kind of confirmation from Kesairl and Perin.

Kesairl nodded, finally rising to speak. "Worthy Kelish and my honoured sire are right. We are best suited to this task. We will undertake it."

He held his head high, touching his horns with both hands lightly before extending his hands forward in the manner of offering. It was the prigon motion for honouring an equal. Many others in the Torzsanag also made the sign. Perin noticed that Darmir did not, and Lyen also stayed silent and immobile.

Later, when the stars had become invisible against a lightening sky, Perin lay down to sleep in the tent arranged for him. Kesairl remained out amongst the other prigon, talking quietly with Kelish and Abrun. The kotuzska had almost dissolved completely in the middle of the meeting area. The torzsanag had officially concluded and the fire rocks had been left to provide light to those still in conversation.

Perin briefly discussed the plan with Medrivar. The king was content; it followed the course he would have taken had the dark mage not destroyed his body.

Kesairl entered the tent when Perin was almost asleep.

"We should both rest now." He spoke in slow Priga, to allow Perin time to work out each word. "Tomorrow we go. Nagyevo!"

The golden light of the fire rocks spread briefly up the length of the cold meeting stone in the dawn. The light flickered for a moment longer before fading as the last of the stones burned up. Grey light washed the hillside. The Torzsi slept. Perin's memories of battle kept him awake for an hour or so, and then he slept, as well.

NINE

THE SUN WAS FAINT and the grass damp with mist. It had been hours since Perin and Kesairl had set out. The land was flatter now, the hills of Csus and the moors of Helynvale both far distant. Perin felt the pace. Kesairl did not travel at any great speed for a prigon, but even with Medrivar's strength aiding his own, Perin tired quickly.

After an exhausting day of travel and an uncomfortable night, Perin shrugged off the blanket Kesairl had given him. The fabric, which swamped Perin, had gathered a coating of dew. As soon as Perin sat upright, blinking blearily around, Kesairl passed him some food.

The dried mushroom was, without its stalk, about the size of a plate. It had been treated in the Helynvale fashion and was, therefore, very strong in taste and served to wake Perin up. The mushrooms did not look nearly so large in Kesairl's great, purple-brown hands as they did in Perin's.

The two spoke in Priga to help Perin practice the language as they got their packs ready. By the time they were up and walking again, the sun had risen. Perin's head had cleared a little and his muscles had warmed through.

More evidence of settlement appeared as they travelled along what had become a road. The dirt path spread about six paces wide and was obviously not that well travelled. Behind, the rolling hills blurred together. Perin experienced another pang that Csus's invisibility persisted, even in this slightly clearer weather.

The land around them was totally flat. Occasionally, a wooden hulk would mark where an old homestead had been, and the wild grass grew in regular shapes, marked out like fields. Hedges formed curving boundary lines. It all seemed strange to Perin, who was used to foliage being wild and uncontrolled, and stranger to Kesairl, who remarked more than once on the oddity of seeing trees growing in lines.

The evening returned too soon. Perin pushed himself harder in response to the darkening landscape, matching Kesairl's stride and exceeding it in the hope that they would come to better shelter than last night's.

Kesairl paused and looked around.

"This isn't right. It isn't late enough to be so dark." He said it in Priga, and then repeated it in Claimic so that Perin could fully understand. The prigon's large nostrils flared as he sniffed the air. "Rain."

Perin groaned. The area around was devoid even of hedgerows now.

Kesairl shook his head. "Wear that coat of yours high about your neck and be ready to run your fastest. We need to get out of this before it gets too bad." He sounded serious. A rainstorm out in the open would challenge even a prigon. Perin had dressed well for travelling, but he would not survive a winter storm on the flatland.

Perin nodded grimly and made sure the brass buttons were done up on his dark leather coat. The high collar would come in useful now. He set out running with Kesairl, loping along easily beside him. The clouds issued a rumbling bellow, the first hint of what was to come.

In a matter of minutes, the sky seemed to fall around them as they ran, turning the dust road to mud. The rain hammered down with force, slicing at his cheeks with a harsh cold, despite the wide brim of his hat. Perin ran faster than before, his heart thudding and his chest aching from the effort.

A shape loomed up out of the dark. It was evening now, and both Perin and Kesairl were totally soaked, despite Perin's thick coat and the prigon's canvas cloak. The shape turned out to be a barn with a gaping door. They made for it at once, Perin sobbing now with the pain of running through the tempest.

Out of the rain, Perin collapsed onto the straw-strewn floor. A rat ran out of the way, burrowing deeper into the old bales that were heaped against the wall. The sound of the storm thudding on the roof was punctuated only by the sound of the two travellers' breathing and the dripping of water where it had found gaps.

Perin stripped off his wet clothes until he was shivering in his underwear. With one arm held across his chest for warmth, he checked their packs.

"Kesairl! The water's got into everything. The blanket, our food, everything!" Perin sat back on the nearest bale, wincing at the prickling straw against his bare legs.

Kesairl turned away from the door without answering Perin, who had spoken in quite competent Priga.

"We have no kotuzska. However, there is more than one way to make heat." Kesairl retrieved a bowl from his pack and placed it on the floor. He held out his hand and stared intently at it. For a moment, nothing happened, but then fire burst into life, flickering up the edges of the container. The prigon sat down, plainly wearied by the deed.

They dried the blanket first, and hung Perin's clothes over a beam above the fire. Kesairl's cloak hung next to them, dripping onto the straw below. Perin wrapped himself in the newly dried blanket and lay back on the straw.

Kesairl sat, dressed only in his loincloth and talismans, humming a song that Perin had heard around the fires of Torzsa Kelish.

After listening to the tune for a while, Perin found that he could remember the words, even though they were in Priga. He joined in, his faltering voice gaining confidence as Kesairl's rolling, bass tones carried the song. Kesairl sang verses that Perin had not heard before, even with Torzsa Kelish. Perin listened as they were sung the first time, and as Kesairl repeated them, Perin joined in. Sometimes he could understand lines of the song at a time, and at other instances, he knew nothing more than the syllables that passed his lips.

Eventually, Kesairl reached up and shook out his mage's cloak. It was still damp. With a shrug, the prigon sat once more and lay down beside Perin, coverless. Perin felt a little guilty that he was using his friend's blanket, but he knew that Kesairl would not allow him to offer it back. The prigon seemed content anyway, his thicker skin keeping him warm. He was hairless, aside from the crop of dark hair around his horns. The patterning of colour on his hide might have been tattooed there; it seemed so dramatic and symmetrical to Perin's eyes. The mix of deep purple and rich brown was seamless.

After a time, Kesairl spoke. "You know what that song is?"

"No. I've heard it before, though."

"Before the time with Kelish?" Kesairl asked without emphasis on the importance of the question.

Perin frowned. "It must have been the first time. I had not met any prigon before that, except for you, and you never sang it."

"True. But when I first met you, you were making the tune."

"Was I?"

"Yes, you were whistling or humming something. Remember what it was?" Kesairl eagerly awaited Perin's answer.

Perin responded slowly, speaking now in Claimic, so that he would be able to easily understand the conversation from then on. "Yes, it was the same tune. But I had not heard it before then. Graves certainly never sang it. He wasn't very musical." Perin paused, caught by his fondness for his old mentor, saddened by the memory of their parting.

"It is the song every prigon youngster learns first. It is our peoples' song, in many ways. Did you understand it?"

Perin shook his head. "Only some. Something about, 'Self and others.' And love. Not the Priga for romantic love though."

"No. The word describes a love demonstrated through putting others before oneself. Many of our elders refer to the time that a prigon went to man and suggested the Alliance. I do not agree with that. There was mutual benefit in that Alliance, not sacrifice. That does not make the Alliance a bad thing. It is a very good thing, even as it seems to be falling apart.

"The song is older than the rest of our artistic tradition. I have heard it sung by the elders, by Abrun, by Kelish more recently; even cowardly Lyen sings it. Yet I have heard it from one other person. Though with different words." Kesairl looked straight at Perin, meaningfully. "In a different tongue." Perin already knew who he meant, knew on a deep level.

"Medrivar," he breathed, and felt a small affirmation from within.

Kesairl nodded slowly. "When I first met him I was in Darmir's territory, making a nuisance of myself. I was highly suspicious of him, as I had been taught since birth to hate the undead. I was just beginning my magistry then and knew little battle magic. I carried a sword, a proper, wide-bladed prigon sword, and I was about to bring its edge down on him."

"But?" Perin asked, propping himself up on his elbow.

"But Medrivar started to sing."

"His people know the song! The Bright Dead know the so…"

"Shush! I'm telling the tale, am I not?" Kesairl said grumpily, but with a flicker of amusement in his tricoloured eyes.

Perin grinned and held his silence.

"The Bright Dead know the song. It is their hymn. I told you that it is our song, the song of Priga. Well, the Bright Dead *are* the song. They embody its message. They fight those spirits that, like them, have taken bodies to use, but who long to take their evil against the living.

"We have been given this time. We were born normally into this realm, but they, the dead that walk, are invaders, imposters. Even Medrivar admits as much, his race are not meant for this time. Yet his Bright Dead follow Order even at their own expense. They fight for people they have never met simply because Medrivar believes.

"Even after travelling Helynvale with me, meeting many of the people he protects, and seeing their blind hate, even then, he still believed—he still *believes*—that it is his purpose. He has lost his very flesh in the battle, and even now is still fighting on."

For a moment, Kesairl was silent. "I miss being able to speak to him," he said simply, after a long time of staring at the ceiling.

Perin reached out and touched his companion's hand. "Kesairl…Medrivar regrets what has happened. He is touched by your love and deeply proud of your continued loyalty. The time where we could walk together is over. Our work is not. We still have much to do. While Perin is now my main instrument, you are, as you have always been, invaluable to my cause."

Kesairl blinked slowly up at the ceiling before patting Perin's hand, giving a quick smile. For the first time ever, Perin saw tears appear in his friend's eyes. So prigon did cry, after all.

Perin returned the smile, slightly shaken by the way Medrivar had spoken directly through him. It had been natural and unforced, but still... the experience had been truly new.

"So," Perin said quietly, after some time had passed, "the song. The *Song of the Bright Dead*."

"No." Kesairl spoke before Perin could continue. "No, it is not the song of the Bright Dead. It is their song, but that is not its name. It is the *Song of Valo*. The *Song of Valo* was on your lips, Perin, when we met. Something is leading you. It led us to you, Medrivar and I, and now it is leading all of us. The time is coming when great things will be done. I believe it."

TEN

AT NOON THE FOLLOWING DAY, Kesairl halted in his stride. Perin ran forward to catch up, wondering what had made his friend pause.

Visible now past the hedgerow they had been walking beside was the east wall of the city of Nagyevo; the wide, paved road leading toward it. A river flowed alongside the road, then through a gap in the stone wall. Ornate bars had been fixed in place so that the river was the only thing freely entering the city. The walls went on from left to right almost to the extent of Perin's vision.

A small group of people were at the gate ahead of them, probably labourers and merchants from the little villages Perin and Kesairl had passed that morning. All stopped to stare at Kesairl. Perin wondered what it was they found stranger, the height and breadth of the prigon, his features, his nose-ring and clothes, or perhaps the horns rising from his hair. In any case, the whole queue into Nagyevo stood silent and open-mouthed.

As they got closer to the front of the line, Kesairl muttered urgently to Perin in Priga. This only drew more looks, but Perin ignored the attention they were getting. While Kesairl spoke, he casually tied his blanket around Perin's pack, concealing the spade head and part of its shaft.

"Listen, Perin, when we reach the gate warden, you are not to tell him your real name. You are not to tell him who you are, or where you come from. No mention of Erdhanger, your real name, your old life, none of it. If the Tacnimag are already aware of the loss of their fellow, then you are in grave danger."

"Ygen. Za ah asas, estevar." Yes, as you say, brother, Perin answered in Priga, pleased that he had remembered an appropriate response.

Kesairl smiled but did not have time to praise Perin's effort. They had reached the gate.

The gate warden stared up at Kesairl, mouth open.

"Ah..." Kesairl smiled in a friendly manner as the gate warden completely failed to speak. Unfortunately, showing his large incisors to the man had the opposite effect to the one intended. Kesairl's brow wrinkled in concern as the man backed away, calling out someone's name.

"Uh...Bistas...there's a... Bistas! I think a drizen...at the gate... Bistas!"

Kesairl snorted, making several people jump. "I am not drizen, man. I am prigon! I just want to enter the city." His good Claimic surprised the man more than anything else had.

The man called Bistas appeared and took a moment to get over his surprise. He was a greying, paunchy man with a drooping moustache. Kesairl waited patiently until he was asked a tentative question.

"Erm, what's your name, please?"

"Kesairl uto Abrun."

"Ah, all right, and your occupation?"

"I am a skirmisher. I act as a scout and a guardian for members of my clan."

"I'll put you down as prigon guard, shall I?" The man had regained his composure, obviously reassured by the heavy ledger in front of him.

Kesairl nodded, pleased with the description.

"What do you want in Nagyevo, Master uto Abrun?"

"I am to deliver a message. I am an envoy to the city."

"Oh! That's important, that is. Hal, run and see if you can find a dignitary to meet with Master Abrun, here. Hurry, off you go!" Bistas watched as his subordinate rushed off. "Sorry, master, we just don't get many of your folk here, is all."

"That's quite all right. May I enter now?"

"Certainly. We'll send someone to find you when someone of the right quality is found. I don't imagine you'll be difficult to find."

Perin suppressed a laugh.

Kesairl passed through the little gate and out of sight.

Perin swallowed. He was next.

"Name?"

Perin said the first name he thought of, the name he had seen on the headstone against which Graves had been thrown.

"Reger Myrvo."

"Ah. That's a Csus name, right?"

"Yes," Perin squeaked out, close to panicking.

"I have a sister lives in the fold of Csus. Quite rainy there, isn't it?"

"Uh...yes."

"Right. Occupation?"

"Oh. I used to, well... I don't anymore...that is, once I was a thatcher. I thatched houses. Not me, my father, I mean. I just helped."

The warden looked at him, bored after the excitement of Kesairl. "Oh, aye, Reger? All right then. And what do you want in Nagyevo?"

"A change of... I want to get a job." Perin fixed upon this lie with an odd certainty. Bistas nodded as he wrote it down.

"I can understand that. Thatching can't be much fun in the rain, not like what you get in the fold of Csus. Go on, in you go."

Perin breathed a great sigh of relief as he passed through the gate. Immediately, he drew a sharp intake of breath back in as he stared around.

Nagyevo was enormous. Everywhere he looked there were sturdy stone buildings, sometimes two or more storeys high. Wooden rooms had been added on top of existing stone ones to create a wonderful mess of haphazard structures, sometimes joining together above narrow alleyways. The main thoroughfare was filled with people, clustered around hundreds of portable stalls and the shops behind them.

Kesairl stood a short distance away, frozen in an attitude almost identical to Perin's. The prigon pulled his hood back from his head as if this would help him take more in. Plainly it didn't, as he promptly pulled the red and blue garment back up over his horns, as if to defend his senses.

"It's amazing, isn't it?" Perin murmured in Priga.

Kesairl nodded silently. Finally, when a crowd of people had gathered to stare at Kesairl in much the same way as he stared at their city, Kesairl shook himself and began to walk. "Let's find something to eat."

There was no end of places that served food along the street. Bakeries fed stalls selling breads and pastries, and one butcher's shop had an open front where a man cooked cuts of meat over a charcoal grill. Kesairl chose a fixed stall at the edge of a busy square, which was dominated by an enormous stone building. The stall consisted of a brick oven with several spits in a rolling cage. A system of weights at the side of the oven served to keep the spits turning, and on the spits themselves were chicken carcasses, gleaming with juices. Perin actually felt his mouth water.

Kesairl examined them for a while. Then Perin realised something. "You don't eat meat!" he said, looking up at Kesairl. He hadn't realised that none of the food stalls had been serving anything other than meat. Although there had been that bakery...

"I can, if I choose. My life in Helynvale does not call for it. But here, everyone seems dependent on it. My teeth are perfectly suited to meat, fear not."

Perin relaxed, glad because this meant he might get some chicken. The vegetables of Helynvale dishes were delicious, but he had missed meat all the same. Kesairl raised a hand to get the attention of the man behind the stall. The gesture was unnecessary. Since Kesairl had arrived there, the man had been staring at him.

"Two chickens, please. And one for my friend," Kesairl said clearly.

The man nodded. "Three chickens. That's two ranars and one fel."

Kesairl thought for a moment. "Would you allow me to pay you with magic?"

The man's face lit up. "You're a mage, are you? What are you offering?"

"I can place a watchward on your stall. If someone tries to trick or swindle you, the ward will break and you will feel it, if I tie it to you."

The chicken seller reached forward and shook Kesairl's hand. "I'll be glad to see that! Let your friend take the chickens. One moment..." He stopped the weights so he could remove one of the spits from the oven. Perin waited with the cloth bag they kept food in. The top chicken stuck out of the top and Perin was forced to stand there with the scent in his nostrils while Kesairl raised a watchward over the stall.

Kesairl and Perin chose a quiet place to eat. An area of stone pillars with canvas strung up as roofing nestled against the back of the enormous central building. The only people there were those deeply absorbed in debate. Most of them were bearded men of some age and wealth, although there were a few notable women with watchful expressions and quick-witted responses.

An old man not participating in the debate sat down next to Perin and Kesairl, barely giving Kesairl a second glance.

"Do you speak Claimic, prigon?"

"Yes. Would you like some chicken, man?" Kesairl offered the man a leg.

The man shook his head, smiling. "We haven't had a prigon in Nagyevo for a great pass of time. Welcome! The last time one of your people studied in the library, I had my hair. What do you think of our debating circle? It was formed a few years ago by some of my learned friends and I, but it has sadly been overrun by people with more money than wit."

Kesairl didn't say anything. Perin thought that it was possible the prigon didn't know the meaning of "debate" in Claimic. He had only some idea himself.

The man leaned back, yawning. "Anyway, prigon, if you have the time, we'd greatly enjoy to debate with you, though perhaps on a different topic than this. I can't imagine many prigon have heard of the current situation with the Nation of Seven Cities?"

Kesairl said that he hadn't. The old man proceeded to tell Kesairl and Perin about the great nation to the West near the ocean. Perin had heard snippets of this in Erdhanger, but nobody had bothered to speak to him long enough to elaborate before.

"They were looking to expand their empire in our direction, you see. Problem they have, you see, is that they are a democracy. Means that they're run by the people. Never get anything done. Now, I'm not one to sing the praises of our Tacnimag, although if they ask, I never criticised either, but one thing they can do is make decisions. Anyway, the Seven Cities have been doing just what we do here, arguing. About whether to invade or not. This discussion is about what they will decide and when, and why. And of course, what we should do about it."

Kesairl took this in with an unreadable expression. Perin was amazed. It was difficult to grasp that the world could be so much bigger than the Claimfold, Helynvale, and the North. He'd never thought about what lay beyond.

After a time, the man introduced himself. "I'm Cama. Cama Konyva. I run the library. At least, I run most of it."

"Kesairl. Of the Abrun clan."

"Perin. I mean Reger!" Perin stared at the paving. He had just revealed his name! How could he have done that so soon? He glanced up at Kesairl, who gave him a look that only increased his sense of shame.

Strangely, Cama didn't react, except to say, "Your secret is safe with me, Reger. Now, are you supposed to be meeting with someone, as an envoy perhaps? I can take you to a spokesman of the city, if you like."

It wasn't as cold inside the city as it had been outside, Perin noticed, as evening drew in. The sky finally cleared, and the sunset left a red burn across the western horizon. Cama led them through streets that were emptying of people, until they came to a small stone building near one of the gates out of Nagyevo.

They entered the low door, Kesairl with some difficulty. The interior was warm and dark. A curtain made of wooden beads separated two rooms. Cama went up to a counter and ordered some drinks, paying with a silvery ranar. The librarian motioned for them to go through the curtain into the other room.

A man with an impressive physique and a stubbly beard got up to greet them as they entered. He wore expensive cottons, and he had a sword leaning against the wall. It was the first weapon Perin had seen that had not been in the hands of a guard.

Cama smiled in greeting, following Kesairl into the room with the drinks on a tray. "Kesairl of the Abrun clan and Reger Myrvo, this is Adamun, Knight of Nagyevo. He is charged with the welfare of the people, his duties extending even to the last defence of the city."

Adamun bowed. "I have been wanting for a very long time to have a conversation with a prigon," he remarked. "Welcome to Nagyevo, Kesairl uto Abrun."

Kesairl sat, impressed. "You know the correct word."

"Aye. I study your people in Cama's library, whenever I have free time."

Cama passed a cup of something hot and fragrant to Perin. "It's a drink from the Nation of Seven Cities. They make it from some kind of bean. Unfortunately, products from that land are looked down on by the authorities, so we are forced to enjoy them in private establishments like this one."

Kesairl raised a brow. "I thought you were the authorities. Knight of the City, Chief Librarian. Is that not power?"

Adamun grimaced. "We all know who the real power are in Nagyevo, Kesairl. The Tacnimag would not want you in the city. Recently they have been very edgy. Like a horse that has been frightened by something, they are more ready to kick out than in the past." Perin and Kesairl exchanged a glance. "This meeting was brought about because the young man at the gate, Hal, is the son of one of my disciples. He knew that if one of the city officials heard of you before us, you would be banished. Perhaps worse."

"I was on the lookout for you," Cama confessed. "We want to have a conversation that will mean the Claimfold and the Torzsi of Helynvale have actually communicated. The Tacnimag are obsessed and withdrawn at the moment. They are never seen leaving the Observatory, although occasionally one of the junior magi enter the city from outside. Apart from a few exceptions, the council are very unfriendly at the moment."

Perin sat and sipped the drink made from beans and listened until he was close to nodding off in the quiet chatter, comfortable in the cushioned chair. After a time, Cama left them to attend to some duties, and Kesairl continued to talk with Adamun. Adamun was soon deeply in the prigon's confidence, and it was clear to Perin that a friendship had been forged.

Rather than sleeping, Perin allowed himself to enter the mind chamber where Medrivar watched the conversation himself.

The king nodded to Perin as he approached. "How are you finding your new company?"

"I like them well enough, Medrivar. I wish they would stop talking soon, though. I can't keep my eyes open."

"A child grows tired where he should listen," Medrivar softly rebuked. "It might be of great use to you to pay attention. There is...ah!" The king stopped, holding up a hand, his head held to one side. He frowned. "Something isn't right, Perin. Leave the chamber. Get hidden!"

For the first time, Perin experienced the sensation of being pushed out of his own mind. He stood up abruptly at the exact same moment a heavy knock came on the door of the bar.

Across the little table, Adamun's expression froze with fear, partly from Perin's pre-reaction. "Hide!" Adamun whispered.

Perin pulled back his chair so that he could see the gap behind the long-cushioned couch on which Adamun sat. In a moment, he had wriggled in behind it, pulling his feet out of view as the door burst open. The bead curtain rattled from the entry of several people.

"Prigon! I am authorised, as an Observatory Guard in service to the Tacnimag, Nagyevo, and the Claimfold, to put you under—"

"No!" Adamun shouted, rising to his feet. "He's done nothing wrong. You can't…he's an envoy!"

"—Under arrest by order of that same Tacnimag, as you are believed to represent a threat to the interests of the Tacnimag, the city of Nagyevo, and the people thereof. You will now come with us, freely and unharmed, to the Observatory cells—"

"*No trial*? You aren't even giving him a trial?" Adamun was plainly enraged. Perin saw the sword move where it still leaned against the wall. It was the only thing he could see.

"Put your sword down, Lord Adamun! You yourself are not beyond the arm of the Tacnimag!" The guard shouted back at Adamun. For a moment Perin thought Adamun might actually try to fight. The room was too small for combat.

A moment later Kesairl spoke. "Sit, Adamun. I will go with them. There is no other choice."

No! Perin bit down on the urge to cry out. No sound came from him, but his whole body fought with the emotion rising in him. They couldn't take Kesairl away!

Kesairl continued, but now he spoke in Priga. "Stay where you are, brother. Lose your name…you know who you have to be now. Stay in the friendship of Adamun. He is a good man, it seems to me. Think about what is best for Medrivar's cause!" There was a short silence. One of the guards sniggered.

"We don't speak your tongue, bullface."

Perin clenched his fists in anger; his whole body tensed.

"What was that he said?" the lead guard demanded.

"He was blessing me for showing him honour," Adamun said bitterly, "an attribute you and your masters plainly have none of."

"Careful what you say now, Lord Adamun," the guard warned. "Like I said, we have cells for any man, lord or no."

There were the sounds of the men exiting. Then the couch was pulled back and Perin looked up at the dark ceiling. Adamun gazed down at him, but Kesairl was gone.

ELEVEN

PERIN WALKED BESIDE Lord Adamun, having almost as much difficulty keeping up with the knight as he would have done with Kesairl. The knight said nothing until they had passed well beyond the area in which Kesairl had been taken. His expression was grim and angry when he finally turned, stopping in the shadow of a three-storey terrace.

"The Tacnimag appear to have discovered that one of their own has disappeared. It would also seem that they believe a prigon was involved. Kesairl will be held for interrogation. If they get nothing out of him, and I have no doubt that he will defy them, then they will simply keep him in a cell until the problem is solved by some other means." He put a gentle hand on Perin's shoulder. "I do not think they will kill him."

Perin shivered. The thought of his friend stuck in a cold cell, perhaps undergoing some kind of torture, hurt a lot. "Will he ever…" He could not finish the question.

Lord Adamun sighed and looked away, down the length of the street. The dark sky seemed darker still, background to the lights of the city.

"You should stay in the city. Now would not be a good time to flee. If my associates can contact the prigon torzsi, they will. For now, we should stay calm and avoid conflict. I will pay your costs for a year in a building I own here in Nagyevo. After that, you will need to be able to pay for your own food and warmth. The best hope Kesairl has now is that you make something of yourself.

"The Tacnimag have long showed little care to the people they are supposed to serve, and someday the folk of Nagyevo might remember that and things might change. Then you will be in a position to help Kesairl. Learn how to live in your own right. I will help you. Do not let me down, Perin."

Perin nodded mutely. The world seemed to bear down on him. The city's immensity no longer seemed wondrous, but frightening. He did not have much choice—he certainly could not return to Erdhanger. The idea of going back to the Torzsi without Kesairl was unbearable.

Adamun gestured up at the end building of the terrace. A sign showed that the ground-floor rooms were the property of a 'Quality Confectioner', but the steps that ran up the side of the building led to a first floor room with darkened windows. An equally small room with lit windows made up the final floor.

"Up those stairs. The room will be dark and cold at the moment, but clean. A good place to start. Cama lives in the top room, and he will help you as well. You won't be alone. He will be upstairs. All right?"

Perin nodded again.

"Now." Adamun took out a leather purse. "This is for the coming week. I will pass on each week's money to Cama when I visit him at the Library. It would not do for me to be seen with a strange lad when the Tacnimag will no doubt be on the lookout for one. If they are aware of Kesairl, then they will be looking for a youth from Csus as well."

"Thank you." For a moment, Perin was completely overcome by the man's generosity.

The knight smiled, his eyes crinkling as he put a hand on Perin's shoulder. "You'll be your own man very soon and be able to help others in much the same way. Don't forget kindness! It is an underused weapon." Lord Adamun bowed and strode away.

Perin climbed the steps to the apartment, pausing at the door to look back down the street where Adamun was passing out of sight. Then he took a deep breath and entered.

The apartment had solid stone walls with one window looking onto the street. A sink beneath the window had a bucket sitting beside it, and the last inhabitant had polished the wooden counter on either side to a reasonable finish. A low couch sat at an angle not far from the fireplace. Perin felt a breath of cold air as he passed its dark grate. A bed occupied most of a raised section at the end of the room farthest from the door. A heavy looking curtain half obscured the bed from view, and the floorboards were hidden by several mismatched and threadbare rugs. The bed itself was vacant looking, clean sheets and covers untouched.

"Welcome home, Perin," Perin murmured to himself. Medrivar's voice mimicked his own at the back of his mind, fondly amused. Sitting heavily on the couch, Perin escaped into the throne room.

"Kesairl will be strong." Medrivar was already walking toward where Perin always appeared, the middle of the mysterious space, opposite the throne. His ringed hand rested lightly on Perin's shoulder. "He perhaps considered the chances of this happening. I don't doubt that he can handle whatever the Tacnimag might…"

"And if they kill him?" Perin winced at the high pitch of his voice. "Maybe you didn't think about that! I have. If they do…"

Medrivar looked solemn as he stepped away, his hand stroking his beard. "I don't think they will. And even if… Listen Perin, death itself is nothing more than separation. As painful as that might be, it is not discontinuance. Do you understand?"

"No."

"I mean that death brings the next realm into being around the one who has died, the old realm falling away and taking with it their physical form. They are still there—wherever there is—but they are in a new territory."

"I still don't understand."

"Gods of Valo, Perin, am I talking Claimic or not? Stop thinking of this—" Medrivar pinched Perin's wrist without warning, "—as who you are! Your physical shape is less real than you are!"

Perin frowned. "But in here, my physical shape isn't real anyway because I'm inside my own mind. So here my shape is just this way because that's the way I see myself—"

"Yes! Exactly! It's the same on the outside. Your body is how you identify yourself, but without it you would still be the same person. Once you understand that a person's spirit is who they are, and not their body, you can understand death."

There was a pause as Perin considered this, rubbing where Medrivar had pinched his arm. "Who you are goes somewhere else when you die?"

"In a way. Another realm perhaps, where you don't need a body."

"Is it better than this one?"

"I don't know. I have never actually died."

Perin stared.

"Oh, I know I am called dead, or undead. But remember, I came into being undead, because I had no body when I started out, and the only one I could find was no longer being used. My body—when I had it—was physically dead, although magically altered, but my self is as alive as you."

"I knew that," Perin said, truthfully.

Medrivar nodded. "That's because you were gifted with far better instincts than you were sense. No, I'm being unfair. You are not unintelligent, just…pre-intelligent." He winked, and Perin scowled back as if offended.

"My point, Perin, is that Kesairl's death—which, may I remind you, I do not think will come all that soon—would merely be a separation from us, perhaps even a temporary one. Who knows what awaits us, after all?"

"That doesn't really make me feel much better though, Your Majesty."

"Kesairl will be all right."

Perin accepted the comforting weight of Medrivar's be-ringed hand on his shoulder for a moment before he returned to the world like rising from sleep. But the sensation of protective comfort did not go away, and Perin put aside his worries.

When Cama knocked on the door and entered, Perin was lighting candles, carrying a taper to and from the stove oven.

"There's more fuel for that stove upstairs if you run out. And I've brought some food for you tonight. It's not much of a welcome to Nagyevo, circumstances considered…" Cama trailed off. He placed the cloth bundle on the table. "I'm sorry that it happened. I had no idea they were watching that carefully. Now you understand why the learnéd here are afraid to voice an opinion directly opposing the Tacnimag."

"Thank you, Cama." Perin unwrapped the cloth. There was a small round loaf, a slab of white, crumbly cheese, and a second cloth warm to the touch, from which a spiced, meaty smell arose.

"A delicacy from the West. The man who runs the bean-drink house trades it in. If the Seven Cities do decide to make war, the trade routes will close, so that may be the first and last time you eat it!"

Cama seemed tired and nervous. Perin smiled and sat down to eat. It had been a while since the chicken in the market. Cama's mood lightened as he watched the young man enjoy his meal. He finished lighting the other candles for Perin, making conversation as he moved around the small living space.

"You'll need to fit in and make yourself unnoticeable now. Thankfully, the Observatory Guards are mostly idiots, so they won't make a link between Adamun and this place. He puts up the menel for this place, but it's in someone else's name. I work in the library, so falsifying records is easy." Cama continued his chatter. "What kind of work are you going to do then, Reger Myrvo? Not thatching, I assume?"

Perin frowned, remembering his lies at Nagyevo's gate.

Cama smiled. "The young man on the gate is part of the same society as Adamun and I. People who appreciate Western thinking and other more material benefits from the Seven Cities. Your arrival's coincidence with Kesairl's will be missing from the gatehouse records. But your name and details are on there, so you'll still need to be careful."

Perin swallowed, idly pushing the last piece of spiced meat across the plate with his knife. "I have some time before I need to work. But if I can't be a gravedigger—" for a moment his vow to Jesik rang in his ears,"—then I don't want to do heavy work again. I wish I could read."

"I have a job for you." Cama's eyes gleamed with his idea. "I'll take you on as an assistant at the library. That's a little pay straightaway, and in the meantime, I'll teach you how to read and how to write. Then you can teach me the Priga you know—I have their alphabet, and they write phonetically, so we could start translating the few prigon works the library has—on the quiet, of course. There aren't many, as I say, the prigon mainly have an oral tradition rather than a written one..."

Cama shook his head slowly, finishing his utterance with a sigh. Then he made fists of his hands and said, "We'll get Kesairl out of that Observatory cell one day, Perin, mark my words. The Tacnimag won't be able to get away with mistreating the people forever! We just have to wait for our time."

Perin smiled fiercely. "And I'll use it. I'll do what Adamun says. Teach me to read, Cama, and write, and maybe then I'll learn something in your library that will help." *And one day Kesairl will be free and I can be a gravedigger again.* He didn't voice his confirmation of his oath, but he meant it with every moment he held the thought in his mind.

It was strange, waking up after sleeping in a proper bed rather than on the floor, exhausted after walking a long distance in Kesairl's footsteps. Perin had heard that some outdoorsmen had difficulty sleeping in comfort after time in the wilds, but that problem certainly hadn't affected him.

The room was cold. Perin lit the stove, remembering freezing mornings in Erdhanger when he had rushed to get the fire going in the stove in Jesik's cabin. The Csus winds would be colder than here in Nagyevo, he supposed. The land was flatter around here. The city made that difficult to remember, with all its overhanging building fronts and crooked alleyways, but Perin felt he could tell a difference in his bones. He grinned. That thought might have been voiced by Jesik.

Perin's reminiscing was interrupted by Cama knocking on the door. They shared a hasty breakfast standing at the counter rather than sitting at the table, while Perin tried to take in all Cama's advice about living in Nagyevo.

It was impossible to feel secure when walking through the city, Perin discovered. In Erdhanger, there had always been someone watching and listening, but here, nobody seemed to notice anyone else in the crowd. Despite this fact, Perin had to stop himself from averting his gaze every time they passed a guard.

There were two types of guards, Cama explained. The men that had pushed into the Seven City-style drinking house and arrested Kesairl had been dressed in shining mail that suggested constant maintenance. They had all worn expensive-looking surcoats over their mail, and their helmets had been different from the gate guards' simple steel caps. A ridge on the helm tapered down to the nose-guard in a long asymmetrical triangle, bisected vertically with a narrow lightning line. Perin could see no guards wearing that uniform nearby. The patrolmen and gate guards here, though equipped a little differently from one another, all wore the same battered-looking gear, emblazoned with the Nagyevo crest. The faded blue shield symbol was dominated by a silhouette of the walled city.

Perin's insecurity heightened when they entered an open square which was already filling up with a higher class of market stall than Perin had seen before. Looming at the opposite end of the square was the enormous central building that Perin remembered from the debating area, its towering dome dominating the city around it. From the front it was even more impressive, partly because the stone blocks that made up the smoothly curving walls looked cleaner, and partly because of the tall wooden door and the emblem affixed there.

Visible even from the other side of the square, the image was wrought from iron. It showed a ring, suspended horizontally, with a long asymmetrical triangle passing downward through the circle. The triangle, ending in a sharp point at the bottom, was bisected by a jagged scoring line, dividing it down the middle with lightning.

The symbol of the Tacnimag and the immediacy of the Observatory itself made Perin stop in his tracks. Cama's hand gave him a subtle push to get him going again. Perin swallowed. Somewhere in the depths of the Observatory, they were holding Kesairl.

"Come on!" Cama said cheerfully, his eyes scanning the crowd with a manner unlike his tone, "let's keep moving or we'll be late." Perin guessed he was looking out for Observatory Guards.

"It's so close," Perin muttered.

Cama nodded but kept a wide smile as he guided Perin toward a shop.

"You need different clothes. In case someone has a memory, and the Observatory Guards do ask questions…"

A little later, all of Perin's travelling clothes, including his wonderful coat, were packed away and he was dressed in warm clothes suitable for a clerk or a scholar. Without his tough travelling gear, Perin felt underdressed. Now, at least he was in a disguise of sorts.

As Cama led Perin directly past the doors of the Observatory, as if making a point, he explained why the door was so firmly closed. "Very occasionally, a mage comes in through the city to the Observatory, although we never see them leave the normal way. They don't use the front door either. Must have another way in. Either that, or they can pass through it like smoke."

Perin shuddered. Kesairl and his people had many magi among them, and perhaps it was his bias, but he had never felt so cold and threatened among their magic users as he did now, passing the door of Nagyevo Observatory, the seat of power in the Claimfold, fortress of the Tacnimag.

TWELVE

WEEKS HAD PASSED since Perin's first steps into the Nagyevo Library, a square, dignified building a few streets east of the Observatory. The trees lining the square outside were coming into bud and the sharp air gave way to warmer days. The grey stone of the Library became almost radiant in the brief bursts of good spring weather. Inside, dust gently stirred in the columns of sunlight coming in through the high, latticed windows. The occasional sounds of feet on the polished marble floor, and the gentle whisper of pages turning, replaced the sounds of the bustling city.

Perin had worked hard, his anxiety about Kesairl motivating him to progress. His reading was now at a level that pleased Cama, his patient teacher. His writing was a little worse, but good enough for helping Cama with his illicit pastime of translating prigon documents. Of course, it had helped having a second teacher within his own mind, even if Medrivar had influenced him to write in a distinctly archaic style.

The other apprentice clerks respected Perin for his hard-working attitude, but his intensity meant that he was viewed as "the serious one." When the other apprentices went into the city for a drink, he wasn't invited.

Cama pored over the instruction sheet Perin had copied. "Your hand is improving," he remarked with a quick smile. A glance around confirmed the presence of nearby clerks. "Good job, Reger." The man ran a hand over his bald scalp, handing the sheet back and looking away distractedly. "I know I've forgotten to do something…oh, yes, the topographical commentaries we just re-shelved…" He paused, searching his desk for the relevant information. The door from the library atrium closed behind a visitor.

"This one's for you, Reger."

Perin nodded, going to meet the newcomer halfway. A noblewoman with a severe expression nodded curtly to him as he bowed.

"My lady, how may I help you?"

"I would like information on the lands that border the Claimfold to the north. I was told that new geographical studies had arrived."

"Yes, my lady. But I'm afraid the documents on the northern borders have been confiscated, my lady. We don't...we do not know why. Many apologies."

Perin had to endure the woman's biting commentary on the Tacnimag's censorship as he showed her around, from shelf-stacks to the back room archives, and all the way around the iron-skirted gallery above the library's main floor. He agreed wholeheartedly with her vitriol against the magi but kept his input in the conversation to a minimum. There was too much risk in gaining attention for holding a negative view of the Tacnimag.

After lunch, Perin studied alone at Cama's desk, partially hidden by a shelf set aside for the head librarian's private use. He was talking with Cama about what they could do to brighten up his apartment room when the older man suddenly stopped in mid-utterance and stared, alarmed, down toward the atrium. Perin frowned, peering around the edge of the stack.

The figure approaching them wore a garment that made Perin's heart lurch. In design, it was very similar to the black robe worn by the mage Perin had killed in Erdhanger. This robe, though, was not black, but blue and cream. The wearer was young, perhaps a little younger than Perin. He came to a halt in front of them, a slightly uncomfortable smile on his face.

"Master Librarian."

"Welcome, young master." Cama took his cue from Perin, who had recovered enough to look merely attentive rather than afraid. "We don't often see Tacnimag mages in here. How can I help you?"

"Thank you, Librarian. Actually, might I talk to your apprentice?"

Alarm fired Perin's mind toward panic. Medrivar's calming presence kept his anxiety from showing.

"Yes. Of course, sir, follow me." Perin led the young mage away to the other side of the library hall, offering him a chair on one side of a study desk. Cama stood for a moment, clearly worried, before he pulled himself together and went about his work.

Perin watched the mage across the desk. Was this a Tacnimag investigator? Was this how they would go about it?

"You're a mage," Perin said bluntly.

The boy across the desk grinned wryly. "It's the robes, isn't it? People always guess because of the robes."

"No...I mean, yes, but...it's like Master Cama said. We don't get Tacnimag in here. Ever."

"Yeah. Well, they probably wouldn't like it if they knew I was here. The elder mages, I mean."

Perin considered this for a moment. His heartbeat was still way above normal, but so far, this young mage didn't seem like an accomplished and ruthless investigator.

"So why are you here? I mean, how can I help you?"

"Look." Now the young mage looked uncomfortable again. "I'm a junior mage. I'm *the* junior mage. I'm the last young one that they've recruited, for years. There are no other mages my age. I'm…I'm saying mage too much." He took a deep breath. "I spend most of my time in the Observatory. Alone. I came because of you."

Perin raised his eyebrows. Beneath the desk, his hand became a fist as he controlled himself. "Why me? What for?"

"You haven't got any friends, either." The boy started to run his fingers through his close-cut, auburn hair but stopped self-consciously. "I don't mean that as an insult. I've just been watching you. The other library boys don't spend time with you."

He's been watching me? "How have you been watching me?" Perin tried to suppress the strength of the question.

"It's a skill, my skill. I'm a telemage. Magic over distance. I can see places that I've seen before, if I concentrate on the memory. As they are at the time that I look. That's just one of my skills." The mage said this with a growing look of guilt. "Look, I'm sorry. I've essentially been spying on you."

Perin swallowed. Medrivar's suspicions were diminished, but still present. "Why?"

"I've been here before," the mage dodged the question, "when I first came here from Temlan. I figured that the Tacnimag elders would never allow me to have ties with the ordinary people, the commoners. But a library clerk's assistant seemed more possible. They respect the learned, despite their feelings about how superior we are as magi."

"You want me to be your friend?" Perin almost sounded incredulous.

The young mage's face fell. "I'm sorry again. I should just stay at the Observatory. They don't like me leaving anyway." His lip trembled as he rose, and Perin was struck by the realisation that the robe meant little, in this situation. This boy was younger than him. He had probably been through less, but in other ways was certainly less fortunate than Perin himself. Kesairl might be incarcerated, but at least Perin had him as a friend.

"I didn't say that we can't be friends," Perin said bluntly, "it's just strange. I mean, it's an odd way of making a friend."

"I don't have a normal life."

Well there's something we have in common. Perin smiled in spite of himself. "So, what's your name?"

The boy grinned, sitting down again. "Neva Yenesen."

"Reger Myrvo," Perin lied, offering his hand. Neva shook it, his smile lighting up the rest of his features.

"So, Reger. How about we get drunk after you finish today?" A confident, humorous smile appeared.

Perin laughed. "You're eager to get on with making up for lost time then."

"I've never been out for a drink." Neva shrugged, getting to his feet. "I have to go back to the Observatory now, but I'll be back when they're closing the library. See you later, Reger."

Perin watched Neva walk away, nodding in passing to Cama, who shot a worried and wondering glance in Perin's direction.

For the rest of the day Perin shelved and archived incoming texts and documents for Cama, explaining quietly to him what had taken place. The librarian was plainly not convinced of Neva's innocence, but bravely put the final judgement in Perin's hands. As the afternoon faded, Perin walked the gallery balcony, wondering if Kesairl was in a cell that let the spring sunlight in.

It was quite cold as the evening came on. Cama wrapped himself in a cloak before checking he had left nothing important at his desk. The other clerks were gathered together, a short distance from the apprentice clerks in the atrium, washed in the gold light coming in through the great, gleaming double doors. Perin could see his breath misting in the air as he threw on his own cloak. Clerks and librarians were not expected to wear the simpler but practical coats of the working classes.

When Perin came out onto the cobbled street, the sun was setting behind the buildings and the town wall beyond on his right, west of the city. A glory of gold and red touched the rooftops, giving the grey city an impression of exotic grandeur under the setting sun. Looking south and slightly east, Perin could see the glass panels in the roof of the Observatory catch the streaming rays of the sun and send back a rose-tinged glow, as if the building was alight.

The clerks headed home. Their assistants and apprentices had already left in search of drink at one of the favoured taverns. Cama stayed a little longer, obviously reluctant to leave Perin to an unknown fate. Eventually, he left with a word of caution. Perin watched him walk away, swaddled in the fir-green cloak that made him recognisable in a crowd. For an instant, doubt rose, and he found himself hoping that Neva would not prove to be false. If he was an investigator and Perin revealed his true identity, then Cama would be at risk as well.

Perin made sure that the circular gold shape of the amulet that Kesairl had given him was hidden out of sight under his shirt. It was the kind of detail that might have been noted at the gate on his arrival in Nagyevo, but he couldn't bring himself to stop wearing it.

When Neva appeared, Perin had to double-check to make sure it was him. He had doffed his mage's robe in favour of ordinary breeches and shirt, and he looked like any tradesman's apprentice.

He grinned at Perin's reaction. "My disguise! It'll be fun to hide my identity for a while, don't you think?"

Perin appreciated the irony in the question. If he was under investigation, it was unlikely that Neva would risk such an appropriate sentence. He smiled and nodded affably.

"So, where are we going to drown our indifference?" Neva was clearly in a good mood. He was almost bouncing on the balls of his feet as he fell into step with Perin, who was moving toward the Observatory Square and the South Way thoroughfare.

"In the trade and industry district, near the south gate," Perin answered, thinking through the overheard conversations of the other apprentices. Medrivar's ability to seek through his memory was useful; he could choose a taverna based on how well it was thought of by others. However, he decided to choose one that was visited less than the others by his colleagues, rather than run into them and create an awkward social situation.

The two young men pushed their way through the jostling crowd on the road as it curved around the bulk of the Observatory. Perin noticed with interest that Neva strayed farther from the building than even he did.

The taverna Perin chose sat a short distance from one of the larger markets on the eastern side of the South Way, but not far from his home, which lay to the west of the road. Carters hurried to leave the city before the City Guard set the watch; the gates would not be closed, but everybody entering and leaving the city after that time would be put through a checkpoint procedure. Neva and Perin dodged creaking livestock carts, now mostly empty, and picked their path around the leavings of the horses. The sunset was a fading, red-gold line behind the dark shapes of the city by the time they entered the taverna.

The crowd of customers within made the large, well-lit room seem cramped and busy. Tables were placed haphazardly around the space, with a variety of mismatched chairs and benches loosely associated with them rather than tidily arranged. The customers were in a similar state of contented disorder, with a cluster of tradesmen and trade apprentices standing around the wooden bar and earlier arrivals sitting at the tables or in alcoves against the old stone walls.

Neva's eyes lit up as if he had discovered treasure. Perin stood, looking around warily, choosing a long table near enough to the wall to be unnoticeable, but still close to the door. A variety of chattering youths his age joined the table without so much as a glance in his direction, and by the time Neva returned, one ranar and six feli poorer, but with a beer jug in each hand, their conversation was well underway.

Neva, his top lip glistening with foam from his jug and eyes gleaming with interest, wasted no time in entering the conversation. His presence was accepted as if they had always known him, and before long Perin was voicing his own opinions.

One boy a little younger than Perin, with wildly untidy hair, seemed to be the dominant presence.

"—taxes get higher. If you complain, they just set the Oh-gees on you. If you pay late, they set the Oh-gees on you. If you don't pay at all, you'll be running and hiding from the bloody, filth-eating, whoring, swindling sons of maggots, until they finally catch you and drag you off to the Observatory cells."

There were murmurs of agreement. Neva frowned. "What's an Oh-gee?"

"Observatory Guard." One of the girls gave him a strange look. "How come you don't know what an Oh-gee is?"

Perin intervened, outwardly casual. "We're library apprentices. What d'we know?"

The girl laughed, reaching for her jug. "I thought it was your job to know things, being a library apprentice," she said to Neva. "You should try 'prenticing down here in the trade district. Try weaving hessian into sacks all day long."

"Try butchery," one of her male friends interrupted with a grin. "It's lovely. Knee-deep in blood all day. Up to your elbows in internal organs." He leaned forward, closer to Perin than Neva. "They start you in the slaughterhouse. I still dream about the sounds the cows make when the steel comes..."

"All right, all right, we understand," Neva laughed. "Your jobs are all hard; ours is easy."

"Easy as pissing," the leader said with a wry smile. There was no sense of threat in his tone. The talk changed, and Perin went up to the bar with the butcher's apprentice to bring in another round of the thick, dark beer the taverna was serving. When he had returned to his seat, Perin could hear that the conversation had returned to the subject of the Observatory Guards. Apparently, Aranyo, the messy haired youth, spent a lot of his time hiding from the authorities.

"Been beaten more'n once. If they catch you, they give you a kicking. Broke my ribs the first time 'cos I shouted at them when they arrested that Seven Cities carter. Wasn't his fault things got jagged the moment a'fore he got into the city, was it? And they were goin'a put 'im in a cell for the crime of bringing drinking beans to sell in the market."

"I'd lock him away for that," one of the others remarked, sniggering. "That stuff's disgusting."

"Yeah," Aranyo countered, turning round to stare at his companion. "But you wanna be careful who hears you say you drank bean-drink. They'd put your family under watch, maybe. In case you were up to anything else subversive."

"But that's ridiculous!" The weaver girl spoke out, sounding tired rather than outraged. "Our cotton comes from the Seven Cities. A lot of the spice and herbs we get here come from there. Even bloody hessian relies on the Seven Cities. We don't grow the jute here."

"Yeah, but people don't know those things. Bean-drink is obviously Seven Cities. So are the other expensive things, like silk and some of the spices. The obvious ones get banned because the Tacnimag want to make it clear that they reject the outside influence." Aranyo explained this wisely, his hands moving as he spoke. "But really, it's just an excuse to let the Oh-gees interfere with our lives. Tacnimag aren't afeared of the Seven Cities. They're afeared of us."

He let the statement hang in the air, taking a long draw from his jug. He nodded to Perin, smacking his lips as he put the jug down. "Thanks for the fetch, book-boy."

"It's Reger."

"Right, Reger. I'm Aranyo. So. You gonna be a library man forever? You wanna be a clerk?"

Perin considered. He had been thinking a lot about what he intended to do. It wouldn't be long before Lord Adamun's money for his upkeep stopped coming and he would have to rely on more than just the allowance Cama gave him for the library work.

"I was thinking of becoming a City Guard. Not an Oh-gee, obviously."

"Obviously! Scum, bootlickers, powermunchers. But my uncle was City Guard. You might have a problem, though, Reger." Aranyo leaned lop-sided across the table. "They don't let you into the City Guard without experience. You gotta have served a term in the army or a five-year in the Borderers."

"Oh." Perin shrugged, drinking more of his beer. It really was very good. Was this the third, or fourth? Aranyo turned his attention back to the subject of the Tacnimag, taking hold of a conversation already in progress.

"They're a joke though! They claim all that power, the only magicals in the Claimfold and all...but they never go out and get new magi in. I'm sure there's a few in this city that could be trained into it. I don't think they care. I think they don't give a flying sheepshit about the whole damn city." He paused to gratefully accept another jug. "If I'm honest, mates, I think they're exaggerating their great and majestic powers to keep us all in line. I mean, they still haven't caught that fugitive from Csus yet. He came into the city with a prigon, apparently. The Oh-gees are searching for them, I know, 'cos my old dad is in the know, you know? They got the prigon locked up, and what for, I ask you? What for? But anyway, he's locked up, and for nothing, but they still haven't found his mate."

"Oh," Perin said, lazily. The drink was obviously affecting him, because he felt supremely comfortable. "You mean the gravedigger, right?"

"You know about him?" The whole table's attention was suddenly on Perin, including Neva's.

"I mean, yeah, it was news at the time. I came into the city at the same sort of time, and I come from Csus as well, so I was going to remember it, wasn't I?" Perin reached for his jug, found that it was empty, continued. "I seen him once."

"Offal," the carpenter's apprentice said with a snort. "You seen—you saw a man that the Tacnimag can't catch?"

"Not a man." He definitely had most of the room's attention now. "He's a boy, I mean, a young man, about my age."

"What does he look like, then?" Someone breathed the question.

"Oh, about my height and build." Perin belched loudly, breaking the tension of the moment somewhat. "His clothes though, that was what was interesting. He wore a really long coat made of leather, with a broad-brimmed hat."

"That's what all the gravediggers wear," someone smirked derisively.

Perin shrugged. "Just saying what I saw. He had a spade, as well. A big one." He paused, feeling that this should have been met with a more significant reaction. "A *really* big one."

Aranyo took him seriously, at least, if only because they were both drunk. Neva was listening with the fascination of a boy starved of social interaction.

"What do you reckon? What do you think he wants? Just to keep out of the way of the Oh-gees? Is he the enemy of the Tacnimag?" Aranyo clumsily tipped a little of his beer into Perin's jug, as if encouraging him to answer. "Is he a friend of the city?"

"What do you think?" Perin answered mysteriously, downing the newly added beer in one gulp.

"I think… I think…" Aranyo slumped back against one of the girls.

The butcher's apprentice let out a loud laugh, "You think? First time I noticed, Aranyo!"

"Yeah, I think…" Aranyo chuckled, momentarily distracted. "I think that this gravedigger sounds very, very, very interesting. I think he deserves us a drinking one to 'im."

There was a ragged cheer as those that heard agreed enthusiastically with the idea, and the ones that hadn't heard cheered because people were cheering.

"Everyone brimming?" Aranyo asked genially. When it was clear that everybody had at least some beer in their jug, he lifted his toward the low ceiling and called out the toast. "Here's to the gravedigger! May he elude them Oh-gees forever!"

Amidst the cheering, with Neva clapping him on the back and spilling beer down his front, Perin smiled. *I'll drink to that.*

THIRTEEN

PERIN WENT AND STOOD on shaking legs with his head over the sink. After a little while of numbly studying the grooves and marks of wear in the stone basin, he risked lifting his head. It felt as though his brain had become some sort of hypersensitive pickle. Every movement threatened to cause irreparable damage. Perin drank a little water from the bucket, seeing that the level was low. Then he sat down on the threadbare rug where he had slept, contentedly insensible, with a spare blanket wrapped around him.

The throne room was normal in appearance as he entered. He had expected it perhaps to have crumbled away, or maybe to have filled with poison-moistened spikes. Medrivar stood by a table—it had appeared there presumably in the same way that any object did—looking unconcerned as he pored over a sheet of parchment.

"Enjoy yourself last night?"

Perin bowed, wincing. "It doesn't seem fair, Your Majesty. How can my head hurt even when I'm inside it?"

"It merely proves that there is no escaping consequence," Medrivar said philosophically. "Incidentally, I am very impressed with your bravado. Propagating your own legend, are you?"

Perin snorted. "Some legend. I'm a fugitive working in a library. That's not very impressive."

"That's the truth though. You didn't—thankfully—tell them the truth. You gave them minor, yet important, details."

"As you say," Perin groaned, kneading his temple with his left hand. "Ooohhh. What are you doing there, anyway?"

Medrivar smiled, ignoring Perin's hangover-fuelled irritation. "I'm making a basic map of the Claimfold. You've never seen one. However, you've seen paper, and you've learnt how to read maps; so once I've made this, I will have effectively transferred my knowledge of the country's geography into your mind."

"That'll be useful," Perin said dully. "If I ever need to make a living selling maps, that is."

Medrivar merely shrugged. "I've filled in the details I wouldn't know about from deductions made observing the conversations of those around you. Did you know, for instance, that I can replay a time period but turn my attention to the background, rather than your focus at the time?"

"I didn't know." Perin closed his eyes. "I feel sick again. What...what do you suppose would be the consequence of throwing up inside my own head?"

"Someone is coming anyway," Medrivar responded mildly. "I think Cama."

Perin withdrew from the throne room and had to sit very still for a few seconds to recover. Then he heard the knocking on the door. It felt like someone was driving coffin nails through the sides of his head.

He let Cama in and sat down again. The bald man entered swiftly, with a cheerful greeting that made Perin groan. Then he stopped in his tracks, turned, and made an observation.

"There's a mage in your bed."

"Yes. Is he alive?"

"Why? Did you try to kill him? How much did you drink last night?" There was a distinct note of disapproval in Cama's voice. Before the trade restriction, he had drunk little, save water, wine, and bean-drink. Perin guessed that beer was no doubt well beneath the level of an intellectual such as Cama.

"No, I did not try to kill him. He was just...much more drunk than me. I had to mostly carry him here. I thought it would be a bad idea for him to return to the Tacnimag like that."

"Well. Yes. Well. But I mean, talk about sleeping with the enemy! If he was a spy against you..."

"If he is, then you might be giving away too much right now."

"He's unconscious." Cama leaned closer to check. "Very."

"I wish I was."

"Won't they wonder where he is this morning? Notice that he didn't come back last night?"

"I don't think so. He says they never notice him. He says they have no interest in him. He sat happily through a load of apprentices speaking curses on the Tacnimag. I think he's confused."

"Confused? He's in *your* bed."

Perin didn't rise to the jibe. "I'm not confused. I think I can trust him."

"Fine." Cama shrugged. "Do as you will. Just be careful." He retrieved some money from his purse and put it down on the table. "One menel seven ranar—that's for this week. It's more than normal because I'm not paying you a proper wage. Most apprentices live with their masters, but Adamun gave you your own abode. I'm assuming that's because he wants you to stretch yourself, go for more, and I agree with him. Have you thought about the coming year?"

Perin had, but the effect of last night, and Cama's questions necessitating him to actually think with what was left of his mind, put him in a mood reluctant to reply. He shrugged and waited for Cama to realise that he was late for the debating circle. When the library was closed, the librarian spent his days in the shadow of the Observatory, disputing the speculations of other Nagyevo intellectuals for most of the day. Perin had gone once or twice at the prompting of Medrivar to gather potentially useful political information, but sitting and listening to people argue about things with very little importance—to Perin's mind—was not his idea of how to spend a free day. For instance, today he intended to occupy his time with not being sick.

When Cama had gone, Perin went and checked that Neva was actually alive. The young mage was apparently still unconscious, yet safe enough. Perin wondered how he would feel upon waking and groaned. Perhaps he should fetch the spare water bucket, just in case...

When Neva was able to move without making a sound like a half-dead animal, Perin guided him down the steps and into the street. Most of the little industries that did business on Sixthday had been up and trading for hours.

"You think they'll notice that you were gone?" Perin tried not to appear nervous on his own behalf.

Neva shrugged, his eyes wrinkling in his freckled face out of dislike for the bright sun. "Sometimes, no one there will talk to me for weeks. I doubt that I'll have been missed." He paused, eyeing the looming shape of the Observatory at the end of the thoroughfare. "Thank you for everything, Reger. Someone else might have left me in the run-off ditch. I like your home." He stood awkwardly, pinching the bridge of his nose as if he could draw the headache out through that point. "It's nice," he added, somewhat pointlessly. "I'll see you in a few days, hopefully."

"Well, you know where I live," Perin said with a slight smile. He waved goodbye as Neva set off, somehow making it possible to move gloomily. Perin watched his shape pass in and out of view due to the crowds and occasional carts, slowly but steadily being swallowed up by the dark shape of the Tacnimag Observatory. Perin shuddered and turned to walk back into the trade district, nonchalantly managing to change direction and avoid a trio of Observatory Guards on the way.

Perin's route skirted the southern edge of the warehouses and surrounding workshops known collectively as the Lower East. The city wall stood indomitable and grey to the right of the wide but relatively clear road. City Guards could be seen at the doorways leading to walltops, gathered outside the guardrooms while off duty. Occasionally, messengers on horseback would clatter along the paved roadway. Horses were not allowed to be ridden on the inner roads except by lords and high-ranking officers.

The road curved round to the point where Perin almost faced north again. He knew from Medrivar's internal map that there was another thoroughfare ahead, the East Way, along which Perin and Kesairl had come after entering Nagyevo for the first time. Perin paused, accepting Medrivar's help on remembering the way to go and headed off the Wall Way into one of the narrower roads. Clusters of residential buildings were interspersed among other larger structures. A hospital sat, grim and solitary, reminding Perin of the tanneries because of the space between it and the surrounding buildings.

The ground rose here as he went onward, the houses becoming grander, the wider roads often lined with trees. A very expansive green space had been given over to use as a cemetery. For a moment, Perin stared over the painted wooden fence into the densely populated graveyard, observing the mausoleums and monuments peacefully cohabiting with the crude markers of the poor. The sign over the iron gate dedicated the occupants of the cemetery to the keeping of the Nameless Gods of Valo.

Perin moved on. It might be tempting fate to be seen near a graveyard. It was entirely possible that the poor groundskeepers and gravediggers here were under investigation by the Observatory Guards.

On the other side of the broad hill, the city was more built up. A few specialist shops appeared among the grand houses they served, along with upmarket tavernas and guesthouses.

Separated from the East Way by a cluster of buildings and the attached park, sat a solid building with an official shield hanging above the wide door, contrived to look unobtrusive. A stone wall with a tiled rampart surrounded an area of ground to the building's rear, and a brewhouse stood conveniently opposite. It was named The Borderer's Rest.

Perin stared up at the Nagyevo Borderer's Headquarters. It was not a fortified building like the duty houses used by the City Guard, but the architect had nonetheless decided to make it defensible.

The door was open. Perin crossed the threshold cautiously, unsure about how wise it was to enter a building occupied with law enforcers—even volunteer law enforcers—with a fugitive status. The first three rooms, including a kind of reception and hospitality room, were empty. The building clearly did not get much proper use; the walls were mostly bare and the floorboards dusty.

Bemused, Perin left the building. He was met by a man coming the other way across the road from the Borderer's Rest.

"All right, are you friend?" He was a slim man with a way of standing that implied strength belying his height. At a head shorter than Perin, he still managed to give a sense of authority. "What did you want with the Borderers?"

"To join," Perin said simply.

"Oh." This seemed to surprise him a little. "Why?" Intelligent brown eyes examined Perin.

"Why would anyone?" he said defensively.

The man shrugged. "Can't think of a single damned reason, and I've been a Borderer for eight years." He grinned suddenly. "Swordsman Kard. Swordsman, that's the rank second in command to Response Leader, for your information. And a Response is a unit of six men, not counting myself and the Response Leader." He offered his hand.

Perin shook it, noticing the calloused palm. "It's good to meet you, Swordsman Kard." Perin smiled nervously. "If I'm honest, it's because I want to be able to join the City Guard."

"Ah. Well, the pay is better. Borderers are paid a pittance, apart from commission. That's based on kills made. Commission rate is very high because banditry and similar is so rare, so it's a bit of a joke really." He pointed with his thumb at the Borderer's Rest. "Anyway. Come in and join up."

"You're based in the brewhouse?"

"Now, son, that's a public house, not a brewhouse. Brewhouses are where you go to get drunk. Public houses are where things happen."

"What kind of things?"

"Anything. All kinds of things!" His eyebrows jumped suggestively.

"Sounds like a brewhouse to me," Perin said dubiously.

Kard grinned. "Only certain people go into a brewhouse. Everyone's welcome at the Borderer's Rest." He paused, frowning. "As long as they haven't got anything against Borderers. Obviously."

Perin followed Swordsman Kard into the low-ceilinged interior of the public house. Grouped around a table and arguing vociferously were several other men, all quite lean and a little shabby. They stopped talking as Kard came across, whistling. All of them stared at Perin.

"Hello, Kard. Who's the citizen?"

Kard moved aside to make room for Perin to identify himself.

With a quick breath, Perin stepped forward, ducked to avoid the ceiling beam that Kard had casually walked beneath, and introduced himself. "I am Reger Myrvo. I'm here to volunteer for service with the Borderers."

There was a muffled laugh from one of the men, who sat with his head resting on his arm. A mixture of grins met his announcement.

"Let's get a round in, Kard. An actual volunteer, no less."

The oldest man waved to the barman to follow up on his companion's suggestion. "Capital. Good to know that the volunteer spirit still lives on in Nagyevo."

"Gotta admit though, Captain, it's pretty poorly, this volunteer spirit. He's the first volunteer for over two bloody years."

The captain ignored his subordinate and pushed a newly arrived flagon of beer across the table, clearly intending for Perin to take it.

"Here's the first and last drink you'll be having with us, boy, for a long time at least. I'm the captain of the Nagyevo City Borderers. My job is to manage all the Responses—that's the squads of men—through the Response Leaders and pass on needs and requirements to the Tacnimag, as well as coordinating with the City Guard. These here are my Response Leaders, all eight of them, plus Kard and these two others, who are Swordsmen. Seeing as he brought you in, I'll get you put in with his Response for training. Is that all right, Törodè?"

The Response Leader glanced up from his flagon as if seeing Perin for the first time, looked across at Kard for a moment, and then nodded. "Certainly, Captain."

Kard waited politely for Perin to finish his beer and then steered him out of the Borderer's Rest. "Right then, Borderman Mryvo. We have to get your mark put down on a piece of important-looking paper to show you've volunteered, and then you can go away and see your loved ones for the rest of the day."

In a sideroom in the headquarters, Kard oversaw Perin's signing of the Volunteers' Log.

"Turns out you were just in time for this season. Just turn up here before it gets light on Firstday. Your training will begin as soon as you get here." He gestured around as he led Perin through the doorway of the headquarters into the closed yard, empty except for some old packing boxes and firewood. "The door will be open, and we'll be awaiting you here in the training yard."

"Unless…" Kard turned around and winked, "you don't get here before dawn, in which case you'll have to run double quick to catch up with us at the south gate."

The next day, Cama sat silently for a few moments after having been told Perin's plan. Then he brought out his purse, opened it, and handed over a couple of ranar.

"Not much, really, but it'll do for buying you and a pair of friends a drink after training. That'll be the key, you know. Getting on the right side of the other Borderers."

"Why?"

"Because these days, Borderers are rarely volunteers from the city, like you. Most of the Responses are full of young men who were volunteered for service by their noble—or not so noble—fathers because they were too much trouble at home. They might be somewhat resentful of an actual willing volunteer."

"Oh." Perin took the ranar and pocketed them gratefully. "Thank you, Cama. You've been very good to me. You and Lord Adamun. When you see him next, pass on my gratitude." He stood and offered an embrace, which the librarian accepted with a brief smile.

"You're a fast learner. You'll be fine as a Borderer. And who knows where you'll next end up?"

"I'm not worried about that, as long as it isn't the Observatory cells," Perin answered seriously. "This is all so that I can get into a better position to free Kesairl. Even if it means I work my way year by year into the Observatory itself."

Cama nodded slowly, seemingly a little shocked by Perin's intensity. "I can see you doing it, as well. You're not a fugitive gravedigger anymore."

"Oh, I don't think I'll ever stop being that." Perin smiled broadly. "At least I'll always be a gravedigger at heart. I owe it to someone."

Perin assumed that his meeting with Cama would be the last until the Borderers let him back from training. However, as he ate alone in his room the following day, silently conversing with Medrivar about what he could expect from the training programme the Borderers went through, Cama rushed in without even knocking on the door.

"Perin...look—look at this!" He draped a piece of parchment over the table in front of him. It was a large poster similar to many that the Oh-gees posted in the rougher areas of the city, warning citizens to keep the law. This one, however, had a heading saying, "Dangerous Fugitive" and beneath that in great, dark letters, "The Gravedigger."

There was a picture of a tall young man in a long leather coat and hat. A spade was visible, strapped across his back.

"The Tacnimag Investigator can replicate images and words exactly! Straight onto paper! Hundreds more like this have been posted around the city!"

Perin swallowed his mouthful. The likeness was quite good. It was worrying, of course, that they had such an accurate image of what he looked like in his gravedigging clothing, but, of course, he would have been caught immediately had he carried his spade around in public anyway.

"Well?" Any composure Cama might have had vanished. "How did they get this information? I went and had a word with a friend I have who deals black market goods to one of the Observatory Guards in return for inside information, and he says that the guard said there had been eyewitness accounts. That there have been accomplices and associates caught and questioned. It's not two days since you went drinking with that Tacnimag mage, and the city is suddenly in uproar!"

"I doubt it's in uproar." Perin felt strangely calm. "And if Neva had found out who I was, the Oh-gees would be here already. Anyway, how can they have caught accomplices and associates? I don't have any!"

Cama sighed. "It's a way out, isn't it? The Observatory Guards, the Oh-gees as you call them, they start to make things uncomfortable for subversives and petty criminals, and because of that conversation you had in that brewhouse, where your loose words must've been circulated throughout the entire criminal fraternity of the entire fornicating city and—" Cama took a deep breath to try and recover before finishing, "Before they can react, the authorities are receiving confessions and information referring to you as some kind of outlaw genius! The lawless in the city are going to throw their lot in with this non-existent gravedigger folk hero, just so that they can lessen the threat to their freedom. Just for the sake of hope."

Perin thought for a moment. "This is all right though, Cama. Tomorrow morning, I'll be training with the Borderers. No Tacnimag investigator is going to start off looking for a criminal in the Borderers."

Maybe it was the level of emergency that Cama was feeling, but this brought out his sense of humour. "Perin, do you listen to the brewhouse talk about the Borderers? They don't have pure-white reputations."

When Perin didn't respond, Cama sat and immediately began to calm down. "Look, you're probably right. You're far safer training on the city outskirts with the Borderers than you would be walking past the Observatory every day on your way to the library. But you must take this seriously, my lad. The search is going to heat up now. The Observatory Guards are going to feel the pressure. The Tacnimag can't be seen to be weak, unable. They're all going to be on a much closer watch for you now."

Perin finished his meal in a sober silence after Cama left.

"Ah, well," he murmured to Medrivar, "so be it."

FOURTEEN

THE AIR WAS COLD, but the light rising across the cloud-streaked sky promised warmth. Perin shivered a little in his light shirt and hempen breeches. The others that had arrived stood around the dishevelled training yard, each attempting to appear unconcerned and ready.

Perin nodded to the nearest boy. He acknowledged this with a terse nod in return, his hands thrust firmly into his pockets. Judging by the cut of his clothing, he was probably either the son of a nobleman or of a wealthy merchant. His dark eyes watched Perin warily, and one hand ran nervously through his blue-black hair.

Only one of the new Borderers seemed comfortable waiting for Swordsman Kard and Response Leader Törodè to stop conversing by the headquarters door. The recruit's unkempt mop of blond hair stood out as much as his preposterously rich clothing. There was so much gold thread in his shirt that a mage might have used it to conduct magic. His tired, early-morning expression smiled comfortably out at the world. Seeing that Perin and the dark-haired boy were watching him, he smiled widely and waved like a child.

A slim, delicately featured young man with a quirky mouth and cropped brown hair leaned against the wall of the yard, watching everyone with fiercely critical eyes. A short distance from him stood a broad-shouldered lad with longer brown hair and striking green eyes in a face so smooth and well formed that it seemed almost unnatural. He kept his eyes on the ground, studying the dirt as if it had wronged him somehow.

According to what Kard had said two days ago, there should be six new Borderers, five apart from Perin. Therefore, one was missing. Dawn had technically broken, so this latecomer only had Kard and Törodè's conversation between him and a conspicuously late arrival.

It was as the Response Leader brought his talk with Swordsman Kard to a close that the last volunteer entered the yard between them, walking as if anything that got in his way would receive a blow. He ignored their startled and watchful reaction and came to a halt a short distance from Perin. His head was closely shaved, a style Perin hadn't seen before. His grey eyes were not as sleep-blurred as most of the others, but they had an intensity that made Perin wary. He was taller than everyone in the yard, even Response Leader Törodè, although the blond-haired boy was probably broader in the shoulder.

"You're just in time," Törodè said mildly, coming to stand in the centre of the yard. "Bordermen, let's come to order."

Kard, grinning like a fiend and with the slightest glance in Perin's direction, strode forward in a way that made the shaven-haired boy's entrance seem positively effeminate.

"*All right, my beauties! Line up!*" he roared.

The volunteers formed a line as if the sound of Kard's voice had direct power over their muscles. The latecomer glared back at Kard, but stood alongside the others.

"With a little more *poise*, if you please, lads! Straight-backed and with hands *at your sides*! Welcome to the Nagyevo Borderers! You're all here because you volunteered, or because someone with more sense than you, volunteered you. I'm Swordsman Kard, which makes me second only to Response Leader Törodè. That means you do what I say, and *you damn well do what he says*! It's called the chain of command, lads!"

Kard paced up and down the line of young men as his leader looked on with mild approval. "Right, to get you started, the quartermaster has come down here from the Nagyevo Committee building especially for you, to make sure you're turned out in the best defensive wear that Nagyevo can offer. So let's get those citizen rags off've you!"

"I mean *now*, lads!"

Kard returned to Törodè's side to mutter something quietly to him as the boys hurried to undress. The latecomer tore off his rough shirt and breeches with a violence clearly intended to be noticed by the unconcerned Response Leader and Swordsman. Within a few seconds, Perin stood like all of the new volunteers, naked and shivering. Kard nodded in agreement to Response Leader Törodè's reply and stepped forward again.

"This is what we call the social leveller, mates! Some of you are noble, and some of you aren't, but that doesn't matter when you're standing in the stark, now does it?" Kard gestured to where a man approached across the yard. He sized up each boy by eye and marked down his conclusion on a pad of paper with a thick pencil.

"Right. Introduction time. One after the other, starting with the bald feller at the end there, I want to hear you call out your name, *your place of origin—* that means *where you come from, lads—* and what you used to be before you came here to become a Borderer. *Lesshearitthen!*"

Gritting his teeth as if he hated even the sound of his own voice, the shaven-headed boy complied. "Name's Forgos! Claim of Nagyevo!"

"And what were you before this, lad?"

"None of your business!"

Kard grinned and shrugged, nodding to the next boy, the dark-haired one.

"I'm Uno Sudar from the Claim of Nagyevo. I—my father is on the Nagyevo Committee of Trade. He volunteered me."

Perin swallowed, standing straighter before calling out the required information.

"Reger Myrvo! I'm from the Claim of H—of Arpavale, in the Fold of Csus. Last week, I was a library apprentice."

"Harco Oksen! I'm from the Claim of Solorin in Narsun Fold. Lord Oksen owns some vineyards. He's my father, by the way. I used to do, well, nothing really—"

Kard cut the blond boy short. "That'll do, Borderman." He nodded to the attractive, green-eyed boy.

"I'm Maka, son of Lord Nyacus of Nagyevo. Used to do whatever I could get away with." There was no appreciative chuckle to meet this joke, although Kard suppressed a smile.

The young man with the judgemental aspect managed to appear faintly disdainful despite his vulnerable, skinny body being on show in the early morning air. "Gyorva Jolsen. Claim of Nagyevo. I'm not fit for haulier work, and I'm not fit for this, but at least here, my father can't see me." This cold statement was met with uncomfortable silence. Forgos turned his shaved head to stare down the line at Gyorva, who smiled crookedly at Kard.

Törodè stepped forward and spoke in his calm, measured voice. "Welcome to Second South Response, Bordermen."

Half an hour later, all six new Bordermen were dressed in fair-quality, cotton shirts beneath a leather lamellar cuirass. A long, awkward hessian coat stained with dirty greens and browns fitted—sort of—over the top. Perin's canvas breeches had been replaced with leather ones in the same undyed colour as the cuirass. The armour shirt was buckled with a stiff leather belt covered in tabs and loops obviously designed for fixing equipment to, and the whole thing was completed by scuffed, solid-looking boots.

"Hey, don't we get helmets?" Harco asked after they had all been marching for ten minutes or so. They were approaching the Wall Way along the same route that Perin had first taken to find the Borderer Headquarters.

Kard glanced back at the blond Borderer. "This isn't the army, Borderer Harco. Borderers are about the business of being seen—or not being seen, if we wish—while patrolling the surrounding country of the city." Kard's voice managed to sound fierce, even hushed, as he spoke now. "That's why we march in file and why there are hoods on your hessians. Also, lads, unless the Response Leader or myself have told you otherwise, you are to keep silent on the move, right?"

Perin decided that Kard's forceful whisper was even more potent than his shouting.

Medrivar appeared to be enjoying himself immensely. The memories he had inherited from the original owner of his lost body included a great deal of military training. He was experiencing a kind of nostalgia echo. Perin couldn't help but be buoyed up by Medrivar's emotional impressions.

The sun was climbing through a pale-blue, cloud-scudded sky by the time the Response reached a long, low hut someway eastward of the South Road. Nagyevo lay a league behind. Törodè nodded to Kard and entered the hut, closing the door behind him. For a moment, Kard watched approvingly as Perin, Forgos, and Uno Sudar stayed standing and ready. Perin had taken longer walks for his own enjoyment back in Csus, so he had been untroubled by the swift march, and his time following in Kesairl's large footsteps had been perfectly adequate as physical training.

Forgos was breathing harder than Perin. His expression, as Perin had been ordered ahead of him in the file, had been a mixture of respect and resentment. The quiet young man with the dark hair was also on his feet, although his slim chest heaved with exertion.

The others had fallen behind with Maka leading them. He now sat with his hands behind him, looking moodily up at the sky. His good looks were marred by his attitude; Perin could tell he was clearly unhappy with the level of exertion he was being forced to make.

Forgos nudged Perin and nodded in Maka's direction. "Lords' sons don't get out much."

Perin shrugged noncommittally in answer.

The worst off in the group was Gyorva Jolsen. His thin body had little muscle, no doubt one reason why he had been unwanted in his father's haulier business. He hunched up a short distance from Maka, not looking at anyone. In contrast, red-faced and sweating, despite his broad shoulders and naturally muscular frame, Harco lay flopped unashamedly on the grass.

Kard went and helped Gyorva to his feet. "Stand straight, son. It helps you breathe.

"Now listen up, you lot! That was a short stroll in Borderer terms. In a day, we'll often need to travel as far as six leagues without stopping for a rest. Today we let everyone go at their own pace, to see who can do what and for how long. You're all at different levels of fitness, but those of you who dropped behind today aren't gonna have that problem for too long."

He gestured around him as Maka and Harco got to their feet. "This is where we train Borderers. The hut's for Leader Törodè and any paperwork that needs doing—which is the worst thing we've come up against as Borderers for years. As for sleeping, everybody gets paired off. One man carries the ground canvas, and the other the top canvas and struts. You'll be issued with your canvas soon. It's stored with weapons and other equipment in the hut."

Kard looked around once more, his hessian hood troubled by the steady wind coming from the southwest. "Ah…that's good. Breeze from Solorin and steel from Nagyevo…this is what it is to be a Claimfold man, boys! This is what it is to be one of the Hillspears! Yes, you heard me right. You're about to see your tools of the trade for the first time. File up then, if you would. *Quickasyoulike!*"

Törodè and Kard spoke together in the doorway of the hut for a moment after the Response Leader had unceremoniously thrown four sets of canvas out onto the thin grass. Left without orders, Perin and the others stood in an awkward line opposite the hut. Finally, Törodè stepped inside for a moment, handing out six spears to Kard, who briskly distributed them. Perin felt the weight of the dark wood in his hands. The head of the spear was not as long as the boar spear he had seen the hunters use in Csus, and it wasn't exactly gleaming.

Kard noticed Perin's inspection and nodded. "Some of you are already thinking like a Borderer should think—like, what condition is my equipment in? What are my priorities? Where do I get a drink around here?" he chuckled.

"Incidentally, you should feel lucky. Funding we used to get, back in the hundred-and-forties, meant that we could only afford iron spearheads. It served, but good steel is better. Forty years on, and there are only a few Responses left, but at least we can afford better gear. We're only maintained, as you well know, so that the gentry and the rich have somewhere to send their sons."

"Are you a historian or a soldier?" Maka asked in a dry, cultured voice.

Kard shot him a steel-edged look. "I'm a Borderer, and a damn good one; so shut it or I'll shut it for you."

"But come on." Maka had gone red from being told off. Perin supposed that he was not used to the humiliation. "It's not as if you're the army or anything. Father says you haven't had to defend yourselves for years. This is just a glorified patrol!"

Kard looked at Maka for a moment, then turned and pointed to a large butt at the side of the hut. There was a brass tap in the side.

"That's the water supply. Containers are in your equipment rolls. Get yourselves watered."

Kard put an arm out to block Maka as he made to follow the others. "Not you, son. We're going to have a chat about what you know about the Borderers."

Perin took the second drink, turning back to join Uno Sudar in watching Maka, his poise defensive and wary, versus Swordsman Kard, confident in the face of the young man's height. He was explaining something to Maka in low tones, but using harsh terms. The young nobleman didn't seem to like what he was hearing. Even from thirty feet away, his pretty face was visibly flushed with anger. Kard shrugged, picked up one of the spears, and stabbed it into the soil next to Maka. Then he took three steps back and gave the young man a nod.

"What's going on?" Harco said bemusedly, taking a slurp from his container.

Uno Sudar frowned. He still hadn't spoken, not since his introduction that morning. Forgos and Gyorva swapped opinions on Maka in quiet voices. For a moment, Maka stood frozen, before slowly pulling the spear out of the earth and levelling it inexpertly in Kard's direction. His flush had faded and he now looked pale.

It took about a second. Maka made a violent, half-aimed thrust in the swordsman's direction. Kard didn't blink, and in one swift pull and turn, he had disarmed Maka and laid him flat on the ground. Harco gaped. Gyorva snickered and nudged Forgos who was now watching Kard with deep interest.

Uno Sudar spoke at last. "He shouldn't have accepted the challenge."

Perin nodded in agreement. "Yes, but I didn't expect him to do something like that. Kard, I mean. Just…he dared him to have a go, wouldn't you say, Uno?"

"I'd say so. I'd rather go by Sudar, by the way."

"Got it." Perin smiled. "Sudar. Nice to meet you."

Sudar nodded and went back to the water butt for another drink.

Perin privately agreed with Medrivar's soundless advice that Swordsman Kard would be a man to learn from. And a man to stay on the right side of. Filling up again after Sudar, he took his bottle over to Maka, whom Kard had left prone, returning to Törodè in the hut.

Maka looked furious when Perin offered him the bottle. He scrambled to his feet, pushed past him, and went through the canvas rolls to find his own container. Harco and Sudar came over to pick up their spears again.

"Never mind, Reger," Harco said cheerfully. "He's just fed up with this whole thing. Being dragged out of comfort and made to walk awfully long distances and all that. Luckily for me, I'm an optimist." He slapped Perin on the back.

Sudar glanced sidelong at Perin with a look that carried so much amusement about Harco's happy, unreserved manner that Perin nearly laughed.

Training with the spear took only a week or so, much to Perin's surprise. The weapons were designed for thrusting rather than throwing, although Kard demonstrated their effectiveness when hurled over short distances—limited by the expertise of the thrower. After being taught the correct way to hold an infantry spear and the sequences of offensive and defensive moves—lessons that Perin did very well in due to Medrivar's extensive memory of the subject—Kard set up sparring sessions.

Apart from the hard, physical challenge of consistently having to pit himself against other Borderers every day, the march routes around the training area were long and the amenities and weather less than hospitable. Disappointment came with the archery training—Perin was fairly bad at it, to say the least. Perin and Sudar shared their canvas, while Maka had partnered with Harco, who was the only one willing to put up with him. Forgos and Gyorva took the third. In better weather they removed the top canvas to breathe the night air and watch the stars.

Perin sat against the back of the cabin on a late spring day near the end of the training period. Nearly one-and-a-half months had passed since he'd joined up. Kard and Törodè were going over the Response Leader's notes inside. Törodè had been absent for much of the training and needed to confer with his second on the Borderers' progress. The other Borderers were resting. Perin took every opportunity that he could to overhear what his superiors were saying, without being noticed. Törodè spoke too quietly to be heard, but Kard was easily audible.

"They're not bad, really. Let's start with Gyorva Jolsen. 'The Mind'. He's not exactly a prime physical specimen, but he's a brilliant archer. Had trouble at first with the higher ranges due to the pull-strength, but he puts in more practice on the range than any of the others, so that and the stews Reger cooks up for them are putting muscles on his arms."

Perin smiled to himself. His cooking was, in his and Medrivar's opinion, terrible. But it did the job.

"Forgos hasn't been trouble, though we thought he might be. He puts in the work, expresses his anger in appropriate ways…that's all good. He's teamed up with Gyorva, so that might have something to do with it. Gyorva's bitter, but he knows how to restrain himself. He learns from him. I like to call Forgos, 'The Storm.' I haven't seen a Borderman with his fighting energy for a long time.

"Uno Sudar is the quiet one. 'Quiet Spear,' if you'll forgive my sense of drama, sir. He has the best technique out of all of them. The only one apart from Reger who can beat Forgos. On top of that, he's a great bowman, which Forgos isn't, and Reger certainly isn't. Reger spends a lot of time with Sudar, but unfortunately, it hasn't made his marksmanship any better."

Perin winced and tried to ignore Medrivar's chuckling.

"Speaking of Reger Myrvo…yeah. He is interesting. It's like he's handled weaponry before. He learns fast, damn fast, and does everything like he has a real reason to. Naturally, I call him what the others call him: 'The Volunteer.' Speed and physical ability are good, and his stamina's the best in the Response. He can march forever. Him and Maka are at odds half the time, but it hasn't come to blows yet. And with the exception of our young Lord Nyacus, Reger gets on with everyone. He'd be my recommendation to watch for leadership in the future."

Perin bit his lip to control the huge smile that he felt coming. He didn't want to give Medrivar another reason to make fun.

"Maka's applied himself, thankfully. His spear work is good. His bow is better than Reger's, and his fitness level has improved as well. Still don't like the bastard yet, though, Leader. His arrogance is riding him too hard for my liking. He's 'Twice Stubborn' Maka in my book, until he's earned a better nickname.

"Lastly, we've got the 'Blond Warrior,' Harco Oksen. He's a bit of an idiot, to be blunt, but he's decent, works hard, would make a great spearman if he'd remember his footwork, and can shoot competently. Doesn't realise his own strength now that he's hardened up a bit after years living on a vineyard. He's friends with everyone as well, even Maka, which is a relief."

There was a short silence. Then Perin heard movement, and suddenly he could hear Törodè's voice. "All right, Kard, good job. We wait for one more supply delivery from Nagyevo, then we head them out into duty. Orders from the Tacnimag say that we'll be taking over where First South Response left off. We'll be covering West Mezyro or East Solorin, covering their patch and ours as necessary.

"The Tacnimag just raised taxes again. High. Really high. The city's rioted twice already since we left, and we have to make sure the landowners out here pay theirs as well."

"Fine, noble work for us lucky lads."

"Yes. It's not the work I'd like for the Hillspears either, but Borderers do as Borderers must."

"As you say, Leader. Orders?"

"Get them filed up. Let's tell them they've passed the training."

Perin slipped away to join the others.

FIFTEEN

PERIN HANDED OVER the money and grinned as Sudar and Forgos nearly knocked over their drinks in their haste.

"Easy, lads. If you spill them, then they can't be drunk."

Forgos grinned widely. The change in his demeanour over the weeks seemed quite dramatic to Perin and the others. "Here's to the man with the menel. The buyer of our drink. Reger of the many ranar. The purveyor of our happiness!"

"Reger. Hoorah," Sudar said without much enthusiasm, although he winked at Perin and took a long draw from his flagon.

"So, how come we're called volunteers and yet we get paid?" Forgos wondered aloud, searching through his pockets for hastily stowed coins. "Not that I'm complaining or anything."

"Not wages," Sudar said, tipping back his flagon. Despite his lack of bravado and often words, the Hillspears had quickly discovered their first day back in Nagyevo that the quiet one could out-drink any of them.

"Swordman Kard says that they call it 'allowance'," Perin said.

"You listen pretty hard to what the Swordsman says," Forgos teased lightly.

Perin shrugged. His reputation for hard work and near-obsessive dedication to the training earned him the occasional backhanded compliment. It meant that Maka, who still harboured resentment for the Borderers, openly despised him.

Gyorva also seemed to have a bad opinion of him, which he expressed by avoiding all interaction. The cynical young man's strong friendship with Forgos, who respected Perin's attitude as much as he made fun of it, meant that he didn't bring his feelings into the open.

"Hey! Library boy!" Perin turned and nearly spilt beer on Aranyo's shirt. The boy from Perin's first drinking outing, the butcher' apprentice, stood in front of him. The messy-haired youth grinned, but his face fell at Perin's reaction.

Aranyo's features were disfigured by an ugly red-purple bruise that spread from his chin, up across his face, enveloping his left eye in puffy, livid flesh.

"Oh, yeah. The bruise."

"That's not a bruise. That's an attempted murder," Forgos said, leaning back on the bar on his elbows. The barman stared over at Aranyo, who grimaced uncomfortably.

"Close to the truth, mate." He nodded gratefully as Perin threw down another coin and Sudar passed him the resultant flagon. "What are you up to these days then, Reger? Haven't seen you or your redhead pal since we met that first time."

"I joined the Borderers," Perin answered, making room for Aranyo. With a pang akin to guilt, he wondered what Neva had done in the past weeks—he hadn't told the mage that he had joined up, after all.

Aranyo froze up for a second, and then slowly took a drink. "Oh. Better than library work, is it?" There was a cold edge to his voice.

"We get a good allowance," Forgos said cheerfully, "but I doubt it's as comfy as clerking, eh, Reger?"

"Collecting tax for the Tacnimag," Aranyo stated quietly. "No. Doesn't sound that comfy to me. Me, I wouldn't be able to sleep at night."

There was a cool silence where Forgos and Sudar looked from Perin to Aranyo uncomfortably. "Steady on, mate. It's a job—" Forgos started to say, his fists clenching involuntarily.

Aranyo sat up straight, a tear resting in the eyelashes of his bruised eye while his good one stared fiercely, furiously, at Perin.

"My family's been streeted cos of the tax rise. I've been laid off my job, so don't talk to me about jobs, you glorified Oh-gees."

Forgos got to his feet in a rush, pushing his flagon aside. "Don't you dare call us that! If you weren't already bruised, then I'd put my fist through your face!"

"Easy now," Sudar murmured, slowly standing to make a slim, slight, but relentlessly determined obstacle between the two. His dark eyes urged caution.

"Go ahead. Don't let this worry you. It'd be the second Oh-gee fist in so many days to make my day worse."

"I *hate* Oh-gees, all right, puffy? And I'm not a fan of the mages in their whorehouse either, but I didn't have much choice. Borderers do what they're told, but we *don't go beating on folk* who've done nothing!"

"Oh, yeah? Yeah?" Aranyo bobbed from foot to foot, seemingly unaware that the entire taverna was staring and edging away. "What if they don't got the menel to pay those taxes? Do you just smile and go on your way?"

"No. We file a report." Perin felt Medrivar urging him to stand strong, back-to-back with Sudar, facing Aranyo down. "Then the officials send out a representative from the city, a few Oh-gees and some workmen to cart off some of the property in payment. Usually that means the homestead falls into a situation where they can never pay back the money; and, eventually, they're turned off the land. Then corrupt city officials who've pleased the right people get to set up house there."

"Is that supposed to make me feel better?" Aranyo muttered. He was calming down.

"No. It's so that you can see that we know. We don't like it either. But have you got a suggestion about what should be done?"

"One that won't get us all arrested by the Oh-gees?" Forgos added angrily, sitting back down at the bar. He pulled his flagon toward him and downed the contents.

Perin pushed his own flagon toward Aranyo.

"The Gravedigger would do something," Aranyo said bitterly. He took the flagon, drank deeply and messily, and banged it down on the bartop. "That's why I got worked over. They thought I had something to do with him. Said next time they'd break something. Fingers, maybe. A wrist." For a moment he stared at nothing and then shrugged disconsolately. "Thanks for the beer, Reger."

Perin watched him go with sadness. Sudar shook his head, but he stayed typically silent.

Forgos swore loudly. "This is all so torn. Torn as cess. City's going to the shiteheap."

Perin sat in silence, studying the wood grain of the bartop with Aranyo's words echoing in his mind. Since re-entering the city, he had been barraged with poster after poster describing and decrying "The Gravedigger." His former life had taken on an epic importance all of its own. At one of the riots in the previous week, jobless workers had chanted the name until Observatory Guards killed four men, one of them a new apprentice. Forgos was right. Things were indeed torn when fifteen-year-olds were having their skulls crushed by guards.

"I'm going to meet Gyorva." Abruptly, Forgos left.

Sudar watched him go, eyebrows raised.

"I'm done here, as well." Perin sighed, getting up. "You coming?"

Sudar nodded, watching his friend's uncharacteristically glum face as he followed him out onto the street.

Spring rain made the cobblestones shine dully under a strangely luminous sky. Strong sunlight shone behind the dense, rolling cloud, reminding Perin for a moment of the skies in Csus fold, as he headed out toward the South Way. The Observatory was visible behind the rooftops of the nearby trade houses and city courts.

Sudar followed, slightly behind Perin.

"Reger!" came a familiar voice.

Perin turned, well used now to answering to his false name. A figure, mostly obscured by his raincloak, came running across from a small group of youths huddled beneath an abandoned wayside produce stall.

"Neva?" Perin asked, seeing auburn hair and blue eyes. The young mage came to an awkward stop, glancing at Sudar, who stood ready, perhaps thinking that he was about to bring a knife out from beneath the cloak. The dark Borderer relaxed on seeing the younger boy put back his hood.

"What are you doing in that thing, Neva?" Perin asked, grinning. "It's spring rain, not a thunderstorm."

Neva muttered something about disguise, turning his head away from Sudar, who looked up at Perin, nonplussed.

"Neva Yenesen, Uno Sudar." Perin introduced them for the sake of appearances. Neva shot him a look that might've been anger. "Look, he's not going to tell, Neva. Sudar, Neva's a junior mage."

Sudar raised his brows again, no longer completely relaxed.

"Just don't tell the Tacnimag," Perin joked. "He's not supposed to wander around the city."

"That's all I've been able to do." Neva's voice cracked as he raised it. "You vanished for weeks. I spent days on my own in the Observatory or watching your house. Where did you go?"

"Borderers. I volunteered," Perin explained uncomfortably. Sudar had been put back at ease by Neva's plaintive tone, but he was clearly a little surprised by the strain of emotion in the mage's voice and face.

"Did they drag you off?" Neva asked.

"What?"

"Did they kidnap you? Because you didn't tell me you were joining up." The look on Neva's face was stubborn and made him appear all the younger for it.

"Well, no, but did you expect me to knock on the Observatory door?" Perin answered, annoyed, aware of how embarrassing the situation was becoming. "Look, your life doesn't revolve around me, all right? You…I mean, I only met you once, three weeks ago. It's not like I suddenly became your brother." *Your friend.* His voice rose to cover his own feelings of guilt. He hated the hurt in Neva's reddening face.

For a moment, Neva seemed to be considering a reply. Then he blinked, angrily crushing a tear, and stormed away.

Perin turned, exasperated. He rolled his eyes for Sudar's benefit.

"Dependent, huh?" Sudar asked, turning back to see where Neva was. He had vanished, possibly obscured by the gaggle of pedestrians.

"Do you think?" Perin said with half-hearted sarcasm. He began to walk again and Sudar followed.

"So. You're his only friend."

"That surprises you?"

Sudar didn't answer this. "Everyone needs companionship."

Perin swallowed and sped up slightly without realising.

"He has family in the city?" Sudar asked.

Perin shook his head.

Why had Neva reacted like that? It couldn't be helped. There had been no time to contact him before Perin joined up… It had been a surprise for him as much as anyone, really. Hadn't it?

Medrivar stayed tactfully silent throughout this mental questioning.

"Then you are the only one he has to depend on."

Sudar's statement made Perin stop. "What's your point, Sudar?" he asked in a low voice, turning slightly.

With a mild expression, as always, Sudar looked up and answered in his own quiet voice. "You have a responsibility to him then, wouldn't you say?" His dark eyes were full of gentle reproach.

Perin stared in astonishment. "I think I prefer it when you keep quiet," Perin said, affecting annoyance.

His heart wasn't in it, and either Sudar could tell or he chose to ignore it. "It's often more useful to listen than it is to talk."

Perin nodded at this, feeling suitably admonished. "I'll talk to him when I see him." He paused, looking up at the distant Observatory. They started to walk again, Perin leading off South Way into a long alley connecting with the network of residences and private businesses of the Lower West Quarter.

"You're a good man, Sudar."

"I know," the seventeen-year-old responded.

"Where are we going?" Sudar asked after a few minutes of seemingly random turns down narrow, twisting corridors. The path ran between sloping, overhanging timber buildings of a much older design than the richer Lower East or the sophisticated Upper City. Perin didn't know either, having been driven to follow his feet by nothing more than his love of walking.

A couple of barefooted and tatter-clothed children ran out of a broader alley, their heads down and legs flying behind them as they came around the corner. As Perin opened his mouth in a soundless question, dodging up against a crumbling wall, the shortest boy glanced up and yelled back as he passed, "Oh-gees, pal! Pick another path!"

Sudar glanced at Perin. As Borderers, no matter how bad the reputation of the Observatory Guards, surely they were safe?

"Come on." On an impulse, Perin nodded and led the way down the alley from which the children had come. Two corners later, with Medrivar cautioning alertness from within, Perin stopped, listening to the clearer sounds that he and Sudar had been trying to make out since the departure of the escaping children.

"No need to take this one back. He's a troublemaker already. City'd be glad to be rid…"

"…can't just decide that fast, man. Put some thought into it. We've got nothing in the way of reason…"

"Come on, boss." This voice was different, indicating at least three people. All the voices were audible over an occasional muffled groan. "Give us a chance. Haven't put my boot in something for a while, and I missed out on that last riot."

"Look, here's how we do it," the lead voice said, sounding bored. "I've nothing to file him for. So far as I'm concerned, we leave him here to catch something nasty. But you two enjoy yourselves. You dropped behind to… investigate something and caught up with us later. All right?"

The second voice sniggered. "We hear you, boss. See you back at the guardrooms."

"Don't take too long."

Perin turned to see Sudar with an ugly expression on his face. The normally calm and neutral Borderman clenched his fists, wincing at the sound of a whimper. Whatever the scene was, it was taking place on the other side of a cluster of communal privies.

The tramp of three or four pairs of feet moving away was followed shortly by one of the two subordinate voices rising again. "Nice bruise we gave you yesterday, ratfilth."

Perin and Sudar's eyes widened in horror, and as one, they began to move swiftly and quietly along the battered fence. In moments, they were looking out and down into a small, scrubby square designed as some kind of playground. A child's ball was lying against the far brick wall of a converted tannery, and some kind of goal had been painted sloppily on the near wall of another unidentified building. Also lying in the dust, his hands over his face and his legs pulled up to protect his groin and stomach, was Aranyo.

"We did his dad, wasn't it, weeks ago?" One of the two Observatory Guards realised aloud, turning to his partner, a taller, broader man with a similar expression of vacant cruelty. "Same hair, same build, I could swear… oy, ratfilth! Your dad's a criminal, right?"

"They're all criminals in here, pal."

"Well, certainly. All right. Your dad—we done him before, didn't we? Hey, ratfilth, answer when I ask!" He kicked out and caught Aranyo across his shin. As if suddenly motivated by his friend's violence, the larger man put his foot on Aranyo's neck.

"We did do his dad. Taking stolen stuff—black market stuff. Seven City stuff. Stabbing our city in the guts to put food on his table. Selfish bastard."

Sudar looked up at Perin, his eyes filled with a mixture of fear and rage. Borderers had no authority as lawkeepers inside the city. And never over the Observatory Guards who often superseded the City Guard.

"You're doin' better than your dad did," the smaller of the two sneered, crouching next to Aranyo as his friend put a little more weight on the boy's neck. He reached out and grabbed the shirt Aranyo wore, slowly tearing it for no apparent reason as he spoke.

"Your dad, he wet himself by the time we put him on the floor. But then, we'd hit him 'arder than you. So you're lucky, really."

"Hey…" The big one stepped off Aranyo, cracking his knuckles. "How about we take a piss on this one…"

Perin had had enough, and so had Medrivar. He stepped forward all the way into the small yard, walking with purpose. After a momentary hesitation, Sudar forced himself to follow. Both Oh-gees looked up in surprise. Their reaction was annoyance, not guilt.

"Clear off, lads. This is none of yours."

"It is now," Perin answered clearly, with barely a tremble in his voice.

Sudar said nothing.

The Observatory Guards both had swords at their belts. Sudar and Perin were not even dressed in their Borderer uniforms. They had no weapons.

"Tell me," Perin started, swallowing hard, "how did they work out what bits to put armour on, after you rolled down off the shiteheap?"

"More like dropped out of a pig's arse," Sudar growled fiercely. His fists were raised in the stance of someone who not only knew how to fight according to the Borderer manner, but had been trained previously how to use his fists. No wonder he made a good spearman. His tradesman father had obviously paid for more than just academic tutelage.

The Observatory Guards were not men who extended arguments. The big one took two steps forward, received Sudar's punch with a grunt, and then laid the boy flat and unconscious with a swing of his own. The short Oh-gee drew his sword and pointed it at Perin, grinning maliciously.

"If you need to go, Szagu, feel free to use this privy." He caught Aranyo with a back kick. "In the meantime, mate, I'll put some scars on this one's face." He leered pointedly at Perin.

"If you can!" Perin fired off, overcome by some mad confidence. *Don't slip and fall on it.* "And you, the big bastard, if you dirty that pal of mine, I'll cut off whatever first comes to mind and then hit you with it!" Perin tensed, ready, watching for the first sign of movement from the short man. Medrivar ran memories of disarming techniques through Perin's mind at an alarming rate, unfortunately forgetting to leave out the ones where the one doing the disarming ended up horribly impaled.

"Who in a whore's bed do you think you are?" Szagu roared, coming to stand next to his companion, drawing his own short sword. Behind them, Aranyo immediately began to crawl away, glancing up only once. All he could see of his rescuer was Perin's legs, seen through the legs of the short guard.

Perin swallowed. Well, it hardly mattered now, considering he was probably about to be spitted by two swords simultaneously. So much for it being safer for a fugitive in the Borderers. Or maybe his mistake had been to challenge two armed men with nothing but his fists and hasty insults…

But there was no way he could have let Aranyo suffer while he hid.

Oh, well, then. In for a fel, in for a menel.

"I'm the Gravedigger. And…and…you're both about to die!"

SIXTEEN

PERIN STOOD, FROZEN IN SHOCK at what he had just committed himself to. Sudar was out still, thoroughly unconscious. Aranyo had almost crawled as far as the opposite alley.

When the short man rushed forward and thrust his blade toward Perin's unprotected belly, Perin completely failed to disarm him. Instead, he succeeded in pushing aside the sword by sidestepping and grabbing at the guard's wrist. The result was an avoided early death, coupled with a misstep that led to him stumbling backward against the wooden fence of the privies. With a yell, the short guard slammed his shoulder into Perin, throwing aside his sword and nearly impaling his larger companion through the foot.

Perin felt the rotted wood of the fencing cave behind him, and he kicked and scrambled his way backwards into the space behind. On his right stood a heap of fresh-dug earth and the wooden structure of the toilet itself.

Perin realised with a bizarre level of clarity that he had just crushed someone's violets. Someone had grown flowers in the small, dingy space to brighten it up. Perin stumbled to his feet, avoiding his opponent's attempt to grapple him through the gap in the fence. Putting out his hand for balance, he found himself seizing a garden implement in his right hand.

Well, that at least explained the heap of earth. The tenants had probably been about to do some work on their privy. Perin grinned madly. He was holding a spade.

It wasn't much, not compared with his paragon of a spade that was hidden in his room in Cama's building. But it was still a solidly made affair, well jointed to the shaft and rust free.

Both Observatory Guards were openly astonished when Perin came back through the fence in a rush, holding the spade high above his head. Then the larger of the pair, Szagu, laughed.

"I think he means this rubbish! He might actually be this Gravedigger they're going on about!"

"Nah," The smaller one disagreed, grabbing up his fallen sword, just in case. "The real Gravedigger's older."

Perin stepped forward, sidestepped again as his opponent lunged, this time successfully. The blade of the guard's sword passed through the enclosure made by the shape of the spade's handle. Perin, gripping the spade midway up its length, made a fierce twist, trapping the sword securely against the inside of the spade's handle and simultaneously slapping his enemy in the face with the back of the spade head.

As Perin pulled back, the sword went spinning, clattering up against the wall. Perin levelled the spade at the short guard whose larger friend pushed in to protect him, holding his own weapon more cautiously.

"I'm gonna..." his demented snarling didn't quite form into actual phrases. Perin waited for him to move and was rewarded as the big man came forward, bringing his sword across in a tight swing.

Perin dropped to his knees and twisted to avoid the blade, bringing the spade up hard. The head of the spade punched heavily upward into the fork of the man's legs, causing him to double up as Perin scrambled to his feet. Without pausing, experiencing a frightening thrill as he did so, Perin brought the spade's handle down on the back of the man's head as hard as he could.

"*Filth!*" The shorter guard drew a knife from his boot, pushing past his collapsed comrade. He threw the short blade at Perin as hard as he could, but on prompting by Medrivar, Perin was already swinging the spade across to counter. The blade glanced off the spade's head and skittered off to the right, coming up short of where Aranyo was getting unsteadily to his feet. As Aranyo looked round, the short guard threw himself after the knife, blocking the young man's view of Perin. Seeing that he was in danger again, Aranyo stumbled to his feet and disappeared around the corner.

The guard didn't throw his knife this time. He watched Perin nervously, fear now present in his narrowed eyes. Perin casually began to spin the spade from hand to hand. It was half the length of his own spade, much better suited to this kind of close-up fighting. His heart was still beating furiously, but now Perin felt that he could win.

"Tell the Tacnimag that I'll start digging some more graves," Perin announced ominously. It was a meaningless threat, but fitted the persona that the city had created for him. "But I can start with yours, if you like." Perin stopped twirling the spade and held it with the handle pointing toward his enemy.

Seeing this as an opening, the short guard made a wild rush forward and was met with an edge-on blow as Perin flipped the spade in his hand and brought his arm up and around in one movement. A long, dark spatter of blood darkened the dusty yard-floor as the guard smashed face first into the ground, knocked insensible by the damaging blow. As Perin watched, newly horrified, blood began to pool slowly under the man's right temple.

Perin took a moment to wipe the small amount of blood from the spade, using the fresh earth in the garden from where it had come. Then he propped it back up in approximately the same place he had found it.

Sudar came round as Perin half-dragged, half-carried him in the general direction of his room. Perin propped him against a wall, ignoring the passing looks of the people coming from the South Way.

"So much for my superior combat skill then," Sudar said with a rueful smile, "how did we get out of that one? I thought they were going to cut us into very small pieces."

"Me, too." Perin shook his head, taking in an exaggerated breath. "Squad of City Guard came by. Oh-gees are arrogant, but not so stupid as to kill a pair of citizens in front of City witnesses."

"Close call," Sudar said slowly. "Odd for the City Guard to patrol so far in from the wall…"

"I know."

Nursing the steadily developing bruise as they stepped out into the diminished flow of pedestrians, Sudar followed Perin to the South Gate. Forgos and Gyorva were there, in conversation with a pair of City Guards.

"My room isn't far from here. I'll be back here at sundown."

Sudar nodded. They both knew that he would, unless Perin wanted to be verbally destroyed by Kard when he did arrive. Perin headed off with a cursory wave to Forgos and Gyorva, jogging as soon as he was out of their sight. He went up the rain-slicked steps to his room with reckless speed, falling through his door as he slipped on the top step and found it to be open already. He tumbled onto the cool, hard floor.

Neva jumped, putting his hand to his heart and making a distinctly un-masculine noise. He slumped down into a crouch out of relief when he realised that it was Perin.

"Reger! Hello…Cama must've been in earlier…door was open…"

"What are you doing here?" They both spoke almost at once. Neva flushed red and ran a hand through his red-blond hair.

"Curse it…I'm sorry."

"No." Perin stood up, remembering Sudar's quiet expression. "You don't apologise. I am sorry. I'm sorry I didn't let you know somehow. Didn't think how you'd feel."

"Abandoned," Neva said softly and then looked away, ashamed. He had spent so little time with the strange library apprentice-turned-Borderer that it seemed ridiculous to have become so attached to him. Perin read the conflict in Neva's body language, caught the sidelong look of admiration. Medrivar's perception aided his own, and now Perin understood the extent of the hurt in the young mage.

Perin swallowed, surprised by emotion. Empathy was not a word he had even heard until he had become involved with the library, and he scarcely knew its meaning now, but he suddenly felt Neva's loneliness like a blow to his heart. He remembered the rain-drenched hillside of Csus, where he had known Graves and no one else. But, even there, he had been in better company than Neva. Neva's life since entering Nagyevo had been cold stone walls and silence.

"Will you forgive me?" Perin managed to say without his voice trembling. Neva gaped at him for a moment, astonished at the sudden role reversal, before nodding emphatically.

"Thank you."

Despite his time with Kesairl and his kin, Perin obviously had not learned to become immune to awkward silences.

Neva actually started to examine the wood grain of the table out of embarrassment. "The Elder Mages know," Neva said suddenly.

Perin's heart began to pound as he forced his expression to neutrality.

"About me going out into the city," Neva explained, and thankfully glanced away, missing Perin's inappropriate expression of relief.

"Oh, no! They haven't locked you up then?"

"Found a way out of it. This was ages ago, before you left even."

"Then why were you so afraid earlier?"

"I wasn't. I was angry that you introduced me so casually to your friend, after...but that doesn't matter." Neva grinned nervously before going on. "They found out, but I found a way to keep going outside."

"What's that?"

"Oh, I'm sort of like their spy."

"Oh," Perin said, hoping his face didn't look nearly as cold as he suddenly felt. Neva seemed proud of himself.

"Yes. You know all the posters that started? It's because of that night at the taverna, when the trade apprentices were talking about the Gravedigger, remember? I told one of the mages, and he told the Guard Mage, who has charge of the Oh-gees."

Perin sat down. "You're the one who started all this fuss over the Gravedigger?"

Neva nodded. "Yes. All I had to do was mention names that I remembered. They let me out to do what I like now, long as I remember people and what they say."

"Did you tell them about Aranyo?" Perin said cautiously, his hands gripping his knees. He could no longer look at Neva's bright, pleasant, friendly face.

"The blond one? Yeah, he was the only name I could remember at first. What's wrong?"

Neva seemed to finally have realised that Perin's face had become a mask of anger and sadness. Perin got to his feet slowly and went over to where Neva stood, pushing the table out of the way. He stopped inches from him, putting a hand on his shoulder.

"Neva. Listen to me. Minutes ago, two Oh-gees nearly beat Aranyo to death. He's been questioned about this Gravedigger person, and you know that they sometimes ask questions with their fists, don't you?"

"Beat?" Neva's voice actually quivered. His eyes dampened, partly because Perin was so close, and so angry. But it was a restrained rage and Perin was sure to balance his anger with something softer.

"They were going to leave him for dead. They were going to piss…look, you don't even need to know just what they were going to do. He got out of it alive, barely. If a few more minutes had gone by…he would have been crippled, at the very best."

"He nearly died?" Neva whispered in horror. "Because of me? Gods of Valo!"

"Yes. Gods of Valo," Perin said harshly. "You didn't do it to him, Neva. And I'm not going to hold the blame to you. But anything you say that gets back to the Oh-gees is going to…" Perin stopped, unable to continue because Neva had burst into silent, uncontained tears, as he slid down against the counter. Perin found himself half holding the younger boy up, feeling very awkward.

"No, come on, stand up." He sat Neva down on the edge of his bed, putting a hand on Neva's shoulder and squeezing. "Shh. Come on."

"I…can't do…anything….anything right!" Neva clenched pale fists and beat them a few times against his legs, ineffectually.

"He's alive. He'll heal. Stop crying."

Let him cry. Perin felt Medrivar advise. The king had, up until now, been taking a distanced position on what he saw as a situation personal to Perin.

"Don't feel too bad. It was a mistake. A big one, but not something you did out of hate. You don't hate Aranyo."

"I liked him! I didn't think...they wouldn't...how can they let them get away with it?" Neva's shame had become anger.

Perin nodded. "They shouldn't. But this is Nagyevo, Neva. This is the way things are. I go out...I have to go out to the South Gate at sunset before they close the gates, and then I have to go out into Mezyro with the Response and collect money from people who can't afford to give it to the Tacnimag. Or else the Tacnimag take away their living. And yes, the Oh-gees tried to take away Aranyo's life. But you need to know this and realise it more than you need to feel sorry for yourself."

Neva quietened down, his blue eyes reddened by his tears, his body taut with emotion. "What do I do then?"

"Don't stop informing. That'll just mean they stop letting you out. I don't want that."

"Thank you."

"Tell them about the Gravedigger instead. Just...don't link him to people you don't want hurt."

"But...I don't know anything about the Gravedigger."

"That's fine." Perin took a deep breath. "I'll tell you what I find out from the other Borderers. For some reason, I seem to be the first to know when he does something."

Neva nodded, swallowing and rubbing his sleeve across his face. "Do you suppose they'll reward me if they catch him because of my information?"

Perin looked back thoughtfully, his arm still draped companionably across Neva's shoulders. "Yes, Neva, I imagine they would."

There was another silence, this one less awkward than the previous ones, which seemed strange to Perin.

Finally, Neva stood up. "I wish you were my brother, Reger."

Perin blinked, looked away, stood. "Yes. Er... You...you all right then?"

"Yes." Neva paused in the doorway, shrugging his hood back up to cover his head from the rain. "Reger...how did Aranyo get away?"

Perin grinned. "Guess."

"You mean...*him?*...no!"

"Yes."

"You were there?" Neva's eyes widened. "Did he see you?"

"Oh, no." Perin answered seriously, secretly enjoying the irony of the question. "He couldn't look in my direction. But I saw everything that happened."

"You were close?"

Perin nodded, keeping his expression straight. "Very close."

SEVENTEEN

KARD RAISED A HAND to call a halt. With what was becoming practised ease, Perin and the other Borderers dropped into a low crouch.

Törodè turned to address them. "Swordsman Kard will pick one of you to scout the perimeter of the copse ahead." Törodè gestured up the sloping ground to a thick birch stand on a slumped curve of scrub-bound earth. "The rest of you, partner up. We'll start to establish a temporary position up ahead. Borderman Jolsen, you're with me."

Kard nodded to Perin and moved on, heading out to the left of the Response. Perin joined him, flexing his shoulder muscles in an effort to keep his pack from jolting uncomfortably as he ran in a partially stooped manner toward the trees.

"Just a cursory sweep around the curve of the rise. You look inward; I'll look outwards. Go." Kard set off at once, one hand resting casually on the lower shaft of his spear to keep it from jiggling in its bindings on his back. Perin followed, glancing across to where the others were entering the copse. Considering the complete absence of human existence other than their own in this desolate area of Mezyro, the taut, military wariness of the manoeuvres were beginning to wear thin.

"Back round to the hollow by the split beech," Kard muttered tersely as they confirmed that the countryside around the copse was bare of movement, as bare as the copse itself was of anything other than squirrels, densely growing ivy, and bracken. And six less-than stealthy Borderers.

"Swordsman. They're not even bothering to be discreet!" Perin murmured as he leant against the broken carcass of the damaged beech tree. Leaf mould and beechmast slid beneath his feet. Kard smiled slightly, peering out onto the landscape ahead.

"That, Borderman, is because there has been no event of banditry south of Nagyevo for several years now. It's our job to make sure the first one doesn't come as too much of a surprise." Perin nodded, following Kard's gaze out over the Mezyro plain. The hills were a vague cloud of blue-green on the horizon. A poorly marked road crossed the otherwise unremarkable view, visible only because of the cart using it. Perin frowned.

"Swordsman…"

"Yes, Borderman?"

"Shouldn't that cart be moving?"

Kard examined the immobile object for some time before giving a brisk nod. "Well noticed, Myrvo. We'll have a look at it. You tell me how we should proceed."

Perin recognised this as a test. "Borderers should always be in pairs when separate from the Response. Scouts run in pairs, but investigating an object or place of interest should be carried out by two pairs, one Borderer being of Swordsman rank or higher."

"Well done, Reger. Bring Sudar and Oksen back here after reporting to the Response Leader."

"Yes, Swordsman."

For a time, the sounds of leaves moving gently were joined only by the creaking of grasshoppers. Then, almost invisible, as they travelled fast and low through swathes of meadow grass toward the road, four Borderers added the sound of their booted feet to the quiet. Kard kept the hood of his hessian up as an example to his subordinates.

They slowed as they surrounded the cart, no longer bothering to keep low, now that they had left the cover of the grass. Harco looked around briefly for appearance's sake before turning to Perin to say, "I almost stepped on some kind of snake!"

Kard's frown silenced him. The Swordsman stood and watched the abandoned cart as if waiting to see what it would do. The shafts rested in the dirt of the road, and one was cracked most of the way through. A jumble of wire cages were in some disarray on the back of the vehicle.

"All right." Kard breathed out eventually, pulling his hessian hood down and running a hand through his short, thick hair. "So. No pony in the traces. No carter in sight. The goods are all assumedly accounted for. Sudar—investigate and explain, if you would."

The Swordsman's keen eyes watched Sudar closely. Sudar nodded and immediately began to circle the cart slowly, running his hand over the wood, leaning in to examine the damaged shaft, all the time holding his peace.

"Gyorva would have this figured quicker than me." He stated matter-of-factly. "But I've noticed that the damage isn't isolated to the shaft. The footrest has been cracked as well." The Borderers began to come around the cart to see what he meant. The footrest was indeed damaged and when Harco pressed at it gingerly, the wood splintered still further, making him jump. Kard glanced briefly at this but did not give it his attention. Instead, he turned and surveyed the road and the nearby grass verge.

"Bandits after all?" Perin suggested, looking up from a gouge in the dirt that looked as if the nearside wheel had been forced to travel sideways, as if the cart had been pushed against the direction of its wheels. Kard snorted softly.

"Maybe I should have sent for Borderman Gyorva Jolsen after all. No, Reger, this isn't bandits. Thieves wouldn't waste their time on a ponycart full of empty traps. This was bound for the Mezyro fur runs. This is a personal cart; the carter is almost certainly a trapper himself.

"Pay attention to the marks in the soil and the way that shaft has broken." With that abrupt order, he went to the grass verge nearest the snapped shaft and crouched down, hands gently moving through the grass.

"It looks like something rammed into the side of it or made it judder sideways," Perin said, hoping to regain some respect. "The dirt's scuffed and the cart's not in line with the road."

"Here's why." Kard stood, looking around with a sudden return to vigilance. For a moment, his hand rested on the hilt of his shortsword. His left hand pointed into the grass at his feet. "Did you notice that the traces themselves are missing? They must have been torn from the cart, which is connected to the reason for the broken shaft."

One by one, the Borderers noticed the crushed grass stems; the pattern of nodding, seedless grass heads; and, finally, the spatters of dark colour amongst the green. Harco reached out toward the nearest glob, face white. Perin suddenly found himself remembering the broken crown of the Observatory Guard in the dust.

"Blood."

"That's right, Reger. This is where it gets confusing."

"No…" Perin's mind, unaided this time by Medrivar, finally pieced together what Sudar had already realised, judging from the look on his face. "I see it. Something rammed into the side of the cart, and then threw the pony out of the traces, breaking this shaft and tearing the leather traces away with the beast. The animal was dragged away through the meadow in that direction, but only after it had been struck down from the side of the road because that's the way the blood falls…"

"What about the crack in the footrest?" Harco asked, standing up.

"Carter dodged a blow by jumping off to the side. He was dragged off, too, I would guess."

"Isn't it more likely that the pony was led away? I mean, obviously injured, but still able to walk?" Sudar said mildly, glancing at Kard. The Swordsman scanned the horizon again and then raised his hand in the "return to file" signal.

"Let's fall back to the copse. Sudar, Harco, you take first watch at the southeastern edge of the camp. Reger, you get to repeat what you just said to me to Response Leader Törodè, son."

Several minutes later, Perin finished re-describing his understanding of the mystery. Törodè frowned at him for a moment and then looked up at Kard whose expression gave away nothing. Maka openly sneered at the surmisal.

"All right, Borderers. Reger, you get those supplies handed out, and in the meantime, you all have freedom of speech. Feel free to put forward your opinions on this." Törodè sat back on his bedroll, watching Kard's expression above all others.

Perin tried to ignore Maka's superior smirk as he made use of the already-lit fire and began to sort out field rations. "Reger...don't tell me that you're saying there's a monster out there."

Perin looked up at Maka and passed him his ration, keeping his face expressionless with effort. "I didn't say that."

"Maka, as strikingly unintelligent as he is, has nonetheless managed to grasp the essential absurdity in your suggestion," Gyorva interjected with a sardonic drawl. "You are suggesting that something dragged off a pony. What do you suppose? What do you imagine we must suppose from your analysis?"

Forgos looked up from his bedroll, where he had been casually whittling a knotty piece of beechwood. "Leave it, pal. Either he's right or he's wrong." His gaze immediately returned to his work.

Gyorva was almost surprised by this, but shrugged and withdrew, muttering, "Clearly. But do we need to guess at which?" Maka watched this exchange warily and then returned to his sport.

"I heard you were a librarian before, Reger. Maybe you read too many books. Made your brain go wrong."

"Made my brain go wrong?" Perin responded incredulously, trying to model a little of Gyorva's sarcasm into his speech. "The library would have done you some good."

Forgos suppressed a smile at this, and Gyorva looked up with vague interest.

The following morning the Response left the copse under cover of a light mist. Perin kept his hessian hood up only when moving as it obscured his peripheral vision at the same time as breaking up his outline, a trade-off that made him uncomfortable.

They moved out into a sloping field dotted with exuberant patches of wild flowers, occasionally disturbed by lone-standing trees. Kard had a few words with Perin. The Swordsman had spent some of the previous night threading dried-grass stalks into the hessian cloak he wore, giving the impression that he was wearing part of the field.

"Reger, you feel bad about your guess about the cart?"

"Yes, Swordsman," Perin admitted.

"Don't. I'm taking you seriously." Kard nodded to Törodè for confirmation and then gave the hand-signal for the Borderers to spread out in pairs. "I'm taking you seriously because, strange as your analysis was, it also made sense. Which is not something I say gladly."

Perin said nothing. Kard glanced across at the young Borderer, noticing again the strength of resolve that he had noticed before. He had seen it sometimes in people he knew, people who remembered the last conflicts in Koban back in the year 135. You could see it in experienced soldiers, yet Reger Myrvo was a young man of eighteen years.

"I read reports that come in to the Borderer Captain's office, Reger," Kard began abruptly, "because for every hundred reports of tedious thefts and disputes that are sent to Nagyevo by local magistrates and Tacnimag assessors, there's maybe one good report. Sometimes there've been rumours about the north, but the Tacnimag have classified and restricted reports from beyond Helynvale now. Recently, there was a story from the east, from the fold of Csus."

Perin stumbled in his tracks and hurriedly turned the action into a slightly exaggerated turn of the head, as if he had seen something. Kard's quick eyes followed his gaze and then slowly returned to Perin.

"You're from Csus, eh?"

"Yes, Swordsman."

"Claim of Arpavale, was it?"

"Yes."

"You wouldn't've heard of it then. There were a few rumours raised by huntsmen in the Hanger and Varo Claims. Seemed unlikely. But you wouldn't have travelled the Varo route down from Csus, not if you're an Arpavale lad."

Perin nodded in agreement.

"You talked about that pony's fate as if you were seeing it happen in the eye of your mind," Kard said softly, checking that they were sufficiently distant from the other Borderers. "You seemed...strangely certain. Now. I'm taking you seriously. I'd like you to take me seriously." His eyes stared deep into Perin's. Perin swallowed.

The target of the mission had come into view. A squat, thatched farmhouse sat beside a bedraggled vegetable garden with a stand of out-of-place fir trees some distance beyond. An old chicken-run occupied one corner of the fenced-off area. Some form of hedge had been encouraged along the near edge of the homestead, and Kard signalled for a halt there without dropping his gaze.

"Borderer, stay low and quiet. We're going to scout on."

Perin felt decidedly tense. The possibility that his fears would be realised was manifest in two areas—firstly that his supposition about the missing carter's fate would be proved correct, and secondly, that Kard's sharp mind had brought the Swordsman close to Perin's true, fugitive identity.

"That's interesting," Kard murmured as he wriggled backwards, extricating himself from the ditch beneath the hedge. Perin peered through a gap in the branches, where an abandoned bird's nest mimicked the silent and lifeless home on the other side. "Chicken coop, but no chickens," Kard explained, frowning up at Perin from where he lay on his stomach. "Come on, follow me round behind these firs…"

The ground was dark and cool beneath the motionless canopy of the evergreens. Perin and Kard crept forward, watching the house for movement through the trees. Wordlessly, Kard pointed to where the near windows had been barricaded from the inside. The shutters hung off their hinges, swaying slightly as a breeze lifted.

"That's extreme. We're tax collectors, not besiegers."

Perin rested his hand on the rough bark of the fir above him and felt resin beneath his fingertips. For a moment, he examined Kard's statement and the evidence of clumsy fortification. The door of the house had been damaged and was cracked vertically, and yet it still stood in place. Clearly, there was a thorough barricade set up. Perin frowned, idly pressing the sticky sap of the tree between his fingers.

Kard narrowed his eyes, as if suddenly convinced that he had caught movement behind the ramshackle outhouse and storage shed annexed to the closest end of the cottage. Perin looked down at his fingers; he swallowed slowly before reaching out with his free hand to nudge Kard.

The sap on his fingers had not bled from any tree.

"Blood," Kard whispered starkly, his hand darting to the pommel of his sword. As one, they both looked up into the dark architecture of the fir trees above them.

The pony hung across two overlapping branches. It hung with ribs torn loose, the forelegs completely dislocated. There were a few flies alighting on the torn hide of the beast, and the freshness of the carrion coupled with the strong, resinous scent of fir trees hid the smell of death that only now began to register with the two Borderers, aided by rapid imagination and a total, shock sensation that seemed to have spread throughout Perin's body like the stabbing of millions of icy pins.

One dead eye stared down from above the gaping, twisted horsey skull.

"Withdraw!" Kard muttered in a cracked voice.

The withdrawal was barely more than a panicked scramble back along the hedge to where the other Borderers of the Second South Response were waiting in stealthy positions.

"We found the pony," Kard reported bleakly in hushed tones. Törodè's eyes widened, and he motioned for attention. It was unnecessary—all eyes were firmly on Kard, save Sudar's, which were watching Perin wipe blood off his hand with a wad of grass.

"Something's thrown it up into one of those trees."

"Impossible," Gyorva stated with an expression of sudden fear. Forgos immediately checked that his spear's cloth hood was loose.

"It's drizen. It's got to be drizen," Perin said with certainty, his nerve returning. Medrivar's presence was a calming force. He was no longer shaken. At least, it had been the pony they had found and not the carter…

"I think there's someone in the farmhouse," Kard said bluntly. "There's signs that the occupant barricaded himself in. That means he's aware of the presence of the hostiles, whatever they may be…"

"Drizen," Perin repeated, sliding off his pack and unhooding his spear.

"There haven't been drizen south of Nagyevo in, well, ever!" Gyorva pointed out, simultaneously copying Perin, on the off-chance that he was wrong.

Törodè waited for the tense silence that came once each Borderer had divested himself of his pack and had taken up his spear. Sudar, the only one whose expression showed no concern, tucked his spear hood into his belt and drew his hessian cloak closer about himself.

"One moment, Leader." Kard waited for Törodè to agree before drawing Perin aside.

"Now. Take me seriously, Borderman. You seem damned sure that there are drizen nearby, damn sure, despite the fact that they're supposed to be nearly extinct. Explain."

Perin weighed up the situation. He had never been more certain in his life than he now was that they were facing drizen. Before, when there had been nine drizen in the Varo pine forest, there had been more than a dozen hunters armed with weaponry appropriate for dealing with drizen: long spears as well as bows. And, of course, there had been a prigon skirmisher with him then. Perin wondered for a moment how Kesairl was coping in his cell. He needed the prigon now.

"I...I've seen them before. Drizen. In Varo. Please don't ask me how or why I was there."

Kard's eyes widened. "I don't care why or how! But no one has seen them since...the only people I know who have seen combat against those monsters are now so old they have forgotten how to fight! You fought them?"

"Yes, Swordsman."

Kard nodded and returned to the circle of ready Borderers. "Response Leader Törodè. We are up against drizen. Borderer Reger Myrvo will take over and brief us. He has more experience with drizen than I do."

Maka and Gyorva stared blankly at Perin while Forgos leaned forward, showing respect to the young man who had volunteered.

"Right," Perin murmured with a slight tremor in his voice. "If there's two or three of them, I think we can do this. If there's more, then we're going to join the pony."

Medrivar's inner voice cut through Perin's hasty strategising.

We need to work on your understanding of morale.

EIGHTEEN

"SO NOW WHAT?" Maka whispered nervously. His eyes, like the eyes of all the Hillspears, were fixed on the boarded-up, barricaded house. The wind moved the grass, causing another whisper, and the trees replied. No birdsong sounded on the air. Perin's imagination kept returning to the image of dark blood dripping gently onto pine needles.

"Shush." Kard spoke with unusual quietness. "Reger said that they fight as individuals—disorganised. We need to take advantage of that."

"Yes. Yes." Perin swallowed. His heartbeat raced. The lives of the others would be put to the test according to his advice, bad or otherwise. Medrivar gently encouraged him, calming him down.

The plan is good. I have fought before, remember?

"Keep your spears between you and them. Don't break out on your own, don't back out on your own."

Kard relayed the information he had gleaned from Perin's hurried briefing into workable strategy. "Gyorva, Sudar, stay hidden here at the hedge opening. Don't loose until you're sure that you'll hit well."

Skinny Gyorva and slight, silent Sudar both nodded. Their bows were out and strung.

"Aim at the head," Perin suggested.

"No, aim central. Try to hit high up the chest. There's a good chance then that the arrow will lift and strike the head, but you're likely to miss entirely if you aim higher. That's why you're such a poor archer, Reger. You aim with too much optimism." Kard loosened his shortsword in its scabbard, glancing around. There was still no movement around the quiet yard beyond the curve of the hedge.

Törodè directed a question at Perin. "You're not leaving any information out?"

"No, sir."

Kard picked up his spear and nodded. "Harco, Forgos, go now. Keep quiet, Harco, for the sake of the Nameless Gods, or this will all fall apart." Harco nodded, his normally cheerful countenance closed and fearful. He followed Forgos along the line of the hedge, gripping his spear with white knuckles. Response Leader Törodè put a hand on Maka's shoulder once Forgos and Harco could just be seen near the end of the hedge, peering round into the yard. If there were drizen behind the nearside of the building, they showed no indication.

The Response Leader and Maka both checked their bows before Törodè nodded to Kard. "All right, Swordsman. When you're ready. Gyorva, Sudar, I wish you good shooting."

Maka, with a face like pale stone, followed Törodè out into the yard. They moved low and silent. The pretty-faced Borderer stared around, unblinking. When they reached the vegetable garden, both sank down in the stand of meadow grass that had escaped through the hedge to border the bedraggled plot. With their hessians up to cover their heads, they were difficult to make out, even from such a short distance.

"Let's move," Kard said abruptly to Perin. He stood, shouldered his spear as if about to casually walk along a Nagyevo sidestreet, nodded to Perin, and stepped past Gyorva and Sudar into the yard.

Perin gripped his spear in as controlled a way as possible, despite the fact that his hands wanted to shake. Kard was a picture of iron, looking around with thorough, sweeping turns of his head, taking his time, watching for movement. After what felt like drawn-out minutes, they reached the front door. Perin forced himself not to jump when he heard the sound of movement behind it.

"H-hello?" A voice came from inside. "Who's there?"

"Nagyevo Borderers," Kard said, loud enough to answer, fixing his gaze on the dark pines and the corner of the building.

Perin turned and faced toward the other corner, seeing that Harco and Forgos were visible at the end of the hedge. That meant there were no drizen around that corner, or they wouldn't be showing themselves so clearly.

"Thank the Nameless Ones! I thought... My husband went to our neighbours as soon as he'd blocked the door. I don't know if he's still alive. He said they'd gone, he said they'd gone..."

"Madam," Kard interrupted, "what are they? Are they still here?"

"I don't know! Monsters! I don't know if they went. I don't know. I don't know!"

"Calm yourself. You're in the safest place you—"

Swordsman Kard cut himself off, his eyes widening. Two shapes were emerging out of the dark beneath the pine trees, trudging steadily into the sunlight. Their rough, hairy bodies were larger than he had imagined.

Kard swore as the two drizen let out guttural noises of realisation. As one, they drew hooked swords from their ragged belts and came forward at speed, their weird, toe-hoofed feet pounding the ground. Together, Perin and Kard ran backwards, levelling their spears until they were not far in front of the vegetable plot. Both dropped to one knee, a manoeuvre rarely used in training, one designed to repel mounted enemies.

Everything slowed down. Then it began to move very fast. Perin braced himself. Shouts came from behind. An arrow flew past Perin's shoulder, hit the drizen on the right just above its stomach, but did not hinder it. A second arrow, poorly loosed, glanced off a blackened shoulder plate, followed fast by an impossibly good shot away from the right that slammed into the side of the drizen closer to Kard, punching through its jaw beneath its raw, quivering snout. It stumbled away toward the house wall, and as one, Perin and Kard rose up from their ready posture and drove their spears into its companion.

Perin felt the metal of his spear grind against bone in the drizen's chest, then against the head of Kard's spear beside it. The drizen exhaled explosively, spattering Perin with blood as the young Borderer dug the butt of his spear into the earth and rolled sideways. Kard twisted his spear to free it and spun around to pull it clear. The drizen fell forward, and Perin's spear came through its back before the shaft snapped under the weight.

Kard, now facing toward the end of the hedge, saw the reason for Harco's shout. Four more drizen were coming steadily toward where he stood, as if to cut off Harco and Forgos from joining him. Making the correct decision, both the Blond Warrior and the Storm sprinted to where Response Leader Törodè and Maka were hurriedly notching new arrows.

Both loosed, missing with one arrow and striking one drizen in the upper arm with another, before throwing down their bows and unslinging their spears, standing side by side with Kard. Two more arrows flew past, hitting the same drizen in the chest and making it falter and fall behind. Despite their slower, warier paces, the other three were almost upon Kard, Törodè, and Maka.

Gyorva and Sudar were suddenly at Perin's side. Gyorva turned so that Sudar, who had thrown down his own bow, could retrieve the spear from Gyorva's back sling and hand it to Perin.

"Don't break this one," Gyorva cautioned Perin, raising his bow, pulling back, taking in a breath, releasing. The arrow hit the twice-stricken drizen just below the previous two, and this time the creature went down for good.

With a glance at one another, Sudar and Perin ran forward to join either end of the spear line.

One of the drizen paused and roared its hate in a snarling, high-pitched voice. This one had no hook sword. It held a rock in its human-like fingers. As the two charging drizen were driven back by all seven spears, it hurled its rock over-arm. It smashed against the side of Harco's head and he went down like a dropped sack of grain. Perin gasped, stepping in beside Maka to fill the gap and keep the near pair of drizen on the retreat. There was blood in Harco's blond hair.

Gyorva shouted a warning and ran. The drizen with an arrow in its face was rising. Blood poured steadily down over its lower tusk, staining its chest hair. Swaying, it came to the realisation that it was mere feet away from the line of Borderers, and they had their backs to it.

Even Törodè panicked for a moment before Kard called out, "Steady!" But it was enough.

The line broke. The two drizen, both bloody from many spear wounds, stepped back a few paces, snorting and squealing, aware that only Maka, Perin and Sudar were still facing them. Forgos, Törodè and Kard had all turned to deal with the other threat, more than was necessary to fight one, severely injured opponent. Kard's spear snapped as it drove between two armour plates and destroyed the rising monster's heart. In that moment, a thrown stone hit the back of Kard's head. He swayed, drew his sword, and thrust it unnecessarily into the dying drizen before collapsing.

"Back to the line!" Törodè roared, drawing his own shortsword and turning.

The first of the two drizen to plough back in came through unscathed, knocking Maka down and sending his spear spinning into grass. For a moment, it stood over the nobleborn lad before Perin desperately launched Gyorva's spear at its throat. The resulting injury caused it to stagger back, a hand rising to the wound.

Sudar stood face to face with the other drizen. He snatched up Harco's dropped spear with his free hand, bracing both spears against the ground. A third stone whistled past his head and hit Gyorva before he could loose another arrow.

"Get the stone thrower!" Sudar shouted as Perin, driven by something akin to desperation, chose to run and jump onto his injured opponent, his fingers gouging at the bright semi-intelligence in the small black eyes. Törodè and Forgos heeded Sudar's call and both ran past, Forgos throwing his spear and grabbing up Maka's as he ran.

Perin experienced a jolt as the drizen he was attacking fell to its knees, nearly equalling their heights. The monster had weakened from blood loss, blood that spilled all over Perin, but it had the strength to grab around the young man that had torn its throat, attempting to crush him. Perin, feeling the air being driven out of him, punched upward with his right hand.

The air filled with screams. The blue sky waited serenely above the turmoil of bright blood, stench, and pain. Perin felt the drizen's eyeball burst under the fingers of his left hand, heard the shriek of pain and horror from the monstrous creature that was crushing him, the vibration of the scream echoing in his bones. Perin's right hand had punched up into the tear in the drizen's flesh. Slippery with blood, his fingers tore at the resistant, taut tissues within the creature's throat. His hand dug inside the monster's neck. For a bizarre, clear moment, he realised he was choking it.

Then the madness returned. The drizen pitched backward and began to thrash on the ground, the light in its remaining eye dying.

Törodè stabbed at the rock thrower's face as it stumbled back. Forgos's spear tore at the back of its ankle. It flailed, tripping, falling. Forgos let out a wild yell and drove his spear all the way through the drizen into the earth beneath. Pinned in place, it squealed a string of incomprehensible words before Törodè silenced it by hacking once, twice, three times. The head parted from the shoulders.

The Response Leader and Forgos took in the scene as the last drizen scream faded. Perin was locked tight in the arms of his twitching opponent, eyes squeezed tightly shut, his hand held out away from himself, shining with blood.

Gyorva stood a few paces back from it all, nursing an injured arm with a scowl. He kicked at the loose piece of masonry the drizen had flung his way. His bow was broken.

Maka got to his feet, his eyes wide and horrified, mouth tightly shut, his normally attractive lips sealed in a thin line. He stared down at Perin in shock.

Kard lay senseless beside the drizen he had thoroughly despatched. Harco, too, lay still, silent, fully stretched in the grass beside the vegetable garden. His blond hair was soaked with blood.

Sudar stood over his defeated foe with wild eyes and two broken spear shafts. The greater parts of both weapons were buried deeply in the drizen that slouched, dead, on its knees, partially held up by the spears that had killed it. The spearheads had crossed diagonally to drive their way through, their points emerging some way beneath the shoulders on its back.

Perin realised a hand held his. He looked up, startled and then calmed by the face of Medrivar. The king comforted him, his other hand on Perin's shoulder.

"Come back to yourself, Perin. Forget the blood. Forget it."

Perin began to sob. He felt as if he had been damaged deep within his being. The first time he had killed had not hurt like this, sending the crooked mage down to his death in the Erdhanger well. The second time had not hurt like this, though he had been sick from the horror afterwards. This time it was different. He had been drenched, surrounded, assailed on all sides by the work of his hands, the spilled...

"No," Medrivar said firmly, "forget the blood. Put it from your mind. Let it go. Let it go. Let it go."

"Is he all right?" Sudar asked anxiously. They had rested Perin against the wall. Törodè had checked that Perin still lived and then entered the house to calm the distraught owner. Kard lounged along the wall down from Perin, holding his head in his hands and murmuring words as if to make sure his mind had not been damaged.

Perin's eyes were still closed, and his body hunched around the sobs that issued from him.

"It's as if he's gone inside himself," Forgos murmured, tearing off his shirt and using it as a cloth, wiping blood from Perin's face and forearm. Forgos's hessian and cuirass lay where he knelt. "He saved your life," he said to Maka as if stating the weather.

Gyorva paced back and forth, his teeth gritted. The pain in his arm was good, in as much as he knew that it signalled the bone was probably unbroken. A bitter, ironic smile showed that he was less than overjoyed.

Perin opened his eyes slowly as if he had been very deeply asleep. He looked around, saw the expression of relief on Sudar's face, saw Forgos at work on cleaning his arm, saw Gyorva pacing, Harco lying still a short distance away...

"Get off!" he gasped out. "Harco! Go help Harco!"

"I don't think we can," Forgos answered with surprising gentleness. The shaven-headed Borderer had put aside his tough exterior.

Sudar stood and walked a short distance away, his face expressing pain that wasn't physical in nature. Everyone loved Harco.

Perin realised that Maka, silent for once, held his other hand, the cleaner one. "Is he...?"

"There's a lot of blood," Forgos said, by way of an answer. He stood, his features tight as he breathed, more in the manner of one preparing to fight than a man who had just finished. One grimy hand rubbed at his shaven head angrily. He threw his sodden shirt aside.

"Did you check?" Perin asked, pushing himself more upright against the wall. "Did you check to see?"

"No." Forgos, like the others, had not wanted to confirm what they all felt they knew.

Gyorva's sardonic tones spoke through the pain in his voice from where he stood, bending over Harco.

"You know, he is actually breathing."

"Oh, thank the..." Perin subsided with relief.

Forgos strode over to check and then settled to his knees in the grass as if he could take no more.

Törodè, done with advising the woman to stay in the house, re-entered the yard. He approached Harco, muttered a thankful sentence, and paused just to peer up at the sky, his fists gently closing and unclenching. After a few moments, he looked down, took in a deep breath and spoke.

"Right! Come on Hillspears! On your feet, those that can. We have wounded to tend and bodies to shift." He hesitated as Forgos pulled on his cuirass over his bare torso.

"I have a spare shirt for you, Forgos. Wait until we get back to the packs.

"Well done, all of you. Sudar, astonishing spear work. Gyorva, your shots were brilliance itself. Reger, good strategy, good work. Forgos, I'd be happy to fight alongside you any day of my life."

Maka did not seem to notice that he had not been mentioned. His gaze was on the ground, and his eyes were wet with tears.

Perin felt he understood. Maka would have died. If Perin had not jumped so stupidly, so desperately, onto that wounded drizen, Maka would certainly have died. There was an element of satisfaction in that. For weeks, the supercilious young nobleman had been getting at Perin whenever possible with his jibes and insults.

"You would have died," Perin said, ignoring that it was perhaps unfair to Maka, especially at the present time.

Maka looked up, then away, blinking tears across his cheeks. "I'm a coward."

Perin wasn't sure what to say to this. It clearly wasn't true, which surprised him. He would have marked Maka down as a coward easily, hours ago. Finally, he squeezed the other youth's hand in return.

"You might want to let go. The hand you're holding has got eye on it."

Maka helped him to his feet. They both stared at their hands. The gore seemed somehow innocuous now. For some reason, it seemed like time to start laughing.

NINETEEN

THE SECOND SOUTH RESPONSE stood in a loose circle by the entrance to the Borderer's Rest. Perin ached all over, new burnings starting with each movement. From their haggard expressions, he could tell that it was the same for the others.

Maka slid down against the wall of the taverna with a groan. "They can flay me to death here in the street," he said with typical defiance. "I'm not standing anymore."

"He won't stand for this kind of treatment," Forgos said, without smiling.

Sudar grinned wearily at the joke and sat down with a little more élan than Maka.

When Törodè stepped out of the Borderer's Rest, all four Borderers were seated in the dirt. The Response Leader surveyed them critically for a moment. Then he sat down beside Maka and tugged his stained Hessian off, throwing it aside. "You're all off duty now, so if you want to get yourself the attention of a physician, now's the time. Swordsman Kard is being seen by the Borderer medic."

"Which infirmary did Harco and Gyorva go to, Response Leader?" Perin asked, struggling to his feet and offering a hand to Forgos.

"The one on Temple Garden Way."

"Nice!" Forgos remarked with enthusiasm, accepting Perin's help and brushing dust, somewhat pointlessly, from his torn and soiled clothing. When the others looked at him quizzically he shrugged. "I've been in houses on Temple Garden Way." His face gave nothing away.

Törodè smiled to himself and began to lead the way.

Harco was unconscious again. The wound on his head had been cleaned and the bloodflow had ceased of its own accord. The physicians had left the wound open to the air. Herbs simmered gently in a clay bowl over low blue flames beside the bed. The fumes made Perin feel vaguely unsteady.

The Borderers stood around Harco for a little while before Forgos said, "This is pointless. He'll laugh at us when he finds out we just stood and stared at him sleep."

"Harco doesn't laugh at people," Maka remarked, but he followed the others out into the courtyard anyway.

Gyorva was white-faced and more sardonic than usual when they found him in a room on the other side of the courtyard. Perin stayed in the doorway, looking out on the enclosed square, rich with herbage and swarms of butterflies. He watched them dance above the buddleja and kiralszenta flowers. The sweet smells of the garden and the continuing good weather kept him in a strange, alert state, so that he could see his extreme tiredness as if from a distance. It had taken all night and most of the morning to make it back to Nagyevo, carrying Harco and assisting Gyorva.

"Physician says that Leader did a good job of setting my arm right. Broken after all, but I'm lucky it was a closed break. Bastard drizen," Gyorva remarked. He looked up at where Perin stood staring out of the doorway. "See him watch the butterflies. Mental deficiency must be liberating." When Perin did not appear to hear, he grabbed Forgos with his free arm. "Tell Reger, thanks. He helped me along more than his share.

"Where *is* Response Leader?" he added as if Törodè had been the topic of conversation all along.

"Physician's with him," Sudar said.

Perin went out into the early afternoon sunlight. Cirrus clouds broke the hard blue of the sky like the transition between spring and summer. The roof tiles that surrounded the sky, the walls, even the grass, glowed warm with light. Perin lay down on his front, feeling the cool tickle of the grass stems against his cheek and arms.

After a moment, Sudar approached to covertly assure himself of Perin's wellbeing before, silent as usual, he left him be.

The following day was ushered in by a swift dawn, promising clear skies resting on a heat haze. Perin woke a long time after dawn, and when he finally forced himself to leave his rooms, the heat had become uncomfortable.

Cama met him on the steps and listened intently as he explained what had happened in Mezyro. After Perin had watched the changes of expression in the older man's face, he felt positively cheerful. Cama's breathed thanks to the Nameless Gods brought a smile to his lips and he embraced the older man before heading out into Nagyevo.

One thing was certain, Perin decided, as he picked his path through the throngs of citizenry—early summer heat made Nagyevo stink. It was this above all that made him stay away from the trade districts and the Lower West city. This route to the Borderer Headquarters was longer, and it would take him past the Observatory gate but he didn't care. He had fought and survived again.

When he arrived, Törodè was talking to Kard quietly by the back wall of the training yard, similarly to the way Perin had seen them on first joining. Kard seemed to have fully recovered from his knock and was smiling at something Törodè was saying.

"Second South!" Kard stepped forward and called them into line. Perin went quickly to stand between Forgos and Sudar. Kard grinned widely and strode up and down the line. "Hillspears! The Borderer City Liaison would like to congratulate you on your worthiness as Borderers. However, he has decided to do a better thing, a far better thing. He has gone to the Tacnimag, just for us, to request better equipment. Apparently, yesterday he was told that the drizen in Mezyro were a freak occurrence, but today they have changed their magical minds!

"The good that will come of this, we hope, is a more suitable form of spear. Too many good weapons were broken on Fourthday, not least Borderman Gyorva Jolsen's arm. It is expected that Harco will be back with us by Firstday of next week, as his mind has not been damaged. Nor improved, I'm sad to say!"

Wry smiles greeted this, though Kard beamed as if they had all laughed uproariously.

"How long will it take Gyorva to…"

"Hush, Borderman Forgos! Gyorva will be returned to fitness soon. Normally, it would take between seven and twelve months for a break to be declared safe, but a Tacnimag healer has expressed an interest. It's wonderful to have such helpful magi within the city walls." His tone was difficult to read. It would have been impossible to claim that he was expressing sarcasm, although his eyes flickered toward Perin as he spoke.

"Finally, the Borderer Liaison has approved your bonus payout for the drizen we slaughtered. Your normal allowance of one menel each is due, of course, but the commission rate for killing drizen has been set at six menel per creature. That's thirty-six menel, for the slow of thought. Shared equally between the eight of us, that comes to four menel and five ranar each."

There was a collective intake of breath and a whistle from Forgos. Each Borderer privately calculated how many drinks that would mean.

"I'm going to buy a coat," Maka said with unusual fervour. "With gold-thread embroidery in the collar."

Forgos made a face at this before winking lasciviously at Perin. "I'm going to buy a woman."

Perin coughed to cover his amusement.

"Coats and women aside," Törodè interjected mildly, "this may not be a usual occurrence. At least I hope not. So spend carefully."

"Yes." Kard nodded seriously. "Don't waste your menel. First rule of a smart Borderer."

Törodè put a hand on Kard's shoulder. "Now would seem the best time to let you know that your pay is going up. I'm being assigned to First Northwest Response. You're the new Leader of the Hillspears."

There was a short period of silence, broken only by murmured congratulations from the four Bordermen to their new and former Leaders.

"Right!" Kard said with a renewed vigour, rubbing his hands together. "I'm buying me a coat and a woman!"

Perin laughed out loud with the others, relieved. The blood-soaked memory of Fourthday was fading.

"That'll do, Hillspears! Swordsman Myrvo!" For a moment Perin seemed to have forgotten his assumed name. "Yes, that's you, Reger." Had Kard said Swordsman?

Perin stood frozen. Today was a good day. It didn't matter that the city stank of tannery and livestock in the hard sun. It didn't matter that yesterday—no, the day before—he had come within moments of death.

He had just been promoted!

Forgos, Sudar, and Maka broke ranks to clap Perin on the back under the delighted gaze of Response Leader Kard. Törodè watched for a moment or two before briefly clasping Kard's shoulder and heading for the Headquarters door.

Forgos grabbed Perin and spun him around, all propriety and discipline forgotten in an excitement that brought a boyish grin to his hard face.

"Hey, Reger, want me to buy you a woman, too?"

Take order, Perin.

"That'll do!" Perin heard Medrivar and spoke almost simultaneously. "That's enough!" Turning to Kard, Perin asked, "Would you like me to bring them to order, Response Leader?"

Forgos fell back into line, still grinning. "He's good, isn't he? Don't you think he's good?" he whispered to Sudar, who was smiling quietly away, studying Perin's expression intently. Perin shot Forgos a look, making him face forward for a brief second. When Perin turned once more for Kard's answer, Forgos's voice could again be clearly heard in its stage whisper, "I think he's good. He'll go far."

Perin suppressed his own smile.

"If you would, Swordsman." Kard nodded to Perin with a strange expression on his face. It carried expectancy of a proper attitude in the young man before him, a reminder of the weight being placed on his shoulders.

"*Line* up!" Perin roared, for the first time in his life giving orders. "I want to see an orderly line of Bordermen leaving this place."

Kard nodded approvingly and then ruined Perin's first work as Swordsman. "Very good, Bordermen. Now. Who wants a drink?"

The next week was full of activity, albeit activity where Perin found himself drinking with his subordinates far too much, or spending time attempting to escape from the constant presence of either Maka or Neva.

Neva had a way of picking his appearances when the other Hillspears were not nearby, which at least meant that Perin could handle his incessant questions with a clear mind. The young mage had become both more serious and more flippant in the past few days, it seemed. When Perin had described the drizen encounter to him, he had pondered quietly for a moment. Then he had earnestly told Perin he was glad he had not been hurt. At the same time, an increasing confidence brought back the cheerful, witty enthusiasm he had shown on approaching Perin for the first time.

The Hillspears were off duty for a month to give the Tacnimag healer time to work with Gyorva, who claimed vocally whenever asked that the mage was a detestable imbecile.

Perin sat, watching the sky through open shutters in the window of his favourite trade quarter taverna. It was midday and summer thunderclouds were rolling heavily across the sky, spreading an ominous, purplish hue over the grey city, reminding Perin pleasantly of home. Forgos had drunk up and left for some mysterious arrangement, leaving Sudar and Maka alone with Perin.

Harco had returned in good health, but for some reason, he no longer saw any point in pretending he liked beer. The blond warrior was acknowledging his aristocratic background, and two days ago, he had treated himself and Gyorva with a trip to his father's vineyard in Solorin, so that his common-born but aspirational friend could experience a more expensive form of drunkenness.

Maka, much to Forgos's amusement and Gyorva's disgust, had begun to show symptoms of jealousy when alone with Perin and Sudar. Sudar was by far the closest of the Borderers to Perin, despite—or perhaps because of—the lack of direct conversation between them. Maka, who had followed Perin doggedly since Perin had saved his life, clearly resented the strength of Sudar and Perin's friendship.

Perin had been content in the last golden week to watch all this happen with a calm detachment. Maka's devotion made him uncomfortable, but it was at least more positive than the derision the handsome young man had held for him before.

"Do you want another beer, Reger?" Sudar asked casually, nudging Perin across the divide between their chairs with his foot.

Perin turned his gaze away from the lowering sky and nodded, pushing his jug across the table. Maka stood abruptly and took it, muttering that he'd get it, he was closer. Sudar shrugged. Perin understood that Sudar was more aware and perceptive than he ever let on. The dark-haired Borderman was the embodiment of the western proverb about wisdom, "He who shows himself to be wise, does so in secret."

"The Seven Cities began to restrict trade last week," Sudar said quietly, demonstrating that he, like Perin, had his thoughts elsewhere.

"That doesn't mean war," Perin answered lightly, wondering how Cama and the other debaters had taken the news. Western philosophies would be viewed all the more poorly in the light of probable conflict.

A spot of rain made a broken whiplash across the panels of the shutter. Perin put out his hand to touch the water with calloused fingers, and the second drop landed on his arm, accompanied by a rare stirring of cool air. Moments later, the possibility of storm-break had passed; the air became hot and sticky once more.

"Reger?" A person Perin didn't quite recognise appeared, pushing through the cluster of tables and chairs that filled the taverna. It was a young woman, perhaps one of Forgos's numerous courtship attempts...

"Reger Myrvo? The library boy?"

Perin sat up straight, remembering her. "You're Aranyo's friend. The hessian weaver?"

"Yes, yes. Look, I didn't know what to do. I was told you'd gone and been made a Borderer, and then you were promoted. Aranyo needs..."

"What's wrong?" Sudar interjected, realising faster than Perin that the girl held back panic. "Is Aranyo in danger? Oh-gees?" The girl blinked, not knowing that Sudar had tried to help Aranyo last time he had been threatened by the Observatory Guards.

"Yes! They're hunting him in the Lower West City. He was caught daubing slogans."

"Again?" Perin got to his feet. Sudar shot him a look that said, what can we do about it? But Perin ignored it. "I'll run off and see what I can do. How many of them are there?"

She shook her head, either not knowing or not trusting herself to remember.

"Sudar, look after her. I'll go on my own."

"Reger…" Sudar began to protest, pausing at the look in Perin's eyes and the reappearance of Maka.

"What's going on? Has something happened? I got your beer, Reger."

"I'll go on my own," Perin repeated firmly, "and that's an order from your Swordsman. Su, mate, explain to Maka."

"I'll come if you like…"

"Maka! You have got to stop." Perin's self control broke. "Shut up, sit down, stop following me. I'll see both of you later."

"You better," Sudar said quietly, putting one hand on Perin's shoulder and the other on the girl's, as if expressing wordlessly his intent to uphold Perin's order.

"I will," Perin told himself as he left the taverna, moving into a street mostly empty of people. He broke into a run, heading not directly across the South Way and into the Lower West City, but toward the crescent of more affluent housing on the Lower West's Wall Way where his room above the confectioners stood.

Minutes later, biting his lip against the fear that Aranyo—brash, common, exuberant, thoroughly decent Aranyo—could be lying at the feet of an Observatory Guard, Perin took one of the alleyways up into the Lower West City. A climb along a broken wall and up the side of a skewed timber building brought him onto one of the many flat, or nearly flat rooftops. Some of the roofs were attempts at gardens. Most had a water tank of some kind, and more than a few hosted holes caused either by overfull water tanks, neglect, or people like Perin.

Ducking behind an architectural obtrusion, Perin hastily changed. The clothes he had gathered from the hiding place in his room had been heavier and harder to hide than he had thought, let alone his spade, which he had wrapped in a sheet.

Everything in Perin's mind, including Medrivar, told him that he was making a mistake.

This is not the time to reveal your old identity! Medrivar's mind-voice filled Perin's inner ear. *There is nothing you can do to help your friend. Not alone.*

"As your voice is reminding me, I'm *not* alone," Perin muttered angrily, admitting that he was being foolish, but he continued anyway, driven by his fear that Aranyo was about to die.

The figure that stepped out of cover, moving stealthily along the baking-hot roofscape, looked decidedly different from Reger Myrvo, Borderer Swordsman.

Perin felt very stifled now, with his long leather coat draping about him as he walked. He peered out from beneath his broad-brimmed hat for sight or sign of the Observatory Guards or Aranyo. The benevolent-eye amulet winked at his throat, reflecting the odd light above. It was good to wear Medrivar's symbol openly after so long keeping it hidden.

He had to acknowledge, despite his fear, that somehow this felt right. He was a gravedigger, even when wielding a spear for the Borderers. Gravedigger was written on his heart, penned by his oath to Graves.

Memories of burying Graves returned. Perin resolved once again that Aranyo would not die because of him. By now, Medrivar had stopped advising him against the path he was set on, and instead, rapidly informed Perin of the best strategies available. The heat really was intolerable.

A short distance away, a desperate Aranyo, fresh blood caking in his wild-blond hair, struggled up the bared structure of a dilapidated storehouse, rolling onto the rooftop beneath the scorch of the sun. Observatory Guards ran beneath, shouting out reports and curses. Then one of them called, "The roofs!" and Aranyo moaned, struggling upright, hearing boots, and gloved hands grasping at the wall.

The sun sank behind a mountainous wall of glowering thundercloud, shading the world beneath in subdued tones. A robed mage stood in one of the yards of the Lower West City, surrounded by guards, grim with determination. He was aware of his target, and intent on capturing him, but he was blinkered to the other, to Perin.

Perin moved fast despite his long coat, striding across the Nagyevo rooftops with a sky full of thunder above him.

TWENTY

WATER GATHERED IN the darkness of a high stone arch, dewing up in the rounded crack between two deep-set stones. Distant footfall and the approaching glow of a torch set the condensation aglitter with an echoing brilliance. For a moment, the dank walls shone.

The guard crossed beneath the arch, casting shadows of his fully armoured form along the grey, stained walls. The hand that held the torch was over-warm, enclosed by a thick leather gauntlet, but the cold seemed to encroach at the gaps in his mail.

The Observatory symbol flickered in and out of sight on his surcoat, the monochrome lightning design only emphasised by the torchlight. Turning the corner, the guard stepped back from the wall to allow two visitors to pass. Their coloured robes brushed the filth of the cold floor as they walked, a fierce, pulsating light going ahead of them, suspended inches above the right hand of the foremost.

The guard saluted as they passed, ignoring him in their conversation.

"The solidarity campaign is clearly failing. There is simply no trust. No magic can win the minds of men!"

"None yet found, brother. Espionage and action then, if there is no other route. The loss of the Northern project has limited our options."

"We committed too soon…"

Their voices faded away. The guard followed the curving corridor to an intersection, one of four within the Observatory. On his right, a door in the outer wall led to tributary corridors designed as a defensive measure. On the left, the room opened into a great central space brightly lit by many torches.

The broad archway revealed an expansive raised floor, seeming to reflect its burnished metal to the glass dome above. Stormlight poured in through the Observatory roof. There were telescopes in the alcoves surrounding the central area, raised on tall plinths and decorated with ritual embellishments. A thick glass mirror in a twisted frame sat at the base of each, connected to the telescope itself by a spiral of gold that wound along the length of the devices.

The floor itself was a series of concentric, dizzying circles bound together like a stylised metal grille. The guard had walked across the Floor Gate before and remembered the draught that rose from beneath. It made the otherwise beautiful room cold.

Two more magi were conversing beside one of the telescopes. The guard recognised one as the Guard Mage, the mage in charge of ensuring Nagyevo's security. He looked tense, his movements quick and his gestures terse, accompanying a fierce frown. The other mage appeared to be expressing disappointment; the Master of the City seemed to seethe with frustration. The conversation ended with the sedate withdrawal of the superior mage. The Guard Mage gripped the hem of his red robe angrily and then crumpled up a paper in his hand, letting it fall to the floor. The guard guessed that it was a poster, a tool of the solidarity campaign. He hurried on.

Stairs led down beneath the level of the Nagyevo streets, down into a darker, colder world than before. The aired, pipe-heated upper rooms of the Observatory that ringed around the domed roof were as different from the slimy stonework and damp air in the lower passages as it was possible to be.

In one of the cells, in the foundations of the building, light came faintly through the iron grille from the corridor. The occupant of the cell was seated on his bed, two normal-sized palettes pushed together, hard and cold in the dark. Sometimes the torch in the corridor went out, and it was a day or more before it was replaced or relit. The prisoner shivered for a moment, pulled his thick cloak about his shoulders, once again grateful his captors had allowed him to keep it.

The walls of the small cell were lined with many bars of iron, thickest about the door itself.

Footsteps made the prisoner lift his head. The corridor resounded with the echoes of light footfall, although no new torchlight appeared on the dank walls beyond the grille. The prisoner relaxed. He knew who his visitor was.

"Are you there, prigon?" The boy's voice came clear in the silent dark.

Kesairl chuckled. "Where else would I be, mageling?"

"Sorry," the young mage apologised, as he frequently did. "Has it been bad this week? I noticed that the torch was out the day before yesterday."

Kesairl stood and bent so he could peer through the grille of his door. He could make out the nervous features of the young man on the other side, but only when straining his night eyes. "My weeks have been better since you came to talk to me. How have you been?"

The boy paused. "Afraid," he said at last, "that I am doing too much that is bad and not enough that is good."

Ah. Kesairl smiled to himself. Sometimes his visitor was cheerful and cocksure, full of witty remarks and enthusiastic conversation. Other times, and more frequently of late, his voice was filled with doubt.

"We all have that fear, my friend. At some times more than others. You have been telling your superiors about the Gravedigger?"

"Yes, but every time I do, another house is broken up by the Observatory Guards. I only tell them that someone in a taverna said something or that I've seen 'Gravedigger' scrawled on walls in a certain place. But someone specific always ends up getting hurt."

Kesairl listened to the hurt in the mage's voice. "My friend, you are in a difficult position." His rumbling voice filled the silence. "You have a job to do, and you do your best not to hurt anyone. It is the Guards who injure and destroy, is it not? Can you blame yourself for their actions?"

"I don't know. Can I?"

Kesairl let that question go unanswered. "Mage, I do not know your name, and you do not know mine. That is well, as we are enemies by circumstance. If one day they killed me, I would not want that guilt to go to you just because you were friendly to me. Likewise, if one day I should break out of here," he laughed to disguise his sadness, "and I accidentally blasted you apart as I brought this place down, I would not like to know the name of the innocent I had killed.

"I do not think you are doing evil in the city. But tell me about the Gravedigger. Tell me everything that you tell your superiors, as well as the information you keep from them. Please."

The mage shifted in the dark corridor. "There are a lot more slogans painted in the Lower West City. The people use him to raise their hopes that things will change. But he has done nothing out in the open. I spend time with my friends from the tavernas, my friend in the Borderers, ask them what they know. No one knows anything. Sometimes I wonder if he's real at all."

"He's real," Kesairl said firmly. "I know he's real."

Perin's spade crashed down on the back of the guard's head. The man fell forward, smacked his face hard against the brickwork, lay still.

Aranyo looked up, hand shielding his eyes. "Nameless ones! Gravedigger!"

"Yes." Perin kept his hat tilted low and affected his voice so that Aranyo wouldn't recognise it. "Hurry, you need to get out of the Lower West."

"You really are real!"

"I should hope so, yes." Perin scanned the surrounding rooftops for movement. Aranyo got to his feet hurriedly. The man Perin had struck moved, groaning.

The man had not seen Perin's face, but he would if they stayed. The search for the Gravedigger would only intensify. Aranyo and others would only be more likely to fall prey to the Oh-gees. Perin turned the guard over, his pulse racing.

Aranyo and Perin gasped simultaneously. It was the survivor of the pair that had attacked Aranyo before, big Szagu. The danger was suddenly much greater than before. It was thanks only to the Mezyro trip with the Borderers that Perin had been out of the city while this guard had been describing his attacker. Perin had never found out for certain whether the shorter guard had died or not.

"I remember him." Aranyo spat. "Was it you saved me from them before?" He stared up at Perin as he crouched down over Szagu.

Perin looked away just in time. He scanned the rooftops as a cover. "Yes, that was me."

"Well, this one won't bother me or anyone again." Aranyo's voice shook.

Szagu groaned, his eyes crossing and uncrossing as he tried to focus on the world around him.

Perin watched in shock as Aranyo gripped the large Observatory Guard around the throat, clenching tightly, a growl rising in his throat.

It is his right. Medrivar murmured before Perin could interfere. Szagu's hands were beginning to flap and dance, knuckles battering on the hard roof.

Perin strode away to the edge of the roof, to stare out into the complicated tangle of alleys and yards. He swallowed, forcing down his shock. When he returned to the boy's side, Aranyo shook all over and Szagu was dead.

"Come on, Aranyo."

"Coming, Gravedigger," Aranyo murmured at last. He followed Perin away from the site of the kill, as the clouds broke. Rain began to pour down on Nagyevo in great columns and curtains, driving across the city like only a summer storm could.

"We need to get off the roof before we slip and fall to our deaths!" Perin called out, heading for a stairway. When they were halfway down, an Observatory Guard appeared at the bottom. Perin just managed to leap the remaining steps and knock the man down before he could let out a warning shout. The rain pounded down on the pair as they struggled, until Perin was able to bang the guard's head against the floor, knocking him unconscious.

Under the sound of drumming rain and rolling thunder, Perin could just make out the sound of distant, booted feet running in his direction.

"Aranyo. Do you know any friends who live near here?" He spoke urgently, pulling the boy after him into a recess between two buildings.

"Um...Hasna, but she's past all the ones that were chasing me...or the Borderer boy, Reger Myrvo, I suppose... I know he's close, because we met once for drinking..."

"Concentrate! Do you think you can get to his house?"

Aranyo blinked rain out of his eyes. "Yes, I think so."

"Go ahead! I'll come after and try to cut followers off. Go!"

Aranyo nodded and started out running. Almost immediately, an Oh-gee dashed past in hot pursuit. Perin swung his arm around and caught him across the throat, tumbling him to the cobbles. Excitement rushed through Perin, warring with fear and the calm encouragements of Medrivar. With a murmured thought to his king, Perin ran after Aranyo, aware of the shouts of guards coming from behind.

At the next crossing of two alleyways, Perin dodged past a woman running from the rain, or the guards, or both, and turned around to face the three men. Thunder cracked overhead, a mere second or so after a bright flash of lightning cast Perin's imposing figure in sharp relief. His coat flapped around him in the rain and wind. With one hand, he adjusted his wide brimmed hat. With the other, he lifted his spade high above his head, as if tempting the lightning.

"I am the Gravedigger! I am the City! Nagyevo! Valo!" The Observatory Guards stopped short, readying their shortswords, their faces grim. There was room for them to come two at a time, and then only with restricted movement. Faces looked down on the scene through opened shutters. The Lower West City would know all about this tomorrow, whatever the outcome.

"Go on!" The guards all tried to come forward at the same time.

Perin used a chopping, circular downswing to push them back. The backswing knocked a guard's sword to the ground, breaking his hand. He stumbled back into his fellows, hindering them, as Perin rushed forward. He struck out long, his spade in his right hand, his left drawing a coffin nail and driving it into his disarmed opponent.

The man's hand shot up to ward off a spade blow, and the nail bit deep into his underarm, finding no armour to block its cold inches. Blood spurted suddenly from around the iron spike, and the guard screamed, pushing backward to get away.

Perin let out a high warcry, his spade clubbing one of the guards unconscious. The last ran, his sword discarded in a swelling, reddening puddle.

Without pausing, Perin turned to continue in pursuit of Aranyo. Medrivar was silent for the moment. A tune rose in Perin's mind, haunting and beautiful, a melody he had once hummed in a Csus graveyard nearly three years ago.

The boy on the other side of Kesairl's cell door suddenly fell silent. He put a hand up to his head, wincing.

"I hate it when they do that," the boy said, smiling sheepishly.

"Telepathic summons?" Kesairl asked.

The young mage nodded, his expression suddenly excited. "They want me to know that the Gravedigger is fighting Observatory Guards in the Lower West City! My information actually led somewhere! He can't hold them off for long.There are so many, and I know that the Guard Mage went with them... There's no way he'll escape. Do you think...do you think they'll reward me, prigon?"

Kesairl swallowed in the dark. "Perhaps." He kept his sudden fear from his voice with some effort. Was Perin in danger?

"This is great!" The mage grinned. "I can't wait to tell Reger about this..." He turned to go, sweeping his blue robes about him.

Kesairl rushed to the door, put a hand up against the cold, magic-suppressing iron. "Reger?" Kesairl questioned urgently.

"Reger Myrvo, my friend who's a Borderer. I mentioned him before," Neva explained, looking back. "I really should go now..."

Reger Myrvo! Kesairl remembered the name. So this mage knew Perin— knew him without knowing that he was hunting him.

"Yes," Kesairl said, calming himself. Perin had Medrivar with him, after all. "Farewell, mageling."

The boy's footsteps echoed away, leaving Kesairl alone in the dark.

Perin skidded around the corner, seeing with satisfaction that Aranyo was not in sight. The diminishing crowd of Nagyevans were drab and uniform in the rain. But now Perin had a problem. He needed to escape as well, but could not hope to be hidden in the crowds whilst wearing his Gravedigger apparel.

Making a sudden decision, Perin turned and ran into a neighbouring passageway, by chance picking one that did not immediately link back to the one he had just left. His running feet took him through winding pathways, slipping and sliding in the mud and puddles, dodging people who had not yet taken cover from the weather.

The wall beside Perin suddenly cracked with heat, then exploded violently. With a startled yell, Perin spun and looked out into a courtyard surrounded by trade buildings, balconies hung with cloth. Standing between two covered dyeing vats, his robes heavy with rainwater, was an Observatory mage, his hands extended in a magic-wielding stance.

Perin dropped on one knee as if damaged by the attack, gathered a coffin nail, and threw it as he rose, running away along the nearest passageway. Unseen by him, the mage knocked the nail aside by exerting a wall of force, hands clenching momentarily before he began to chase the Gravedigger. His attack had been so close…and after all this time of doubting the man's existence…

Perin scrambled over a temporary fence that blocked off privy yards from surrounding buildings, hoping that the mage would not anticipate this change of direction. Now he scrambled desperately from yard to yard, in some places pushing through damaged fence sections, always seeking for a way out.

Behind him, wooden slats exploded into dust and splinters as the mage approached.

Perin changed tactics again, recklessly hauling himself up a drainpipe, his spade in its baldric belt across his back. The drainpipe held, and once again he found himself on the roof, the storm rushing down around him. A blast of force and heat smashed against the edge of the building behind his feet, and he stumbled forward, swearing as he almost fell to a messy and undignified ruin in the privy yard below.

Shite, how do I get out of this one? Perin wondered.

Medrivar was silent, although Perin could sense the king's anxiety. Another force-blast hit the building's edge.

There! Medrivar spoke suddenly, directing Perin's attention to a raised garden across another alleyway from the rooftop that Perin stood on. The building trembled, as if at any moment, the roof might give way.

Perin stared up into the rolling, thunderous clouds for a moment as if to centre himself, and then he ran for the edge of the roof. The building slumped inward on itself as he leaped, barely catching the edge of the garden wall, legs dangling above a cobbled surface some twenty feet below.

On the other side of the falling trade building, the Tacnimag Mage stepped backward, raising a ward to prevent falling debris from hitting him. His mind was having trouble seizing hold of the Gravedigger's position amid the chaos.

Perin rolled over onto somebody's attempt to grow vegetables. The beanpoles he had just crushed were empty of bean pods, the dried-up stalks now crushed into the soil. As he stood, wondering how much longer he could go on, the doorway into the terraced apartments opened, and a woman came out into her small garden. She did not even glance at her destroyed beanpoles but immediately beckoned Perin.

"Gravedigger! Hurry!"

The small trade building finally finished its collapse. Perin followed the woman, disappearing from view.

With a curse, the mage surveyed the wreckage he had caused, then lifted his hood to cover his head from the rain and withdrew, leaving behind wreckage and failure.

TWENTY-ONE

THE CANDLES AROUND Perin's desk guttered briefly as Kard entered the room, closing the door on the rest of the headquarters. Perin looked up, smiled to acknowledge the Response Leader, and returned his laborious attention to his quill.

"Just the training reports?" Kard asked, sitting across the small room at his own desk. The week had been slow since Perin had returned from his narrow escape, at least, slow for the Borderers.

Perin nodded. "Yes, sir. What's the Liaison asking of you?"

"Nothing, really. Requested a report on the reliability of the new spears out on Response."

Perin nodded. The Borderers of Second South Response had taken the new weapons on short patrol circuits outside the city wall. They were heavier than the traditional Borderer spear, designed not for functional flexibility but for standing up to the stresses of heavy combat.

"First South should get that report to the Tacnimag Liaison first, I should imagine," Perin said grimly, remembering the neighbouring Response returning from a costly victory over drizen in Solorin.

Kard nodded slowly, deep-brown eyes studying the floor. "I don't think that report will be written. Not with their Response Leader dead."

"One death isn't bad, considering. Six drizen is a good account, even with the new spears."

"One death is still bad," Kard corrected Perin.

Blinking, Perin sat back, feeling a chill creep around the back of his shoulders.

Kard watched Perin for a moment in the manner that always unsettled him. "We talked once, back when you were a Borderman, and I was still Swordsman," Kard began.

Perin nodded. "At least once, sir." Something in the way Kard looked at him made him focus his attention on Kard very closely.

"Yes. About your home."

"Csus. Yes." Perin swallowed, putting his quill down carefully so that it did not drip on his paper.

"Arpavale Claim," Kard said, resting his elbows against the low back of his chair, leaning as if to take in Perin from a better angle. Perin said nothing. He now had a good idea what was coming. Medrivar had become alert in Perin.

"You said Arpavale, Reger, and we talked about the route down from Csus onto the Nagyevo plain. How it wouldn't have taken you through Varo, coming from Arpavale."

Perin said nothing.

"And then when we were about to meet drizen for the first time—in my case, at least—you changed your mind. You had been in Varo. You'd fought drizen in Varo."

"I asked you not to ask why," Perin managed, resting hands that weren't shaking on his desk.

"And I said, I didn't care why." Kard locked his eyes with Perin's. "I still don't. Not really. But I'm no fool."

Perin slowly relaxed. He nodded, smiling to show his relief. "I know you're not, sir."

"Good. Don't start thinking any different, Reger. If that is your name."

"It's not."

"I don't want to know." Kard shrugged, standing up. For a moment, he looked toward the door, and then he sat down again, another question on his lips.

"Swordsman…"

"Yes, sir?"

"Is there a significant difference between killing drizen and killing men?" The question hung in the air.

Perin swallowed hard. "How do you…?"

"Oh-gee deaths are hard to keep quiet, even if you're the Tacnimag. I won't ask why or how or even when, just…"

"It's easier," Perin answered abruptly. "The killing, I mean. Smaller, softer, weaker. Easier than killing drizen. Apart from later…"

"Later…" Kard stated, sitting motionless opposite Perin in the candlelight.

"Yes. Later, when you think about it. Who they were. If they had family. Whether or not you care." Perin's voice was taut.

Kard watched him for a moment more, his eyes shining. Then he got to his feet once more and broke the tension by changing the subject. "Another riot yesterday. Right outside the Observatory. The city must be becoming an uncomfortable place if you're a mage, don't you think?"

Perin nodded gratefully. Kard's quick smile was followed by a hand on Perin's shoulder, briefly tightening there. "Who else knows?"

Perin smiled again, remembering the reproving look given by a typically silent Sudar when they had met after the collapsing of the warehouse in the Lower West City. "Sudar. At least, I think so. No one else, as far as I know."

"Sudar is sharp. And he is a support for you, if anyone is. More loyal than Maka, although that's not for want of Maka trying," Kard said wryly. "If you or I die, then Sudar will be the next Swordsman of the Hillspears."

"Good choice," Perin said quietly.

"One more question." Kard stood, this time actually reaching the door before turning back. "Why the Borderers? Because you didn't think you'd be found here?"

"Honestly?" Perin grinned. "I wanted to get into the City Guard. I heard Borderer experience was required."

"Yes. I remember now. The City Guard? Why? You're earning more now, what with likely drizen commission."

Perin shrugged and smiled. Kard took the hint and left with a smile of his own. Perin's good humour faded instantly. Kesairl was in the Observatory cells. The problem was, if he got into the City Guard, he would be no closer to his much-missed companion than he was now. The masterplan did not seem to be working.

Don't give up, Medrivar murmured.

Perin picked up his quill and started a new sentence with fierce determination. "Never said I was."

Neva appeared more strained to Perin than he had done on their last meeting. He accepted a drink gratefully.

"How are you?"

"I'm well," Neva said in a strange tone of voice. His blue eyes glanced around the room, taking in the blanket roll on the floor by Perin's bed. Aranyo had been sleeping there since the events in the Lower West City, to stay hidden from the Observatory Guards. Neva didn't comment on the blankets. Something more important appeared to be on his mind.

"Just dealing with the weight of knowing things that are difficult to know." He grinned briefly, a shadow of the carefree manner from the days when Perin and he had been new friends.

"Do you want to talk about any of it?" Perin prompted.

Neva nodded. "Well, for a start, you should know that the Lower West City won't be safe to enter from tomorrow morning. The Tacnimag are conducting a purge of the dissenters there." Neva's voice had become uncharacteristically grim.

Perin put his hands in his pockets to keep his fists from clenching. For the first time, he was aware of Medrivar rising to his feet without having to be present in his own mind to see it.

"Why?"

"The recent failure to capture the Gravedigger. The mage that destroyed the building in the Lower West City reported that the locals are hiding him."

Perin remembered the woman who had led him down through her house to a drained water-channel, giving him clothing belonging to her dying son, and a sack to hide his coat and hat, another to hide his spade. He had walked past the room where her only relative, her firstborn, lay dying of water sickness. The memory made him wince.

"I told them that my sources suggest he's no longer in that part of the city," Neva said tightly, his voice almost cracking from emotion.

"Thank you for telling me." Perin put a hand on Neva's arm.

"That's not all. I overheard the Master of the City talking with the Borderer Liason. Since your promotion, there's been one too few Bordermen in Second South Response."

"That's right."

"The next volunteer is going to be planted by the Master of the City. The Tacnimag want eyes to watch for dissent in the Borderers. I'm only telling you because I know that there are sometimes good people that are also dissenters."

"Yes. Thank you." Perin took a deep breath. If Neva hadn't chosen to tell him this…

"You can get round it. But you'll need a volunteer before tomorrow evening to fill the position. I don't think the Master of the City expects anyone to step up. Thankfully, it isn't a priority as far as I can gather from listening in on conversations. It's their own fault really—they trained me to spy." There was a long pause. "I'll come tomorrow. I just…just want to come and see you and just talk or go drinking or something normal." The statement came from the young mage in something of a rush.

Perin smiled sympathetically. "That would be good. You know where to find me, Neva. I can see you're doing your best."

"I'm following balance," Neva said slowly, looking away. "I won't do anything I think is wrong, but I will support the Tacnimag. Without their rule, there will be chaos."

"Quite possibly."

"It seems that sometimes it's about which sacrifices to make." Neva's eyes evaded Perin's for a moment, and his posture fell, making him appear defeated.

Perin resisted the urge to ask the young mage what he meant.

The week grew quickly worse. The Tacnimag and the Observatory Guards moved through the Lower West City arresting and beating inhabitants almost indiscriminately. There were further riots, and an altercation of sorts outside the Borderer Headquarters, when an Observatory Guard captain tried to order some of the Responses into the streets of the city to assist with law-keeping.

The Borderer Captain had made his point a little short of violence; the Borderers were constitutionally forbidden from interfering with intra-city affairs, and the Observatory could stay out of Borderer affairs as well.

The Observatory Guard Captain, for his part, left with threats of Tacnimag punishment, the Borderer Liaison running after him. The Borderers were well within their rights. Perin and Kard were not worried; the Tacnimag were unpopular enough as it was. Breaking more of the fragile peace would not help them.

In a further subtle blow against the Tacnimag, the new Borderer recruit for the Hillspears was not a spy for the Observatory. Instead, Perin oversaw Aranyo in the training yard, rushing him through training in spear and bow, knowing that the need to get Second South out into Mezyro and Solorin was vital.

First South awaited resupply and a new Borderer of their own, so the Solorin routes were suddenly as abandoned as the Mezyro patrols. In the past, that would not have been a problem. The Claim north of the city, Cserys, had not experienced drizen attack. However, thanks to the dense grouping of taxpaying lords and homesteaders to the south of the city, the drizen attacks were happening frequently in Mezyro and Solorin.

The vintages of Solorin were suffering greatly now, according to report. The Tacnimag had stopped sending commands to collect money from the Mezyro homesteads, perhaps finally realising that the folk of the Claim had none. In comparison, the very wealthy lords and gentry of Solorin were going untaxed, as every day another dignitary who owned estates in the northwestern corner of the Fold of Narsun chose to defy the Tacnimag.

In short, the Tacnimag had never been so disliked by so many, and tensions had never been so high. Perin found it difficult to construe it as coincidental that drizen attacks on the tax rebels were also so high. Yet the sudden appearances of the monsters remained a mystery.

Neva sat half asleep in a chair in Perin's rooms. The door stood open to let in air. Summer was well underway, to spite the curses of the Hillspears against the heat. Perin had returned the day before from another campaign into Solorin, the second in the month. Both routes had seen fierce action against more mysteriously appearing drizen, the monsters appearing from nowhere both times. Aranyo had proved himself, his kill easing his acceptance into the Response. It helped him that he had his tales of the Gravedigger to tell.

Perin's thoughts ran over the stories as he busied himself with the food he had cooked to entertain Neva. Aranyo always told the tales with wide-eyed sincerity, honouring the Gravedigger beyond the station of a hero, while Sudar, smiling, glanced back and forth between Aranyo and Perin, appreciating the way it affected his friend, enjoying every wince Perin made as Aranyo obliviously praised him.

"Are you tired, Neva?" he asked, carefully placing a clay bake on a countertop and separating the halves of the urn. Aromatic steam rose from the meat within.

Neva shrugged himself fully conscious and smiled. "That smells better than Observatory food. You'd think that mages would be able to apply some magic to their food, wouldn't you? And you'd be wrong. Yes, I am a bit tired."

"Any reason out of the ordinary?"

"Not really. Been spending more of my nighttime talking to a prisoner in the cells." Perin stiffened at this, but carried on as soon as he was able. It was tremendously unlikely that Neva had been talking to Kesairl.

"I'm sorry, Reger. You were telling me about the mystery of the drizen." Neva stretched as he got up, coming to sit at the table. Perin smiled faintly, placing a plate heaped with lamb and rice in front of his friend. Neva began to eat at once.

"Yes. Well, I've said it all really. They come out of nowhere. The greatest wonder of it is that there is nowhere in Narsun, or anywhere else, for them to be camped. The land around is well mapped, and the terrain isn't nearly dramatic enough to hide whole camps of the creatures. That's why the Borderers and the people who suffer drizen attacks are whispering that there must be a magical source."

Neva frowned in thought, but was distracted by the food. "This is good. A little heavy on the carum spice, but I like that."

There was a short pause as both young men ate.

Neva was still considering what Perin had said. "Do you have a theory?"

"Sort of. Well, it seems obvious in a way. Here, you brought the document I asked about, didn't you?"

"Oh, yes," Neva mumbled through his food. He put down his knife and passed a roll of paper to Perin. It showed a record of missed tax payments by citizenry of Nagyevo living outside the walls of the city, especially in Mezyro and Solorin.

"Here. Yes…" Perin compared the dates to those on a sheet of his own that he had brought home from the Borderer Headquarters. "Every attack has happened within three days of the victim or victims' refusal or omission of payment."

Neva shook his head slowly. "That does seem very suspicious. But those monsters murder, don't they? The Tacnimag have their flaws—although I never said that, if anyone asks—but we magi, we wouldn't go as far as to set beasts on our own people!" He gestured at the room at large with his knife. "I mean, apart from anything else, that's just stupid."

"I don't think all the magi are as decent as you. Or as you might think them to be," Perin said kindly.

Neva shook his head emphatically. "They've been clumsy and heavy-handed, but they're not evil. I don't think they are."

Not since he's been given a useful role with them. Medrivar's analytical mind-tones spoke in Perin's inner ear. *I wonder how much more he has been accepted into their circles.*

Perin ate silently for a moment. That was an uncomfortable thought.

"Anyway," Neva continued, "I've never heard any of the mages talking about secret plots involving drizen. If it was one mage working separately, then I'm sure it would have been found out. I mean, the most secretive thing in the Tacnimag is something to do with a Northern expedition or experiment, and while I've heard barely anything about that, I've still heard *something*."

"Besides, there just isn't a way, by magic or otherwise, to transport drizen in the numbers you describe…" Despite his obvious belief in his argument, doubt began to enter Neva's voice. "Although…the weaponry is puzzling."

"Go on," Perin urged.

Neva sat back, his frown more pronounced than ever. "I did some reading about the creatures. Incidentally, I had to get the book from the Observatory library, the confiscated section. They've always used hook weapons like their hook-swords in the past, but they were different, then." He changed tack with a question. "The drizen you've killed often have had different tribal markings on their hide and armour, yes?"

"That's right."

"Well, that's strange of itself, but also, the weaponry that drizen used in the past was different. They can't forge. The drizen only beat. Apparently, they can light campfires, but nothing as sophisticated as a furnace. They used to use stolen farm tools like sickles and scythes, beaten into a shape that suited them."

"Their weapons now seem purpose built," Perin pointed out.

"More than that," Neva agreed, "purpose forged. Which means not by them. Which means that men must be supplying their weapons."

They finished their meal, Perin now firmly convinced that the Tacnimag were behind the drizen attacks. Neva's doubt overrode his other instincts. The facts that supported his friend's theory were undefeatable; yet, as far as he was concerned, the facts defying Tacnimag involvement were also perfect.

It did seem to trouble Neva, Perin noticed, perhaps because the situation seemed to be taking Perin down a route further into dissent. Away from Neva's strengthening position within the Observatory.

"This is confusing," Neva stated with obvious frustration as he pushed away his plate. "It doesn't make sense. It isn't my job though, thankfully. All I have to do is...well, you know." He was almost apologetic in tone. Perin merely nodded in answer.

"The city is so close to collapsing on itself." Neva scowled at the wood grain of the table. "Nobody is listening to the Tacnimag anymore. An Observatory Guard was murdered yesterday."

"Every day some citizen or other turns up dead in the Lower West City," Perin reminded Neva as carefully as he could.

Neva's expression darkened. He didn't want to think about that. "It'll finish if we get him. It'll finish then, finally," he said, one hand unconsciously forming a fist, "if I can just hunt down the Gravedigger for real. If he's out of the way..."

"You intend to kill him?" Perin asked, slightly shocked.

Neva looked up, surprised. "It's war, Reger. He's killed guards. I only mean to catch him, but all this horror in the city is driving me mad, everyone mad. Reger, if I catch the Gravedigger, for the good of the city as much as anything, he will be killed."

Neva's blue eyes filled Perin with cold fear.

"Out of interest..." Perin tried to sound casual, "...if it was down to just you... Would you kill him yourself?"

Neva nodded slowly. His left hand appeared to unknowingly trace the lightning and circle of the Tacnimag symbol on the tabletop.

"Yes. I'd kill the Gravedigger."

TWENTY-TWO

"I HAD A WORD with my friend, the junior mage, yesterday," Perin murmured, passing a parcel of dried fruit to Kard. "He said that Lord Asutan has just passed the deadline on his taxes."

Kard looked up, brow furrowed. "You're suggesting we take our route past the Asutan estate?"

Perin grinned. "Depends on how much action the Hillspears want to see."

The Observatory was silent and nearly empty. The upper passageways normally echoed with at least the occasional passing of magi, both higher and lower, following projects of their own interest or seeking to fulfil a task from a superior.

Master of the City Varostan walked the corridors alone. He had made many circuits of the building since the last of the magi had left the Observatory. The manner of their exit had changed since the beginning of the riots. Nobody used the front door any more. The magic being used to help Tacnimag members leave the Observatory in secret had drained many of the telescopes in the central Floor Gate room.

Varostan was the highest authority in the Claimfold. This was true, but it was a fact that gave him little pleasure and no comfort. As far as he was concerned, it just meant he could cause more problems to more people in less time, and just possibly get blamed for it.

Footsteps made Varostan hesitate in mid-step.

The Master of the City swore quietly under his breath. His day always got worse when his immediate underling approached him in such a way. The younger mage walked with fierce purpose along the corridor toward him.

"Master Varostan, I need to speak to you."

"Indeed, Tulbu. Again?"

"Yes, again. I would like to speak to the junior mage about…"

Varostan sighed. "Nobody takes information from the junior except myself. He's young. His task is emotionally taxing. He needs to act without feeling like he is being set against the…"

"Against the city?" Tulbu interrupted. "He is against the city. We are…"

"Supposed to be for the city! We were created to serve Nagyevo!"

"And are forced to control it! You know what is at stake. You established the Northern Venture; you know that only we have the ability…"

The Master of the City raised a hand and the candles in the corridor flared suddenly and went out.

"Keep your voice down, Tulbu!"

Tulbu sneered and concentrated for a moment, until the candles flickered back into life. "Master Varostan, every mage knows of the Northern Venture. Many would like to know what it exactly is, but do not know, and besides… there's nobody here but us."

Varostan subsided a little, conceding this point with a nod. "What information are you seeking, Tulbu? You're still chasing the Gravedigger?'

Tulbu scowled. "I destroyed an entire building trying to catch that creature. No, where the dissenters are, there we will find him, like the King of Vermin amongst the filth of his rats! I'm committing my time to our other…venture."

"Thank you for your discretion this time," Varostan said quietly, although he had just become far more tense. He glanced up and down the corridor. "But Tulbu, you are the head of the Observatory Guard. The taxes of the Nagyevan Lords fall to me to manage. I do not need your assistance."

There was a frosty silence. The candle flames flowed one way, then the other, as if swayed by a breeze.

"Then perhaps you would like some outside assessment of your success, Varostan." Tulbu's expression was fierce, his sneer venomous. The Master of the City considered reminding the younger mage that he was the elder, the highest rank in the Tacnimag. But it was true that Tulbu had destroyed a warehouse with a single exertion of heat and force; and true, too, that it was far harder to relight a candle than it was to snuff the flame.

"You have something to say?"

"The first time we used the Floor Gate, it was in response to a thought missive from the head of the Tacnimag's research division, am I right?"

"Yes." Varostan looked profoundly uncomfortable.

"A High Mage's call always merits our attention, for sure, Master Varostan. But…research? The lowest of the high, and we all know it. Yet you ordered the first use of the Floor Gate for him. All the way out to Csus?"

"How...how did you know about that?" Varostan began to re-evaluate Mage Tulbu hurriedly. There was only one mage other than himself that should know about the first use of the Floor Gate, and he was reputedly dead. Killed by the Gravedigger, if the city legends were to be believed. All of Nagyevo knew that a mage had been killed in Csus, and that a Csus gravedigger was to blame. None knew what that mage had been doing there. Or what he had been doing in the North.

"He was working on the Northern Venture, wasn't he," Tulbu stated. "So that's why you activated the Floor Gate. Such a waste. He died in some Hanger hamlet, and local hunters cleaned up after you."

"It was a mistake, a mistake I'd make again."

"And you kept making it. Your plan to scare the lords and claimholders into solidarity? That might have worked, but for one thing."

Varostan knew what he meant and hated it. "What might that one thing be?"

"The Borderers. Instead of sending folk running scared into our arms, they've turned to the Borderers, who have been doing some clearing up of their own. And it's getting worse."

Varostan's heart sank. "Second South Response."

"Yes, Second South. They've not lost a single man. Yesterday they rescued the servants and assets of one Lord Asutan from..."

"Don't say it aloud!" Varostan looked defeated, although his tone was strong. "All right. It isn't working."

"It won't work while the Borderers are getting in the way."

"I am not going to lean on the Borderers. We have enough unrest in the city as it is. The City Guard is difficult enough to control without throwing angry Borderers into the mix as well."

"No need to exert political pressure, Master of the City." Tulbu's smile grew.

"The...Floor Gate?"

"Exactly."

"But they know how to fight them...they've killed so many and—"

Tulbu cut him off. "But that's just it. They can only kill so many."

Varostan's eyes widened with realisation.

Sudar kicked Aranyo's pillow out of the way as he sat down in the chair nearest Perin's bed.

Perin glanced up from the document he was reading. "He won't thank you for that."

"Wouldn't expect him to. When does he get back, anyway?"

Perin laughed. "Who knows? Every jug he drinks makes him a little later."

"Is it wise, going out and drinking all the time? Isn't he still wanted?" Sudar demanded to know.

"I think they've forgotten about him, at least as long as he doesn't get into trouble."

Sudar shook his head. "Reger, Aranyo was made for trouble."

"Good Borderer, though."

Sudar nodded. It was true. Aranyo had killed two drizen practically unaided at the Asutan Estate. The massacre had been wholly in the favour of the Borderers because the vineyard had been empty of unarmed humans. Lord Asutan had perhaps guessed at a link between his taxes and the drizen as well, as he had left for Nagyevo the moment his deadline had passed.

There was comfortable silence for a time. Here at home, with only Sudar with him, Perin wore the gold eye-amulet above his shirt. Sudar, true to form, never mentioned it. Now Perin put aside his document, the latest given to him by Neva, and lay back, conversing with Medrivar in his mind. He idly turned the amulet over and over in his fingers.

You are going to attract attention to yourself with each success you make.

I know. But would you rather I left people to face drizen alone?

No.

Perin smiled at the warmth in the king's mind-voice.

Sudar spoke suddenly, making Perin sit up. "When does the next grace period end?"

Perin checked the list. "Just under a week...the Lord...oh!" Perin looked at the taxation document in surprise. "Lord Adamun!" Memories, some from his perspective and some from Medrivar's, flashed across his mind's eye. Perin couldn't help looking around his room, the home Adamun had essentially given him.

"The Lord Knight?" Sudar asked, brow quirked at Perin's alarm.

Perin nodded, his expression returning to normal. "I wouldn't have expected someone of his...in his position to go against the Tacnimag, you know?"

Sudar shrugged. "Lord Knight is an ex-military position. The military have been sitting, guarding our western border for months. They've always resented the Tacnimag, since they took power after the failure of the Senate."

"Which was when...?"

"Only one hundred and ten years ago. Give or take a few months."

"They've resented the Tacnimag for over a hundred years?"

Sudar nodded. "Mainly in the higher ranks. Lord Coronar rank, that sort of thing. To be Lord Knight, Adamun must have been a Coronar at some point. But normal soldiers benefit from the Tacnimag."

"How?"

"The last generation of junior magi are spread throughout infantry ranks. Some with communication abilities, others with more combative skills."

Perin nodded. He could see why that might give even the Nation of Seven Cities pause for thought. "I need to go and talk to Response Leader."

"Think we should be there to give Lord Adamun a helping hand?" Sudar asked casually.

"After the service he's given the Claimfold; I think it's only right." Perin winked as he slid off his bed and went to the door.

"Hold up, hero." Sudar hurried to follow.

The hills of Solorin were gentle and rolling in comparison to some of the Mezyro moors, and the rich soil was the most fertile of any Claim in the Fold of Narsun. The Hillspears moved in silent single-file along a sun-flooded hillside. Flowers created a heady fragrance in the dry air. Birdsong and the sawing of crickets lent the afternoon an atmosphere of calm.

This was not expressed on the faces of the Borderers. Only Aranyo's manner suggested he was relaxed. Sudar and Gyorva took the head and rear respectively, each with bows strung and one cautious hand on the flight of an arrow.

Perin followed in the footsteps of his friend, holding his spear low and parallel to the ground. The others followed his example, to keep from presenting hard lines against the sky.

"Nothing at the moment," Kard muttered, exercising his prerogative as Response Leader and breaking the ordered silence. "Let's circle closer to the estate."

"Yes, sir." Perin nodded. "Hillspears! Take the brow of this hill. Gyorva, Sudar, move to the centre of the line. Let's go!"

The Second South Response spread into a loose line, moving in twos. At the crest of the hill, Perin relaxed a little; there was no creature in sight on the fields below the long, low house.

"This is strange," Kard murmured as they approached the broad, wooden door of Lord Adamun's modest country home, "it's been three days since his deadline passed. You said all the previous attacks took place within three days, and always in daylight, am I correct?"

Perin nodded. "Yes, sir. They say that different types of magic work better depending on how high the sun is in the sky."

"Information from your friend the junior mage?" Kard asked, lifting the iron ring of the door to knock. "You know that most of the Response don't trust this friend of yours," he added in a low voice, nodding over his shoulder to indicate the Hillspears who were waiting on watch by the path.

Perin nodded. "I'm not sure I do, either. He's..." Perin's frown became pronounced as he remembered the vulnerable, brotherly emotion Neva showed when at his most insecure.

Perin swallowed. Since he had met Medrivar, the king had shown steadfast intent to protect him and Kesairl. It was something to emulate. The urge to protect and defend was strong in Perin. Despite this, he knew Neva was dangerous, all the more so because he was vulnerable. Trapped in Tacnimag robes.

Kard did not wait for Perin to continue his sentence. He reached up to knock on the door again, but it opened before he was able to. A young female servant with large, dark eyes looked out in surprise.

"Yes?"

"We're here to see Lord Knight Adamun, miss." Kard pushed back his hessian hood respectfully.

"Yes, sirs, please wait here." She vanished, closing the door behind her.

Perin and Kard exchanged glances, brows raised. Moments later, Lord Adamun appeared in the doorway. He was armed as he had been when Perin had first met him, but now he was also armoured. His beard was fuller than Perin remembered, and he looked older than he should. Could it be only six months or so that had passed?

There was a moment of recognition on Adamun's face as he looked down at Perin. His hand immediately left the hilt of his sword, but his expression became neutral and he examined Perin as if he were a stranger, his eyes scanning both Borderers.

"My Lord Knight. Forgive the intrusion. I am Second South Borderer Response Leader Kard Yenesen." Kard saluted. Perin hid surprise as he copied his leader's salute. He hadn't known his friend's family name and wouldn't have guessed that it was the same as Neva's. No relation though, he supposed.

"The Hillspears, yes?"

It was Kard's turn to look surprised. "Yes, sir! How did..." Kard started to ask, before Adamun made it unnecessary.

"Drizen have been attacking lords that have failed to pay their taxes. Most times, Borderers have intervened. The most successful Response is yours, Leader."

"Yes, my Lord. Thank you," Kard acknowledged. "We're here for that reason today."

"The Tacnimag put an end to the pauper's purse," Adamun said, referring to the fund that had formerly been used to support citizens in penury, "and I haven't paid my taxes since, nor do I intend to in the future, if it's all going to be spent on magic nonsense and councillors houses."

"We will convey your refusal to the Borderer Liaison at the Observatory," Kard said politely. Adamun grunted his acknowledgement.

"The monsters are late," he remarked, scowling out at the sunny afternoon as if it were the fault of the weather. "Perhaps the Tacnimag are delayed somehow."

Kard swallowed. Nobody had yet gone so far as to explicitly state their belief that the Tacnimag were behind the drizen, not even Aranyo. It was still difficult to believe.

"Come in," Adamun said, swinging the door wide. "This place is small, but all the more fortifiable for it. When they come, they'll have to come through the door. Difficult to take a hallway full of spears."

Kard nodded and waved the Borderers in. "That's sensible. We'll help you barricade the windows." He didn't mention the unpaid taxes again.

The Borderers entered, most bowing nervously to the Lord Knight as they passed him.

In the hours before the sun had fully set, the young servant cooked food for Second South and her master, while Perin and Sudar alternately kept watch through the only clear window. While Sudar went to accept a goblet of watered down wine, Adamun joined Perin at the window.

"Hello, again...Reger," he said in a low voice. Perin smiled in response.

"Lord Knight."

"Call me Adamun, please. You've been moving along then, since we last spoke. Joining the Borderers...I wouldn't have expected it."

"Do you approve?"

"Not my place to say, Reger. I've tried to request information on Kesairl, incidentally. Every month since he was falsely arrested. They're now refusing to acknowledge he exists."

"You don't think...?" Perin gasped, but Adamun waved his reaction down.

"Be calm. No, I believe he is too valuable for his knowledge of prigon techniques of the magical arts, if for nothing else."

There was a long pause while Perin considered this. The sky, visible through the window, was spread with gold clouds, the clear-blue darkening into evening.

"It will be night soon. Don't they normally attack in daylight?" Adamun's question made Perin study the hillsides with renewed urgency.

"All the previous attacks, yes."

"Contrary to natural drizen tactics. They did make war during the day, but for isolated strikes, tribal drizen used the cover of darkness much as we do. I studied history in my spare time until all the books worth reading were confiscated by the Tacnimag," Adamun explained. "It's on the Tacnimag's part that all these attacks have happened under the sun. Only a few forms of magic work better at night. All can be performed regardless, but I wonder if the Tacnimag aren't trying to conserve energy."

"That would make sense," Perin agreed, remembering the few hints Neva had given him over the last few weeks.

"And would imply a vulnerability," Adamun said grimly. He said no more on that matter, although Perin waited for him to speak again. The Lord Knight changed the subject as Sudar returned, offering his goblet to Perin. "There's been more unrest in the outer Claims. The Fold of Joval's been quiet; in Temlan they've had good harvests, so the taxes haven't taken too much of a toll. But some of the lawkeepers in Vada have supported an uprising against the Tacnimag magistrate there."

"What about Csus?" Sudar asked, glancing at Perin.

Adamun frowned for a moment and then shrugged. "They've always kept separate there, for the most part, so they resent the stronger hand the Tacnimag are exerting. The Tacnimag still haven't replaced the magistrate they lost a year or so ago. A local murder, I understand. Nothing especially violent has happened, but they haven't paid their taxes in Fenyado, Varo, or Hanger Claims. Sporadically in Arpavale, where the Tacnimag still have a magistrate at work.

"Anyway, the point is, the Tacnimag need to be careful. It's possible for them to lose control of the Claimfold, whatever they may think. Especially with all the regiments away west. Except the one they have guarding a supposed prison in the outskirts of Csus."

"A whole regiment? For guarding a prison?" Perin asked, surprised.

Adamun winked. "That's what they're saying. It's probably coincidental that the regiment is only twelve leagues from Helynvale."

"You mean...? They wouldn't! The Torzsi will tear them apart!" Perin said with conviction. "I'd like to see the Tacnimag order an attack on the prigon people!"

"No you wouldn't," Adamun replied.

Perin stopped, sobered.

No. Perhaps not.

The sun set, fading into deep blue.

TWENTY-THREE

THE SECOND SOUTH RESPONSE trod the hill path in silence. The day was as fine as the last, and the crickets were as loud as before, heat and sound combining to challenge the patience of every Borderman. The drizen had not appeared during the night at Lord Adamun's house, and in the morning, he had sent them back to the city with the promise that he would follow. If the Tacnimag wanted to deal harshly with him, then they could do it themselves, openly.

Perin didn't know why the drizen had not appeared. The central mystery of how the Tacnimag were manipulating and placing them had not been solved. Perhaps they had a dwindling supply. Perhaps their stored energy was running low and that was why no drizen had materialised.

The Borderers reached the top of the hill. This was the last of the Solorin downs, and now Nagyevo became visible, grey and distant through the haze, yet still seeming to fill the green plain. The grass had turned yellow with the summer's heat. The Hillspears paused their march without needing consent from Kard. The road snaked away toward the city, still leagues from their tired feet.

"So much for the chances of a good fight," Aranyo muttered.

Forgos nodded in agreement.

Harco shrugged. "It'll be nice not to put our lives on the line for once."

Response Leader Kard nodded in silent agreement, resting his spear for a moment on his shoulder.

Gyorva laughed sharply. "I think that's the first smart thing I've heard you say."

Harco took the jibe good naturedly, but Perin frowned at the sarcastic archer.

"It's not too far now. If you don't want to run in front of us, Jolsen, keep it pleasant, please." It was the first real tension arising from Perin's promoted position. Gyorva's sneer stuck for a moment. He glanced at Kard to see if the Response Leader would countermand Perin. Kard's expression was neutral. Maka, predictably, came to stand at Perin's shoulder, backing him up. Sudar watched Gyorva closely.

"Sorry, Harco." Gyorva shrugged. He took a couple of steps back and looked away. Perin left the issue, turning away. Grinning, Forgos moved to walk behind Gyorva as the Hillspears continued their journey down toward the city.

"Hey, Gyorva. How do you feel about that, then?" His eyebrows were high with suspended amusement.

Gyorva frowned at him. "Don't be pathetic, Forgos. It was his place. I don't bear grudges, even against those lesser than myself."

"Which is just about everybody, eh?" Forgos rolled his eyes.

Gyorva smirked, increasing his pace. "Of course."

The crickets and the crunching of the road dirt again became a constant. After nearly an hour of continuous walking, the sounds were joined by a distant, rhythmic thumping, growing louder, with the clinking of tack and armour.

Lord Adamun rode up at speed, reining in his horse at the head of the file. Kard bowed immediately, but the expression on Adamun's face distracted Perin from formalities. The Lord was distraught.

"Response Leader Kard!" He forced the words out. "You and your men need to start running—*now*!"

"What? What's happened?" Kard unslung his spear.

"That won't do any good!" Adamun gripped the reins too tightly and his horse reared, trying to turn. "Run! You can't fight this time!"

"How many?" Perin asked.

"Where's your maidservant?" Forgos asked out of turn.

Adamun turned in the saddle to stare back at the hilltop. "Thirty. There must be as many as thirty!" He turned to look back at Forgos. "I'm sorry. She's dead. I'm sorry. There wasn't time."

"Lord Adamun." Kard's face was pale. "My Lord, I want you to ride on to the city. Have help sent out to us. Borderers!" He turned and reslung his spear. "*Run!*"

At first, it seemed almost absurd, running with no visible pursuit, putting energy behind each running step, arms swinging, backs already aching from the weight of their packs. Perin glanced back, saw that all were doing as well as he, Forgos better, thanks to his longer legs...

And still no sign of pursuit, the sky a hard blue at the hilltop. Perin concentrated on running. Adamun's horse was already too small to see against the outline of the city.

Suddenly, Gyorva let out a cry. Kard and Perin turned, saw that drizen were cresting the hill behind, made deceptively small by the distance, ten, twenty...

"There are *at least* thirty!" Kard gasped. He shrugged off his pack in one movement, loosing his spear from it and then casting off his hessian. Perin and the other Hillspears copied him, stumbling as they went, discarding weight but retaining their weapons.

Now they ran with real urgency, fear high and hot on their shoulders. Perin stopped noticing the ache of movement, his legs carrying him faster. Thirty drizen were too many, too many for two Borderer Responses, let alone for one...and the city seemed no nearer.

By the time Nagyevo's walls obscured the low clouds on the horizon, Perin was sure he could run no farther. The drizen were behind, and close. Gyorva had never been the best runner of the Hillspears, yet he was still running with the complete commitment of a man who wanted to live. He had thrown aside his spear, but still gripped his bow in one hand, three arrows in the other.

The drizen were making war cries. The strangled, high-pitched crowing had begun when Maka had fallen, to be dragged upright immediately by Forgos and Harco. Stones had been hurled, but they had fallen short. Now, the city was close, so close that the South Gate was clearly visible, wide open, a few hundred paces away. Tiny faces could be seen on the walltop, staring out at the chase.

I'm surprised they haven't closed the gate, Medrivar murmured. He had kept quiet, impressing encouragement without words from within. Perin felt as though he was running alongside him.

They haven't closed the gate for years. Perin remembered, sharing his thought with Medrivar. *After the Senate were disbanded, the merchants handed over control. The great gates cannot be closed, except by the Tacnimag's command.*

Perin tripped, only to be steadied by Sudar who was running beside him, a physically real version of Medrivar.

I'm surprised they haven't closed the gate to shut you out. Medrivar explained. Perin frowned. Did that then mean that the drizen were after Second South rather than Adamun? Thirty drizen were far too many for one Lord Knight.

The gate came closer, and now the Hillspears put on a final burst of speed. Gyorva cried out with the pain of it. The drizen fell a little behind. The South Gate remained wide open, and there were two City Guards in the centre, spears at the ready.

"Get the gate closed behind us!" Kard roared, waving at the guards. "Close it up after us! If they get into the city..." He didn't need to finish the sentence. The market just beyond the gate would be packed with citizens.

The Hillspears came to a scrambling halt in the gateway. And then they turned and levelled their spears as one. Perin felt proud, suddenly and emphatically proud of the fact that none ran on, not yet, with the gate still open.

The drizen slowed. Perin grabbed the shoulder of one of the City Guards. "We need to get the gate closed! No, you stay here..." He turned to Gyorva who was almost doubled up panting for breath. "Gyorva! Borderer Jolsen, get on the wall!"

"No..." Gyorva breathed.

Sudar gave him a push to get him farther into the archway tunnel. "Go on. You can't shoot safely from there."

"I'll get the gate closed." Gyorva Jolsen promised breathlessly, and went.

The gateway was now held by nine spearmen. There was barely room for them to stand in the gap in one line, and Kard quickly took control, his breath already settling.

"Two lines! We need room to move! Guardsmen, I'm taking command."

"Not a problem, Borderer," one of the City Guards muttered, wide eyes staring at the steadily approaching drizen. Perin realised with surprise that it was one of the guards that had been at the gate on his journey into Nagyevo, months before.

Perin found himself in the front line of the formation. Kard was at the other end of the line with the two guards and Forgos taking the centre. Sudar, Maka, Harco and Aranyo took the reserve line.

Perin could hear screaming coming from the city behind. Standing in the dusty portal between Nagyevo and the monsters, Perin shivered. It was as if the city had built up into a weight behind him. There were people behind who must be running for the walltop, for their houses. Some, perhaps, would even run toward the screaming. If the line broke, then they would pay for it with their lifeblood.

"Get archers on the walls!" Kard shouted back through the gateway.

A drizen, closest of the foes, let out a bellow and threw a stone that sailed past Kard and cracked into shards against the wall behind him. Now Perin appreciated the extra room between the defenders. It felt less secure, but at least they might be able to dodge thrown stones.

"There aren't any archers!" One of the guards said, eyes fixed on the drizen as another stone flew through the air, falling short. "Most of our boys are attending to a protest in the Upper City—they won't get here for minutes!"

"We don't have minutes," Forgos observed, grey eyes narrowed. The drizen had halted completely. Perhaps they were about to charge...

"Get the gate closed!" Kard roared up at the walltop again. His face showed near-panic—not on his own account, but because of the innocents behind the outer defences. There was an answering shout from the walltop, and then an arrow sailed across the brightness of the sun, slashing the blue sky and burying itself in the skull of a nearby drizen. The creature toppled, its skull punctured.

"Arrraaagh! Gyorvaaa!" Forgos roared triumphantly.

The drizen screamed back. Stones flew, most smashing on the wall or falling past the defenders.

"Thirty-two," Sudar concluded in a mild tone.

The thirty-two drizen charged.

"It's been good, lads," Kard said, steeling himself. There was an immediate chorus of acknowledgments, and tears came to Perin's eyes even as he gripped his spear and went down on one knee to make ready.

"Thanks, brothers," Forgos muttered.

"Same from me." Harco said.

"I'm sorry if I die first," Aranyo added his voice surprisingly firm.

Sudar said nothing, but his hand briefly reached out and squeezed Perin's shoulder.

"I love you!" Maka shouted, looking around him with a fierce expression.

One of the City Guards cracked a wry smile. "Thanks, mate."

Despite everything, this made Forgos chuckle.

Collision.

The screaming and roaring boomed suddenly in the archway as Borderer spears caught and bent under strain, impaling their targets and driving them back. The shorter spears of the City Guards jabbed at the drizen trying to come through the gaps, dissuading them, for the moment. Another drizen fell dead at the rear, one of Gyorva's arrows protruding from its upper chest, the other having passed through its eye and into its throat from above. Blood spurted in the sunlight and in the shade of the wall.

A stone flew past and smacked heavily into Harco's head. Perin felt the shock of it reverberate through him, knowing that this second time, Harco could not survive. Blood rushed through his blond hair as a screaming Maka dragged Harco's limp form away from the line. He returned in a rush, reddened eyes streaming, his spear thrusting violently, catching a throat and turning its owner back and out into the sunlight.

"Aaagh! *Harco! Harco!*" They were all shouting his name with Maka. There were drizen heaped about them, some scrambling upright, hook-swords clashing against the obstructive gateway wall. There was a high scream as Forgos's arm burst bloody from a sudden sword-blow. The shaven-headed Borderer bit down on the pain and fought back.

Unexpectedly, the drizen were drawing back. Another stone, the last, thudded ineffectually against the breastplate of one of the guards. In the sudden withdrawal, shouts could be heard from the walltop. It sounded like conflict. Perin risked turning to look behind him and saw an armoured figure running toward the gate from the wide roadway. A chill went through Perin as he saw that people were indeed gathered at the edges of the South Way. The murmur of anger was there, a mystery amongst the obvious sounds of fear.

Adamun ran to a halt and drew his sword. His face turned red with violent anger.

"The bastards! Bastards!"

"Looks like they're gathering for another charge," Forgos said between clenched teeth. He was leaning against the stonework, his face pale below his shaved hair. Sudar was tying the arm of his shirt around Forgos's wound. The fabric was already richly scarlet.

"The Tacnimag," Adamun spoke, gesturing at the curved ceiling of the gateway. "There are Observatory Guards on the walltop. They're blocking us from the gate mechanism. Your man with the bow, they knocked him down the steps!"

Kard gaped in astonishment. Forgos swore foully, possibly from the pain as Sudar tied off the bandage. Perin listened to hurried advice from Medrivar for a second or so, his eyes back on the drizen, who were pacing some way off, apparently arguing in their thick, nasal tongue.

"Forgos." Perin was surprised by how steady his voice sounded. "Go and make sure Gyorva is all right. You can't help us here, not with that arm. Lord Adamun, we need that gate closed. Do your best, please, for the sake of the citizenry." Perin could hear Medrivar's words in the phrasing.

Forgos went at once, passing his spear to Sudar. His expression was taut with guilt at leaving the danger of the line, but perhaps he hoped to take some of his anger to the Oh-gees on the walltop.

Lord Adamun hesitated for a moment. "Reger..." He caught the masterful look in Perin's gaze. His head bowed briefly and he went, but he did not sheathe his sword.

"Here we go!" Aranyo called shrilly, lifting his spear. The fifteen-year-old was a picture of terrified defiance. Perin returned to the line immediately, standing with the other six and levelling his own spear at the drizen, who were coming again at pace, this time in something more akin to a formation.

"Bastards are learning," Kard said tersely to nobody. Sudar had moved into the front line in Forgos's place. He crouched low in a strange stance, his spear braced against the line of his leg and leaning body, Forgos's spear in his other hand, held aloft.

"Seventeen," he intoned quietly.

The first drizen swatted aside Kard's spear and ran full length onto the Response Leader's drawn sword, spraying blood onto the Borderer's face. Kard roared and pushed, a guard helping him, and the drizen stumbled back into its brethren, Kard's hilt sticking out of its ruptured flesh just beneath the collarbone.

Another drizen ran onto Sudar's spearpoint deliberately, his hook sword slashing down and breaking the shaft. Sudar dropped the broken weapon and thrust his reserve spear upward as the monster roared out its pain and fury. The spearhead took the creature's throat up through its head and out the other side in an explosion of gore and splintered bone, the tines of the spearhead crosspiece preventing the shaft from going further.

Perin's wrists ached desperately as another drizen stumbled backward, fumbling with Perin's spear-shaft, the weapon's head lost in the creature's innards. It fell and snapped the spear under its corpse, a choked squeal fading out as it bit the soiled earth of the gateway.

A much longer version of the usual hook sword cut the air as the largest of the drizen shouldered others aside. It came on alone toward them all, its awful, bristled face set in an expression of glee at the slaughter.

All their spears and Perin's sword bit the creature together, as Borderers and Guardsmen pushed forward, their cries of defiance crushing their fear. Even as blood rushed from many places on its broad torso, the monster laughed, snorting a red shower in the sunlight. One arm reached out, backhanded Aranyo hard enough to send him flying against the gateway. Its hand closed on the face of one of the guards and crushed it, even as the lengthy hook sword wheeled in across the face of the bright sun and brought sudden darkness to Maka.

The handsome boy fell, cloven, his hand reaching out toward Perin.

Aranyo slumped motionless, blood trickling down from beneath his blond fringe, much as it had when Perin had saved him from the Tacnimag mage.

The drizen champion fell, still clutching one of the guards, taking the dead man down to the soil with him.

"Back! We are too far forward!" Kard choked out, bodily pushing those nearest him backward. Sudar and Perin covered the hasty retreat back to the shadow of the gateway.

Now the defenders numbered four. Thirteen drizen regarded the survivors with glowering eyes, their gaze intent on the vulnerability of their enemies. Their small minds did not wonder at the lack of reinforcement from the city. They saw four—two adults, two mere youths—standing, barely, swaying from their emotional and physical exhaustion.

The defenders were woefully spread out. A strong drizen would be able to push past. Snouts wrinkled wetly, smelling the fear of the softer ones that were beyond the gateway. One more charge, and they would be through.

One more charge, and Nagyevo would be open to their swords.

One more charge...

Sudar passed his unbroken spear to Perin. "I'll trade you." He said thickly. Perin understood, passing his sword to his friend. Sudar was now armed with the top half of his broken spear. In his other hand, he wielded Perin's sword.

"Thank you, Swordsman."

"No need, Borderman," Perin replied quietly.

Kard let out a low groan that became a sigh. At the end of it, a smile spread across his pain-wracked, tear-stained face. "This is it then."

"So it seems," the remaining guard agreed. He had swapped his short spear for Maka's. The remaining Hillspears would not begrudge him it.

Kard's smile became grim as he saw that the drizen were slowly and steadily approaching, unhurried in their confidence. "One last favour, Reger," he said quickly, levelling his spear, ready.

"Anything, Response Leader," Perin replied at once.

"Your name. Your real name."

Sudar's eyes flashed between Kard and Perin.

"I am Perin," Perin said simply. The shambling walk of the drizen gathered speed.

"Perin," Both Kard and Sudar murmured the name together.

The guard, unsure of the significance of the conversation, fixed his eyes on the drizen, which were now running. "Not that it matters, but my name's Hossa."

"It matters," Perin murmured in reply.

Kard grinned broadly. "I'm fed up with being charged at. Come on, lads. Our turn!"

Without hesitation, the four lifted their weapons and ran toward the drizen.

TWENTY-FOUR

THE NEXT DESPERATE minutes of combat rushed into a chaotic, painful blur. Spears thrust and were eventually broken. Hook swords sliced the air and caught nothing. There was some miracle in the carnage—the defenders were yet unhurt and still fighting.

Sudar fought with his half-spear and sword as if they had been designed for use in that manner, as if he had been trained in such combat. Perin forced burning muscles to comply with the complex, illustrative movements Medrivar conveyed to him. It was as if the king fought from within the throne room, his subject fulfilling the movements simultaneously. Kard fought beside the guardsman with his teeth bared like a wild animal, using a discarded hook sword, now that his spear was useless.

One drizen made it through, stumbling from its wounds into the open space beyond the arched entrance to Nagyevo. It blinked in the horrified stares of the gathered citizens, raised its sword and collapsed, squealing, as Adamun and Gyorva converged on it, spear and sword flashing. Silent and confused, the Observatory Guards that had denied the lord and the Borderer access to the gate control, watched both sides of the wall as the battle ended.

Perin kneeled in the muck of the battlefield, the sun hot on his face. Sudar was similarly positioned, his back to Perin's. Their hands were empty. Even Sudar no longer had the strength to hold his makeshift weapons tight.

Kard and Guardsman Hossa lay dead a short distance away, beside the motionless corpses of the drizen that had ended their lives.

"Nameless Gods…" Sudar whispered. One of the drizen nearby was trying to rise to its feet.

"Gods of Valo…" Perin agreed with his friend, watching the drizen with some detachment. It was over. How were they both alive?

The silent gateway echoed suddenly with the sound of approaching feet. A file of City Guards hurried out into the field of battle. The forerunners made it to the struggling monster as it took to its feet, and struck it down, their spears darting again and again into its body. Its arms flailed to ward off blows that were already tearing it apart.

One of the City Guards stopped to dry retch. A Guard Officer stopped beside him to rub his back, looking around with hard eyes. He saw Perin and Sudar and strode toward them immediately.

"Borderers."

Perin looked up at the guard, eyes narrowed against the sun. He made out the small gate symbol that was worked into the guard's gorget. "Commander?" he hazarded a guess. The man nodded and offered a hand to help them both up.

"Are you injured?"

"No, sir."

"I apologise, Swordsman, Borderman," the Commander said, having caught sight of Perin's empty scabbard. "We had to disobey direct orders to come here, and yet we are too late. I am truly sorry." He bowed his head. "The city owes you."

The noise from the city had risen and grown tumultuous. Perin swayed, managing to stay upright. "It owes more to Kard and Maka. And Harco. And… Hossa." He looked toward Response Leader Kard and the dead City Guard. Some of the Commander's men were already gently lifting them from where they had fallen, to bear them back to the city.

"Come on, Sudar. Let's walk in with them."

With the help of the City Guard Commander, Sudar and Perin walked beside their dead leader until they reached the gate. Wordlessly, Perin stepped across to help the guards with Maka's body. Sudar went and crouched beside Aranyo, seeing that he was breathing.

Finally, they came through and into the city, and the noise of the crowd dropped.

Lord Adamun stood with Gyorva, his bloody sword pointing toward Perin and Sudar. "Here! Here are your protectors! Swordsman Reger Myrvo held this gateway with his comrades, to keep your lives safe! And what did the Observatory Guards do?"

He turned, spitting with anger. "They kept me from closing the gate! The order of the Tacnimag was that I could not save these Borderers, my friends, guardians of this city! Does Nagyevo deserve such heroes? Does she deserve the ministrations of the *Tacnimag*?"

There was a roar of anger. The Observatory Guards on the walltop had gathered together in a tight group, back to back, eyes fearful. A stone was thrown from the crowd and struck one on the shoulder. He hefted his spear, panicking, only to be calmed by another wiser man.

"That is not all!" Lord Adamun continued. He turned and began to stalk across the South Way. Their fury rising, the crowd followed him, making room for the City Guards and Perin and Sudar. The Lord Knight led them all to the stone steps of the City Guard barracks on the Wall Way. At the top of these steps, above the barracks themselves, sat the residence of the Captain of the Guard. The captain himself had come to stand at the top of the stairs.

Beneath him swam a sea of irate faces. Citizens that had known their lives to be in danger were prepared to express their rage to anyone, and Lord Adamun was now their compass.

"A full company of Guardsmen were within this barracks, within a hundred paces of the South Gate!" Adamun roared, pointing his sword directly at the Captain of the Guard. "This man did not order the men forth to aid the Borderers! He listened instead to some Tacnimag Mage, and the guards that are here with us came against orders from further in the city!"

Perin glanced at Sudar. He felt numb from the fight, but there was danger of another sort here. Adamun was close to instigating a riot.

Another figure left the Captain's residence, coming to stand beside the man, whispering in his ear. The Captain of the Guard stiffened. Then he nodded slowly, his head low.

He lifted his voice above the noise of the crowd. "I resign my position. I have misinterpreted orders. My position is forfeit." He intoned dully. The figure beside him looked satisfied, and some in the crowd lifted jeering cheers. Perin found himself being raised up by nearby men, his bloodied and exhausted form held above the crowd.

"Swordsman! Swordsman! Swordsman!" The chant began as he was borne to the steps. Sudar struggled through the mob, falling twice, trying to follow his friend.

The unknown figure on the steps came down to meet Perin.

"You are a survivor of this debacle?" His smooth voice infuriated Perin, but he kept the reaction hidden. This man had Tacnimag written in his posture and attitude. His dark-brown hair was short and slick, and he had sharp hazel eyes a similar shade to Perin's own, staring out of a thin face.

"Yes. Who are you?" Perin said bluntly.

"I am the Tacnimag's Investigative Officer. I have little magistry, but I am adept at understanding people, and that is a skill they sorely need. Well, Swordsman, your popularity is well deserved. You have saved many lives, nearly at the cost of your own."

"No thanks to the Tacnimag!" Someone in the crowd shouted. There was a roar of approval. The Tacnimag Investigator raised his voice.

"Indeed! It has been a failing on our part, and I will readily admit it before you all!" The noise died away after a few jeers. Perin could feel Medrivar's distaste in his mouth. The king was well aware of this investigator's tactic. Calm the mob with lying truths…

"It seems we have need of a new Captain of the Guard!" The Investigator called out loudly, a slender hand coming to rest on Perin's shoulder. He smiled at Perin, ignoring Sudar, who wearily climbed the steps.

"Here's an opportunity for you to advance yourself, Swordsman. Just stay quiet and stay useful, and life will be sweeter than patrols and drizen, mark my words." The Investigator spoke softly through his smile. Perin didn't react, although he caught Sudar's eye.

The Investigator lifted his free hand. "Due to our mistake, it would not be fit for us to choose the new Captain." He spoke loudly again, his hand on Perin's shoulder tightening. "Who would you, people of Nagyevo, choose as *your* Guard Captain?"

There was a roaring response. Perin could see Aranyo, dazed but alive and upright, supported by Gyorva in the crowd.

Adamun's voice became audible in the cacophony. "Swordsman Reger!"

"There…" The Investigator looked sidelong at Perin, still smiling. "I have favoured you. Remember it when you come to make important decisions, Captain Reger Myrvo." He bowed deeply to the crowd, descended a few steps and bowed again, this time to Perin.

"I present to you, your Guard Captain, Reger Myrvo!"

"How in hell did that happen?" Forgos said, shaking his head in amazement. He reclined on a long couch in Perin's new rooms, Aranyo sitting near his feet, his head as heavily bandaged as the taller boy's arm. Sudar stood quietly by the door, which was locked. Gyorva had taken a chair by the fireplace, which was cold and empty. The candles around the room spread enough heat with their golden light.

The room was well-furnished, the walls hung with paintings and heraldic banners. A great scarlet and gold rug that had almost certainly been imported from the Seven Cities covered the stone floor.

Cama and Sudar had helped Perin carry his few belongings to his new home above the City Guard barracks the day before.

It was the second night since the battle of the South Gate.

How in the hell *had* it happened?

"I have no idea," Perin said. He sat in the captain's chair, which he had brought around from behind the broad, dark-wood desk.

"It's to keep from having the city rise up in full revolt," Gyorva said bitterly. "Reger…I mean, Perin is being used as a pawn."

"Perin," Aranyo considered. He still looked a little distant after the knock his head had taken. "I still don't know why you kept your name secret from us. It's a nicer name than Reger, though."

"I am going to explain," Perin started, looking around at his friends' patient faces. "This is something that I thought I could not safely tell anyone. But I know that I can trust all of you. I only wish…I only wish that Maka and Harco…" He paused, emotion surprising him.

Forgos nodded quickly. "We know, Reger. I mean…Perin…you know what I mean."

Perin blinked fiercely for a moment and then nodded to Sudar. The dark-haired boy pushed away from the wall to stand upright, coming to his friend's aid. "Perin kept his name secret because the Tacnimag may know it."

Perin regained his composure, hands gripping the arms of his chair. "I came from Csus, which you know, but I didn't come from the Claim of Arpavale, like I said. I'm from Hanger, from a village called Erdhanger."

There was a pause. Gyorva's bright eyes stared at Perin in realisation, but Forgos and Aranyo seemed none the wiser.

"Erdhanger is where a Tacnimag mage was killed. He was killed by a local gravedigger." Perin stood up and turned, taking his hat from the desk where he had deliberately placed it once the door had been locked. Turning again to face the room, he stepped forward, trembling a little.

"The gravedigger's name was Perin. The gravedigger's name is still Perin, but now…now he is the Captain of the Guard of Nagyevo."

There was a short silence. Aranyo stared at Perin in shock. "But…you? I…you were…?"

"I think the answer to that is yes," Forgos said, grinning at Aranyo's amazement. He got to his feet, holding his injured arm carefully as he approached Perin, holding out his good arm.

"It's nice to meet you, Perin Gravedigger."

Gyorva chuckled, the laugh quickly becoming uncontrollable. When he realised that all eyes were on him, he wiped his eyes and explained. "I just realised. One of your duties as Captain of the Guard…Perin…your job…"

"Is to catch the Gravedigger," Perin finished, smiling despite himself. "Yes, it is a bit…complex. But that's why I wanted to tell you this tonight. I'm going to need help. The Tacnimag Investigator is going to put pressure on me, and the only way I can do what's right for the city is if I divert his attention toward the Gravedigger.

"In short, I'm going to promise the Tacnimag that I will catch...well, myself."

There was a shocked silence. Sudar, who had already heard the plan, was the only one that didn't look incredulous.

That's a dangerous game, Medrivar said quietly, sitting back in his throne. He was smiling as he said it, his tone approving.

"It is a dangerous game," Perin agreed aloud. "I will need all your help, my friends."

There was no hesitation. The remaining Hillspears raised their hands and their voices at once. Unheard by all but Perin, Medrivar added his own promise.

"I'm meeting with the Tacnimag Investigator and the Guard Liaison tomorrow, in the late afternoon," Perin explained, going to the safe box that lay behind one of the wall paintings. He opened it and put his Gravedigger hat back with the rest of his clothes. His spade was hidden behind the false partition of a wardrobe, a space that the previous Guard Captain had used for the storage of illicit goods.

"I'll want you to be nearby for that." Perin locked the safe and regarded his companions seriously. "But first, we'll go and say goodbye to our friends."

The sun shone brightly through a brisk wind, easily felt on the low hilltop. The graveyards were spread across the rise of the Lower East city, nearer to the Eastern Wall Way than it was to the Borderer Headquarters. The beautiful, empty chapel of the Nameless Gods of Valo caught the morning sun nearby, as Maka Nyacus and Harco Oksen, and Kard Yenesen with them, were lowered into the rich soil.

The Hillspear remnant were not alone at the gravesides. Borderer Response Leaders who had known Kard stood in silent ranks, giving room to the families. Maka's father, Lord Nyacus, and Lord Oksen—Harco's father—stood with their wives. Lord Nyacus was straight-backed and fiercely dry-eyed, though his wife wept into his shoulder in abandonment.

Lord Oksen had tears in his eyes. His strong resemblance to his son—he was a little fatter—was a warm reminder of Harco in life. He had a similar, unsure nature and open friendliness. He had embraced each of the remaining Hillspears freely on arrival, and Perin's heart ached for the lord and his wife as much as it did for his own loss.

Cama and Lord Adamun had both come as well, separately, standing at opposite corners of the ceremony. Perin knew that Cama was there to support him.

A priest spoke the Ritual of Farewells over the graves as they were filled in, layer by layer. Perin waited until most of the grievers had left, watching quietly as a gravedigger diligently smoothed the earth over. He felt a strong urge to go and help. He made do with approaching each grave and gently leaving a handprint in the soil.

"Are you well?" Sudar asked him as they joined Cama in walking back down the hill toward the centre of the Lower East side. Perin experienced a deep calm in the wake of his sorrow and looked up to see that Sudar's dark eyes were red in his fine-featured, steady face.

"Yes, my friend." He put an arm about Sudar's shoulders. The quieter boy accepted the comfort with a light frown.

Cama said nothing as he walked alongside, his bald head bowed in thought.

"Why are we alive?" Sudar finally broke his customary silence. Cama glanced at him, but the question had certainly been put to Perin, and no other. "Because we fought better?" Sudar's frown became fierce, his brow trembling. "I will not believe that! We were fortunate...Maka and Harco had no time—" he choked on the phrase.

"It's not our fault," Perin said, unsure of the fact even as he spoke, passing on Medrivar's words. "We deserve life no more than they did."

"I won't waste it, Perin," Sudar said darkly, fists clenched. "I won't waste my life."

Perin nodded.

As they neared the city barracks, he let fragments of a half-remembered tune reach his lips. Sudar listened to the broken melody in silence, feeling almost as if it was a song he had heard before.

The Tacnimag Investigator stepped casually into the Master of the City's chamber. Varostan sat opposite, resplendent in his long robes, seated in a grand chair behind his desk.

"Master Varostan." The Investigator bowed.

"Mage Isdar," Varostan acknowledged. A figure on the right shifted his position, and Isdar saw that Mage Tulbu was present.

"I can scarce believe that you are allowed to take the title of mage," Tulbu said derisively, sitting back in the alcove he had taken, holding his head high and looking down at Isdar.

Isdar smiled thinly.

"I may not be able to destroy a building, Mage Tulbu, certainly. You or the Master could easily crush me magically and I could do nothing. But where you were gifted with energies, I was gifted with brains. Something you lack."

Tulbu's anger came out of him in a hiss, but he dared not strike against the slim, black-clothed Investigator, not with the Master of the City present. Smiling coolly, Isdar continued, "Incidentally, whose idea was it to simply throw drizen at the Borderers?"

Tulbu stayed furiously silent, knowing that Isdar knew the answer already. "Who was it that just elevated one of the troublesome Borderers to the position of Captain of the Guard?" He tried to inject poison into the weak question.

"It was I," Isdar said mildly. "And the city has not risen up around the hero, as they might otherwise have done. He is within our reach. Within my influence. He is young, and he owes his position to me." Isdar smiled, completely at ease with the more powerful magi.

"Master Varostan, worthy Tulbu…this is one we will be able to control."

Perin finished explaining his plan to Forgos, Gyorva, Aranyo, and Sudar. Each had understood, their faces serious in the candlelight of Perin's locked rooms. Sudar, who had been keeping an eye out through the one shuttered window, turned and nodded. The Liaison and the Tacnimag Investigator were on their way.

"They are almost here." Perin smiled confidently. "They know I have some weight behind my decisions, because of my sudden popularity, thanks to Lord Adamun. They will not be surprised by some stubbornness on my part. What is important is that we make the Gravedigger issue fundamental to our bargaining. It's our great hidden trick. The key is to give the Tacnimag the illusion that they are in control."

"And then…?" Forgos asked, breathless with the excitement of subterfuge.

Perin thought for a moment. Medrivar's calm urged patience in him, and he shrugged, lifting his open hands. "And then we wait."

TWENTY-FIVE

THE BROAD DESK now occupied the middle of the room. Extra candles had been lit, and Sudar stood silently in the flickering shadows. Perin's two visitors sat in the chairs provided them, with their backs to the door and Sudar.

The City Guard liaison sat uncomfortably beside Isdar, his pale face taut as he waited for the argument to continue. Isdar smiled wolfishly, putting a slender hand on the tabletop.

"Captain Reger. Be reasonable. The Observatory Guard will not respond well to any suggestion that limits their power or—"

"Isdar," Perin cut him off, enjoying the heady sense of power that came with calmly interrupting the Tacnimag Investigator. "The City Guards were established to defend and keep the city. They hold the responsibility for order. The Observatory Guards are security for the Observatory alone. The people resent their invasion into a territory that is not theirs to police."

Isdar frowned.

Perin knew that he was correct, of course. The Tacnimag had become used to having their armed men in the city...without official legal sanction. Judging by his expression, the mage knew it as well.

"That is true," he said slowly, watching Perin. "You don't need to tell me that the City and the Tacnimag have not benefited from the situation."

"Exactly." Perin hid his surprise. "I will gladly serve the City and the Tacnimag in keeping order, but only if the Observatory Guard are returned to their proper posts and duties."

"Fine," Isdar said bluntly. "You have what you want—the Observatory Guard out of the streets—now listen to what we require of you. Malcontents and tax evaders plague this city. If the Observatory ceases to punish and collect, then the City Guard will have to do so."

"I understand that," Perin replied lightly. "I will choose how best to do that. It is my opinion that public anger grows if you feed it violence. We shall see if my lighter hand will better affect the citizens."

"Ensure, though, that this light hand of yours can be firm, if need be," Isdar cut in. The Liaison nodded emphatically, trying to give the impression that he was contributing.

Perin smiled. "Of course."

"Captain Reger. The main assurance that the Tacnimag requires of you…" Isdar paused, shifting in his chair. This youth was far more of a man than he had expected. This would need to be worded carefully. "There may be occasions when the services of the City Guard will be required by the Tacnimag. On those occasions, we want to know that you'll provide us with the manpower." His eyes met Perin's.

Perin leaned forward. "You insist entirely on this?"

"Yes."

"And if I don't?"

"That which is made can be unmade."

"It's easier to destroy than it is to create," Perin responded immediately. Isdar blinked. Perin smiled, the phrase had issued straight from Medrivar's throne. "By which I mean, Isdar, that if you were to destroy me, there's no telling where it will end. My popularity with the people right now is hard to calculate, but judging from last night's graffiti alone, it appears that I'm too high a tower to attack. If you bring me down, my fall will crush others."

"Threats!" The Liaison decided it was time for him to express outrage.

Perin ignored him. So did Isdar.

"Point well made, Reger. Our relationship is for the purpose of returning the people's trust. You're right. You are too well-liked for removal—not that I want you removed. For now, anyway."

Perin nodded slowly. "I think I understand you. For the information of your superiors, I assure that the City Guard will be used for keeping order in the City. Any threat to public safety will be removed. I promise you that." Perin reached out and snuffed the candle on his right to demonstrate.

Isdar wasn't sure he liked this assurance.

"For example." Perin folded his hands on the desktop. "This Gravedigger character."

There was silence as smoke wavered from the candlewick. Isdar gathered his composure. He had not hoped for the captain to bring the issue up himself.

"He certainly needs to be removed," the Tacnimag Investigator murmured. Perin bowed his head in agreement. Isdar watched him very carefully. "There'll be a trick to that, Captain. He's nearly as popular as you."

"Don't flatter me. I imagine we're equally popular, the Gravedigger and I. The people believe he is their voice for justice, as they do me. The difference is I have the official position."

"Quite so. He is also a murderer and a rabble-rouser. You have a method?" Isdar wondered aloud, genuinely interested.

"I cannot hide my pursuit of him from the people," Perin stated. "Instead, I will attempt to exploit the Nagyevan sense of honour. I will be his worthy opponent, and he mine. The city will learn that I respect him. They will become spectators to see which of their champions triumphs."

Isdar nodded slowly. "That might work."

"Only if I can also express my dislike of the Observatory Guards. Openly."

Isdar frowned. "You'll end by destroying them, Reger. If the City Guard and the people are united in their hatred of the Observatory forces…"

"They'll learn to stay indoors. As they should. Unless, of course, the Tacnimag require them for something that directly affects their safety."

Isdar leaned back. "Very well. The thugs will take this badly, of course; but that's not my concern. Damage them all you like in your announcements, Captain. But paint the Tacnimag in a better light."

"I'll use a fine brush, Investigator."

"And the Gravedigger. You believe you can succeed where the last captain and the Observatory failed?"

"Tell the magi that the Gravedigger will be put in his proper place within a year," Perin stated, voice firm, eyes steady.

Isdar rose to his feet. "Good. With that, I think, they will be satisfied. Good afternoon, Captain. And Good luck." He followed the Liaison through the door as Sudar held it open for them. On the step outside, he paused and looked back. "My condolences. I understand you buried friends this morning."

Sudar closed the door gently.

"I'm glad that's over." Perin stood and went to the window. "I think we did well."

"*You* did well," Sudar corrected him. "I was just an unsettling presence."

"It was performed perfectly." Perin grinned. "Can you take the news to Forgos and Aranyo for me?"

Sudar nodded. "Are they still in the Lower West?"

"Should be. I asked them to spread the concept of Captain Reger Myrvo and the Gravedigger as honourable foes. I imagine they'll be found in a taverna."

"You give them the best jobs." Sudar smiled wryly. "I'll go hunt them down. See you later, Perin."

Perin finished writing in his slow, careful hand. The documents made his friends' positions and pay official. The last sheet, however, was a reminder to the Borderer Headquarters that Second South Response was, although technically disbanded, still entitled to the bounty money from the slain drizen.

The money, when divided, would come to twenty-four menel for each member of the Response. Harco and Maka's money would be given to their families. Kard's was to be divided again and shared, as he had no family.

A knock on the door came just as Perin signed the parchment in his uneven, scrawling hand.

Somehow, Perin knew even as he opened the door that Neva would be standing there.

The boy stepped inside cautiously, his blue eyes fixed on Perin.

"Reger."

"Neva?" The young mage appeared to be in his near-to-tears state. When Perin gestured for him to come inside, the younger boy fell forward and wrapped Perin in an embrace.

"I'm sorry I didn't come before!"

Perin staggered backward, pushing Neva's shoulders to disentangle himself.

"Whoa! Neva...what's going—"

"I couldn't get a chance to come and see you after the battle. When I found out it was your Response fighting...I...I'm glad you're not dead," he finished, dropping his open hands to his sides.

"So am I," Perin said quietly. "Thanks, Neva. I...appreciate your concern."

"You're Guard Captain now." Neva grinned suddenly. "Isn't that great? I have a legitimate reason for visiting you now!"

"Did you need one?" Perin asked, warily. "I thought the Tacnimag were giving you free run of the city. For your spying." Neva winced at the word.

"Yes...but I've been honoured by the Master of the City. That's like the closest the Tacnimag has to a leader. He's told me to work with the City Guard. So that's you!"

"Yes, I suppose it is." Perin smiled, relaxing a little. "Come and sit down, Neva. I've got something to drink somewhere..."

Neva visited occasionally in the following days. Perin found himself invited to banquets and dances in the Upper City and had Sudar coach him in protocol for such occasions. Sudar's father had made himself an important man in Nagyevo through trade, despite the fact that he was a commoner, and Sudar was best suited to teaching Perin how to bridge the class gap.

Everywhere he went, Perin proudly boasted that the Gravedigger would soon be in his hands. The nobility found him to be a charming oddity, but the tradesmen and merchants took him very seriously, and thanks to Forgos and Aranyo, the ordinary citizens also watched the Guard Captain with rapt attention, some cheering him on, others making no secret of their preference for the Gravedigger.

Barely a week had passed before Perin was challenged. Gyorva had gone to work in an administrative position at the Borderer Headquarters. It was the best way for Perin to get news from the surrounding Claims, as the Borderers often got it firsthand.

Some of the noblemen that, like Lord Adamun, had begun to distrust the Tacnimag openly, were of the opinion that the Gravedigger did not exist. It was their belief that the Tacnimag had invented him as a scapegoat—a plan that had obviously failed. The opinion irritated Perin because it implied that he colluded with the Tacnimag in his boasting.

Almost two weeks after his captaincy had been attained, Perin decided it was time that the Gravedigger reminded Nagyevo of his presence.

"This is madness," Forgos said bluntly. Perin looked up from under the brim of his broad hat. He wore his long coat, as well. Sudar had helped him rest his spade in the arrangement of belts on his back. He felt whole again and grinned at Forgos's disapproval. They were on a rooftop near the city barracks, and the clouds muted much of the pre-dawn starlight above.

"I think it's a good plan," Perin replied lightly. His one regret was that he had used up his supply of coffin nails. "Did you get me the spikes?"

Sudar nodded. "Aranyo to thank for it. Carpenter's stuff." He handed three to Perin. Each was nine inches of dark iron. Perin hooked them onto his belt. He looked out across the city, imagining his route to the Observatory. It would not take long, and at this time in the morning, he shouldn't be seen. Not until he reached the square, anyway.

This is madness, Medrivar murmured in his head. The king spoke in a tone that was half weary, half amused. Perhaps Medrivar was becoming used to his subject's recklessness.

"You can't follow me," Perin said, looking from Sudar to Forgos and back. He spoke earnestly. "It's too dangerous. This is my job."

"Your job..." Forgos shook his head. "You're doing your job already, Perin. You're making the city better. There hasn't been any violence since you became Guard Captain. The Tacnimag recalled the Oh-gees—"

"It's not good enough!" Perin snapped. "I came here...to do something. I don't know what. I followed my friend here to help another friend...but I couldn't do that! Kesairl's in the Observatory prison..."

"The prigon?" Sudar asked softly.

Perin nodded. "That's not all. The whole reason we came here was to help my…my king…but I don't think you'll understand."

The expressions of his two friends confirmed this.

"Anyway. Every time I think to put on my real clothes, these clothes, I can hear the song in my head. If there's something I'm supposed to do…then it's this."

Sudar looked down in thought at this, but Forgos shook his head. "I think you're a little bit mad, Perin. Nameless Ones know, I love you, but you're not normal." He grinned to show Perin that he didn't want to offend him.

Perin smiled back. "Trust me. I sound crazed to myself, as well. I'm sorry to involve you in this. Both of you."

Forgos shook his head and Sudar put a hand on Perin's shoulder.

"I'll never regret getting volunteered for the Borderers, pal. I wouldn't have met you otherwise." Forgos shifted his grip on the foul-smelling hessian sack he held. "I was a thief before all of this; dunno if you worked that out? Proper thug. I'm the bastard of a Nagyevan Lord—not saying which one—so instead of a flogging, I got volunteered. Best thing that ever happened to me, I swear."

Sudar didn't say anything, but his hand remained on Perin's shoulder.

"We're in the Gravedigger Ring now, too far gone to back out, or to want to," Forgos finished. He handed the sack to Perin, his nose wrinkling. "That was easy to get but hard to smuggle in. Don't know if anyone will notice it's missing."

Perin grinned grimly. The row of stakes lining the southern approach into Nagyevo would be sporting one less drizen head. "Gravedigger Ring. I like that, Forgos. What do you think, Sudar? Should we make that an official name?"

Sudar shrugged.

Smiling, Perin rose to his feet, clutching the heavy sack in one hand. "This won't take long, I hope. See you afterward. Stay away from my rooms at the barracks, just in case."

"We'll go see if Cama's up," Forgos joked. Since Perin's move, the so-called "Gravedigger Ring" had become good friends with the bald librarian.

"Good luck, Perin," Sudar murmured.

Perin nodded once, turned, and began his climb down into the dark city.

In his cell, deep beneath the Observatory, Kesairl sat in his meditative posture. The prigon's thick limbs and broad shoulders were slimmer than before. He had been fed well, for a prisoner of the Tacnimag and had spent much of his time exercising to the extent the cell allowed him to. As a result, his powerful frame had become leaner, his muscles more defined and his proud, taurine face slimmer. His skin was paler, too, from lack of sunlight, the mottled, purple-brown hues faded.

They had taken his arm rings, of course. Without them, he could only store so much magic. Thanks to the fascination of the Master Mage, who had visited Kesairl once after his first, fruitless interrogation, he had been allowed to keep his nose ring. The band was a small one, but it gave Kesairl enough energy storage to practice techniques in the long, dark, cold hours of his imprisonment.

Thanks to the iron bars that lined the walls and door of the cell, Kesairl could not affect his environment magically. The metal functioned in a manner opposite to gold and silver, which conducted energy. Good iron would not only refuse the passage of raw magic, but it would also draw, absorb, and nullify it. Regardless of any spell or technique Kesairl could perform, the cell would remain undamaged.

The young prigon went back over memories in his mind.

His coming of age in his torzsa, Torzsa Abrun. His father's pride in him. His expectancy of one day becoming a good leader for the clan. His mind ran through it all, passing his first, unlucky romance, his desire to be a good skirmisher, his goal of attaining the more prestigious rank of a Battlemage.

Then he had met Medrivar on the northern borders of beautiful Helynvale. The alien figure had entered his homeland and changed everything, in much the same way that their arrival in Erdhanger had changed Perin's life. The king had horrified him at first, an undead, the enemy of childhood tales. Then he had heard the song, the *Song of Valo*, and it had broken his heart. He had left all his goals behind. From that moment on, he had set out to serve the king.

His travels with Medrivar, when the king had been corporeal, were a comforting time to lose himself in. Despite the disapproval and fear of his family and his people, despite the loss of any chance of leading a torzsa, despite even the loss of fulfilling his magistry, the time had been a good one. He had been serving a higher purpose.

He still was. Even here in his cell, he reflected, he faithfully waited and worked as best as he could toward the day of his release. Perin was out there in the city, and Medrivar with him. They knew the *Song of Valo*, and they knew he waited. Rumours of the Gravedigger, heard from the young mage, lifted his heart.

Perin served the same higher purpose. The Bright Dead, no doubt, were yet awaiting the aid Medrivar had set out to bring them. The time in the cell might drag, and his frustrations might mount as the months passed, but Kesairl remained fiercely sure of one thing.

Perin would come. The king would come. And Kesairl would be set free. Valo would see.

TWENTY-SIX

PERIN SLIPPED THROUGH alleyways, passing the back doors of shops and houses, walking in shadows with his coat draped around him. Even the drunks and the criminals were absent from these alleyways, their revelry and business taking them into more entertaining districts. This part of the city formed a loose crescent facing the southeast curve of the Observatory, across the broad, circling boulevard. Small trees in full-leaf decorated the now empty space, known to the Nagyevans as "the square" despite all geometric sense.

Perin halted in the dark by a flight of steps at the edge of the square. Aranyo, cloaked and hooded, moved quickly out of a side alley and crouched beside Perin.

"Here it is." He passed Perin a small, battered can. There was no lid, and the handle of a brush stuck out over the rim.

"I got it ready for you. It's as close to blood red as I could find. Are...are you sure you don't want me to help you?" Aranyo asked, nervous and eager.

Perin shook his head, his face hidden by the brim of his hat. "You can't afford to get caught again with a paintbrush, my friend."

"And you can?"

"I won't." Perin tugged his hat a little lower, nodded to his companion, and left the shadow, moving upright and quickly across the square.

Thanks to his negotiating with Isdar, the observatory guards had stopped even patrolling the square. Very occasionally, a pair would leave the Observatory to make a quick circuit of the building. These cursory patrols typically happened earlier in the night, and Perin was sure he would be able to finish his task without being interrupted.

He followed the curve of the Observatory's forbidding stone wall until he could see the South Way on his left. The great wooden door, complete with the iron emblem of the Tacnimag, reared up on his right. The metal symbol spread high up the great wooden door, higher than Perin could reach. That was good. The wood was clear for his work.

Perin began to paint hurriedly, aware that the emptiness of the square might not last forever. The red paint ran a little as he pushed the brush across the weathered wood. When he had finished, the sentences ran in a slight arc across the entire width of the door.

HERE I LAY THE BLAME

And beneath that...

I AM THE GRAVEDIGGER

Perin glanced about him. There were footsteps approaching from a fair distance away. Recklessness pushed excitement through his blood, and he ignored Medrivar's warnings to be cautious.

Perin unhooked one of the nine-inch nails from his belt. The long, pointed iron cooled his hand. Taking a deep breath and holding it in, Perin unwrapped the hessian sack from its burden.

The dark, ragged drizen head reeked with decomposition. The eyes were gone, taken by crows, and in places, the bone bared. Grimacing, Perin lifted the macabre thing up against the door. The wood was all in one piece, opening not outward or inward, but lifting up into the archway above, the centre of the door undivided. Perfect for what Perin had in mind for it.

The spike drove through the knot of hair at the back of the monster's head. The point bit a little into the wood, but it took several blows to drive the spike a few inches into the door. The sound resounded with a *boom*, like the slow echo of Perin's thundering heartbeat.

On the sixth blow, a shout rang out. Perin turned, saw that a pair of Observatory Guards were running towards him, pulling their swords free and throwing down the torches they had been carrying. Perin stood in the pool of flickering light, spreading from the torches ensconced on either side of the vandalised door. As the two guards drew closer, Perin reached behind him and lifted his spade free, letting it make a few revolutions around his hand as he brought it up into the ready position.

The guards slowed.

"Will you be the first to pay for the Tacnimag's crimes?" Perin roared in as deep and loud a voice as he could muster from his body. The spade rose and pointed directly at them as he stretched out his arm.

Completely carried away with his role, Perin strode towards them. The Oh-gees had halted and now they turned and ran, one of them calling out as he went, "*Gravedigger! Gravedigger!*"

Perin would have laughed, but his voice had gone too hoarse from shouting at the two men. This was perfect. Nobody in the buildings opposite would fail to wake up on hearing such a cry. His work on the door would be seen by many, at least by enough to spread news of it around the whole city. He turned and headed down the South Way, returning his spade to his back.

Suddenly, the streets were full of guards. Perin could see them running in pairs from sidestreets and alleys that he would have counted on as clear escape routes. Putting on a burst of speed, Perin made for the nearest street that he knew would lead him into the complex Lower West, where he had evaded pursuit before. Where had the guards come from?

Little houses and dark shops passed in a blur as Perin ran, his boots stamping through the rubbish in the gutters. He made as many turns and changes of direction as he could, but always behind him, he could hear the sound of stampeding feet.

Perin stumbled into a pitch-dark alley. He pressed himself up against the wall and tried to steady his breathing. His chest burned and his legs ached. Borderers were fitter than Observatory Guards, to be sure, but there were more of them. And it seemed like they always knew where to follow him.

"He's over here!" shouted a voice, horribly near. It sounded like it had come from above, but Perin couldn't be sure. An Oh-gee made a fast turn into the alley at that moment, slipping in a puddle, his hand slapping against the crumbling brick wall to keep him upright. Perin gritted his teeth, drew another spike, and leapt forward as the man continued to run.

Their collision was awful. The guard's legs shot up and out as Perin tackled him at chest height. He didn't move again. Perin had driven the spike halfway up into the guard's skull from below the man's chin. Blood began to paint the cobbles.

Perin stood, backed away again, farther into the shadows. He was fed up with running. Maybe if he killed enough Observatory Guards, they would lose hope. Perhaps the legend he had created of himself would become too terrifying a truth to face.

The next guard that took the corner was able to scream out as he died. Perin had driven the spike up beneath the man's arm, where no armour protected his side. It was another move of Medrivar's, and though it guaranteed death to the victim, it did not bring about the guard's relief as quickly as the last kill.

Shivering, Perin backed away again. His bravado seemed to have fled. He felt trapped, completely trapped, in a way that drew the hope out of him in a steady stream, as steady as the blood soaking the alley floor.

You need to leave this alleyway, Medrivar whispered urgently.

Perin could hear pounding footsteps, a lot of them. He shook his head. In the alleyway, they would come one or maybe two at a time. Outside, in the broader street, he would become surrounded.

How many do you think you can kill in here before a mage comes? Medrivar asked.

Perin felt as if the king was trying to push him out of the alley and back into the city. He looked up, saw stars through a break in the thick cloud. "If I die, this is where it'll happen," he said darkly, to Medrivar and the sky.

Medrivar fell silent.

The sound of footsteps had paused, as if the pursuers were halting to discuss their quarry's position. There was no sound except Perin's breathing and the *click-clack* of roof tiles in the dark.

I didn't know you felt so guilty, Medrivar said in a tone of realisation.

For a moment, Perin could see himself in the throne room staring out of a window.

The king had come to sit beside him. *You know that when they died, when Harco and Maka and Kard died...you know that they did not cease to be, do you not?* He was trying to comfort the boy. Perin's tears were visible, here, in the throne room.

Their spirits were not extinguished by death, Perin. You feel at fault for your survival. I apologise. I should have seen it.

I hid it well, Perin replied, watching the stars through the window. *I worked hard. I led my friends.*

You have a gift for leadership, Medrivar said softly. *But you will not be able to lead anyone if you allow yourself to die here.*

There was a pause as Perin stood, fists clenched, biting his lip until he could taste copper. It felt like waves were crashing over him. The throne room trembled under the assault of doubt, though Medrivar stayed still and unaffected beside him as the blows came.

Kesairl in his cell, Maka, Kard, and Harco in the ground. The City of Nagyevo and all her inhabitants. The unaided Bright Dead far in the north.

I can't do it all, Majesty. Now Perin was kneeling.

The undead king rose slowly, his expression kind but stern. The gold of his torc and circlet flashed as torches lit on the walls of the throne room. At once, he held a long, leaf-bladed spear.

I will help you, my dear friend. Get up. Fight. Dying here will help no one. I would pass with you, and then who would help my kindred in the north? Get up!

Perin stood again, horrified. His selfishness sickened him. It was not just *his* life he gambled with in the dark alleyways of the Lower West; it was Medrivar's as well. It was the future of Valo. It was the Song.

Perin stepped out, dropping his gaze from the night sky. The mouth of the alley had cleared, but he could hear footsteps again. No matter. He would go out and face them. He would survive.

A figure dropped lightly from the roof near the opening of the alley.

He was not tall, and his robes were not so voluminous as the robes of an Elder Mage. As he came forward steadily, the clouds broke further, and moonlight shone on auburn hair.

Neva's blue eyes were shadowed as he spoke. "Perin."

Perin's heart froze.

Medrivar was silent and still in his throne room, as shocked as his servant.

Neva halted a few paces in front of Perin.

"You know that name?" Perin swallowed. Then there was a chance that Neva did not know, had not made the connection between his friend Reger and the Gravedigger. Perin was the name he had left behind. The Tacnimag must've discovered it...

"I know who you are. I never thought that it would be you, Reger, after all this." The sentence came like a blow. Perin pulled his spade free and held it at the ready, his heart fluttering in his chest. Prickles of shock raced across his cold, sweaty skin.

Neva lifted his head and shrugged off his outer robe. Beneath it, he wore a loose, short-armed shirt of pale-blue cotton held by a black belt above the dark-blue cloth of his breeches. His right forearm was enwrapped by a magic ornament in the shape of a serpent in red gold, the snake's head facing forward above the wrist. His left forearm was similarly adorned, but with a slimmer, silver serpent with three separate tails circling up beyond Neva's elbow.

"Careful, Reger." The warning sounded like a genuine caution.

"Do you mean to take me alive?" Perin spat, disgusted. "And my name *is* Perin, and thus, seeing as you've found it out, you should use it!"

"Perin," Neva murmured, nervously watching the other boy. "The Gravedigger. Why didn't you tell me?"

"Why do you think?" Perin's voice rose high with sarcasm.

"You were like my elder brother!" Neva's composure broke. He no longer seemed like the calm capturer, his vulnerable nature tearing through the mask.

Perin felt a bitter tug on his heart. He had always felt protective of that side of Neva...

"I wouldn't have cared! You were my friend!" Neva continued, nearly shouting. He was not crying, a fact for which Perin was grateful. "The Tacnimag didn't mean as much to me, not then!"

"And now?" Perin asked, sounding cold, distant.

Neva's fists clenched. "Now... Now I've worked for them. I've gained their notice. Even Master Varostan pays me attention. I said I'd catch the Gravedigger, and I have! I'm the hero of Nagyevo!"

"The Gravedigger is the hero of Nagyevo!" Perin shouted, surprising himself with his anger. "The Tacnimag have been setting drizen on their own people!"

"I know. I saw the head you pinned to the Observatory door." Neva's voice sounded haunted, his expression twisted. "I've seen it. Just yesterday I've seen it. Beneath the Floor Gate in the centre of the Observatory is a great pit. The Floor Gate is the ceiling. Wires dangle from it into the pit. They've bred drizen down there, given them armour, fed them prisoners to keep them docile... The wires carry the magic down, and the Floor Gate sends them out to where the Tacnimag needs them."

"You've seen it?" Perin sounded disbelieving. "You've seen proof, and you're still faithful to them?"

"They're in charge," Neva protested. He stared at Perin. "I'm on their side. I'm a mage! I can't help that!"

Perin stared at Neva. He had never considered that fact. Neva was defined by what he was. Outside of the Observatory, magi had no place, no home. They did not exist beyond the walls, away from expert training.

"Just because...just because you're a mage, it doesn't mean you have to fight on the side of the Tacnimag. You know they're murderers now."

"And I'm one of them," Neva said bitterly, raising his fist. Light sparked off the scales of his red-gold serpent. Perin stared at him and slowly returned his spade to his back. He spread his open hands and took a step towards Neva.

"I'm sorry, Neva. I haven't been a very good friend."

Neva choked on a sob. "Don't do that. Don't...don't..."

"I'm sorry," Perin repeated, his heart racing. "I've let you down, Neva."

"Shut up!" Neva gasped. A cobble tore away from the alley floor and lifted, spinning gently, to hover inches from Neva's fist. Perin stared at it.

"I can kill you. I can kill you!"

"I know." Perin's blood pounded in his ears.

Medrivar remained completely silent, watching the scene with hands clenched.

"Neva...I should have trusted you."

The cobblestone shot past Perin's head with such speed that his hat spun away. Brickwork at the end of the alleyway exploded. Neva trembled from head to foot. Another cobblestone lifted clear of the floor, spinning faster than the last. Neva backed away, the stone following him, hovering over his fist as he brought his arm back toward him, his fingers feeling the air. The stone spun so fast, it became a blur.

"I have to choose...Reger! I have to choose..."

Perin nodded, stood still, closed his eyes. "You do. Choose, Neva."

"Choose."

In the throne room, Medrivar began to sing. The melody was pitched lower than the one Perin had hummed before, and there were no words. The king's voice filled Perin's mind.

"Stop humming," Neva whispered. Perin quietly echoed the tune, his hands open, awaiting possible death. The *Song of Valo* filled the silent alley.

Tears ran down the face of the young mage.

The cobblestone plummeted, clattered in the dark.

"I don't know who I am." Neva stared, eyes wide, at Perin. He dropped his hands to his sides. The song echoed in Neva's ears, and he put a hand out against the wall to steady himself.

"Neva. Are you all right?" Perin appeared at Neva's side, and his arm steadied the mage.

"I don't know who I am," Neva repeated. He leaned against his friend like a small child, as the long absent footfall of the Observatory Guards drew closer. "I can't kill you."

It was a simple, inescapable fact.

"Would you like the chance to find out who you are?" Perin asked him, before he was even sure what it meant.

Neva straightened slowly, looked at him in fear and guilt and need. "Yes."

"Then we need to find a way out of here, and I'll try and help you."

"You'll forgive me?" Neva's voice was small.

"I already have."

Neva swallowed. "I can get us out of here." He glanced around, nodded to himself. "Yes. I was only there recently…" He picked up his over-robes and pulled them back on.

Perin retrieved his hat. He looked toward the mouth of the alley. "With your magic, we should be able to fight our way to escape…come on. Little brother."

Neva beamed, a smile brighter than any Perin had seen before. "I can do better than that, brother." He added the word almost shyly. He opened his arms. "Hug me."

"Now's not the best time…" Perin frowned, wondering what had come over Neva.

"No, you idiot…" Neva nearly laughed. "If you want to get out of here, hug me!"

Perin stepped into the embrace, frown still in place.

There was an explosion of air. Perin stumbled out of Neva's grasp and fell onto his hearth rug. The dark shape of his desk occupied much of his vision. Scrambling to his feet, he stared in astonishment at his room. Neva sat down on the edge of Perin's desk, taking a deep breath.

"Whoa. Good thing someone left some candles burning. I couldn't have done much with a dark room. Not without destroying your furniture."

Perin's legs felt weak. He struggled to the mantel, picking up one of the lit candles and taking its fire to the other wicks around the room until he could properly see. It proved no easier to believe than before.

"I didn't know you could do that."

Neva grinned, a little embarrassed. "Nor did I. I mean, with two people. I've only ever translocated by myself before."

"Translocated?" Perin repeated.

Neva nodded. "That's right. I'm a telemage. I can see places as they are, in my head. If I try really hard, I can put myself in the picture. As long as I've been there before, I can go anywhere. It really drains Kigkarmzin, though." He gestured to the red-gold serpent that encircled his wrist and forearm.

"You named your adornments?" Perin asked, surprised.

"They were named when I was given them. Gifts from Master Varostan. Kigkarmzin and Kigzusta. They're not Claimic names, so they must be in another language."

Perin nodded. "Sounds like Priga to me. The language of the prigon people. I know a little. I think it's something like Red-snake and Silver-snake."

"Oh." Neva looked down at his adornments. "I hoped it would be less obvious than that. What's your spade called?"

Perin took his spade off and looked at it. "I don't know...I haven't named it. Spade, I suppose."

"You can't call a spade 'Spade!'" Neva protested. "At least, not one that's a weapon."

"I thought you were supposed to call a spade a spade." Perin grinned. He went to hide his weapon in its place behind the boards of his wardrobe in the next room. Neva followed him to the door of the bedroom and waited until Perin emerged again, back in clothes suitable for a Captain of the Guard.

"I know a prigon," Neva stated. "I used to go and talk to him in the cells all the time."

"You know Kesairl?" Perin asked, turning to look straight at his friend.

Neva nodded, looking embarrassed. "He was quite interested in what I had to say about my friend, Reger Myrvo. Now I know why."

Perin laughed. After a moment, he put a hand on Neva's shoulder. "Neva. You've chosen me, over the Tacnimag?"

"Yes." Neva sounded almost hurt, as if saddened that Perin could doubt it.

"I'm glad. Thank you, brother. I only want to give you the choice. Will you help me? Will you join with the Gravedigger?"

Neva took a deep breath. "Yes, Perin." He smiled at using his friend's real name. "I'll help you with everything I've got."

"We'll have Kesairl free in no time," Perin responded with a fierce smile. "Now, though, I need to call out the guard, and you'd better go back to hunting after me."

"You're calling out the guard?" Neva asked, looking confused.

"Yes." Perin tapped his decorative armour shirt. "It seems that the Gravedigger is out somewhere in the Lower West city. It's my job to catch him. I'm not going to let the bloody Oh-gees overstep their boundaries!"

Perin left the building the conventional way, by the door. A relieved-looking trio of former Borderers joined him as he made his way toward the Lower West.

In Perin's rooms, Neva made sure the door was locked. Then he took a deep breath and vanished in an explosion of air, putting out the candles.

TWENTY-SEVEN

"SOME OF YOU KNOW NEVA," Perin said quietly, looking around the room. They had pushed the desk back against one wall and arranged chairs in a circle. Neva sat nervously beside Perin.

Sudar looked wary and curious, whereas Forgos and Aranyo had expressions of barely suppressed hostility. Gyorva had customarily seated himself in the shadowed corner, and his face was difficult to read.

"He's a mage. Obviously," Perin started, aware that he was going to have to do a good job of representing Neva positively. "Until very recently, he was directly working with the Observatory to track me down. Well, to track the Gravedigger down. Now he knows that I'm the Gravedigger, and he's decided to switch sides."

Neva moved uncomfortably on his chair.

Aranyo lifted his hand, carefully not looking at the young mage. "Perin? What's to stop him from switching sides again?"

Neva bit down on his lower lip and looked at the floor. Perin found himself struggling to cool his anger. It wasn't an unreasonable question, but it was surely hurting Neva.

Forgos nodded slowly. "No offence, mage, but I don't really know you. We didn't trust you before, and it turned out we were right not to, so you understand why we don't really trust you now?"

Perin relaxed a little. For Forgos, it had been a sensitive comment.

Neva raised his head. "I won't fight against Perin. You've fought alongside him, so I know you're probably closer to him than I am. I've never risked my life for him. But he risked his life for my sake, and I will *die* for him in an instant if he ever needs me to. From now on, I'll risk my life for him the same as you."

There was a pause. Gyorva moved a little, watching Neva's face intently. Forgos frowned slightly, pleased by the fervent answer, but unsure whether he should trust it.

Aranyo snorted. "Words are easy to say, mage."

"My name's Neva. And I meant what I said, and I'll prove it!" Neva trembled with suppressed anger and fear. He was magically gifted, but the former Borderers were all bigger and stronger than him.

"I don't think Perin means *anything* to you," Aranyo stated, getting off his chair and standing stiffly, looking at Neva across the circle.

There was a rush of air. Neva blurred. His fist hit Aranyo hard in the face, and the blond boy went down, knocking his chair over.

Perin and Sudar jumped to their feet, and Forgos took a couple of wary steps back. Gyorva didn't move, but his eyes showed his excitement at the change of pace.

Neva had crossed the space in one movement, punching Aranyo. He now stood over him, his shoulders shaking, fists still clenched. Then he offered a hand to his opponent. "I'm not sorry. But I don't want to fight you."

"Too late for that!" Aranyo shouted, slapping away Neva's hand. He jumped to his feet and raised his fists, but Forgos stepped in the way.

"Come on, Aranyo. Stop. Sit down and have a think."

Shocked, Aranyo did as the taller boy had asked.

Forgos ran a hand across his shaved head, as if making up his mind. He offered the hand to Neva. "I believe you. If you were still against Perin, you wouldn't have got so angry."

Neva shook his hand gratefully. "Thank you. Although, it could just have been because I wanted to hit him." He narrowed his eyes and looked at Aranyo.

Aranyo caught Perin's eye and looked away.

"I'm Forgos. The boy you punched is Aranyo. He's a good lad, but he has reason for not liking mages. He'll get used to you." Forgos introduced the companions one by one, and Neva received welcomes, some more reluctant than others.

"It was a good punch. For a mage," Aranyo finally admitted. The last of the tension in the room faded.

"So," Perin said, once everyone was seated again, "we're all going to trust Neva, and that'll be the end of the argument. He's a member of the Gravedigger Ring now."

He waited to make sure there were no open disagreements. When none came, he sighed with relief and slapped his hand down on his thigh as if to mark the end of the conflict.

"Good! Right, the city. We need to discuss what's going on. I've received a formal apology from the Tacnimag for allowing the Observatory Guards out into the Lower West again." Perin's expression was dark. "They nearly caught me. Neva, how did they set up the trap?"

Neva swallowed and began. "That's my fault, really. I was just taking the odd look at places around the city, and I saw the Gravedigger—saw you—walking across the square towards the front door. I translocated to Master Varostan. He called as many Oh-gees to the Floor Gate room as he could, and then he and Mage Tulbu—he's a very powerful mage—sent them out through the Floor Gate."

"This Floor Gate...it sends people places by magic?" Gyorva asked, very interested.

Neva nodded. "It's like an extension of my translocation magic. It enables magi who aren't gifted that way to get out to faraway locations. I'm the only telemage in the whole Observatory, so the Floor Gate is very useful. They don't like walking through the city."

"I wonder why," Aranyo scoffed.

Perin grinned. "Yes, Nagyevo really doesn't like magi anymore. No offence, Neva, you're an exception."

Neva shrugged and smiled.

For a few minutes, the Ring swapped theories on the Floor Gate, with Neva cutting in with corrections. The fact that the Tacnimag had used the device for spreading captured drizen around the Claimfold, was utterly damning. There was no doubt now that the Tacnimag were the enemy of the people.

"The rumour got out to the other Folds," Gyorva cut in, "that the drizen attacks were magical and that the Tacnimag were to blame. In the city, everyone had got used to disliking the Tacnimag. Out in the Folds...the reaction was more dramatic."

"What's happening?" Perin asked, thinking of Csus.

"The unrest in Joval has exploded. Temlan Claim is in something of a revolt, centred around the town itself. Vada will follow, though people won't care about that until the Claim stops sending horses down to Nagyevo. They're a vital trade, after all. The Claim of Cserys has seen an increase in bandit activity. Tax routes are being attacked.

"Narsun Fold has been quiet, really. Thanks probably to us and the other Borderers and the fact that the Claims of Mezyro and Solorin are still trying to get over the drizen attacks. Lord Adamun has been a revolt all by himself, though. He's gathered a fair few nobles, and even some merchants—they're having meetings in the Upper West city. The Tacnimag have accused him of treason, saying he supports the Seven Cities, which is nonsense, but you might be called upon to break up his gatherings at some point, Perin. That would be awkward."

"Very," Perin agreed, frowning. Lord Adamun was in danger of making too much trouble for himself. "So, that's the northwestern and southern Folds of Valo. What about the east? What about Csus?"

Gyorva nodded. "I thought you'd want to know about that. Varo and Hanger Claims have essentially declared themselves no longer under the governance of the Tacnimag. The hunters that have been coming into the city from Csus recently are wondering how long it will be before the Tacnimag sets the Eastern garrison on the towns there."

"You think that could happen?" Perin asked. Despite the mostly poor memories his homeland had given him, he had a fondness for the mountain region. Mistress Hoer in Erdhanger came to his mind. She had wanted him to court her daughter. That was one family he didn't want destroyed by Tacnimag retaliation.

Gyorva shrugged. "It might do. They've challenged the Tacnimag directly."

"What about the Northeast?"

"Well, I've got no news from Helynvale because there hasn't been any trade with the prigon since your friend went missing here, Perin. Nobody's told them that he's in a Tacnimag prison, which is just as well. There'd probably be war, and that wouldn't help any of us."

There was a murmur of agreement.

"Koban, on the other hand, is even more outraged than Joval. There's a whole bunch of fortified settlements up there on Helynvale's western border, and they've always been a hard people, the Koban Claimers. They've threatened to kill any Tacnimag representative that comes looking for tax. They're collecting for themselves now, independent—Koban money for Koban needs."

"The whole Claimfold's ready to tear itself apart." Perin shivered.

Gyorva nodded. "Essentially. If the Seven Cities don't fight our armies in the West soon, they won't need to conquer us. We'll have broken our own gates." This gloomy statement left the room silent, thick with thought.

The following day, Perin received the bounty money for the dead drizen. The Gravedigger Ring, minus Neva, celebrated their riches in customary style. Perin watched enviously as his friends spent the afternoon getting drunker and drunker, aware that he needed to stay sober, in case Isdar arrived with some kind of worrying request.

The Investigator had been a thankfully infrequent visitor since the Observatory Guard had overstepped their bounds. He was apologetic, even though he had not ordered them into the city himself. The Oh-gees had made a mess of the Lower West city looking for the Gravedigger, and while the citizens cheered Perin's public denunciation of them, the Tacnimag quietly fed the few prisoners they had taken to the cells, and to the drizen pit.

Investigator Isdar had personally interrogated them. They were the type usually dragged in, petty thieves or black marketeers, and after he'd exercised his methods of torture on them, most went to their deaths or their cells gratefully. The torture was pointless, of course. Isdar was resigned to the fact that the city, on the whole, was ignorant of the Gravedigger.

Only the Guard Captain, Reger Myrvo, seemed to have any idea. He always seemed confident, always seemed to be following some obscure lead. Recently, he'd ordered a quiet investigation of all the genuine gravediggers in the city. When that had failed, he'd extended his range of enquiry.

Cheerful City Guardsmen, glad to perform a less onerous duty than patrol and wall-work, spent their time interviewing salesmen across the city. No shop that had ever sold any form of gardening equipment went unvisited. Samples of merchandise were all brought back to the City Guard barracks, usually in the form of spades and other soil-turning implements. The Guard Captain even ordered, at the expense of the City Guard budget, a selection of nails from across the city.

There was a logic to it, of course. The several bodies that the Gravedigger had left behind him in his attacks on Observatory Guards showed that nails of differing sizes were something of a trademark, as well as the famous spade. Isdar only wondered how Reger went about converting his research into a plan of action. Was he up to the task? Could anyone catch the Gravedigger?

Perin oversaw the return of all the spades he had borrowed, compensating shopkeepers whenever claims of "damage" were made. He had taken time, in the chaos of it all, to make a now near-untraceable transaction with one of the better artisans of the city. It resulted in a reworked version of his beloved spade.

The weapon had been reinforced; the steel of weapon-grade, honed brilliantly. The craftsperson straightened the shaft, and as it was no longer intended for digging, the circular handle had been removed. An additional circle of iron banded the butt, adding balance. Perin had even had the name of the weapon engraved on the metal where it joined the shaft: *Spade*.

With it had come a smaller spade, similarly fashioned but half the length, like a woodsman's tool. This one had a traditional handle and could still be used for digging, although the primary reason for the redesign was to allow Perin to whirl the weapon more flexibly in combat. This shorter spade would fit on his belt, hidden beneath his coat, for when he needed to fight in close.

Of course, he had also taken the opportunity to stock up on nails.

Sudar had bought himself a pair of short swords with broad blades. Perin had no doubt the talented young man knew how to wield them. He was pleased by the fact that Sudar had also bought a spear, unable to deny his favourite weapon, despite the advantages of the shorter swords.

Forgos had opted for buying some very fine clothes and a good longsword similar to Lord Adamun's. Gyorva had neglected to buy any weaponry, claiming he was done with fighting. None of the Ring knew what their smartest member had spent his money on and soon gave up asking.

Aranyo had not been trained to use a sword. Because of this, he bought a selection of daggers from a shady man in the Lower West city and continued to practice his spearplay on the barracks parade ground.

There was a sense for them all that they were in preparation, especially Neva, who still spent most of his time acting as a loyal Tacnimag mage.

Occasionally, Perin and Neva would work on planning the rescue of Kesairl. Each time, they gave up in frustration. Kesairl would not be rescued while the Observatory was full of powerful magi.

Perin eventually tired of listening to Gyorva's updates on the Claimfold and of reading Sudar's well-written reports on how the city had taken his last announcements. Keeping up the pretence of being just a few steps behind the Gravedigger became wearing. Perhaps there was something mentally damaging about hunting yourself in public.

At the end of a long, paperwork-heavy day, Perin blew out the candle at his bedside and allowed himself to enjoy the feather-comfort of his large bed.

In the throne room, Medrivar ran through Perin's memories of the day, examining events carefully. If Perin had need of a memory, the king would know exactly where to find it.

The king became aware of an increasing drowsiness. He had never felt tired before, not since his last need to regenerate, when he had had his own body. He had never needed sleep while cohabiting Perin's body. The sensation intrigued him, and as it intensified and he found himself lying down, he began to worry a little. The feeling was so natural and so welcome that even his concerns began to fade. There was nothing wrong, nothing wrong with the feeling, nothing wrong with the fading...

The hall soared high and vaulted, the stone distant above Medrivar's head. The king rose, found himself to be not alone. There were others with him, his kin, those that had chosen to be his subjects. The Bright Dead lay all about.

They were moaning. They were in pain. They needed his help.

Medrivar walked from hall to hall, immersed in familiar surroundings. His people were not fallen without reason. The structure of the halls resonated with magical energy. He could feel the disturbance that had cast his warriors to the floor. They felt it acutely; whereas he, not truly there amongst them, was spared. In the South, long leagues from these under-mountain halls, something terrible seemed to be happening.

But what?

With purpose and urgency now, Medrivar strode down from the great, wrought caves of the Bright Dead and into the tunnels that led to the boundary of his territory. Some of the tunnels led through dark and dangerous terrain and would, in a tortuous, convoluted way, come to their destination. But there was a quicker way there. Medrivar made for the Bridge.

The Bridge spanned a great gulf of empty space. High above, the inner slopes of the mountains formed the ceiling, but mist and distance veiled the dark rock. The blue glow of the stones made all visible. The Bridge spanned the border between the territory of the Bright Dead and the Damned. It was a great, twisting, organic column across the divide that had been hewn, in places, into something fit for taking travellers, and it represented the centre of the Meddoszoru, the Dead Hill, both geographically and spiritually.

Medrivar knew that the Meddoszoru, this great cavern of a city under the hill that was his birthplace and battleground, was also known as the Hill of Three Thrones.

The first he knew well, at the highest point under the mountain in his own territory, in the throne room of the Bright Dead. The Bright Throne occupied that chamber, and none were fit to sit there, not even himself. Those that had tried could only feel its power, the raw energy running through the bones of the earth. They could not make use of it. Amongst the Bright Dead it was believed that if one great enough in power could take that seat, then truly, war could be waged across the bridge and into the territory of the Damned. Truly, then there would be victory. Amongst his people, it was the only belief held to as a certainty, though none knew for sure.

Medrivar had never seen the second throne. It abided in the chamber that formed the mirror image of the Bright Dead's throne room. The Bright

Dead themselves were as much afeared of the second throne's power as they were in awe of their own artifact. And as much as they hoped for a saviour capable of wielding the power of the first, they feared the coming of a person great enough to occupy that second seat.

The Meddoszoru formed the heart of power in Valo, Medrivar believed. Nowhere else had he seen evidence of magic running raw and pure through the very rock. Elsewhere, that energy was disparate and weak. Magi needed to gather and store enough to work with, in gold and silver bands. But under those mountains, the power lay unlimited, checked only by the stone that contained it.

Medrivar had always thought only of his brethren, seeing his halls as their home but he had never seen the truth that lay beyond. Now, he had travelled Valo. The doings of the Claimfold, of the prigon, of even the Seven Cities, all were subject to energy. Life was magic, it seemed to Medrivar, and magic had its source in the Meddoszoru.

The dead king had always believed in the principle of a higher power, had sensed spirits beyond his reach. Now he was sure. Whatever and whoever had built Valo had included a heart to the whole land, a place where seats of power waited. One for each dead force that warred over the right to the world of the living, and a third…

Now something was disturbing that order.

Medrivar stopped in the centre of the Bridge. His blue eyes stared, piercing the mist across the way. The Damned waited there, muttering, shaking their spears in the dark. They were aware of the disturbance. They welcomed it. Now, they waited with purpose. With urgency.

He is coming. They are coming. He is Coming. They are coming. Coming. His. They…

Medrivar screamed out and awoke. Perin clutched at his brow, a sudden headache thrusting him up through layers of sleep and into awareness.

"What is it? What's wrong?"

Medrivar's voice shook. It caused terror in Perin to hear fear in the king's voice.

Something is wrong! In the South! No…not in the South, not from here…it would be east of here. I do not know!

Perin rose and staggered to his bedroom window, which he knew looked east, toward Csus. He stared out and blinked, astonished.

Hanging low in the East above the encircling wall of Nagyevo, the moon had changed. Its bright disc did not shine tonight. Its white face was obscured. A black circle shadowed it, eclipsing its light, and even the stars seemed to have forsaken it.

TWENTY-EIGHT

COME DAYLIGHT, the city was full of talk. The sky appeared clear and there was no sign of impending destruction. The omen had passed.

Speculation began. The few learned people, Cama among them, were ignored as they explained that the phenomenon had been observed before, to no ill end. The people of Nagyevo were more interested in inventing ever-worse meanings behind the eclipse. The only people who did not put forth a suggestion were the magi. An official query was made by the Merchants Liaison, but no reply came back.

Perin capitalised on the situation by declaring that it was a sign, a sign that the Gravedigger would soon be found and dealt with. His cheerful hecklers in the crowd called back to him their own theories. It seemed many thought that the Gravedigger would soon issue some great doom upon Nagyevo.

Isdar had been due for a meeting with Perin, but he did not arrive. No explanation was given until Neva arrived at Perin's rooms, where Sudar and Perin were sharing a drink. The evening sun washed in through the open window and door. Neva entered without knocking, stirring the dust that floated in the warm light.

"Through the door, this time!" Perin remarked, smiling a little from the pleasure of seeing his friend, and a little because of the contents of his half-full tumbler.

"I wouldn't translocate in on you," Neva protested. "That would be rude! I wouldn't even look into your rooms—not unless I needed to."

"Thanks for respecting my privacy," Perin replied, only half joking. He seemed to attract companions capable of seeing where they shouldn't be able to. Medrivar found the coincidence amusing, but did not laugh. The night's dream still weighed too heavily on him.

"I've come on business," Neva said importantly, sitting down beside Sudar.

"You won't need any of this, then," Sudar murmured with a little smile, moving the bottle of Western spirit out of Neva's reach.

"It's thirsty work," Neva replied, grinning delightedly at his joke. He lifted a hand and the bottle slid back across the little drinking table and into his grasp. He poured himself a little but did not drink any. "The Tacnimag have gone a bit strange."

"They were always a bit strange." Perin laughed. His laugh fell short. Neva's expression was serious.

"Master Varostan and Mage Tulbu, and a few of the other powerful magi, have been stuck away in the Master's office all morning. The whole Observatory has been talking about the moon thing last night, but we've all been forbidden to discuss it with anyone outside of the building. We're not even supposed to talk to the Oh-gees."

"Do they know something about it?" Perin asked.

Medrivar observed closely.

Neva shrugged. "No idea. A few hours ago, they must've decided something, because orders came down that no one was to enter the Floor Gate room until told otherwise. One of the Oh-gees told me that Mage Tulbu went in there to use the Grand Telescope."

"Which does what?" Perin asked.

"The telescopes all look out through the solid roof, in a circle around the walls of the Floor Gate room," Neva explained, "but the Grand Telescope is in the centre, retracted up into the ceiling. When it's down it hovers above the Floor Gate and draws energy out of all the other telescopes. The others used to be used for viewing, but now they're just storage devices like my adornments." He let his sleeve fall down his raised arm to show them a flash of Kigzusta's silver tails.

"The Grand Telescope, however, is still used for viewing. It can look anywhere in Valo, I think, and the advantage is that it doesn't have to be a place that the user has seen. It draws a lot of power, though. I imagine Mage Tulbu is using it to look about the land. Maybe they think that the moon-dark was a warning of war."

"I don't think he needs to look to the West," Perin said, as if to himself. "It's the East to which he should look."

"What do you mean?" Sudar and Neva asked at the same time.

Perin jerked, as if surprised out of a daydream. "I don't know. Just something in my head." Perin was surprised. Medrivar normally warned him before putting words so obtrusively in his mouth.

"Maybe you said it because east means home to you?" Sudar suggested.

Perin shrugged.

Suddenly, Neva straightened up in his chair as if an idea had struck him. "I've got to go! That was a Tacnimag summons... It must have been Master Varostan—nobody else is as powerful a telepath..." He rose to his feet. "Nameless Gods, he's being urgent!" he exclaimed, promptly vanishing in a rush of air.

"It must have been urgent. He left his drink," Sudar said dryly.

Neva hurried through the hallways of the Observatory. As he rounded a corner, he found himself walking into the middle of an argument between Mage Tulbu and Investigator Isdar.

"I don't care about your theory, Isdar! The...*thing* that is coming makes the Gravedigger look like a blessing!"

"Listen, Tulbu, you slow-witted fool, if it's coming from Csus, then don't you see that they must be connected?"

Both fell silent as they saw Neva standing there.

"Apologies, Masters." Neva bowed and hurried past them. Varostan's summons had called him to come to the Floor Gate room. He had time though—none of the magi knew how frequently he was now able to translocate. His rare gift was prized, but not well understood. With that in mind, Neva hurried down a flight of stairs and turned off the corridor and into a storage room.

Sitting on a pile of blankets, he imagined the corridor where he had walked in on Tulbu and Isdar's argument. With his eyes closed, the dark blur of the back of his eyelids transformed into colours. His ears felt as though he had stuck his head underwater and then suddenly they were clear, and he looked down on the corridor where the two mages stood and argued, as if from the ceiling.

"Just because the Gravedigger comes from Csus," Tulbu snapped, "there's no proof of a connection! And it's irrelevant. The Gravedigger is not magical. He could not have done it!"

"They say that he is not, but he vanished from a blind alley in the Lower West city, with no one to explain how! And the best witnesses have told us that he wears a gold amulet of some kind at his throat, in the shape of an eye..."

"Which means nothing!"

"Circular, gold, nothing? What do we wear beneath our clothes, Tulbu? On our arms? *Circles of gold*. It's the best design for storing large amounts of magical energy, for the sake of the Nameless Gods!"

"So what?" Tulbu sounded defensive.

"That's not all." Isdar's voice lowered and he stepped closer. "I shouldn't know this, but that symbol has been described to the Tacnimag before. To Master Varostan only. By a certain researcher we sent into the North…"

At the word "researcher," Tulbu flinched. His face darkened. "How do you…?"

"Don't worry about that. But I know. I know about the Northern Venture. We rewarded the research mage for all his abstract theories on the so-called 'Spirit Realm' by sending him to find this fabled 'Hill of the Dead' in the North, beyond Koban Fold…he's the same mage supposedly killed by the Gravedigger, am I right? And now the Gravedigger wears this emblem? The very one that is supposed to have come from this Hill of the Dead?"

"Be quiet!" Tulbu's face trembled with fear and rage. "Varostan shared this with me, and me alone! That you know this…can you be trusted?"

"I can be trusted," Isdar said coldly. "But I can't trust you or the Master to think, apparently. The thing that is coming…so soon after the Gravedigger laid the blame at our door… I don't know what's coming, Tulbu, because you won't tell me. But I'll swear it's coming because the Gravedigger arranged it!"

Neva stopped viewing and got to his feet. He considered translocating at once back to Perin, but knew there was a chance that somebody would observe his absence. Instead, he hurried as fast as he could through the Observatory to the Floor Gate room.

Master Varostan stood in the centre of the room, grim-faced.

Neva resisted a shudder as he walked out over the cold metal surface, aware of the drizen deep beneath. The other magi glanced around at him, but Varostan appeared not to have noticed his entry.

"Magi. The Tacnimag is forced to prepare for what may be a dangerous confrontation. I've gathered you all here because you are not suited for battle, but rather to other, nonetheless worthy, arts. All the magi who can fight have been told to withdraw to their rooms and draw energy to conserve, just in case, you understand. Additional adornment devices have been issued to them, and they will store as much magic as possible, the better to defend us, should the need arise.

"You are required for a similar purpose. Recently, this room was used to better our position against a potential foe. All I can tell you is that the enemy is not the Seven Cities. The Claimfold is not at war. But the Floor Gate and the telescopes here are all drained. I need you to draw energy and store it in the telescopes. It is vital that the Observatory is at strength, in case we are needed to perform any great magic. Please, set to it at once."

The magi obeyed Varostan, their faces troubled by the urgency of their task. Neva made his way through until he stood in front of the Master of the City. The man looked old and tired.

"Master, what's wrong?"

Varostan turned to look at him. "Oh, Junior Neva. I wish I could tell you." He looked around the room, and for a moment, Neva could see the fear behind the man's mask of stern calm.

"Master, may I go and help the fighters? I can charge devices for them. There are enough magi here for the telescopes…"

Varostan nodded distractedly. "Go on, Neva. Work hard. The Tacnimag value you." He looked hard at Neva suddenly. "You may not always have felt so, but you have been useful to us. Well done."

"Thank you, Master." Neva bowed and backed off, then turned and ran out of the room. The man's distant kindness surprised him. How could it be that someone could order the deaths of someone at one moment and be warm and human at another?

Neva's feet took him down into the cells. He stayed away from the restricted and secret corridor that led to the drizen enclosure, skirting the dank storeroom that hid the entrance. The torches along his way were lit, for once.

Finally, breathing shallow in the damp air, Neva stopped outside the door of Kesairl's cell.

"Kesairl," he whispered.

There was the noise of the big prigon getting to his feet, and then the tricoloured eyes could just be made out, looking at him through the iron grille.

"How do you know my name, mageling?" The voice rumbled, full of threat.

Neva made himself stand tall. "I am friends with Reger Myrvo, whose real name is Perin, and he told me your name."

Kesairl blinked a few times. "Are you telling me, young human, that you are not my enemy?"

"Yes." Neva felt a swell of pride as he realised that he was really part of a side now, no longer holding a meaningless allegiance for the sake of comfort. "I am a member of the Gravedigger Ring, a friend of Perin, and your ally! My name is Neva Yenesen."

"It is good to meet you as a friend, Neva." Kesairl said solemnly. "Please, take word of me to Perin. Tell him that my love and faith in him have not wavered."

"I'll tell him." Neva bowed. "I'll tell him, and soon, soon we'll come and get you out of here."

Kesairl put a hand to the grille. "Thank you, Neva Yenesen."

Perin listened to Neva's retelling of Tulbu and Isdar's argument. The entire extended Gravedigger Ring were present, including Cama and Lord Adamun.

In the silence afterward, Perin listened for Medrivar, in case the king chose to speak. Medrivar was still considering the information, though, and it was Cama who spoke first.

"It's coming from Csus, they say? I wonder what it is."

"We all wonder that," Gyorva said with a touch of sarcasm. Cama shot the boy a withering look followed by a smile. Of all the Borderers, the librarian liked quick-witted Gyorva the best.

"Are there any myths or legends about Csus?" Perin asked suddenly in response to Medrivar's eventual question.

Cama frowned. "None native to the Claimic people. Csus was a bad omen to our predecessors here, but even they learned to take advantage of the mountain's bounty. It is an especially large mountain, of course, in terms of ground coverage. No one is known to have climbed it. The unknown often generates fear. Of course, it was also one of the last few wild places where packs of raveners hunt. That might be why they feared it so."

"The library has no documents of any stories, myths?"

"No, not now. All the histories of our predecessors were confiscated by the Tacnimag, along with information on the North. Like this Meddoszoru, this Dead Hill. A forbidding sounding place."

Perin considered carefully. The Tacnimag had been conducting research on the Spirit Realm. What that was, he did not know, and Medrivar had yet to tell him. But he knew that Medrivar was a spirit, that all the undead were. They were embodied by the regenerate dust of the ancient people, the "predecessors," as Cama called them. Embodied, even as Perin's own spirit was housed in his living flesh.

So the link between the predecessors and the Meddoszoru was the spirit realm.

"I can find you some documents," Neva said breathlessly. "I'm allowed into the Tacnimag library, as long as I'm accompanied. I'll leave a relevant page on a shelf while I'm in there, leave with my watcher, translocate here. Then I'll look back into the room at the page, and write down what it says."

"That's a fine plan," Adamun said approvingly. He had calmed down a little since Perin had warned him against getting arrested. "We need to know everything we can before this...whatever it is arrives. If the Tacnimag are afeared, then we should make ready."

"Agreed," Perin murmured, "and there's one other thing... Isdar knows enough to destroy me. He's smart. He worked out that Csus and the Gravedigger are linked. He doesn't like me, finds me suspicious as it is. If he finds out that I'm from Csus, that Reger Myrvo is from Csus, the fact that I pretend to come from Arpavale instead of Hanger won't help me."

"You think he'll guess?" Forgos asked in a hushed voice.

Perin nodded. "Yes. It won't be long. I think we need to find out how dangerous this all is. We may have to consider leaving Nagyevo."

A shocked pause filled the room.

Adamun nodded. "That's wise, just in case. I'll draw up some evacuation plans. The lords and the merchants know that the Tacnimag are frightened about something. I should be able to persuade them to prepare for the worst. Just in case."

Perin stood. "Good. I don't think it will come to that. In any case, I'll need to deal with Isdar, and soon."

Alone again, looking out into the night sky, Perin took comfort in the fact that the moon was clear of shadow, although obscured partly by cloud. He entered the throne room.

Are you all right, my King? He bowed at Medrivar's feet, aware of his distractedness.

Medrivar looked down at him and quickly descended from the chair to stand with Perin. *I am better. I am calm. I know that the thing that is coming, it must be of the Damned Dead. Of my enemy.*

Majesty, Perin began seriously, looking directly into Medrivar's blue eyes. *Tell me about what the magi call the Spirit Realm.*

Medrivar sighed. *They are fools. It is just the world seen through better eyes than ours. All beings are Spirit, Perin. There are some spirits that are higher than us, higher than the living, and higher than we spirits that became the undead. The difference between our kinds is that you are in your proper place, while we are invaders.*

Perin swallowed. *The Higher Ones...are they the Nameless Ones? Are they the Gods of Valo?*

Medrivar shrugged. *Maybe. They are the ones that rule the realm below them, that is, this realm. Valo. So yes, they govern Valo, as do the gods you Claimic folk believe in.*

Are they on our side? Perin asked, feeling numbed by all the new information.

Medrivar smiled at this. *What a question that is! Better to ask, are we on theirs? For they have sides, too. Two sides at least, the same as Valo.*

Good and Evil? Perin guessed.

Medrivar frowned. *Yes. In a manner. The Selfless and the Selfish would be another way to see it. More accurately, there are those that serve those higher than themselves, and those that reject all rule but their own.*

Perin sat down on a chair that appeared for his benefit. *Whose rule do they reject?* he asked, staring up at his King.

Medrivar looked troubled for a moment. *They serve and seek power. Those with greater power subjugate the others, but always, they seek for more. Understand that this is a mystery to me, Perin, for I only half sense that these spirits exist and suppose the rest. There is more to know that I do not know.*

Perin sensed that Medrivar evaded the question. He thought back through his memory of his discussions with Medrivar until he found a detail that told him what question to ask.

Medrivar, your Majesty. Who do you serve? Is there a higher king?

Medrivar stared at him. *I serve you and Kesairl, my men, your people, and the* Song of Valo. *Only foolish kings believe that they are the highest of the high. Perhaps there is a Highest One. If there is, I will only serve a servant. If this Highest One exists, I would hope that he—or she—is a singer of songs. Or perhaps there is no one, and all the powers are meant to be in service to one another. I do not know.*

TWENTY-NINE

THE NIGHT OF THE DARK MOON had been followed by Sixthday. It was Firstday when Neva returned from the Observatory with real news. In the preceding time, he had related the increasing fear of the Tacnimag.

By Firstday, the fear had become near panic.

"I think they've been tracking it," Neva explained. His blue eyes were dark with tiredness. "The lower magi have been repowering the telescopes every day. They're all exhausted. The higher magi are restless. They've been gathering energy constantly, but this thing's not here yet."

Perin frowned. Just he and Sudar were in his rooms today. Forgos and Aranyo were helping Lord Adamun organise his evacuation plan. Most of the Gravedigger Ring felt that the measure was wise but unnecessary. Forgos and Aranyo, in particular, looked forward to fighting the emergent foe, not running from it.

Only Neva really believed that evacuation would be necessary. The mutterings of the higher magi seemed to reinforce the belief. Master Varostan's haggard expression over the last few days had not been one of optimism.

"How long?" Perin asked. He had locked the door and was examining his Gravedigger coat for signs of wear. He had already oiled Spade, and the smaller spade that Neva insisted on calling Kisumt. Neva had told Kesairl about Perin's rather literal naming of the larger weapon. The prigon had found it very amusing and had made a joke of his own, giving Neva the name for the shorter spade, from a Priga word meaning *little*.

Neva considered Perin's question. He knew the answer, but giving it would add tremendous urgency to their situation. He hoped they had enough time. "I believe it will arrive this afternoon. Maybe this evening. No earlier. I hope."

Perin started, and Sudar rose from his chair, astonished. "How do you know?" Perin asked.

Sudar shook his head. "From Csus to here in less than three days?"

"That's fast," Perin agreed, his scowl darkening. "Very fast. Kesairl and I took nearly four days at a fast walking pace, and that was from the border of Helynvale, a day closer than Csus. Whatever this terrible thing is, it can run fast."

"Or doesn't get tired," Sudar said ominously.

Neva watched the two of them, waiting for an opportunity to answer Perin's earlier question. "I don't know for sure. But Master Varostan ordered the higher magi to join him on the plain below the South Gate, no later than midday. I think that means noon is the earliest the Tacnimag are expecting it."

"And if I were them, I'd give myself some hours to spare." Perin looked around at Sudar. "Can you get the Ring together, Sudar? Everyone, all of us."

Sudar nodded. "I'll go and find Gyorva, get him to help me. Where do you want us?"

Perin paused. It was a big decision to make. Normally, he felt that Medrivar would have urged caution at this point, but the king seemed to be in favour of action.

"Tell everyone to meet here at noon. By then, I hope to know what we're up against. And what we need to do. Tell them to bring their weapons and any equipment they might need if the evacuation is necessary."

Sudar saluted. "Perin, I'll get it done. I'll see you at noon." He nodded to Neva and left. Perin watched him go.

"You're very close to Sudar, aren't you?" Neva asked, sitting down. There was the slightest hint of jealousy in his voice, but it was outweighed by admiration.

Perin smiled. "I forget how much I rely on him. He's been my best friend, besides you, since I joined the Borderers. He's completely reliable. You're reliable," he added, grinning. "Don't make our friendship a competition. And I need to ask your help now."

"I'll give it!" Neva declared, his face reddening slightly.

"I need you to look ahead at the landscape that this enemy will be travelling through to get here."

"I haven't seen it," Neva said, his cheer falling.

Perin held up a hand. "I have. I've patrolled enough of the Nagyevan area for both of us. I've seen as far east as the border of Mezyro. And if the Tacnimag expect him by this afternoon, he must have passed that point."

Neva shook his head. "But it's still no good. You're not a telepath. You can't put the image out of your head into mine."

"That's what I'm wondering." Perin opened his desk drawer and brought out his amulet. The benevolent eye sat in the palm of his hand. "This acts as a strengthening kind of communication between two minds. It was necessary once for bringing me together with another friend, who you haven't met. But I think that if I wear this, I'll be able to give you my pictures."

Neva looked doubtful, his brows dipping, his eyes narrowed.

Perin put the emblem on, messing up his black hair. "Try it," Perin suggested, tapping the gold circle.

Neva shrugged and reached out, touching the metal and opening his mind for the images he didn't expect to come.

They came in a series of vivid flashes, imprinting each location in his head with such strength that he doubted he'd ever be able to forget them. Neva backed away, startled.

"That's not your mind!"

Perin looked as surprised as Neva for a moment, then nodded. "You're right. Sorry. Neva, meet Medrivar." Perin's calm tone reassured the young mage, and he reached out, frowning, to touch the benevolent eye again. This time, he heard Medrivar's voice. For a few minutes, he said nothing before slowly breaking contact.

"You're sharing your body with the spirit of an undead king?"

Perin smiled awkwardly. "That's basically right."

"Whoa." Neva's eyes were wide. "Whoa. That's... excellent."

Perin heard Medrivar approve the sentiment and laughed. "Good! So, can you have a look along that route for me? For us?"

"Yes," Neva said softly, his eyes still wide. "Are you going to tell the others? About King Medrivar?"

Perin nodded. "When I can."

"Yeah. You'd need to pick your time, all right. Whoa, it's still...unpacking itself, everything he sent to me. I'm going to have a headache later, I know it." Neva grinned and closed his eyes. "Right. Let's look as far out as I can and then come closer to home..."

For a while, he made no sound and did not move.

Suddenly, Neva's body convulsed. He let out a strangled cry and fell like a dropped brick, bouncing off the edge of a chair and hitting the floor hard. Perin rushed to help him up, but the boy was already scrambling to his feet. He grabbed Perin and held him against himself, shaking, his head pressed into his friend's shoulder.

"Oh, Gods...oh, Gods...oh, Merciful Nameless..."

"What is it?" Perin asked, horrified. Slowly, Neva let go of Perin. He seemed so shaken and childlike that Perin reached out and took his hand, not wanting to deprive him of contact. "What *is* it? What did you see?"

Neva shuddered. "I don't know how to tell you. But I don't think the Tacnimag can stop him. Perin, I don't think anyone can stop him!"

Perin was subdued but determined. Neva had largely recovered, although he kept silent, focusing on his own tasks. Perin had sent him to find Investigator Isdar and bring him to his office room shortly after midday.

In the meantime, Neva bluffed his way into the Tacnimag armoury and took possession of Kesairl's confiscated arm bands and bracelets. Nobody challenged him. Most of the adornments and devices had been cleared out already to add to the reserves of the fighting magi. It was assumed that Neva had plans to take them to a mage who would use them.

Neva risked stealing several more articles before he went to look for Isdar, choosing adornments that had been tooled by the prigon people in the days of the tribute. He felt that Kesairl would appreciate his choices.

Perin met with the Gravedigger Ring very briefly. He informed them that they were going ahead with the evacuation, beginning the moment of the enemy's arrival. Lord Adamun left at once to organise the nobles and merchants, those chosen to manage the vast numbers of people.

The sobering truth was that, regardless of what might happen, many people would choose to stay. Many more would be unable to leave, especially the very old and very sick.

Perin sent Forgos to assist with the leadership that would be necessary in the trade district. Aranyo had already volunteered to rouse the inhabitants of the Lower West city when the time came. Gyorva was given the responsibility of the North Way out of the city. As many people as possible were supposed to leave through the North and East Gates.

Sudar and Perin sat behind Perin's desk, awaiting the Tacnimag Investigator.

Isdar entered briskly but did not take the chair offered him.

"I have little time, Captain. I was told this was important."

Perin stood, and Sudar went to close the door. "It is important," Perin said seriously. He nodded to Sudar. "Better lock it as well. Can't have someone walking in."

Isdar frowned. "You have news?"

"Yes." Perin smiled faintly. "It's in my power to tell you who the Gravedigger is."

Isdar gaped. "You have him? It is urgent that I see him—the time has *never* been more urgent!" He grasped the edge of the desk, leaning toward Perin in his eagerness.

"You will see him," Perin promised. "Very soon. First though, I want you to know how I achieved this."

Isdar frowned. He was plainly in a hurry. Yet, Perin could tell that the mage truly wanted to know how Captain Reger Myrvo had done it.

"Tell me."

"I will show you." Perin nodded to Sudar again. This time, his friend went through into Perin's bedroom, returning with Perin's coat and hat. He placed them on the desk. Perin himself retrieved his spades from behind his wardrobe.

Isdar observed the items with curiosity. "Are these his? Or replicas?"

"These are mine," Perin said, with a shrug.

Isdar nodded. "So, you had these made to inspire your thought process. Is that all there was to it?"

"Far more." Perin hid a grin. "There are hunters that wear the skin of their prey, I have heard. I wanted to put myself in the Gravedigger's shoes. Think like he thinks. Be the Gravedigger, as much as possible."

Isdar frowned sceptically. "And this worked? You were able to track him down simply by wearing the clothes?"

Perin donned his coat. Sudar passed him his hat and Perin set it on his head, tipping it down a bit over his face. "His clothes, his weapons, yes." Perin picked up Spade and looked down its length. He placed it in its harness and chose Kisumt, moving it from hand to hand.

"You look very convincing," Isdar complimented coldly, impatient once more. "But I really must insist that you show him to me."

"Isdar," Perin started, coming to stand in front of the mage, "tell me please why the Tacnimag are gathering on the plain beyond the South Gate."

Isdar paled. "There is an enemy approaching," he admitted. "He…it…is linked with the Gravedigger. I cannot fight the one that is coming, but if I can destroy it by killing the Gravedigger, then that is something I can do."

Perin nodded, wondering what Isdar meant. "Very well. I will give you a brief opportunity to kill the Gravedigger. Here he is."

Perin took two steps back, lifted the spade above his head in a stance that came to him through hundreds of years of Medrivar's memory. The undead king had last used the stance with an axe. The head of the spade reminded him of the curve of the axeblade. Raised, ready to fall.

Isdar frowned in incomprehension. "What are you doing?" Isdar showed fear now. "He's here?"

"He stands in front of you." Sudar said calmly. "Perin is giving you a chance to defend yourself."

Realisation struck Isdar, and he stumbled backwards as Perin came at him. The spade smashed through the seat of the chair Isdar had refused and came up again as the mage rolled away. He drew a dagger and raised a palm.

The world seemed to shimmer. Perin frowned, realising that the subtle mage was attacking his senses.

Sudar staggered forward against the desk, completely off balance.

Isdar's true target stood, seemingly unaffected. Isdar stared. "How!? Are you a mage after all?" he asked shrilly, out of options. He held the dagger out toward Perin as if he could match it against the spade.

"No," Perin answered and took the question away from Isdar in a sudden swing. The mage dropped, confusion mixing with pain and shock. Then nothing.

Perin sighed, resettled his weapon at his side, beneath the fold of his coat.

Sudar rose groggily, steadying himself on his friend's shoulder. "I hate magic. So unfair."

Perin smiled mirthlessly. "He's done now, at least. Come on. I need you to wait for me in the Observatory square. I'm off to see what's causing all this fuss." His light tone belied the fear that was steadily rising.

"I've readied your travelling equipment." Sudar followed Perin to the door. "In your bedroom. I'll take it with me. You go on."

"Thank you." Perin considered another fear for a moment, his hazel eyes dark with it. It might well be the last time he talked with Sudar. "You're a fine friend, Sudar. I hope we're never parted." He bowed slightly, awkward with emotion, then left, the coat sweeping around him as the door closed.

Fetching Perin's travel pack, Sudar left the building for the final time.

Perin walked through the street in daylight. The bustle of the market fell under a hush as he passed. A City Guard approached, but Perin doffed his hat without slowing, showing the man his face and lifting the seal of his office for good measure. Bemused, but assuming that Captain Reger played out some strategy, the guard withdrew with a salute. The action caused a hubbub of conversation to rise. Nobody called for his arrest.

Neva met Perin outside Perin's old quarters.

Cama was there, his life packed onto the back of a small donkey-drawn cart. He gave Perin a brave smile. "Strange to see you dressed like that. It suits you, somehow."

"It's good to see you, Cama. You're ready?"

"Yes." Cama's face darkened with irritation for a moment. "The neighbours think I'm mad, of course. But I'll make sure to get ahead of the rush. Don't know what is coming any more than what you've told me, but I trust your judgement." The old librarian looked up at the blue sky. A few clouds wreathed the skyline above the nearby buildings, but the air was fine and warm.

"Seems a strange day for Nagyevo's doom to fall. I would have written in a storm, but it seems the Nameless Ones are not as poetic as me." He grinned. "I hope to see you again, Perin. If I do not, then may all the blessings in Valo follow you. It has been my privilege." He bowed low.

Perin returned the bow, then stepped forward and embraced his former teacher. "You've been too good a friend, Cama. Be well. Go soon."

The older man nodded. "I will. Who knows? I might be able to turn around and come back in a small time. The City may prevail."

"Yes."

Neva's face was set. His opinion was different.

The two boys watched Cama go. "How much time do we have?" Perin asked, as if he were discussing the closing time of a taverna.

Neva winced. "I hate to think on it. Not long. But I'll translocate us onto the south walltop first to get a good look."

"Can you manage two double translocations?" Perin asked, wary for his friend's safety.

Neva nodded. "Three, actually, assuming you want us to translocate back again as well. But I'll be fine." He tugged down the high neck of his robe, revealing one of Kesairl's armbands, which he was wearing as a sort of torc. His forearms held Kigzusta and Kigkarmzin, and above them, on his upper arms, were other charged adornments.

"Well done," Perin laughed. "I'm ready then, if you are."

Neva nodded, took a deep breath and embraced Perin tightly. For a moment, the younger boy's brow furrowed with thought, and then they vanished, the telemage and the Gravedigger, in a rush of air.

Their appearance on the walltop gave two patrolling City Guards a shock. Perin quickly revealed his face and Captaincy badge to prevent them from attacking. The sun, just beginning its long journey westward, lit the whole plain below.

Perin gave the two guards orders, hoping that Forgos and Lord Adamun had been able to integrate the City Guard properly into the evacuation plan. Again, he hoped that the measure would not be necessary.

With a shock, he realised that his order to evacuate would mean the death of Nagyevo. If the city remained abandoned, the Seven Cities would not hesitate in making war to occupy it. The Claimfold would have suffered a great blow, and all at his doing. The responsibility made him choke, and he had to lean on the battlements for a moment under the weight of it.

Neva put a hand on his shoulder. "Are you all right, Perin?"

"I hope so." Perin shuddered. He stood upright, slowly, listening to Medrivar's comforting encouragement. In the Erdhanger graveyard, he had never thought to one day possess so much power.

Out on the plain, the Tacnimag fighters were gathered in a loose crescent, their little shapes suddenly lost in the shade. In the East, a dark cloud spread. It was not large, but it was more intensely black than any cloud

Perin had before seen. It moved westward like the head of a crow, tendrils of shadow making it ragged, the land darkened beneath it. A shadow fell across Perin's face.

The face of Nagyevo fell under gloom, too. Cries of surprise and horror echoed up from the city's streets. Perin felt his heart sharply judder in his chest as his gaze lifted upward.

The sun was going out.

THIRTY

THE SUN SLIPPED BEHIND a black disc, diminished, flame fighting darkness, only the bare edges still glaring. Perin blinked furiously, turning his gaze away from the terrifying sight.

The air hummed with thick electricity, as if the brown gloom that covered the city was alive. The dark cloud on the plain narrowed even as it approached, refining into a spearpoint, a black beak, solidifying and reforming. The Tacnimag fighters stood at the ready, and Neva wondered who it was that stood foremost, closest to the figure that was slowing, steadily treading closer to the magi, its banner of darkness dispersing.

A figure no larger than the Tacnimag fighters.

"Get us onto the plain. We can't see from here," Perin said urgently, despite his strong reluctance to get closer to the mystery enemy.

Neva, shuddering even as he prepared to translocate, took hold of Perin once more.

Partly because of Neva's fear, their landing came closer to the Tacnimag fighters than Perin would have liked. However, the nearest magi made no aggressive move toward the pair. All their attention was focused on the man that now stood a stone's throw away.

The air trembled about his figure as if from a heat haze. The incredible stillness with which he held his body was alarming. Tattered robes hung, stained and rotted beyond recognition.

The man was bald. Crimson tattoos traced across his pallid neck and up across his skull. Perin and Medrivar felt the shock together, and Perin stumbled.

Neva, shivering violently like a man with fever, reached out a shaky arm to support his friend, frightened by the horror in Perin's face.

Tulbu was the mage standing most forward. With a deep breath, reminding himself of his position as most powerful in the Tacnimag, he stood his ground. "It is you, then."

The figure stared at Tulbu with blank eyes. Then the blue lips parted slowly in a gaping smile. The head tilted back and it laughed. The man's throat was ragged, where once it had felt the bite of a spade.

Cold sweat ran down Perin's spine. "It's Keresur," Perin gasped. "The mage I killed! He's alive!"

No, Medrivar uttered. *Not alive.*

"Who?" the figure asked. His mocking voice was raw, a raspy exhalation. "Who do you think that I am?"

Tulbu did not reply. The mage took a deep breath and gathered energy at his fingertips. The heat soared around him as he bent the world to his will, sweat standing out on his brow. With a roar, the air filled with fire.

His target stopped laughing. The fire engulfed the dead mage, but Perin could see the figure walking forward, despite the blaze. As the flames went out, a cold, tattooed arm reached out and took Tulbu by the throat.

The moment the pale fingers touched Tulbu's skin, all light left the mage's eyes. His body fell limp at the feet of the dead man.

"You do not know who I am." The imperious voice cracked, issuing from between the blue lips and from between the livid, torn edges of the throat. "Small spirits, all. You are unfit to face me. I am *Akrash Haal! I am the One and the Many!*"

For a moment, the black cloud from before seemed to coalesce in the air above Akrash Haal, flickering, fading. To Perin, the shifting mass seemed to suggest the twisting and contorting of many limbs.

Fire and shockwaves showered on the dead man from the circling magi. The corpse dismissed each attack with a shrug, lip curling contemptuously as he strode from mage to mage. His touch dropped them like leaves. The screaming began when the fighters realised nothing they were doing was working. It grew, hysterical and barely human, as Tulbu got to his feet again.

Even from where he stood, Perin could see that Tulbu's eyes were dead. One of the fighters that the Dead Mage ignored backed into him. The man spun, shrieking as he stared into the face of his former colleague. Tulbu's hands reached up, seizing, choking, crushing.

The poor man coughed blood onto Tulbu's dead face.

One by one, the killed magi rose. The flickering cloud formed a maelstrom above their animate corpses. Spirits whirled in the air, vying for position, for the next empty body. Vessels for Akrash Haal, the Dead Mage, and his passengers.

The tattooed figure stopped, ignoring the remaining Tacnimag fighters as they struggled desperately with the bodies of former friends at his feet. He raised a hand and pointed straight at Perin.

"I remember *you*. This body remembers *you*." The words came as if forced from his lungs, the rough, gasping inverse of a shout. He began to step closer, his gathering entourage of fresh cadavers leaving the destroyed forms of their opponents to tread in his wake.

"I am the Gravedigger," Perin confirmed, mind reeling. Medrivar was shouting for him to withdraw, and Neva clung to his arm.

"I am Haal," the dead mage responded. He bowed to Perin. "I am come from beneath the mountain. I am come to take my throne."

Medrivar's shouts fell silent. Stark, silent fear reigned.

Get. Away. From. Here!

With a great effort, Neva pulled himself upright, surrounded Perin with his arms, and translocated.

The city had never seen such a day. Families hurried through rioting streets, dragging belongings in tied blankets. Shops sat empty, doors broken. The looting had begun as soon as the evacuation became official. The City Guard were not numerous enough to do anything more than guide the flow of people toward the North and East gates.

The shouts and screams of people caught in the rioting were joined by screeching and wailing as the South Gate splintered. Tulbu's corpse swayed in the breach, his hand still extended from the shockwave he had cast. His head hung to one side, blank eyes watching the panic, the hundreds of people running for their lives.

The crying of the refugees was silent in his ears.

At the door of the Observatory, Sudar watched in bitter helplessness as the river of people coming up the South Way became a panicked torrent. Shouting guards guided the rush towards the East Way and away from the Observatory square. Fires were burning in the Lower West city, and the smoke drifted dark against the false twilight. The body of a woman lay trampled not ten yards away.

Sudar could tell she would never move again.

Aranyo, bruised and bleeding from his lip, pushed through the mob as best he could. He halted beside Sudar, gasping for breath. "It's all wrong," he said when he could force the words out. His eyes were red. "All wrong. They're killing each other."

Sudar bit his lip. Drizen were easier to take than this. He put a hand out to comfort Aranyo, but at that moment, Perin and Neva appeared by the body of the trampled woman. Neva stumbled unsteadily forward before reclaiming his balance. The boy looked older to Sudar, his expression serious and focused. Neva took a deep breath and joined Perin in checking to see if the woman was alive.

"She's dead," Perin said, his voice hollow. For a moment he stared in a kind of horror at nothing, then he turned to Sudar. "We should cut off her head."

"What?" Sudar and Aranyo were united in their shock. Neva shook his head.

"The enemy is an undead. He has an army of spirits with him, and any whole body is another soldier." Perin let this sink in.

Sudar stepped forward, dark eyes wide. "If people see you cut the head off an innocent…"

"Leave her." Neva broke in. He had stepped to stand in front of the Observatory door, now free of the incriminating drizen head. "What difference will it make? He's going to have an army of thousands." With a great effort, he raised his arms above his head. The blue sleeves of his robes fell down his arms, revealing Kigzusta and Kigkarmzin, the silver and red serpents glinting oddly in the half-light.

The Observatory door began to raise into the alcove in the arch. Gritting his teeth, Neva forced himself to continue until the mechanism locked in place. He doubled up, letting out a gasp, as if he'd been physically lifting the door. "Shite…that's the last of my stored energy in Kigzusta and Kigkarmzin…"

"Are you all right?" Perin asked.

Neva nodded, straightening up. "Yeah. I still have Kesairl's arm rings. Let's go in and get him."

"We need to wait for Forgos," Aranyo interrupted, looking at the dark slope of the Observatory entry hall with trepidation.

Perin paused, caught between two loyalties.

"I'll wait for him." Sudar solved the issue. "Aranyo, go with Perin." The look on Sudar's serious features challenged anyone to disagree.

Perin nodded gratefully. "Thanks Sudar. See you in a minute." He drew his spade and led the way into the echoing shadows of the Observatory. Neva followed at his shoulder, with Aranyo hurrying behind, a dagger drawn and held ready.

Sudar turned his gaze back onto the chaos of the city.

Perin followed Neva as the young telemage confidently led them through the labyrinthine lower chambers of the Observatory. A few guards passed them, but were beyond fighting. The Tacnimag were broken and destroyed. The Observatory had become a memorial. Soon it would be a mausoleum.

When they reached the cells, a lone guard saw Perin coming and came at him with his sword raised. Having little choice, Perin readied himself to counterattack, gripping his spade firmly.

But before Perin could strike, the guard flew backward and crashed against the nearest unoccupied cell, buckling the iron-banded door. Perin looked with astonishment at Neva, who brushed by, snatching up the dropped ring of keys.

"I didn't know he could do that," Aranyo said, with a certain amount of admiration. He put his dagger away. "I won't need this with you two here." He grinned, despite everything.

Perin's heart pounded as Neva led them to a cell at the end of the dank, echoing corridor. The old torch on the wall guttered and cast shadows that danced infernally across the stonework. It had taken the crushing of the Tacnimag and the loss of Nagyevo, but Perin would finally see Kesairl again.

Neva said nothing as he turned the key and the door swung open. Now, he stepped back and bowed low, removing the arm ring that he had been wearing around his neck. He offered the device and its twin to Kesairl with outstretched arms.

Kesairl bowed his way through the door and stood tall, his horns brushing the roof of the corridor. He was magnificent in the torchlight, his tricoloured eyes shining brightly, though he was thinner than when Perin had last seen him. His blue and red canvas coat was filthy, but Perin could see him in his mind's eye, as the prigon had been when they had first met in Graves's graveyard.

"Kesairl!" Perin nearly ran forward to embrace his friend. The presence of Aranyo and Neva hindered him, and then he felt ashamed that he had not done so. Kesairl's eyes sparkled as he made a short bow.

"The Gravedigger, I believe? I am honoured." He smiled.

Perin laughed, stepping forward, his own eyes bright with unshed tears. "I promised I would rescue you."

"I will always trust your promises, Perin," Kesairl rumbled solemnly. Perin did embrace him then, dwarfed by the prigon's great figure.

Neva stood aside, still holding the skirmisher's adornments. When Kesairl and Perin broke their hug, he coughed.

"Ah, thank you, Neva." Kesairl took the golden circles back and replaced them on his arms, a smile spreading. "Do you have the bracelets as well?"

"I'm wearing them on my arms," Neva confirmed.

"Keep them for me, for now. I can see you've used a lot of magic to get this far."

"Neva"s been brilliant," Perin said, still emotional from his reunion with his first best-friend.

Neva coloured at the praise, looking down at his feet.

Aranyo had said nothing the whole time, staring up at Kesairl in amazement and a little fear.

"Well?" Kesairl put his great hands on his hips and stood forward, eclipsing the torch. "Haven't you ever seen a prigon before?"

Aranyo didn't seem to understand why this made Perin laugh.

A scream echoed from far along the corridor. Neva, as startled as the rest, knew from experience that the sound probably had come from above. Noises often filtered down from the corridors around the Floor Gate room.

"We have to go," Perin said, turning and taking the lead. "The mage I killed in Erdhanger is back with an army of evil spirits. The city is emptying."

"Nobody tells me anything," Kesairl said, winking at Neva, his freedom filling him with an inappropriate euphoria.

The group followed Neva back up the long stairway.

"The Tacnimag are all dead. Undead by now," Perin said, his words sobering Kesairl's mood. Another scream resounded, louder than before.

"This is a bad day for Valo." The prigon clenched his hands into fists.

Perin put a hand up and patted his friend's arm. "Medrivar says that you don't know the half of it."

The group turned into a wider, curving corridor with a high ceiling. Torches banished the darkness and the walls were well painted and clean.

"He will have to tell me the greater half, then," Kesairl spoke darkly as the group came to a sudden halt. Three Observatory Guards were approaching, their armoured shapes making shadows on the pale walls. Perin felt a chill run through him as Medrivar focused his gaze on the silent guards.

The men began to run toward them as one, lifting their swords. It was only when they were paces away that their blank stares marked them for what they were. A rush of air made the brim of Perin's hat lift, and the three figures were hurled backward by the motion of an invisible barrier. Kesairl lowered his arms, although his hands stayed crooked in the casting position.

"That shockwave would have knocked out a living man," he rumbled ominously. The dead guards were climbing to their feet. One had a broken jaw from the impact. It hung loose, low and twisted, and a long hiss of anger pushed out of him as he rose.

"Shite, shite, shite, shite!" Aranyo swore, backing away, holding his dagger like a charm.

Kesairl readied himself for another attack. His brow set in concentration. Perin wondered if he was out of practice after so long in prison.

Once again Neva interrupted the fight.

His eyes wide with fear, but with his mouth set in determination, the young mage stepped in front of Perin and threw a pebble into the air. It hung there for a moment, spinning faster and faster; and then at a twitch of the boy's hand, it blasted a hole in the forehead of the guard with the broken jaw. The back of the corpse's skull exploded in a violent mess, and the body went still.

"Shite!" Aranyo squeaked, nearly dropping his dagger.

Perin swallowed his shock, noticing that even Neva was swayed by what he had done. Kesairl murmured an approving word. There were still two carcasses to face, and they were animated and angry.

Kesairl clapped his hands together. Heat gathered between his palms as he concentrated on the task. The two remaining corpses approached again, this time with caution, their swords held in appropriate readiness.

A longsword thrust suddenly through the torso of the first, twisting and withdrawing before taking off the head in a single sweep. As the body fell, it revealed Forgos, who kicked the bloody thing away, raising his sword in salute. He and Sudar had come around the corner in a silent but devastating charge. Sudar's two shortswords flashed in the torchlight, painting the white walls ruddy as he left his target headless in two quick movements.

"Perin! Sorry we're late!" Forgos grinned, his teeth white in contrast with the blood the tall boy seemed to be bathed in. Clearly, the two had been through slaughter.

"Speak for yourself. I was waiting for *you*," Sudar muttered, putting his swords into the scabbards at his hips, leaving a few inches of the steel free.

Kesairl let the heat he had gathered dissipate. "Saves me the energy," he conceded, a little disappointed. "Your friends are more impressive than I thought."

"Yeah, well, Neva was underselling us." Forgos winked. "Perin, we need to get going. The big one with the tattoos is in the building." Perin began to run at once, taking Forgos at his word.

"Neva! Show us to the Floor Gate!" The telemage caught up, nearly slipping in his handiwork. The pebble gleamed wetly against the wall, a long way down the corridor.

"Who killed the other one?" Forgos asked, as Perin and Neva passed him. Neva wordlessly raised a hand, pointing with his other at an opening coming up on their right.

Forgos looked impressed. "Remind me not to make you angry." They slowed up in a hurry, as the great vaulted space of the Floor Gate room came into view.

The room was accessed by the ceiling-high gap in the circling wall, both before them and opposite. The Floor Gate gleamed, the circles of metal resonating with stored energy. Aranyo looked around the wide, circular space, marvelling at the gold of the telescopes and the brightness of the mirrors at their bases. There was little light coming through the glass dome of the Observatory roof.

As they stepped forward into the clear space, their footfalls ringing on the Floor Gate, figures stepped into view, filling the gap facing them. The corridors of the Observatory were full of the dead.

They were not all guards. Many were ordinary men and women, most bearing the marks of trampling or the bruises of strangleholds. Their silence and their staring were worse than a war cry. The motionless crowd stirred into action, parting like a curtain.

The mirrors reflected the frightened, determined expressions of the Gravedigger Ring as Akrash Haal took his place, his head lowered, predatory. The blank eyes fixed on Perin.

"You. *Gravedigger!*" He stretched out a long arm. His teeth bared suddenly in a rictus grin. Kesairl clapped his hands together and took a step forward. Terrified, and with good reason, Perin looked to Neva. The young mage's eyes were closed tight and he was muttering to himself.

A beam of tight fire lanced through the air and struck Haal in his chest. The body actually stumbled, and Perin felt a leaping of hope. But the flesh did not burn as it should have done. No neat hole was made in Akrash Haal's chest. Only the ragged robes smoked under the touch of Kesairl's Narrow Fire.

Snarling, the Dead Mage raised a twisted hand and gripped it into a fist. The air in the high room began to howl and the glass of the ceiling shivered, then shattered, rushing skyward in a blast of chilly air. The mirrors cracked in their frames. The telescopes began to shriek as forces gripped and stretched them beyond the boundaries of their endurance.

The Floor Gate hummed under the strain. Kesairl, his own eyes tightly closed, stood with his legs apart, his arms stretched out as he forced a dome of protection around the small group. His teeth were bared with the effort and his long growl competed with the howling wind as he tried to take the strain.

Neva, his robes whipped around him by the increasing wind, also stood in a wide stance, his own hands spread and lifted. His muttering had become shouting, and his blue eyes snapped open and stared at Haal as the Floor Gate's humming became a shrill song.

"See you later, carrion!"

There was a tremendous rush of air and the Floor Gate suddenly emptied. The Dead Mage rushed forward, his torn throat flapping in the howling gale. The shriek of anger that rose nearly covered the crashing as the Floor Gate gave in, collapsing into a destruction of Akrash Haal's own making.

THIRTY-ONE

LIGHT DANCED AGAIN over the sweep of the hills. The sky shone clear. The black disc over the sun had passed, and the grass rippled green on the west-facing slope. The wind was the first thing Perin noticed as his feet met the ground. The relief of escaping Akrash Haal put him in an odd state of calm, even as he tumbled down the incline, colliding with Forgos, who had managed to keep his balance on landing.

Forgos helped him up. Aranyo and Sudar were getting to their feet, looking around warily. Kesairl stared up at the sky in astonished joy, his black hair whipping about his face. It had grown long in his imprisonment. His filthy canvas flapped about him until he shrugged it off violently and cast it away down the hill.

"Now I really feel free." He turned and helped Neva to his feet.

The young telemage was dazed. "We're safe? I got us here?"

"You did. We are safe, for now. Well done, Neva." Kesairl gripped the boy's shoulder. "Perin? Where is this?"

Perin replaced his hat on his head. "Medrivar sent Neva several images of our journey into Nagyevo. I think… yes, Medrivar thinks we're not far from the Helynvale-Csus border."

Kesairl nodded, returning his gaze to the higher hillside. Forgos and Sudar exchanged glances. Perin pulled his hat off and ran a hand through his black hair. He smiled nervously.

"Who's Medrivar?" Sudar asked, brushing grass from his breeches.

Perin paused, wondering how to explain it. Medrivar went unhelpfully silent.

Neva coughed. "Medrivar's a disembodied, undead king. That dead mage destroyed his body, so now he's just pure magic and consciousness and he's sharing with Perin. He's on our side."

Perin stared at Neva.

"Just trying to save us time." Neva grinned. "I think we're fine for now, but this *Haal* thing really seems to have it in for Perin. So we should probably make a plan and move on it, don't you think?"

"The mage is right," Forgos said reluctantly, staring at Perin. "We're lucky. The evacuation in the summer, rather than the winter. Hopefully, Gyorva got a lot of people out through the North Gate. The harvests of Joval will have to stretch to serve a lot of people."

"So...Medrivar shares your body?" Sudar looked intrigued.

Perin smiled weakly. "Not quite. He's in a throne room in my mind. He just...gives me help when I need it."

Sudar shrugged. "Fair enough. Majesty." He said seriously, dipping his head in Perin's direction. Medrivar's laugh and returning comment were silent to all but Perin.

"He greets you back," Perin said. "Commends your valour and your skill."

"I'm honoured," Sudar replied.

Forgos looked very uncomfortable with the exchange. "Can we get to it, Your Highness?" he added cautiously. Perin laughed along with Medrivar this time.

"Medrivar's going to sit back and watch. If you're always talking to both of us, it will get confusing. He wants you to concentrate on me. Apparently, I'm your leader."

"Well, no one else is," Neva said.

Perin smiled. "All right, then. We can't camp here. We don't have any supplies. We've only got our clothes and our weapons, so...so I think we should make for Csus."

"Not Helynvale?" Kesairl looked hopeful.

Perin paused to consider. "From prigon or Claimfolder, we will need help. If we make for the Claim of Varo, we'll pass the southern meeting stone. If there's a torzsa in the territory, we might be able to make contact with both."

Kesairl nodded in agreement. He thought for a moment, looking up at the sky. "If my thoughts are well gathered, I believe my own torzsa will be moving through the south border territories. It was difficult to watch the passing months from my cell, but this should be Abrun's time here. Abrun will help you, once they know what we know."

"Even with their disliking of Medrivar?" Perin wondered.

Kesairl seemed unsure.

"Sounds like it's still worth a try," Aranyo said, speaking for the first time. He peered up at Kesairl in open admiration. "I'm looking forward to meeting your family, Kesairl, sir."

Kesairl smiled. "You're courteous, fair-hair. I think I should learn all your names now. It would seem appropriate."

Perin grinned. "Sorry, my manners are terrible. Cama always said so. This is Forgos, Sudar, and Aranyo. They've all killed drizen. Good fighters. Your clan will like them."

"They will." Kesairl rumbled. "Killing drizen...they are men worthy of renown at the Torzsanag. We have not had men such as these in our ranks for a long time."

Forgos nodded. The praise was only correct in his view. Aranyo flushed with pride.

Sudar's dark eyes watched Perin closely. "When do we march, Gravedigger?"

Perin turned to his friend, surprised. Sudar stood to attention. Kesairl looked impressed.

"Yes, perhaps we should proceed as those who are at war. Gravedigger!" He bowed to Perin, as he had playfully done on his release, but now he was serious. "We are at your command."

Perin fought his natural reaction, receiving unexpected help from the king. Medrivar clearly favoured military discipline, as well.

"Very well. Kesairl, you're my second. Everyone, if I'm not available, he's in charge." There were nods of assent. "Let's march...yes. East. With me, Bright Ones!" The name slipped out at the last. Nobody questioned it as they began their march. Medrivar had added his influence at the end, enthused.

Bright Ones. That's what you call your men, am I right? Perin's silent question fell into the quiet of the throne room.

Medrivar's response, slow in coming, was quite emotional. *Yes. My brothers. My sons. Perin, we will have to go to them. I don't know how much time they have.*

Perin frowned, walking under the weight of Medrivar's dream. He remembered the troubling vision, the images of the Meddoszoru. The agony of Medrivar's Bright Dead.

Medrivar, Majesty... What are we fighting? What is Haal?

There was no immediate reply. Perin could feel Medrivar's uncertainty, his fear, darkening his excitement and pride.

Medrivar, my King. This...this is about far more than Nagyevo isn't it?

Medrivar's voice sounded weary. *It's called the* Song of Valo *for a reason.*

What is it? Perin was surprised he'd never asked the question before. *What is the* Song of Valo? *What does it mean?*

With his eyes half-closed as he marched, Perin could just see the king sitting on his simple throne, head downturned in brooding thought. *I can only guess, but it seems surer to me every day now. It's a call to arms. It's a warning.*

The meeting stone appeared the same as it had those many months ago. It stood against the darkening sky, not quite suitable for shelter. Thankfully, the summer evening was mild, and even the wind across the hills had lessened with nightfall. High clouds were drifting in across the dark blue heavens.

There was already a campfire lit at the base of the stone.

Kesairl and Perin exchanged a glance. "Not prigon," they said together. A prigon camp would typically be marked by blazing kotuzska in a shallow bowl of water. Wood was scarce on the marches of Helynvale.

They approached with caution, hands close to their weapons. Kesairl fell in behind Forgos and Sudar, so that he would have time to gather energy if they were ambushed.

There was no ambush. The sentry was asleep. He was a young man with a mess of dark hair and unconvincing stubble. In the firelight, they could see that his nose was slightly crooked. Perin gaped in surprise.

"Erdhanger's carpenter's apprentice?" He reached out impulsively and shook the boy's shoulder. The boy jumped up with a start, reaching for the modified hoe that Perin had thought was a spear. Then he saw Perin's close silhouette against the fire. He gasped, pointing at the shape of the broad-brimmed hat and the long coat.

"You're the…!"

"He's the Gravedigger," Forgos said, drawing his longsword. "Who are you?"

"He's Veso. Apprenticed to Selhamos the carpenter in Erdhanger. My home village," Perin explained, taking off his hat.

Veso's astonishment doubled. "You're…! It's true!" Excitement had taken the young man over, although the sight of Kesairl renewed his fear.

"What's true?" Perin asked, pushing Forgos's sword blade away gently. Veso smiled broadly, despite his nerves.

"Mistress Hoer started saying it was you ever since them news runners came through, saying about the Gravedigger. We thought she was crazy, but there was folk in Erdhanger looking for Graves's apprentice afore that. It started making sense. But I never thought it. Perin Foundling, the hero of Nagyevo? The Gravedigger?"

Neva looked affronted. Perin smiled uneasily. "Unbelievable, I know. I didn't manage it alone, my friend."

Veso looked taken aback. "Friend? I thought you was goin't lump me! I jumped you last time we met."

"All in the past," Perin said firmly, offering his hand. "Besides, you were paid for that then and there. I broke your nose, I think. Master Graves was ill. I hadn't the patience at the time."

"Oh, yeah." Veso got to his feet. His smile became a grin. "To think! I once had me nose broke by the Gravedigger!"

"Quite an honour," Kesairl rumbled. "Young human. You know that I'm a prigon, I think. Have you seen others like me here?"

"No." Veso shook his head. "The others of us are on the other side of the rock, down the hill a-ways. I'm supposed to be sentry here. Not doing a very good job though, eh?" He looked comfortable enough with his failure.

"Poor conduct." Kesairl growled. "Sentries take responsibility for their whole camp!"

Perin looked around, surprised at Kesairl's tone. Veso began to tremble.

Kesairl glanced at Perin but said nothing until they had walked past the stone toward the main camp.

"So they've formed a militia against the Tacnimag, based on you and their rejection of the mages' injustices. They'll be useful against Haal's undead, but only if they learn properly how to act and how to fight."

Perin nodded in understanding. "All right. It just caught me by surprise."

"Like this camp," Kesairl responded darkly. Perin saw he was wondering why the Claimfolders were here, while his own people were not.

Kesairl moved into the middle of a ring of little tents and bedrolls and let out a loud shout.

The camp's response to this was better than Perin had expected. The figures were on their feet in the dark at once, weapons in hand. It was only when Kesairl ignited and lifted a globe of light above his head that the Gravedigger Ring could see the people. They were mostly youths. Their weapons had once been tools for working the land, or for cutting lumber. In fairness, they still warranted caution. An axe, Perin found himself thinking, can fell a man faster than it can a tree.

"Hold!" A wild-haired figure called out shrilly. The fire had died to embers, but in the light Kesairl cast, Perin could see who she was. His mind ran back over the many months that had passed, and he saw himself standing in her husband's shop, buying dry-cured beef.

"Mistress Hoer!"

"Gravedigger!" Mistress Hoer bowed deeply, then stepped forward, ignoring Forgos and his ready sword, to embrace Perin in a hug. "Perin the Gravedigger! Welcome!" Her men stood down.

A little while later, with the fire relit and banked up, the makeshift militia passed some food around, while spare tents were made up for the Gravedigger Ring.

"We were close to organised when it happened," Yana Hoer explained, looking up at the now starry sky as she continued. "I told anyone who would listen that you were no outlaw, that you were a little hero all in your own right. Bers threatened to leave me over it. He was a silly man." Tears welled in her eyes for a moment, and she made a show of brushing some crumbs off her leather hunting clothes.

"Where is Master Hoer now? Is he with your daughter?"

"He died when it happened," Yana said softly, looking southeast toward the forested hills of Csus. The mountain was invisible on the horizon in the dark. "When that mage came back. I believed you that you had killed him, Perin. But he came back somehow. Haunted with it."

"Haal went through Erdhanger?" Perin asked with a chill pinching in his chest. He had not considered that.

Yana nodded. "Killed a lot of folk as he passed. Some of them got up again afterwards. Took us to de-head them to make them stop. Us that survived were mostly the Erdhanger Rebels. We took to the Varo forests and joined up with the hunters. All of us have lost somebody. But Minya — my daughter — is safe enough with her aunt in Arpavale."

"That's good. And I'm sorry," Perin said soberly. "It's the same with Nagyevo. Everybody living has left the city."

"The Claimfold is falling," Yana Hoer said darkly. "What can we do, Gravedigger?"

"Catch it as it falls," Perin replied at once. There was a murmur of agreement from the rebels around the fire as Perin continued. "It's all going to come to crisis in the North. If Valo can be saved, then that's where we'll need to go." He received some confused looks at this, but no one questioned him.

Eventually, the camp took to bedrolls and tents, as the wind rose again, pulling sparks out of the fire and scattering them across the hillside.

Neva was already sleeping when Sudar and Perin accepted bedrolls on either side of him. Forgos took a watch to keep an eye on the sentries. He talked with Yana Hoer for a time, impressed with her amateur leadership of the militia. Eventually, after making one more circuit of the watch points, he lay down to sleep between Aranyo and Perin.

Only Kesairl stayed awake.

The wind flowing past the tents set up an irregular noise of flapping canvas as the night slipped away. In the grey pre-dawn, Kesairl and Perin walked the crown of the hill.

"You say that we must go into the North?" Kesairl said after a moment, watching the hazy shape of Csus on the lightening horizon. "You do not want to go home?"

Perin bit his lip and turned away from the mountain's distant shape. "Erdhanger is gone. Nagyevo is lost. Medrivar's home is threatened. I do not know if the Bright Dead are holding back their enemy since they lost the ability to regenerate in their burial chambers. But Medrivar is sure that Akrash Haal will march on Meddoszoru. He has not fully explained why. Something to do with thrones."

"We need to contact the Torzsi," Kesairl said with surprising fervour. "Perhaps I misjudged the time of year, but my clan should have entered this land by now."

Perin's brow furrowed in concern.

A sentry shouted something incomprehensible from the northeastern face of the hill. Perin and Kesairl began to run, the great prigon easily overtaking his friend.

A line of rolled tents and marching figures were coming down out of the green-brown slopes of Helynvale. When Kesairl saw them, he sighed with relief and sat down in the grass.

"There they are, after all. Finally we shall have some news."

Torzsa Abrun made their camp in a circle around the Erdhanger Rebels. The prigon moved warily about the shared space, occasionally exchanging a wordless greeting with one of the awed humans.

Perin spoke in his unpractised Priga with Kesairl's father. Abrun was as tall and hale as he had been before, but with more concern in his tricoloured eyes.

"Greetings to you, Perin Gravedigger. You are the leader of these men?"

"Yes, Abrun. It was last night that I found them here."

"Are they aware that they are trespassing?" Abrun rumbled deeply.

Kesairl shifted slightly at his side. "Father. They did not know and I did not tell them. It is good that we are all in one place. We are allies."

"Torzsa Abrun is not allied with the Claimfold! Truly, none of the Torzsi are! You were sent on a diplomatic mission and you were made captive, were you not?"

"I was. Perin was forced to hide his identity while I was in a Tacnimag cell. But the Claimfold are not the Tacnimag. The Tacnimag are now overthrown. These men and women here are rebels who were against them. Now we need solidarity with them for another reason…"

"You overthrew the Tacnimag?" Abrun stared at Perin before raising his hands out over Perin's head, fingers splayed as the enormous prigon bowed.

"He is honouring you," Kesairl muttered to explain.

Perin thanked the clan chief by pressing his open palm firmly against his heart, twice. "It was not my people that overthrew the Tacnimag in the end. They were destroyed by another enemy."

Abrun took a step back.

Kesairl murmured, "*Hilylilana zyist.*" The evil dead.

Abrun made a gesture that Perin did not know but immediately understood. The terror of Haal's appearance in the dead body of the mage called Keresur was not lost on Abrun.

Perin and Kesairl carefully explained the fall of Nagyevo. By the time they had finished, Abrun was seated on the grass, his head bowed with the weight of it.

"We must work together," he said finally, "my warriors and your warriors, Perin Gravedigger, together."

"Agreed." Perin sat down opposite Abrun. "But more, we must call a Torzsanag. All the Torzsi must be together with us in this. We have to cut off any march the enemy makes out of Nagyevo, to protect the Claimfolders who have escaped both into Joval and out towards here, toward Helynvale. These *hilylilana zyist* cannot be allowed to threaten the innocents of either of our peoples."

Abrun got to his feet and offered a great hand to help Perin to his. His eyes were fierce as he stared toward the West. "I will have my Torzsa's Ontava summon the other Torzsi. It will be a war council. And with you, Perin Gravedigger, our people will go to war!"

THIRTY-TWO

TORZSA KELISH ARRIVED FIRST. The forerunners appeared at a steady pace, ascending the hilltop to greet Abrun's sentries. They were six prigon, dressed in a familiar pattern of red and blue patchwork canvas. The gold of their armbands and bracelets caught the evening sunlight. Perin forced himself to approach at a steady pace. The excitement of seeing more prigon skirmishers made it hard not to smile.

"Gravedigger." Abrun's sentry bowed deeply, as respectful as he was to his own clan leader. The Kelish skirmishers took the cue and also made their respects known. Perin's hand went from his forehead to his heart as he bowed back in the prigon gesture of brotherhood.

"Welcome. Are Torzsa Kelish far behind?"

The lead skirmisher nodded. "Torzsa Kelish are taking the slower pace of our elders and weak ones. We were sent ahead. The blades are behind. Ah! Abrun." The skirmisher repeated his deep bow to Abrun, who now towered beside Perin.

"Welcome, Skirmisher. I did not know that Kelish had initiated blades... has she been anticipating war?"

The skirmisher looked uncertain and made the gesture for a mild apology, his fingers briefly touching his closed eyelids. "It was a thing begun after the Torzsanag."

Abrun nodded in understanding. "Please, join us, we will refresh you. As you have seen, Perin Gravedigger is here with a warband of his people. We hope to forge a fighters' alliance at Torzsanag, once the torzsi have arrived." Abrun's rumbling voice had drawn the attention of his son.

Kesairl rounded the nearest tent, smiling broadly when he saw the arrivals. "Sontyra uto Nekari!" He strode past his father and greeted the lead skirmisher warmly.

"Kesairl uto Abrun! What happened to your mantle? Surely…" The prigon's handsome face looked suddenly horrified. "Surely you have not been de-magistered?"

Kesairl shook his head fiercely, still smiling. "No! No. I was imprisoned by the Tacnimag, until Perin rescued me… I will need a new mantle."

"And you will need to tell me everything." Their Priga became so rapid that Perin could no longer follow it.

After a ceremonial drink with Abrun, Sontyra left his group and joined Kesairl and Perin on the westward hilltop. He was delighted to hear Perin's Priga.

"I do not remember you from when I was with Torzsa Kelish," Perin confessed.

"I was on a long patrol. Skirmishers spend most of their time away from the torzsa, checking hunting runs and meeting up with skirmishers from other torzsi. That's how I met Kesairl, years ago, when we were still earning our magistries."

Kesairl laughed aloud, making Perin lean away to save his hearing. "Yes! Remember how long it took me to manage a decent shockwave?"

"You were not apt for some time," Sontyra agreed solemnly. "I hear that you have improved much since then."

"I can use the Burn Grip." Kesairl shrugged as if this was a small matter.

Sontyra nodded slowly. "Indeed. That is an achievement. I only learned Burn Grip this past month." A light sparkled in the skirmisher's eyes.

Kesairl grinned broadly. "Well done! I see you match me."

"As always." Sontyra chuckled. He looked down the hill, eyebrows raised. "What is this?" On the lower slope, Sudar and Forgos were drilling the Erdhanger Militia. They were running with full equipment. Forgos's furious shouting was just about keeping them in a ragged formation.

"These are the human warriors?" Sontyra asked, his eyebrows still raised.

Perin coloured, looked away. "They will be."

Kesairl rumbled in agreement. "A little training will go a long way. Though we have little time. I will vouch though, for Perin's closest companions. They fight well, the Gravedigger Ring."

Sudar was close to expressing the frustration that Forgos freely vented. It was not the fault of the men and women from Erdhanger—they were willing and focused—but they were not soldiers. They were not even Borderers. The worst of it was that they had no proper weapons. Sudar doubted many undead would fall under the stroke of a hoe.

The prigon torzsi arrived one by one over the next three days. Abrun and Kelish were joined by Etzsar and Kimr. Lyen and Darmir arrived last.

The mutual dislike between Abrun and Darmir, both the leaders and their clans, was clearly still present. The welcome ceremony was brief and cold. Darmir's long face wore a sneer throughout.

As the camp grew, the number of sentries at the boundary grew as well. The first refugees from Nagyevo to pass through were offered supply by the Torzsi. Most stayed well away from the shapes of the prigon at the head of the hill.

The ones that did enter the camp brought news.

The undead army had cleared Nagyevo completely. The first advance from the city had been to harry the slowest of the refugees in Joval. The greater number of the dead attacked the claims of Narsun.

The Torzsanag gathered in a great circle of blazing kotuzska bowls and clan banners. The Claimfold Militia and Gravedigger Ring were given their own place in the circle, a human torzsa with Perin at its head. With him sat the Csus hunters and Yana Hoer. Neva, self-conscious but unashamed in his Tacnimag robes, sat beside Perin. He was not begrudged his place. Stories about Neva's magistry were already spreading.

The greetings were swiftly over.

"No!" Darmir almost snarled, his long face lit by the inconstant light of the kotuzska bowls. "We will not so easily give up our young warriors in the defence of the humans! To repay their treachery with sacrifice? Foolishness!"

"What is he saying?" Neva asked Perin in a whisper.

"In short, no."

Abrun rose to his towering height and spread his arms wide and low, hands slicing the air horizontally in a gesture of dismissal. "Your tongue rolls with cowardice, Darmir!"

Darmir growled. "You dare, Abrun? I would have expected more from you. It is not cowardice, but prudence!" He spread his arms open to invite attention. "You say that the Claimfold differs from the Tacnimag. You say they are not all alike. Perhaps you are right. It remains, though, that these ones here have not proved themselves to us."

Kelish stood slowly. "Your true meaning is that they have done nothing for us. Truer still, that they have done nothing for you, Darmir."

Darmir snorted, crossing his arms. Kelish continued. "I do not accuse you of cowardice, Darmir. Your fault is pettiness. You make decisions with a small heart. The Claimfold showed themselves worthy long ago when their warriors and ours united against the drizen."

"Their hero Hanger is long dead." Darmir spat. "I doubt that these humans have the might in them anymore."

Perin stood and made a slight gesture for the others to stand, too. Forgos, Sudar, and Neva got to their feet a little self-consciously. "Darmir!" Perin's voice, speaking Priga, was a shout. "I stand with men who have killed drizen. You know that I am blooded, too. We've fought them while outnumbered, killed them 'til none remained alive. More still, we have faced this new enemy, even their master. We have faced them and you have not, but you doubt *our* commitment? Coward or not, Darmir, Valo does not need you if you cannot bring yourself to fight for her!"

"Well said," Kesairl rumbled.

"Fuaagh!" Darmir brought his fists together at the knuckles, staring over them with a bright fury in his small eyes.

Kesairl made a loud sound like the beginning of a roar and nearly stepped forward into the Torzsanag circle. "He insults you, Perin! He who is less worthy than you to stand here! He…"

"He loses his control like a child." Etzsar, the aged prigon at the head of the smallest torzsa spoke out. "Do not take his foolishness seriously. Nonetheless, he shames us. I agree with Abrun and Kelish. We have a duty to unite with the Claimfold."

"You are all become fools!" Darmir took a step back. "We will not take part in this. We will defend our own territory. That is all. Against *any* trespassers!"

"Those of us who will fight will do so in defence of your territory." Kesairl controlled his anger. "You will benefit from our valour. I cannot believe that your warriors would bear the shame."

"My warriors do as I command." Darmir was already a shadow walking away, his torzsa beginning to follow in uncertain groups.

"Not all of them," a deep voice growled out. From the shaded edge of the torzsa, a very large prigon rose. He was dressed in an enormous cloak. As he stepped forward, it was easy to see that it had been dyed gold. When he turned toward Darmir's retreating back, a large red circle was apparent on the back. "Darmir, your battlemage is about to leave you."

"No betrayal surprises me anymore." Darmir had stopped walking, but he did not look back. "Any prigon that wishes to retain their sanity, follow me."

Most of Torzsa Darmir followed, and half of Torzsa Lyen. Their weak-willed leader had said nothing during the entire Torzsanag.

The entirety of Kelish remained, as did the torzsi Abrun, Etzsar and Kimr.

Kelish cleared her throat. "We have work to do and land to travel. The warriors will march ahead. Perin Gravedigger will outline our strategy. Torzsi! Enjoy your sleep tonight. There is little enough of it to look forward to." She crossed the Torzsanag circle elegantly, the silver of her adornments catching the light. "Perin, you held your place well."

"Thank you. I think I was more nervous than I looked. Medrivar takes over more...which is useful." Perin smiled easily, and Kelish's slight disapproval shifted into a smile of her own.

"I am still a little uneasy. Our stories of the dead-that-walk are not easily forgotten. Evil imposters, flesh thieves...but I understand that Medrivar's heart is different." Kelish stared out across the landscape. The dark hills, far from the light of the slowly dissolving kotuzska rocks, were topped with silver-lit cloud. "It is a beautiful night."

Perin acknowledged this with a nod, made uncertain by Kelish's suddenly distant tone.

Kesairl stepped closer, his eyes tracking Kelish's gaze into the far away. A breeze came across from the lower ground, dancing across the hilltop and making Kesairl's new skirmisher garment flutter.

"Valo is very beautiful. I have seen so little of this land, tied to Helynvale as I have been," Kelish explained, "and I regret that. I do not want to see Valo wasted under the tramping feet of the dead."

"Nor I," Kesairl rumbled darkly. "While I live, I'll stand against that future, blood and bone."

"We'll hold the border of the moorland that spans the gap between the Fold of Joval and Koban," Perin declared, looking from Kesairl to Kelish and back. Abrun, Kimr, and Etzsar were close enough to hear, and they came closer, their great forms towering over the young man. The breeze played with his black hair and he shivered. He did not look impressive. Nevertheless, the attention paid him was absolute. "We'll keep them out of Helynvale from there. With any Claimfolders left who might fight, we'll protect both peoples. The dead are not meant to be here. We are. Valo is ours."

"What about Akrash Haal?" Kesairl asked.

Forgos's expression echoed the prigon's question. The Ringmembers that had been inside the Observatory before the escape could well remember how impervious the dead mage had been.

Perin nodded. "Haal is stronger than all of us. Magic seems not to trouble him, and he has nothing to fear from steel. But we have Medrivar, and Medrivar has a plan."

Neva engaged in conversation with the battlemage formerly of Torzsa Darmir. Perin acted as a translator while he packed a few feet away. The whole combined camp, human and prigon, gathered to leave. The chosen front was nearly two weeks travel away, and it was imperative that they reached the moor at the northwest edge of Helynvale in time to fortify it against the dead. Akrash Haal's horde would not be satisfied by the scarce pickings of Narsun Fold for long.

"You're sort of the peak, the greatest kind of mage?" Neva asked nervously. "I've heard some of the things Kesairl has said, that he's always wanted to be a battlemage, like it's the ultimate aim for—"

The battlemage raised a hand to interrupt, head turned slightly toward Perin for the translation. "No, no. It only seems that way. When I was young, a long, long time ago, the battlemagi felt that way, for certain. There is a great deal of honour attached to the magistry. I do not deny that. And battlemagi are capable of devastating feats of power. Skirmishers often aim to progress to the magistry, but I would not call myself greater. Kesairl is well reputed. A strong skirmisher."

"Yes," Neva admitted, "but he said himself that you were more powerful."

The battlemage nodded his great head slowly. There was little hair between his long, slightly out-curved horns, and the little there was had a distinctive silver colour. The blue-black sheen of his skin also appeared silvery in places.

"Perhaps a quotation will best explain. Great prigon Warmaster, Nemar uto Szalar said: 'To win a battle, best have a battlemage. But to win a war, you will need the skirmishers.' He ruled the Darmir Torzsa shortly after that, leading the united torzsi to victory."

The prigon's frown darkened and he sat silent for a moment, giving Perin a chance to hurriedly catch up. Then he looked away and said, "Darmir were a strong and honourable torzsa once, you see. They are all shame and small-heart now. Hmgh! It makes me angry, young telemage."

Neva swallowed his nervousness and put a hand on the prigon's mighty arm. "You shame them, sir."

"Ha! Perhaps I do. My honour's intact, at least, aah?" The battlemage smiled, showing his teeth. He got to his feet and offered a hand to Neva to help him up. Neva's long, lithe fingers were tiny in the centre of the prigon's palm.

"Thank you, Neva. Forgive me. I have not given you my name. I am Battlemage Magyr uto Hegyr."

"I'm Neva. But you know that." Neva grinned, shaking—or trying to shake—Magyr's hand. "Nice to meet you, Mag."

The march became hard on the Claimic contingent. Prigon could go strong in all weathers, carrying their rolled tents on broad backs. At the head of their file walked the torzsi leaders, surrounded by agile elders and advisors.

Behind, and in wide, block formations, marched the blades. Their swords were fully the length of Perin's body, and half as broad. They were heavy and one-edged, with an acute diagonal near the end, running to meet the tip and giving the blade a third edge as long as Perin's forearm.

As many prigon again were interspersed throughout the file and spread far around the army on scouting detail, all wearing canvas similar to Kesairl's. He led the skirmishers in partnership with his old friend Sontyra. The mismatched patchwork of blue and red was invisible now—they had turned the garments inside out, presenting a discoloured, brownish-green pattern to the watching world.

The sun remained absent. Rain ruled from leaden heavens, as it had for the last few days. The prigon went untroubled; but the militia, and even the hardened members of the Gravedigger Ring, were suffering.

"I keep telling myself that this is just another Borderer patrol," Forgos said through gritted teeth as the landscape sloped again, "and then I remember that there's no warm city at the end."

"I miss Nagyevo," Aranyo agreed. His soaked blond hair, made brown by the rain, clung to his forehead. Sudar, of course, stayed stoically silent.

"I miss Kard," Perin almost whispered, suddenly overcome with an unexplained wave of emotion. "And Harco. And Maka."

Forgos put a hand on Perin's shoulder. "My mam used to say that when it rains, it's time to remember."

Perin half turned, interested. "You never mentioned your mother before, Stormy."

Forgos smiled at the Borderer nickname. Once upon a time, he would have punched Perin for it. "Well, we didn't go into our pasts much, did we? It was enough to out myself as a lord's bastard."

Sudar stared up at the mass of layered stormcloud through narrowed eyes. "It's raining. We're tired, cold, hungry."

"What Su' here means," Perin said, with a smile quirking his lips, "is that now is as good a time as any to bring up the past. Go on Forgos. Tell us things we never hoped to hear."

"Yeah," Aranyo agreed, "just keep it clean."

THIRTY-THREE

FORGOS WARMED TO HIS TALE. It was the only warmth to be had.

"So, yeah. Not what you might expect. Er…do you remember the infirmary where Gyorva and Harco were taken after our first clash with the drizen?"

There were more nods than replies.

"Temple Garden Way, right? Well, do you remember when I told you about my father, the lord who shall remain nameless?"

"I wasn't there," Aranyo pointed out.

"Oh, yes." Forgos's high brow furrowed. "You didn't know me the way I was when I joined the Second South, Aranyo. I was born a bastard."

Aranyo's smile faltered.

Forgos continued, "My father was one of the lords in charge of trade regulation and so on. I lived in the servant rooms, of course. Mother only told me about him when I turned thirteen. I spent the next three, nearly four years, getting into more and more trouble, hitting out at everyone. No wonder you all got to calling me the Storm."

"We did wonder," Perin murmured, nearly slipping in the mud beginning to seep out of the slope as the rain intensified. "At least, I wondered why you were so angry."

"Well, I ended up a thief. Not in the usual, streetgang kind of way, but still. It's how I got into trouble."

"Didn't your father know? About you, I mean?" Neva asked.

"Well, yes. I mean, I wasn't ignored. Not really. Never went poor. Never hungry. Father must have had a guilty conscience. But upkeep isn't the same as acceptance."

"So, how did you end up a Borderer?"

"Well… I got angry, as you might expect. Body built for fighting, as Kard said when I joined up. I nearly killed him. My father, I mean." Forgos looked up into the rain. Perin had never seen the strong Borderer look guilty before.

"What did he do?" Perin wondered aloud. Even the angry Forgos from the old days must have had a reason.

"Nothing, really. Mam—my mother died."

There was a collective intake of breath. Forgos looked down at his trudging feet, aware that even Kesairl, in from the outer scouting line, was listening. "Yes. Not so long ago, really. A bit after my sixteenth birthday. Packed a whole life in since then, it feels like. I went crazy after, and he didn't know how to deal with that; and it led to me doing what I did.

"I hadn't planned to stick it out, not for long. Doing the Borderers thing, I mean. There was places I could go to get lost. Didn't need to stay. But meeting all of you was good for me." Forgos looked up, his grey eyes softened, maybe by the rain. "Getting shouted at by Kard was strange. Made me want to fight him. But he was decent, and so were the rest of you, mostly." He tried to smile. "Found myself belonging. I was the big one. The Storm."

"You still are," Perin said, and then sneezed. Forgos chuckled, patting Perin on the back.

"Yeah. I suppose I am. And you're still the weirdly talented one, although I understand that better now. How did you meet Medrivar?" Forgos's gaze searched Perin's eyes warily, as if looking for signs of the indwelling king.

Perin told them. When he finished, it was truly dark and the marchers stopped under sodden evergreens. The land sloped away dramatically from the path but rose still higher to the north and east, where the shoulder of Helynvale's high moors blocked their route.

The group was quiet as they set up camp in a tight circle. Everything was wet, but Perin's status earned them a bowl of kotuzska to huddle around. The rain had stopped.

The Gravedigger Ring stripped off their soaked outer clothes and wrapped themselves in blankets. Neva found himself feeling quite self-conscious without his Tacnimag robes. He felt uncomfortable enough as it was.

"Do you ever wonder…?" Sudar suddenly blurted out. The others stared at him.

"Go on," Perin encouraged.

"Just…you finally tell us your full story and it's as if you came to Nagyevo to meet us. I mean, do you see how fortunate you've been?"

"Things have just…happened," Perin replied. He felt that Medrivar paid close attention.

Sudar nodded slowly. "Exactly. But the way they've happened, has it been random? Or..."

"Haaah!" Forgos exclaimed slowly. "I see. You're talking about fate." He didn't sound altogether pleased.

"I'm afraid to suggest it. That things might happen because it is intended..." Sudar looked unhappy. Perin had rarely seen him so unsettled.

"Intended?" Forgos's voice rose a little, "By who? The Nameless Gods?"

Sudar stayed silent.

Perin raised his gaze to meet Forgos's, worried by his friend's reaction. "Is that such a terrible thought?"

"The gods? Choosing our paths? Writing our lives for us? Dead can take that!"

"All right!" Perin raised his hands placatingly. "It's all right. Just explain."

"Because it would mean that there was a good reason why—" Forgos cut off the end of his sentence before gathering some restraint. "Harco, Kard, Maka. They died. I won't believe that there was a good reason for that. Of course it was chance!"

Perin was shocked. He sat silently considering for a moment. When Kesairl seated himself at the edge of the circle, he looked up as if hoping for an answer.

"Does it help you if they died due to nothing more than ill-fortune?" Kesairl's deep voice gently questioned.

Forgos slowly unclenched his fists. "Help? There's no help for it. They're dead."

"Yes. We must accept it when the loved die. Heroes do not live; they are made in leaving."

"Valo owes them," Forgos agreed grimly.

"If there was no intention—no meaning—behind their sacrifice, then surely it follows that there was none behind their lives?" Kesairl's tricoloured eyes lit up in the glow of the kotuzska.

"No..." Forgos shook his head. "Look, this isn't what I can do. This is talk for the old men in Nagyevo market. I can't do this."

"You already are."

"I could never ally myself with any power that chose for my friends to die." Forgos was resolute. "Never. Even if it was done for some 'greater good.'"

Medrivar spoke and Perin heard.

Interesting. These young warriors have sharp minds, too, it seems.

Did you doubt it? Perin asked in the quiet of the throne room.

No, no. But I feel the discussion leads nowhere, for all their wisdom.

Why is that?

Because they are talking about what is done. If destiny exists, and I believe it does, then it is forged in the moment of action.

Perin frowned. *That's not destiny, then. If we can affect what happens...*
Crucially, Perin, we can only weave our own threads.
I don't understand you, Perin admitted.

Medrivar didn't respond, and Perin sensed that the king was confused himself. It was as if he had been quoting a text he had never finished or fully learnt.

Are you all right, Majesty?

Medrivar's voice sounded strangely distant when it came.

We all serve. That is all. We serve ourselves and create evil, great and small, or we serve others. You've chosen to serve me. I... don't know who I serve. I have met no gods. If they made Valo, as rumour has it, then I am not their work. I am an imposter. Like Akrash Haal. This land was not made for me or mine!

Perin was shocked. The others could see his sudden change of posture and watched him cautiously, aware that he was probably in conversation.

You are not like Haal!

In action, no. But my origin...

If the Nameless Gods exist, then they could only approve of you, never mind where you come from!

Perin's argument quietened Medrivar for the moment.

Then, perhaps we earn our right to be?

Perin shook himself, realising that the others were watching him. He smiled uneasily, looking from companion to companion. Sudar seemed to regret ever beginning the conversation.

"Gods or no gods, we've chosen to fight. Harco, Maka, and Kard left us behind. Alive. What they did... I don't know, but I think it's somehow supreme. The ultimate thing to do."

Kesairl rumbled, "The highest honour."

Forgos seemed to brighten, and he nodded in agreement. "Yes. I think we envy them, somehow."

There was a pause as the Borderers considered that.

Neva pushed through his fear to finally speak up. "I feel bad now. Is it awful that I don't want to die?"

Perin laughed, because it was the only thing to do.

Forgos shook his head, chuckling, too. "You got it wrong, mage. I don't want to die. But if I have to... I'll know what I'm dying for."

The dawn struggled against the remaining clouds, but at least it wasn't raining. Stoic, despite the lack of sleep, the camp rose and packed again. The march resumed.

The weather cleared slowly throughout the day, though the sun stayed hidden behind cloud. They were better conditions for marching, but the fear of journey's end grew. To be too late—unthinkable. To be just in time, almost as bad. The hard tread, hour by hour, day by day, led only to an unimaginable battle against a foe that was already dead.

Valo's remaining life seemed to be measured out by the count of footfall.

Perin opened his eyes and groaned even as Neva reached to shake him. The world was grey and the camp breaking yet again.

"I'm...yes. All right. I'm getting up." He crawled out of his bedroll and blinked furiously as he stood up.

Kesairl sat a short distance away, his canvas wrapped about him as he meditated. The wind blew strong, even down in the dell where they had camped.

"We're not far away. Scouts from Lord Adamun found us during the night," Forgos said, belting his longsword high at his hip. "He's already organised the line. Damn, but the prigon can run! I thought the messengers had got lost."

"Here." Neva passed Perin his overshirt. He waited patiently until Perin stood and dressed, holding his friend's heavy coat at the ready.

"Thanks, Neva." Perin shrugged into the coat and accepted his long spade from Sudar while Neva buckled his baldric across his back for him.

"Are we expecting battle?"

Forgos looked up from comparing a pair of daggers. "Adamun says that there have been dead scouting parties looking for gaps in the defence."

"Adamun's lines must be spread pretty thin."

Forgos nodded in response, deciding that two daggers were better than one.

The prigon led the way down and out of the more rugged hills, leaving the edge of Helynvale. The evergreens spiced the air with a verdant scent, and the rain held off. Cloud-rags moved high above, brushing across the blue.

The line was thin. Frightened and more ragged than the clouds above, Lord Adamun's militia were dispersed in groups of two or three across the irregular frontier. The Lord Knight had picked a spine of craggy rocks as the defensive boundary. The coarse grass and browning heather sloped away from the militia's positions. The dead would be coming uphill.

The dead *were* coming uphill.

They moved cautiously and were not great in number, but Perin was painfully aware of how much damage so few could do to the struggle of defenders. The prigon torzsi and the Csus Militia were barely in time.

A little breathless, the Gravedigger Ring slowed to a walk, joining the Lord Knight at his central position. The men nearby him were former guards of Nagyevo, and they made room for Perin when they saw him approach.

"Welcome, Gravedigger." Adamun broke a brief smile. "Your friends will make this a lot easier." He gestured to where prigon were reinforcing the Claimfolders. Prigon blades stood alongside Nagyevan spearmen and Kobanite archers.

"This is all you have?" Perin wondered aloud.

Adamun shook his head. "This is all I could get here this fast. The prigon messenger was very clear that none should be allowed through—though, what are we protecting? Koban isn't heavily populated..."

"We defend Koban and Helynvale at the same time from here," Perin explained. "The dead aren't going around. This is the easiest path to take, up the long valley between Koban and Helynvale, toward the mountains."

Adamun rubbed a hand through his stubble. "That makes no sense to me. There's nothing up there."

"Just something Haal—their leader—wants."

"Something to do with the Tacnimag's old obsession for the North?"

"Something like that."

They fell silent, watching the prigon skirmishers spreading themselves out below the defensive line, seemingly vulnerable on the slope. The wind rose and fell, making the purplish moor-grass dance. The dead were reforming in silence, their eyes staring. More rose from hidden positions in hollows and from behind patches of fierce yellow gorse. The sky was clearing.

It was a beautiful day.

"They don't look so dangerous," Adamun muttered bitterly. "I thought that they'd drag their feet or run wild like dogs. But they act like us. They fight like us, if they have the weapons to hand."

"The controlling spirits have had time to grow familiar," Perin said in a low voice, hearing from Medrivar.

Adamun didn't respond immediately. Finally, he replied, "I prefer the drizen. What they did to my maid was terrible, and I hope one day to forget it, but at least they were...alive. These things make the breath in my lungs feel wrong."

Perin could see Kesairl a short distance from his friend Sontyra, in ready stance opposite the closest group of dead scouts. The dead stayed put.

"It's as if they're not sure whether to attack or not."

They resent the birthright of the living too fiercely. They will attack. Make no mistake.

Perin took Medrivar seriously. "What do we know about the whereabouts of their main force?"

"Based on what we've heard from the last of the lucky people that escaped..." Adamun's brow furrowed in thought, "last word was three days ago... There was a suggestion that most of them were still making their way out of Narsun and into Nagyevo province again. If they are coming here, if you're right, then most of them will still be collecting in the city.

"Unless," he continued, suddenly more troubled, "they aren't behaving like a living army. If they're coming in waves, then by now they'll be spread from here to Nagyevo—they don't need to sleep and they don't really tire... We'll be hard pressed if we have to defend this place for more than a few days."

Perin didn't say what he was thinking.

Forgos drew his sword a couple of inches, his eyes narrowing. "Shite. I'm not waiting up here. The skirmishers know where to be. I'm going down." He dropped down onto the slope and headed toward Kesairl.

Sudar strung his bow.

Neva counted stones from his pouch, his young face strangely calm and set. Aranyo had acquired a spear somehow and passed it from hand to hand in anticipation.

Perin counted dead heads. "They haven't a hope of making it here. Skirmishers will tear them apart."

Adamun grunted in acknowledgement. "I hope you're right."

THIRTY-FOUR

ON THE ONE HAND, it was going well. Sudar's accuracy had never been finer, and sometimes the bodies he hit actually fell down and stayed down. Kesairl, Sontyra and Forgos were fighting together, the two prigon competing. A dead warrior went flying violently away down the slope as Sontyra exerted a shockwave. Kesairl rejoined by dropping two dead fighters with the same beam of Narrow Fire. Forgos moved between them on light feet, his longsword already bloody.

"Aranyo. Stay with Adamun in the spear wall," Perin ordered, glancing around him and then returning his gaze to the lower hillside where greater numbers of the dead were moving closer. No shuffling, no odd rhythms. Much the same as a living army, but silent. Completely silent.

"Sudar, direct their fire for me." Perin nodded toward a large group of Kobanite archers, freshly arrived from the nearest Koban fortress town. Perin felt a rush of pride in the Claimfold. Koban had defended the lives of its people and neighbouring Folds since before Nagyevo had walls.

"Yes, Gravedigger." Sudar chose a new arrow as he went.

"Are you taking over my command, Gravedigger?" Lord Adamun asked with a touch of humour.

Perin shook his head. "No, my lord. I want my men to know what they're doing. You have the command of the defence of this hillside. But I'm going to lead a counterattack."

Perin didn't see Adamun's curt bow. He moved through the ragged rocks that marked the defensive line, passing Aranyo and the spears. The prigon had spread their own line in the largest gap between two stretches of human spearmen, with the exception of the skirmishers who were already fighting.

Perin joined Abrun and Kimr. Etzsar, reluctantly acknowledging her age, was with Kelish on the higher ridge, helping to coordinate the prigon defenders in cooperation with the Claimfolders. A break in communication now could be deadly.

The gorgeous blue of the sky and the light breeze made Perin smile grimly. The weather had been fine when his Borderer brothers had lost their lives, too.

"Abrun, Kimr." Perin nodded to them before acknowledging Battlemage Magyr as well. The old prigon had assumed leadership of the few Lyen and Darmir that had committed to the cause. "It looks like the ones here are massing. We're more or less evenly matched, but they're taking it slow. They don't want to rush us."

"Yes," Abrun rumbled. The young man's skill with the Priga language continued to surprise him. "It seems that either they want to draw the skirmishers out too far and so pincer them, or that they are taking it slow to tire us."

"I think so, too. Adamun says more of his militia are coming. It seems my people have had time to get angry about being forced out of their homes by a bunch of corpses."

Kimr grinned widely. "I am prepared to rely on the anger of Claimfolders. Let the dead fight their slow battle. We'll outnumber them in time."

Perin shook his head. "No, we won't. They have reinforcements on the way, too. Even if they're a day away, they're coming. And they don't tire—we do." The three prigon took stock of this in silence. Not far down the hill, a prigon fell, overcome by three dead spearmen. The nearby skirmishers counterattacked with waves of force and blasts of brief flame. But they were slowly retreating.

"Even if we still outnumber them when they're reinforced, we need to eat. We need to sleep. We can't fight the line against all their number. If all the dead gather here, then it will be over."

"What are you telling us?" Abrun sounded angry. Perin knew his words sounded hopeless.

"That we need to clear the field. Wipe out all of these that are here already. It will give us some rest."

"Very good," Kimr agreed after a moment's consideration. "Join the skirmishers so that they are informed. Our blades will lead the charge. The Claimfolders will make good work of finishing any corpses we leave unbroken." The prigon slapped a hand down on Battlemage Magyr's shoulder. "I would fear them more if they were prigon dead. Men won't have much answer for the blades, eh?"

Perin walked away down the hill, trying not to show that he had been struck by a new terror. What if the pit under the Observatory had not been empty when Haal arrived? What if there were undead drizen marching their way north, too?

The thought made him feel ill.

You haven't told them that you cannot stay here. Medrivar gently reproached him.

Perin frowned. *It was the wrong moment, Majesty. First... first let's deal with these Damned Dead.* There was no response, so Perin assumed Medrivar's acceptance. The king was growing anxious. *I have an idea.* Perin thought, to reassure him.

Down the hillside, Forgos ducked under a spear, thrust, and cut his opponent's leg nearly all the way through at the knee. The corpse stumbled, reached for the tall young man, lost his hand. Another body ran forward hefting an axe, its ribs showing red and white through rags of pale skin. The axe wasn't a thing of war, looking to be straight from the chopping block, but it was sharp. Forgos stumbled backwards, tripped. He kicked upward to stop the deathblow from falling, his foot striking the ruined ribs.

The dead man spat blood all over Forgos, regained his balance, swung the axe. Perin's spade knocked it aside and then smacked heavily into the meat of the wielder's neck.

Forgos scrambled back to his feet as Perin brought the dead man down, forcing the sharp edge of Spade through the hard wedges of vertebrae and voiding the corpse of its controlling spirit. Perin found it strange that there was no outward sign of its leaving, just the eyes going dead.

More dead. Properly dead.

"Thanks, Reger."

"You're welcome." Perin stood alongside Forgos, ignoring the misused name. Forgos hadn't even noticed his mistake. The two backed up hurriedly; the massed ranks of the dead were not far away. As they retreated, they joined Kesairl and Sontyra.

"The blades are going to rush in and save us," Perin told them. "As soon as their main line gets close enough."

"The blades!" Kesairl snorted. "Ah, well. Best they have something to do, I suppose."

The dead were in strict formation now, obeying the wordless hand movements of a leader, one who wore the body of a Nagyevo City Guard. They came in two columns, with the spearmen at the head, two partial phalanxes aimed up the hill. Perin stayed calm as they trod nearer. His heart raced but he was able to count the number of the true dead.

The enemy had cost the defenders three prigon skirmishers. Dozens of empty corpses lay alongside. There was some satisfaction to be had in the knowledge that they would never rise again.

"Here they come," Forgos muttered. He didn't mean the enemy. The ground began to shudder beneath their feet.

The blades went past. Perin felt a primal thrill as the formation passed. The hillside resounded like a rolling drum. The prigon weren't running very fast, but their speed was building. The long, squared blades were swept back, balanced on shoulders. The two formations crashed together in a roar. Perin and Forgos were already running to support their prigon allies, but it was clear which group would win through. The prigon formation spread wide on impact, giving each warrior room to swing his weapon. Many of the damned dead were in pieces. Perin saw a dead man break apart along a ragged line from shoulder to hip, bursting like a wineskin.

"Along the flank!" Kesairl boomed. Perin went with him to cut off the dead that were flowing around the melee. Forgos and Sontyra went the other way, as skirmishers and human spearmen ran down the hillside to join the push.

It was a bloody blur, and twice Perin had to dodge a frenzied sword swing made by a battle-mad prigon. The blades were not calm warriors. The air grew thick and painful with their roaring. Only the dead were silent.

Afterward, Perin walked a short distance away to meet Abrun and Kimr. He could hear the cheering of the archers and Adamun's men on the ridge. Looking back, he could see a few prigon stumbling from their injuries or dead on the ground. Perhaps ten or eleven who could no longer fight. Kelish and other healers were hurrying to the field.

The prigon withdrew as the Claimfold militia started to work over the corpses, prodding bodies with their spears. There was a great heap of Damned Dead—as Medrivar couldn't help but think of them—to the rear of the battle line. Perin could see Aranyo, his lip curled with distaste, driving his gore-strung spear into a body. It reached for him as the spear went through the ribs. Perin stopped, frozen with horror as the realisation hit. The pile of corpses was moving. The rearguard dead were fallen, but not finished.

"It's a trick!" Perin screamed, running back down the slope. "They went down false; look out, Aranyo!"

The pile exploded. The dead that had fallen to the ground in the chaos were now back on their feet. Dispassionate eyes, silent mouths, and always the reaching hands. Aranyo crumpled underneath them as under a wave, his spear breaking, thrown aside.

"*No!*" Perin hurled himself into a sprint. Ahead of him were mainly scattered militia, turning their spears to defend themselves. They were already being overwhelmed.

With a roar, Battlemage Magyr overtook Perin. He cannoned into the nearest group of Damned Dead and grabbed two bodies by the necks. The corpses shook violently in his grip, voiding before the smoke began to rise from their skin. Magyr tossed them aside and converted the heat he'd gathered into first one, then two beams of Narrow Fire. His bellow rose in volume as he guided the blasts of heat in an arc in front of him, carving up the scrambling dead before they could reach him.

"Stay back! Stay back!" His yell was in Claimic, so Perin knew the warning had been meant for him and the others. The great prigon had caught the attention of the remaining dead, and the human fighters were running clear.

The wind rose around Magyr until its voice was a howl. The sky above was blue and clear; yet around the battlemage, the air whirled in a tempest. A reverse shockwave hauled animated bodies toward Magyr, some being lifted into the air. The battlemage's dark skin smouldered. Then he seemed to burst into violent flame, and a blast rushed outwards with the winds he'd conjured. After the explosion, there remained nothing but a ring of burnt bodies and Magyr, triumphant in the middle.

Perin stared at the mess as the shouts became cheering again. Aranyo was dead. He did not need to look to know that. He did look anyway because Aranyo had been his to protect since the rooftops of Nagyevo, since the tavern on South Way, though he'd not known that at the time. He'd put on a coat and a hat and a fugitive identity and taken responsibility, person by person, for a whole city.

For a whole nation.

Aranyo was dead because he, Perin, had been powerless to protect him.

Just an image, just clothes, after all.

No. Calm down. This is not your fault!

Perin's heart galloped in his chest and he didn't feel inclined to listen to Medrivar. But Forgos and Kesairl were walking up, faces grim and set. He had to control himself. He found Kimr and Abrun through tears, saw Sudar and Neva coming down the slope.

"Withdraw! Back up the slope! Get the wounded past the rocks and send the skirmishers to scout the lower hills. Start burying our dead. Leave theirs where they lie." Perin strode up the slope, squeezing Forgos's hand as he passed him. Neva's expression was heartbreaking, and Sudar's iron look matched Perin's own.

"As the Gravedigger says, withdraw! Wounded to the rock line!" Kimr called out in Priga.

"Skirmishers, with me!" Kesairl added his voice and signalled to Sontyra. The victorious forces reorganised themselves. Perin waited until the Gravedigger Ring joined him at the peak of the hillside, a short distance from where Lord Adamun barked orders of his own.

"We haven't got much time. I don't know what Medrivar's plan is exactly — he won't say more than that we need to be in the North. We need to be under the Meddoszoru. Under the mountainside where Medrivar comes from."

The lack of objections was heartening. Magyr stepped closer, still breathing quite heavily from his exertions and the climb. "That is past Darmir land. I know the landscape. I have heard all the tales we prigon tell of the hill of the dead. I will come with you."

"Thank you, Magyr uto Hegyr." Perin gave the prigon the sign of gratitude. He turned back to his companions. "We'll go as soon as Kesairl comes back from leading the scouts. We need to explain to Adamun and the Torzsi chiefs. It will be hard. We are unlikely to reach the mountains in time. The defence here isn't likely to last more than a few days. This is the end of the Claimfold. It might be the end of Valo. All I have left is Medrivar and all of you. And belief that we have to win somehow."

There was a heavy pause. Neva coughed. "That's not exactly the most inspiring speech I've heard you give, Perin."

"Aranyo is dead," Perin snapped. Neva rocked back a little, as if Perin's words had physically struck him. "We're all dead if we stay," Perin added. "*Everyone* is dead if we stay."

THIRTY-FIVE

ADAMUN DID NOT fully understand. It was a mark of his quality as a man that he chose to trust Perin's word. To many, it seemed like the Gravedigger and his best men were leaving, running for the mountains. Perin felt ill, as if the distrust of the Kobanites, the militia, and the Torzsi had infected him.

The light glowed golden across the slopes, long shadows running from the odd tree and outcrop to pattern the land ahead. The air was cool. Having left their allies far behind, the Gravedigger Ring had walked for hours at a steady pace, but now Perin's unease grew. They were not making fast progress.

When the shadows deepened and the sky was divided into dark cloud lined in gold and pale sky turning slate, Neva held up both hands and stopped.

"What's wrong?" Perin asked him.

Neva gestured around. "This. Us. We've left everyone behind. We're alone. But more importantly, we're tiring ourselves walking, and I have the ability to translocate."

Perin didn't address Neva's frustration at leaving the allied army behind. It hurt him too, but it was necessary. "You can't translocate all of us," he pointed out. The others were gathering round.

"Maybe I can." Neva shrugged back his sleeves. Kigzusta and Kigkarmzin gleamed red and silver in the last light. "You've shared memories with me before, images of places. That's all I need, to be able to see the place I'm taking us. That, and the power to do it."

"You don't have that much energy stored in those," Perin objected.

"No," Kesairl interrupted, a look of realisation on his face. He pulled off his coloured coat and proffered his arms. His own gold rings caught the light as well. "Kigzusta and Kigkarmzin alone are not enough. But I have these devices, which Neva may use. Not including my nose ring, of course."

Neva grinned. "Thanks Kesairl. I'd rather you kept that in, if I'm honest." He turned towards Perin. "Look, I can do three double translocations over short distances using just Kigzusta and Kigkarmzin. You know that. Long distance is harder to estimate, but I don't think the distance makes *that* much difference. It's the moving of multiple people that will be hard."

Perin ran a hand through his hair. He was caught between fear and need. Being able to disappear and reappear leagues north would save time and preserve physical energy. On the other hand, the risk to Neva, the only person who was capable of the task, was unknown. The strain could damage him.

"With respect, Perin, this is not an area in which you have knowledge." Kesairl's deep voice had a reassuring tone.

"All right," Perin breathed out. "You three magi talk about it then. I'm just…"

He took a few steps away, looking down the slope toward the sunset, now a red line against the black of the hills. He concentrated on breathing. Sudar came and sat down a short distance away, resting his spear on his lap. Forgos took up a watch posture on the other side.

In the throne room, Medrivar listened to the discussion between Neva and the two prigon.

Perin approached and sat on the chair that had been readied for him. "What are we expecting to find, Majesty? At the Meddoszoru?"

Medrivar frowned in thought. "Akrash Haal—no, I mean the man Keresur possessed by Haal—was the sorcerer who sullied the earth under Meddoszoru. We know that now. Before he died and became a shell for the ones from beneath Csus. What we don't know is why he did what he did.

"My belief is that when he was in the North, he allowed himself to be possessed. Or at least influenced. In any case, when he came to Erdhanger, he was interested in personal power, nothing more. He was not truly acting on the behalf of the Tacnimag."

Perin stared at the floor, his original question forgotten. "If I hadn't killed him, Keresur would never have fallen down to Haal and the other spirits trapped beneath Csus. It's my fault that Valo is dying."

Medrivar snorted. "You may as well blame the powers that trapped them beneath the mountain in the first place. You didn't know what lay at the bottom of that well. All you knew was that you were fighting to defend others. The noble act led to evil, but that does not make the act evil. You cannot be blamed."

Perin felt comforted. "What powers trapped them there? The gods of Valo? Why under Csus? Why anywhere?"

Medrivar shrugged eloquently. "The sanctity of the Meddoszoru is protected by layers of earth and rock. It keeps the two tribes of the dead away from the living and protects the balance of the thrones. Csus is a mountain. The largest mountain in the Claimfold."

"They needed a body to get them out," Perin murmured. "You could leave the Meddoszoru because you had a body."

"Yes. As for your question…when I left the Meddoszoru over two years ago, my men were weak. Unable to refresh themselves in the burial ground around the Bright Throne, some of them lost their bodies and were only able to haunt the rooms in spirit, incapable of interacting with their comrades or their enemy.

"The Damned Dead may have destroyed every one of my men. Or else, after the sorcerer left to chase me down, perhaps my men were able to regenerate and recover. I don't know. I don't know what waits for us, apart from the three thrones. I don't know what we will do when we arrive, aside from rally any who remain and defend the hill."

Perin nodded slowly. "That is all we end up doing, isn't it? Defending." Aranyo's face haunted him. Medrivar's blue eyes watched him with compassion, full of understanding.

"Defending and failing all the same, that is what you are thinking, yes?"

Perin nodded.

"To do nothing or to run, to put yourself before your concern for the Claimfold—that would be failure. In trying to save them, you do all that you can. Aranyo's death—all their deaths—are not your burden." Medrivar's expression was stern.

"I felt that way when I only had to bury the dead," Perin murmured, nonetheless comforted by Medrivar's words. "It's harder, now I know how people live."

"Perin." Kesairl's voice pulled Perin out of himself. The two prigon and Neva were turned toward him. "It is decided. If you can give Neva the image of a location to the north—for safety let us say about ten leagues distant—then Magyr and I will commit power to Neva's usage. After translocation, we will meditate and recharge our devices. Tomorrow, we can repeat the act perhaps as many as four times before nightfall, giving us enough time to rest and recharge."

Perin nodded slowly. "And you're sure of this? It is safe?" He looked directly at Neva who had an expression of resolute determination on his freckled face.

"It's going to tire me out, Perin. But I can do it. I will do it. We'll get to the hill of the dead before Haal does. I promise." Perin accepted this with a nod, though his face was taut with worry.

They grouped around the telemage in a close circle. Neva breathed in and out in a deliberate, controlled way, both hands reaching up, placed on Kesairl and Magyr's chests. The two prigon had pulled aside their magistry cloaks and bared their chests so that the young man's hands would be against their skin in full contact with the power flowing through them.

Kesairl and Magyr's arms encircled, so that Perin, Forgos, and Sudar could hold onto them or Neva or both. In that bizarre embrace, they waited until Neva's breath had calmed and his eyes opened slowly.

The world whipped away from them, blurring into darkness. Medrivar's image of a place on the road north became real around them. Neva had been unsure of himself for a few seconds—the king's memory had painted the place in daylight. Other details, such as the growth of vegetation, were also different, but it seemed that Neva's skill was enough to overcome. The group stumbled, feet suddenly on different earth. The terrain was rockier, with scrub bushes dimly visible peppering the uneven ground.

Neva sank to his knees, breathing steadily, as if counting time. Perin put a hand on his shoulder and felt a strong heat emanating from his friend. It was fading, but it was enough to heighten Perin's fears. "Are you all right, Neva?"

"Yes. Just tired. Can I have water, please? And something to eat?" Neva's voice was low, as if speaking was slightly uncomfortable. Sudar opened a pack and brought Neva a flask and some prigon food, a blend of dried mushrooms, sticky with a preserving oil. Neva ate and drank while Perin and Sudar set out bedrolls. Forgos lit a fire.

"Impressive," Magyr murmured to Kesairl in Priga.

"Yes. He took more from me than I expected. My rings are empty. And I'm tired."

"For a human, very impressive. With other skills, he might easily have become a battlemage."

"Mmm." Kesairl looked away at the mention of the word 'battlemage', then went to help Sudar and Perin.

Neva was already sleeping when the camp was ready. His bedroll was the first Perin had readied, and Neva lay, oblivious, as they prepared for their own rest or for watch duty. Kesairl meditated to refresh himself, feeling the cool trickle of energy moving along his arms and into his many gold rings. Magyr sat a short distance away, a larger mirror image, great hands almost touching the gravelly soil.

Perin took the watch. After an hour or so, when the fire was dimming, they finished their meditation and began to talk. They spoke in Priga, and it made Perin wonder if he should be overhearing or not, as he found himself understanding most of what they said.

"You want to be a battlemage, Kesairl uto Abrun."

"Yes. That is true."

"You are wondering what my opinion is."

"Magyr uto Hegyr, I respect your experience. If you have advice for me…" Perin could hear that Kesairl was having difficulty veiling the excitement in his voice.

"I am not certain that the magistry is right for you."

"Oh." Perin could hear his friend shifting uncomfortably. "That…that may be so. May I know why?"

"Remember that I am not certain. And remember, too, Kesairl, it is not a lacking in you. You are in no way unworthy.

"I am uncertain because you are a very fine skirmisher, and I wonder if your skills would be wasted in the battle magistry. Consider: we go into unknown danger. Threat chases us, we know; but it may also lurk ahead. A skirmisher is adaptable. His skills are quickly gathered and as quickly employed. The magic might be slighter, but its edge is keen."

"I do not understand."

"I mean that skirmishers are adaptable. Their skills can be used as easily in flight as in attack. You can be quick. You need not spend valuable time drawing on great resources of power, as a battlemage must to unleash his force."

"I do not have enough power?"

"It is not a question of capacity." Magyr sounded somewhat tired. "We both gave much to the human Neva, and I can see easily that you are no more drained than I. It is more than just youth, I believe. You may have better power than me before too long. Your control is better than mine was at your age. I have seen you use the Narrow Fire. That is more properly a battlemage technique, but you use it well, as do the best of the skirmishers."

"I could be a battlemage, then, in a few years?" Kesairl's hopefulness was not hidden.

"You could. You could be a battlemage now, at need. I could magister you here. It is not a question of could. It is a question of should. Should you be a battlemage? The way you do magic would change. It would require different disciplines to be learned. You may lose much. Please, consider the possibility that you can be a far greater skirmisher than you would be as a battlemage."

Kesairl considered this in silence. After some minutes had passed, he spoke again. "It would mean that I could never use the Flame Capture and Flame Release as you do. I could never perform the Falling Wall technique or the Torn Hold…"

"Probably, they would remain beyond you. But you are young. There may be another way."

"What do you mean?"

"If you live long enough, you may be able to conquer the techniques you mention using your own discipline as a skirmisher. It would make you very great and very rare. Changing magistry is the quick way. But it would limit you to the constraints of battle magistry—it is not a flexible or adaptable magistry. We require defenders to protect us while we gather strength. We cannot concentrate on physical combat while preparing power or using it. In many ways, we are limited. A skirmisher that had learned to use the Falling Wall technique…you would defy the strictures of magistry. In the past, the Narrow Fire could not be used by the skirmishers. The first to do so was your father."

"There is another way…?"

"Yes. Do not place respect on titles alone. The magistry is not as important as the power it describes. And what you do with your skills is more important than the skills themselves."

"Thank you, Magyr uto Hagyr." Kesairl got up and went to crouch beside the sleeping Neva. He laid a great hand gently on the boy's shoulder and back. After a moment, his silhouette looked up in abrupt surprise, his horned head turned toward Magyr in the dark.

"Neva… Magyr, come see what I see."

The great prigon rose as well and crouched so that he obscured Neva's sleeping shape from Perin's view. "Astonishing," he murmured after several seconds passed, "astonishing."

"What? What is it?" Perin called out in low Priga. The two prigon turned toward him.

"Neva is regathering energy in his sleep," Kesairl said in Claimic.

"Your companion is a wonder," Magyr whispered. "It is as if in a dream he meditates. Even his Kigzusta and Kigkarmzin are slowly being replenished."

Perin came and stood with them, looking down at his friend. "The Tacnimag will never know how great an asset they had in him," he said. "They used him as a spy. Fools. He will get us to Meddoszoru yet."

He didn't speak into the darkness about the sad fact that they still had no plan for what to do when they got there. His greatest fear was that they would be made to wait in a great tomb, straining their minds at what might be done, while Akrash Haal; the One and the Many, and his dead horde came steadily towards them, time trickling away like blood from a wound.

He went to wake Forgos for the watch.

The following day, they packed the bedrolls and stood together looking up the slope. According to Medrivar, the rise they were looking at would come to a shallow peak and fall away again, only to rise once more in a series of crooked waves towards the mountains. Eventually, full-fledged foothills would conceal the entrance to the Meddoszoru.

Neva seemed strong and wakeful, but a little subdued. He listened to Kesairl and Magyr as if they were coaching him, nodding without much reaction as they told him of his ability to passively recharge his power.

The land ahead was half-veiled in a soft mist that looked suspiciously like oncoming rain. The group huddled together as they had done the day before. Perin looked up in the moment before translocation. The clouds above seemed gentle, pillowed from horizon to horizon in grey-white layers.

They translocated into light, but steady rain and the clouds above were already darkening. For over an hour, the three magi sat in intense meditation, steam rising from them, while Perin and Sudar and Forgos stood watch. There were more trees here, great pines and clumped firs, in patches and strings across the uneven ground. There was no indication that anything apart from birds moved in the wilderness, but the emptiness and near silence were enough to provoke caution.

"It's like the farther we go north, the less life remains," Forgos pronounced bleakly.

Neva finished replenishing his energy first. He meditated on for some time, supporting Magyr and Kesairl in their own devotions. When he stood up, it was with a jump, and he appeared to be vibrating slightly, as if his body were unable to completely contain the energy he had gathered. He grinned, a flash in his blue eyes that reminded Perin strongly of first meeting him in the library. "What are we waiting for? I feel like I could take on thirty leagues. More if it'll get us out of the pissing rain!"

"Ten leagues. Let us not tempt disaster, Neva," Magyr cautioned. They gathered around Neva as before, and in a moment, were on different ground. The rain was less, but the soil was sodden with water, marshy in a way it had not appeared in Medrivar"s memory. They were in a defile running between steep slopes, overhung with alders.

It took some time to escape the bog and move along the defile to a point where they could climb its walls. Neva was quick to get out of the mud and quicker still to make a suggestion to Medrivar through Perin. "Maybe his Majesty could pick high ground from now on? I think the rain has changed his old path somewhat."

Perin smiled. "Apologies."

They paused to drink and eat. Neva sat down and held his arms in a mimicking of Magyr and Kesairl. Within half an hour, he appeared to be done with meditation. It was still before noon when they translocated again.

This time, the hillside grew thick with woods, high elms and beeches hiding the sky. The rain poured unrelenting. Neva did need to rest properly this time, and the two prigon returned to meditation at once, in silence.

As Perin walked uneasily from tree to tree, Neva caught his eye. "Has Medrivar said anything?"

"Should he have?"

"I just wondered. I skipped an image in the sequence he gave me. This was twenty leagues, not ten. We're making progress."

"You stupid—! Aren't you tired?"

"Very. But I'll be fine in a bit. An hour or so. The distance really isn't the problem. There's not much difference between this and the last translocation."

Perin bit his lip. "You should still be careful."

"Says the man who defied the Tacnimag and is leading his friends into unknown danger without a plan," Neva teased.

The comment, in good humour as it was, still stung Perin and he fell silent. The image of Aranyo collapsing under the cold weight of corpses returned to him like a nightmare. He thought of all the people they had left behind on nothing more than an instinct. Neva could see it on his face. His look of sorrow as he crossed to Perin, followed by the hug he gave him, salved the pain.

THIRTY-SIX

THEY MANAGED TWO MORE translocations before nightfall. Each one was twenty leagues, though Neva told no one else, and Perin followed Medrivar's lead in telling no one. Magyr and Kesairl seemed more tired than the previous night, but not in actual danger. Haste was crucial, and Perin's reservations were slipping away under the weight of urgency.

Neva was already snoring, tucked into the warmest end of a niche below a jutting rock that covered two bedrolls from the weather. The nearest trees were down the slope in a stand of firs. The resinous wood had resisted the damp and the fire lit after a little prompting from Kesairl, who sat beside Magyr under the edge of the rock.

When the morning came, the sky was nearly clear. Blue gaped through the high clouds, enhancing their white. South of them, the sky swelled thicker with grey and purple-smudged cloudbanks. The air turned colder and crisp, and Perin found that breathing was slightly harder than before. They were getting closer to the foothills of the mountains.

These they could see clearly now, grey and white, distinct and huge against the sky. *We are forty leagues at most from the Meddoszoru*, Medrivar whispered in Perin's mind. The thought gave him great encouragement. Two translocations, and they might all reach their destination before midday.

Perin volunteered to fetch water, walking along the hillside to a stream that ran in spate down the slope, cutting a path around the edge of the fir copse. He was returning, weighed down by the filled flasks, when he heard the rumbling voice of Kesairl in confrontation with Neva's much reedier voice.

"You don't understand...it isn't the distance. The leagues..."

"You need to listen! We are elder to you, in years and in magic, and we were worn weary by the work of yesterday—we may be running thin; there has been no real time of rest for many days, not since we left Helynvale!"

"But twenty leagues is twice the distance! We did it yesterday, twice! Didn't you notice?"

Kesairl snarled. "So that is why! I thought that I was losing stamina! You had no right, mageling, to use us that way without telling us!"

Perin hurried up and dumped the flasks on top of the heaped packs. Sudar and Forgos were watching silently. Magyr seemed to be in deep thought, crouched a short distance away.

"You great...lumbering..." Neva stopped himself, took a few deep breaths while Kesairl's tricoloured eyes flashed warning. "Look... Kesairl, you're probably right—that I should have told you. I'm sorry. But if I had told you, you would have forbad it. And we would be worse off. Perin knew! Medrivar knew!"

Kesairl was somewhat disarmed by this and looked toward Perin for confirmation. When his friend nodded, in some embarrassment, he snorted and sat down cross-legged.

"Hmph. Strange coming from one that was so worried, so concerned before. What changed your mind?"

"Neva." Perin answered. "He's right. Doubling the distance fatigued you all little more than if it had been the same. Half the distance is twice the number of translocations. You would all be far more exhausted if we had covered this distance in shorter jumps. We don't have a lot of time. And now we are two translocations from Meddoszoru."

"We were not damaged. The weariness could be borne," Magyr rumbled.

Kesairl relaxed his posture slowly. Finally he nodded to Neva. "I apologise. It seems I overreacted. I can only blame the tiredness—magic expended does not weaken the muscles, but the mind and emotions. It makes us *richstii*...fractious."

"Just two more," Perin promised, backed up by Medrivar.

The king's confidence may not have grown much, but his excitement had. He was almost home.

The second translocation saw them tumbled out as if from an invisible hand, to lie on a steep slope on thin snow. Azure light saturated the sky, and the sun was high, glowing on the lower hills and the thin blanketing of rain or mist that could be seen in the distance. The snow was soft here, despite the cold; but farther up, under the flanks of the mountains, it looked thicker and more permanent.

Neva sat on his bedroll and began at once to meditate. A circle of damp rock and earth grew slowly around him, until even some short grass became visible, crisp with the cold. After a brief look around, their eyes narrowed against the sun. The two prigon joined him. They sat either side, so that Neva looked like a small deity, flanked by horned guardians. The snowmelt increased so that soon, Perin, Sudar, and Forgos were able to make a sort of camp on the bare earth.

The entrance is a short walk from here where the earth turns to rock under a promontory. But there is a long way to walk, then, into the earth, Medrivar explained. As they rested, Perin passed this on. He thought he could see the promontory Medrivar described, jutting into the sky at the head of a swollen prow of earth, grey with shale where the white snow failed.

The air had thinned and the light radiated unearthly. The starkness and the enormity of the rockscape around Perin took on a feeling of monument — for the first time he began to sense a kind of significance beneath his feet that hinted of thresholds and antiquity.

Sanctity.

Kesairl and Magyr did not stop until they were brimming with energy. Neva, who had finished already, now paced on the mountainside, periodically shrugging his sleeves back off his arms so that the red and silver serpents wound up his arms gleamed in the sun.

At last, feeling if not rested, then ready, the mages rose and followed Perin, who wordlessly set off toward the promontory. Sudar and Forgos ran slightly ahead, holding their spears and staying watchful.

Beneath the jutting rock, which cut into the sky like the raised heel of the mountains, a wide, shallow opening gaped. Loose shale lay scattered around the mouth, but the walls and ceiling of the cave seemed stable. A short distance into the throat of the opening, two carved stone figures stood. They faced one another from opposing walls, human and posed, weapons in hand. The clothing they were carved in seemed strange to Perin's eyes. At the neck, the warriors' flesh had been chipped away, and in the place of heads, the sculptor had given them skulls, grinning in silent fury.

They walked between the statues, feeling the air get colder out of the sunlight, seeing by Magyr's conjured light, a globe of pale fire that hovered between his horns like a crown.

There was still no sign of movement.

They walked for a long time until Perin was reasonably sure that evening was falling outside in the world above. The deeper they went, the more comfortable the temperature seemed to get, until it was almost stifling. At last, when Perin was about to call for a break and food, the way opened out.

The cavern's ceilings soared beyond sight. The shapes and shadows of the rock suggested many weaving paths and narrow walkways, skirting the high walls like galleries. Other openings in the walls showed black in Magyr's light. Some appeared to dive downwards, others sloping upwards into the rock of the mountain.

These distractions failed to keep them from seeing the bridge. Like an echo of Medrivar's visions made real, Perin saw the great arching structure, high, high above, traced in a blue light. In fact, it was only when Magyr extinguished his fire that they could see the blue light everywhere. It hung in the air close to the walls and ceilings, without flickering like firelight, yet somehow more evanescent than sunlight. Kesairl put out a hand and traced the webbing of blue mineral under the skin of the stone with his large fingers. The light coming from the veins of crystal did not burn or blaze. It simply filled the air with effortless, faint illumination.

"That feels...very odd," Kesairl murmured.

"What is that?" Forgos whispered in the half-light.

"*Bluevein*," Perin answered. His eyes returned to the bridge high above as if drawn to it. "Medrivar says...*bluevein* or *kykvarc*, in Priga. And that..."

That is the Meddoszoru bridge. And yes, you are right, Medrivar said. *That is where the third throne hangs inverted above the gulf. This is where I stood at the end of my dream.*

"What is the gulf?" Perin asked aloud, though he thought he knew. He walked forward, away from the tunnel they had just left, and stopped when the floor ran out. The light of the *bluevein* was enough to show the stone dropping away smoothly into the blackness. Beyond the blue glow, no light came from the immense void.

"How far down to...?" Neva seemed unable to finish the question.

No one could answer, not even Medrivar. Perin looked up again. No matter what took his attention, it was always dragged back to the bridge. From here, he could see a faint blue light hanging beneath it. There was the suggestion of a stone column like an enormous stalactite joining the light to the base of the bridge. The third throne was made of *bluevein*?

Yes. It's better than gold or silver at conducting and storing magic. And unlike gold and silver, it is not inert. It makes its own power. The power of this entire place is bound by the bluevein. Whatever powers built this place, either took advantage of the mineral or created it and everything else with it.

Gods? Perin wondered. Medrivar's lack of response meant he didn't know.

They backed away from the edge and contemplated their options. The tunnel they had exited was one of many openings in the rock. A broad path skirted the edge of the chasm.

"This way." Perin indicated Medrivar's directions by pointing away from the bridge, along the path and into the shadows where several entrances gaped.

A figure moved there.

The party halted, drawing weapons. Neva tossed a stone into the air and let it hover there while he skirted wide to get a good angle. Perin went forward first, but he did not feel alarmed. The dead man came closer. He carried a battered spear, but he was not levelling it at them.

"Majesty." The voice sounded dry and old, reminding Perin strongly of his first meeting with Medrivar. "Majesty! Medrivar King!" he shambled into a run, and now they could see that his left foot dragged. He had been broken at the ankle, so that only sinew kept the limb in place. His skin was withered and taut on his body, and both his eyes had gone.

"Warrior," Medrivar responded through Perin's lips, "where are the others?"

The dead man knelt awkwardly. "In your hall, Medrivar King. Majesty, forgive me for asking..."

"Yes, I am with trueborn, Bright One. I know this was not my law before I left."

"I sense also that you are bound within a trueborn man. This too was forbidden..."

"Yes. Perin saved my life. My body is lost."

Despite his gaunt face, it was possible to see that the dead man was unsure. The others behind Perin looked similarly uncomfortable to hear Medrivar speaking with Perin's voice.

"Majesty...we must know that you are as you were before. To break your own edicts and take territory that is not yours...do you still serve?" For the first time, the man tightened his grip on his spear as if to wield it against his king.

"Yes!" Perin shouted. "He still serves! And he's welcome to me! We're here...we're here because your enemy is back, the one who cursed your burial grounds. He's coming with hundreds of Damned Dead..." Medrivar calmed him. Perin drew in a breath, still terrified that Medrivar's servants, perhaps his last hope, might turn against their king.

"Sometimes...sometimes you have to follow the heart behind a law and break the law itself. Medrivar is my closest friend. I would have died without him. He would have died without me."

"Your name is Perin, Trueborn?" the dead man asked.

"Yes."

"Perin Gravedigger." Kesairl interjected, emphasising the title. It seemed to Perin that the title was hardly relevant now, but the dead warrior nodded as if considering the name.

"My name is Ondriang, Perin Gravedigger. Hmm. Gravedigger... Medrivar King, you said that you went forth seeking burial. After you had gone, the trueborn foe was seen leaving as well."

"The sorcerer Keresur," Perin breathed.

Ondriang nodded his head, empty eye-sockets turned toward Perin. "Some time after his leaving, our ability to rest returned, though not as before.

Not as good, not as strong. But we feared for our king. The sorcerer went after him."

Perin did not think it was a good idea to tell about his confrontation with the Tacnimag sorcerer and its eventual consequences. Instead he said, "A spirit called Akrash Haal is coming here. He...he's in possession of the dead body of the sorcerer who cursed you. And he has many spirits with him."

"Akrash Haal...The One and the Many. Then he is coming to take the Dark Seat," Ondriang said with grim certainty.

"That is what Medrivar believes as well."

"Then we are wasting time here. Perin Gravedigger, you are not our king. But it is your body, your mind that supports his existence. We will serve you in Medrivar King's place. There can be no confusion—whether it is you or the king that speaks to us, we will obey. We must go to the throne room now. I am not likely to be the only scout walking the bypassages. We do not want to forewarn the Damned Dead."

Without pause, Ondriang turned and limped away. Kesairl and Magyr followed without comment.

Neva put his pebble away, following Forgos and Sudar. "I almost killed him," he muttered to Sudar. "Well, not *killed* him as such. You know what I mean."

The tunnels Ondriang led them through seemed to twist and turn beyond any kind of logic, so that Perin's sense of direction was utterly confused. There was some sense of ascent, but little else to indicate where they were in relation to where they'd been. As they went and as the tunnels widened, other warriors joined them, some in better shape than Ondriang and others with even worse injuries.

The tunnel spat them out into a stepped atrium. In comparison with where they had been, the space blazed with blue light. Bluevein shot through the walls in thick sprays and seams, like streams feeding into a lake. The threads of the mineral in the rock converged on a narrow opening atop the highest tier of the cavern, disappearing into the room beyond.

"This is the hall of defence." Ondriang gestured around. It made sense; the stepped tiers of rock would make it difficult to reach the doorway quickly, especially if the room was defended. At strategic locations, the rock had been smoothed into slopes to allow defenders paths of retreat.

There were perhaps seventy undead warriors in attendance. Ondriang limped into the centre of the lowest tier and began to address them. Looking around, Perin could see that there were two other ways out of the cavern besides the way they had come in. One was blocked permanently with fallen rocks, the other one barricaded with waist-high stones. A watch of three warriors stood there looking out. They didn't turn, even to listen to Ondriang.

The veteran spoke in a language that resembled both Priga and Claimic, but was different enough to confound Perin's ability to understand it. Medrivar did understand, of course, but it would be some time before the meanings would begin to filter to Perin. It might be days or weeks before Perin began unconsciously to learn it, as he had managed with Priga. Perin knew that they did not have weeks. As far as he knew, Akrash Haal was even now climbing the hills outside.

Medrivar's whisper in Perin's mind was pained. *Is this all that remains? Where are the rest of my men?*

As if hearing him, Ondriang turned and bowed. "Medrivar King, Perin Gravedigger. We are eighty standing. Eleven men are in the out-ways, scouting or watching for the enemy." He gestured toward the tunnel which they had used to reach the defence hall. "And ten are in the throne room, at rest. We have blocked the in-ways. If the Damned Dead hear the news you've brought, they will attack across the bridge. It's the quickest route between the two throne rooms."

And the most dangerous. Perin didn't need Medrivar to explain. Any body, living or dead that fell from the bridge would be swallowed by the great black gulf beneath. Perin had never seen anything better encapsulate the meaning of 'no return.'

"Since you left, Majesty, our choice has been to defend and conserve our numbers. The burial chambers have slowed. Ten of our number regenerate as we speak, but I fear they will not be fit before battle is joined." Ondriang bowed his head in what might have been shame. "We are outnumbered, Perin Gravedigger. Majesty, forgive us. We have been outfought this last year."

"The Damned have been able to rest," Perin replied in one voice with Medrivar. "You have done heroically to hold out this long without resting. Now we are here. We need to decide what to do."

THIRTY-SEVEN

THE THRONE WAS MADE of white stone. It had been half carved out of a column of rock, and the convergent bluevein flowed across the roof and down into the seat itself. The room was not large, but around its entire circumference were chambered tombs. Scraps of cloth suggested that once, fine hangings had curtained the openings. Perin could see that horizontal alcoves had been carved into the walls of the chambers. Each niche had been filled, or partially filled, with a decrepit and motionless corpse. Only the blue light, which seemed to pulse faintly here, indicated that they were alive. Perin noticed again, as he had on entering the defence hall, how little scent of rot there was.

"They are sleeping," Ondriang intoned solemnly.

Perin, Neva, Sudar, and Forgos sat down on the narrow steps that raised the throne from the polished floor of the room. Magyr and Kesairl stayed standing, as if out of respect. Ondriang was joined by three other dead warriors.

After an awkward silence, Ondriang said, "I am unsure how to go forward. Medrivar King knows us all; but what he may have told you, I do not know." His eye sockets looked at Perin as if for a clue.

"Medrivar is deep in thought," Perin began. "He'll give me words to say if he gains any understanding. He says that our journey here has been due more to instinct and dream than it has strategy."

"Powers guide him," one of the dead warriors murmured reverently.

"I will address you then, Gravedigger." Ondriang settled himself cross-legged, using his hands to reposition his foot. Neva flinched as the bared tissue of the ankle stretched unnaturally. "These are Hagrimmon, Ranmoril, and Drongarrow. They are captains alongside myself. With us, you may build your strategy."

The three sat down as Ondriang had. Hagrimmon was broader and taller than any of the other dead warriors, with a mass of dark-brown hair flowing down his cheeks into his beard. Ranmoril's hair only grew over half her skull, and a recent-looking wound made sure that it *was* her skull on show, the yellowish bone showing through the ragged scalp. Fierce green eyes watched Perin from under her half-fringe. Drongarrow was the most damaged of the three, with most of his ribs on show. He wore ragged mail in a kind of protective curtain over where his lower chest and stomach should have been. His whole body was battered and gaunt, making Ondriang look almost healthy by comparison.

"The threat is simple." Perin watched the faces of his friends and allies as he spoke. "Haal is coming here because the Meddoszoru holds the key to power in Valo. Medrivar has told me what the bluevein does. The Meddoszoru holds more power than any of us can imagine."

"We can feel it," Magyr confirmed, nodding to Kesairl and Neva, "like the rock is shaking. But in our flesh, we can feel it is not."

Perin nodded and continued. "Nobody knows what will happen if somebody becomes able to wield that power. The thrones both connect directly to the rest of the Meddoszoru and the third throne that hangs from beneath the bridge in the middle, the purpose of which, we do not know. We know that the Dark Seat is probably Haal's focus; we know that his dead are coming north, and we know that he mentioned he is 'come to take his throne'."

"There's no doubt," Ondriang said dismissively. "Medrivar King knows as well as we do, how great a spirit must be to hold hundreds of others in thrall, let alone how great it must be to hold them bound inside one body. It is said that it takes phenomenal power to sit the Dark Seat. Even more to sit the Bright Throne. And if this Akrash Haal is enthroned, with nobody to sit here, we will be overrun."

"Valo will be overrun," Kesairl said darkly. "The Claimfold is already overrun. Only Koban and northern Joval are defended still."

"So what do we do?" Forgos's frustration was mounting. Hagrimmon echoed the young man's body language. For a weird moment, they looked like living and dead versions of each other, despite Hagrimmon's thick hair and beard.

"We have been defending the Bright Throne because the enemy wants to destroy it," Ranmoril said in a surprisingly musical voice, "which means that we have been working toward the wrong end. If we destroy their throne, we triumph. They will fall and not rise, ruin and not regenerate."

"Dear heart, we have been fighting the Damned Dead for centuries, hoping to defeat them," Drongarrow rasped, "and only once in my three-and-a-half-thousand years have we come in sight of the Dark Seat itself. I barely escaped. We left twelve good spirits in that curséd room. No rest for we Bright Dead, not that close to the Dark Seat, no regeneration. Only an agony of incorporeality, for the remainder of this world's time."

Perin felt the shock of that statement, reinforced by Medrivar's own pain at the concept. For the first time he felt truly sorry for the undead. True death must seem like an unreachable gift to them. No wonder the Damned Dead had chosen to channel their rage into self-service and destruction.

"We are a third of the number that we were when we last tried to destroy the Dark Seat," Drongarrow continued firmly, "and while our enemies have lost numbers as well, they outnumber us. We were even then. We would fight to a standstill in the narrows of the out-ways, or lose warriors forever, contesting the bridge."

"That is a fight we cannot win," Hagrimmon rumbled angrily. "Even with the mages, even with Medrivar King leading us."

"Don"t forget about Perin," Neva snapped, opening his eyes. As quickly, he closed them again and went back to what he had been doing. He appeared to be meditating, but the crease of his brow suggested a greater level of concentration.

Hagrimmon bowed his head in apology.

"He meant no offence," Perin said calmly. "I understand what you're saying. Medrivar confirms it. The Meddoszoru seems rigged for balance. They've never been able to break you, and you've never defeated them. But now that balance will kill us—and do worse for the Bright Dead."

Sudar leaned forward. "Is there any way we can fight Haal head on? In the entrance on the mountainside, perhaps?"

"We could try," Kesairl replied, "but it would be a doomed attempt. Even if Akrash Haal arrives alone, which he may, as we know he is fast, we could not hold him long. And we would be vulnerable to attack from behind. The Damned would not leave their new master unaided."

The sense of fear in the small room thickened. Perin looked up at the Bright Throne, trying to find a sense of hope from somewhere. They were trapped. There was no way out and no way forward. Akrash Haal could not be fought with steel or muscle. Even Kesairl's Narrow Fire had left him unharmed.

They sat in silence for a while. Perin's gaze stayed fixed on the Bright Throne while Forgos and Sudar examined the floor in silence. Neva's eyes remained tightly closed and his knuckles were white as he gripped handfuls of his cloak. Perin, aware of him out of his peripheral vision, wondered if the fear was getting to him.

Ondriang raised his head slowly. "How much power does Perin Gravedigger wield?"

"What do you mean? I'm not a mage."

"All magic is power, but not all power is magic."

"He is human," Kesairl said gently. "Like prigon, there is a limit to his capacity. He is undeniably a good spirit…"

"But if he is a special case…" Ondriang rose awkwardly, "if he is greater than most, to have been chosen by Medrivar King, a chosen hero…a champion."

"I have no magic. I'm not special." Perin felt a kind of panic. On the one hand, he could feel the edge of hope coming from Medrivar; but his own confusion merged with the fear in the room, and he was being overwhelmed. "I'm not special!"

"Shite, you're not," Forgos growled. "I've fought for and with you too many times to believe you're not." Sudar's expression echoed the sentiment. Neva's eyes stayed closed, though his muscles seemed more strained than before.

"You knew the song," Kesairl said, like a man beginning to realise something, "you knew the *Song of Valo*, the first time I met you. And Medrivar chose you."

"No!" Perin stood abruptly, the room seeming to spin around him. "I was the only one there! Who else? It was luck!"

"Or fate," Magyr said.

Ondriang's empty eye-sockets stared intently at Perin. "Medrivar is within you. He is a greater spirit than I. If he had chosen to serve himself, then he might have accomplished such deeds as Akrash Haal's. And you are with him. One. Perhaps we do not need to destroy the Dark Seat. The Bright Throne is greater!"

"You want me to sit on the Bright Throne?" Perin's incredulity forced his voice to a high pitch. Medrivar's voice was strangely silent.

"It is that, or fight and fail. We have no choice," Kesairl said.

"You can do it, Perin. I believe it," Forgos agreed.

"You have our trust." Magyr rumbled.

The room was definitely spinning.

Neva's eyes snapped open. "Haal is coming! He is on the low slopes!"

Perin stumbled. Sudar held him up, but the others had their full attention on the young telemage. Neva's eyes were wide. "Twenty leagues away. He's twenty leagues away. He's alone. Running."

"How fast can he cover twenty leagues?" Kesairl asked.

Perin let Sudar help him upright. "In hours. We have hours." He looked around the small room at their faces, alive and dead, caught between fear and hope. "I will try to sit the Throne."

The steps seemed to be a challenge to Perin's legs as he climbed them, as shallow and as few as they were. The ceiling, a foot or more above his head, seemed to be pressing its weight down on him. Trembling, he reached out a hand and touched the seat of the Bright Throne. There was no shock of power, no thrill or sense of foreboding. It felt like cool stone, textured by the bluevein running through it.

He turned and looked down. His companions were watching with unveiled suspense, the undead captains with solemn expectation. There were no arms on the seat that he could grip.

Slowly, he sat.

Sweat trickled down the back of his neck. It was too much. He escaped into the other throne room, the one in his mind.

Medrivar was seated on a copy of the throne outside. His head was bowed, resting on his folded hands. The space around mimicked the real throne room, as if in response to Perin's intensity of emotion. "Medrivar…"

"I know." Medrivar looked up sadly. "I dared to hope, as well. It was foolish. I am not a match for Akrash Haal, no matter what my followers say. And you, Perin, are brave and selfless and faithful. But you are not special in the way they want you to be. You are my champion, but you weren't chosen for this."

"Yes." Perin felt the weight fall away, along with his hope. "I am not powerful. The only part of me that is great is you."

"Never say it!" Medrivar rose, furious. "You were great before I met you, though you didn't know it. Do not deny it now."

"But not great enough to sit the Throne. Not great enough to save us."

"No."

"Not great in any way that counts."

Medrivar stepped down and enfolded him in his arms. "I disagree. Who you are will always mean something, important of itself. Knowing what you are not is different from knowing what you are."

Perin rose. His friends seemed to be frozen in their attitudes of expectance. "I'm sorry," he said calmly, "I cannot sit the Bright Throne. I don't have power. I am not a king."

Their expressions, as hope left them, cut worse than any wound Perin had yet felt. He stepped down, forcing himself through strength of will and Medrivar's presence to stand straight and look forward. "We cannot fight

Haal throne to throne. We have hours left to act and no choice left. If we do not destroy the Dark Seat, all fighting ends in the Meddoszoru; and the rest is slaughter."

He reached up and pulled Spade free. "We are breathing—those of us that breathe. We are all standing. Our weapons are not lost. They are not broken.

"We will die or be defeated. All we have left is one choice: how we will die and the manner of our defeat. We can lie down on these stones and hold to one another for the last minutes of our lives or we can defend each other until…until we can do no more."

Forgos drew his sword. "I'd have sheepshit for brains if I couldn't answer that one."

"Fight. Of course we will fight." Kesairl's voice was ragged with emotion, but his resilience remained intact.

"We love you," Sudar said simply, "and we will do as you do."

"Gravedigger." Magyr expressed his willingness in a word. He looked old now, very old, but his great hands did not tremble as he made a gesture Perin had not seen before, taking his horns in his hands and bowing low as if offering something.

"Fighting is our essence and our nature," Ondriang said calmly. "Since we saw there was a war to be carried out, we have done nothing else. If it ends today with us, so be it."

"So be it," Hagrimmon, Ranmoril, and Drongarrow echoed.

Neva said nothing, but he came and stood next to Perin. Sensing the younger man's need, Perin gripped Neva's hand in his own. "So be it."

Ondriang led them back into the defence hall. He jumped down a tier, landing on his good foot and ignoring his torn ankle. His sockets and his mouth gaped and he roared, "*Bright Dead! Arm! Arm! Today we smash the Dark Seat! Today we earn this dust and steel!*" He threw back his head and roared, an inhuman noise something like the howl of stormwinds, harsh and terrible, yet almost musical.

The Bright Dead were forming up. They roared back in response to Ondriang and the other captains, shaking their spears. Some were armed with nothing more than curved pieces of polished stone. "Clear the way!" Drongarrow commanded, pointing at the barrier blocking the central way out. "Clear the way. Leave no defence. Recall the scouts. We will not be coming back!"

"Captains, to me!" Perin called over the raging voices. "Form a guard. Forgos, Sudar, form the blade to Kesairl's point. Take the front. Direct and support our front line. Magyr, take the centre. Conserve your power for groups or captains. Stay within the defence.

"Ondriang, Drongarrow, until we reach the bridge, command our left flank, Ranmoril, Hagrimmon, our right. When we are on the bridge, split to the front and rear. Give me and Neva ten men, and we will be rearguard until then."

"Gravedigger!" They responded in one voice. Drongarrow clapped a skeletal hand on Perin's shoulder as he went.

"Neva?" Perin turned to his friend.

"I'm all right, Perin. Thank you. Thank you. You're…you're…" He looked around as if fearing the timing of what he had to say. There were tears at the corners of his blue eyes, but his face was set.

"Say it, Neva."

"You're my—my big brother. I won't leave your side."

"Don't." Perin gave him the quickest hug that could be afforded. The Bright Dead were formed and marching. There was no time.

There was no time.

The army resolved their voice around two words. "Medrivar! Gravedigger! Medrivar! Gravedigger!"

I am not a king. Perin knew it. *I am not a king. I am a gravedigger.* Whatever the *Song of Valo* or Fate may have wanted him to be, he knew exactly who he was.

THIRTY-EIGHT

THE BRIDGE WAS in sight when the first Damned attacked. Two paths converged on the broad way that the Bright Army had taken, and the enemy came on three fronts. Kesairl killed four of them before they drew close, and the Bright Dead spearmen dispatched the rest almost without effort. They were just scouts attempting to delay their progress. The rest were still coming.

Perin could see the bridge below and to the right of their position, flooded with packed ranks of the Damned Dead who were surging across to block access. From here, he could see the spike of rock jutting from the bottom of the bridge's high arch with the blue glow of the mysterious third throne outshining the bluevein that threaded through the rocks all around.

The broad place where the near end of the bridge emerged roiled with dead warriors. Perin could see just how outnumbered the Bright Dead were. It was at least five to one. Stones and even flint arrows flew through the dark towards Perin's force, smacking and cracking off the rock walls behind and striking blows amongst the Bright Dead. Few warriors fell. Neva dismissed stones and arrows almost idly, his hands twitching as he deflected the missiles and sent some back the way they came.

As ground was lost to the edge of the gulf, narrowing the way, Kesairl changed his tactics, attacking most of his assailants with blows of force, just enough to send them tumbling into the endless dark beneath. The fear of unending solitude in the black was enough to demoralise many of the enemy. The Bright Dead made good progress, spears and stone weapons striking methodically.

Magyr uto Hegyr's first blow of the battle targeted a large knot of warriors at the threshold of the bridge. He gathered a globe of light much like the one he had used for illumination earlier, hurling it into the midst of the enemy defenders. It detonated on impact with a roar of noise and flame. Burnt corpses were strewn across the rock or went howling into the deep. Magyr grunted with satisfaction, his large prigon teeth on show.

At the bridge, the battle began to change. Ranmoril and Hagrimmon brought their force back to relieve Perin and Neva, becoming the rearguard. With a roar, Drongarrow and Ondriang charged with their own men past Kesairl, extending the front and entering full battle. Perin could see Forgos and Sudar fighting alongside their dead comrades, sword and spear flashing in the light of the bluevein.

Perin's excitement began to fail. There was no more forward motion. All around, behind and ahead, the Damned Dead were wild and numerous. Perin could see them on causeways behind and above him, finding tunnels that Ondriang had called the in-ways, running to attack from behind.

For a moment, Perin feared for the Bright Throne. It was now undefended. If the Damned had the means to smash the stone seat, the Bright Dead might lose their power. As if portending Perin's fear, a thrown spear missed him and skipped off the floor behind him, gouging the bluevein there into crystalline shards. As much as power coursed through the Bright Throne, the fragile bluevein rock that bore the throne reduced its structural strength.

Then the terrible thought evolved and Perin realised that it didn't matter. Destroying the Dark Seat was the end of their plan. And what would that mean? If they succeeded, it wouldn't matter if the Bright Throne also perished. Akrash Haal would have no throne to sit, no great power to wield; but he would still come. He would still lead the Damned Dead.

The finality of the situation was like a lead weight in Perin's stomach. He was going to die, and all his friends were going to die, and the most they would be able to do was be a hindrance to Haal. With both thrones gone, no doubt, the power in the bluevein would leak away or stagnate in the rock...

A stone skimmed Perin's shoulder and reminded him that, for now, he wanted to live. Neva shouted out an apology for letting the missile through. The next moment, the telemage was in the air, his arms sweeping downwards as he rose, suspended upright with his feet treading the air. A pattern of stones spiralled like the trailing arms of a galaxy into the air around him. Their launching made a sound that hurt Perin's ears, and dozens of dead warriors crumpled, torn and smashed by the deadly hail. With a high yell, Neva reached forward and swung his fists outward, even as he dropped smoothly back to the bridge floor. Like a parting sea, the press of Damned Dead were moved, whole groups falling to their ruin.

The telemage's actions gave the Bright Dead space to move into. They were now almost halfway across the gulf, fighting steadily. Their number had fallen and they were trapped on the bridge. The flanking Damned were now numerous enough to harry Ranmoril and Hagrimmon's warriors at the back.

Perin's fear had not yet surrendered to despair. He could feel it waiting, though, like a counterpart to the black space below the bridge, creeping at the edge of his vision. His frustration kept it back; pressed in the centre behind Magyr. He had not been able to strike even one blow.

I'm not a king. I'm not Fate's chosen. His thought, or Medrivar's? There seemed little difference now.

Ondriang was the first. A Damned captain thrust a long dirk through one of his eye sockets. Some wounds were too much. The captain fell silently to the stone. Despite the wound, Perin knew that the chambered tomb in the throne room would probably be able to regenerate Ondriang's body, given time.

There was no time.

I'm not a king.

Ondriang's foe physically lifted his body and hurled it over the edge of the bridge. Forgos and Sudar cried out in anguish and redoubled their attacks, and it was Sudar's spear that drove Ondriang's destroyer over the edge and into the void.

Once again, the Bright Army were held to a stop. They occupied the centre of the bridge, and now the fighting became desperate. Forgos and Sudar were in danger of becoming isolated, and only Kesairl kept them safe, blasting their attackers with fire or force with a relentlessness that would have amazed Perin if he hadn't felt so deadened. Neva could no longer guard against all the incoming stones and arrows, as he was occupied with defending himself personally, blowing heads apart with his own small stones or moving neck vertebrae out of place with swift hand movements, his teeth gritted with the effort of combat.

Ranmoril fell next. The warrior who had beheaded her pulled his axe free of her neck and shoulders, exposed muscles bulging in his arms, one ragged cheek showing his teeth. Perin fought back toward him, enraged, spade finally put to work. The axe missed Perin by inches as he jumped sideways, and more crystals of bluevein scattered under its blade. With a cry, Perin smashed Spade into the dead man's jaw, knocking it loose and pushing him to the edge. Another blow sent him over.

I'm not a king.

Hagrimmon was wounded many times before he succumbed. The last of his warriors fell before he did, torn and battered, under the press of Damned Dead, collapsing the rearguard. Perin did his best but he was forced to fight the enemy on the back foot, retreating toward Magyr.

I'm not a king. I'm not a champion. I'm just a gravedigger.

Of Medrivar's captains, only Drongarrow survived still, swinging a curved axe in each hand, twisting and flexing out of harm's way, his ragged form seemingly immune to peril.

Magyr sent a wave of force back across the bridge, made visible by the ripples of heat stored in it. As it rolled over the Damned Dead, it set them alight and threw them into disarray, giving Perin the breathing space to turn and push forward to Forgos and Sudar. Neva had begun taking out large or authoritative enemies with individual pebbles, taking his time and blasting holes in his targets with a kind of slow rhythm.

Forgos slipped on gore. He fell flat on his back, his sword skittering out of reach on the slick stonework. Spears and bare hands reached for him and he closed his eyes, steeling himself for a horrible end.

Kesairl saved him through sheer physicality, taking spear wounds in the arms and sides as he battered the dead away from Forgos, blue flames leaping as the prigon lost control of some of his stored magic. When it looked as if he was about to be overwhelmed, the skirmisher looked down the length of the bridge and let out a roar. His hands clapped together, swung apart, blurring the air.

A dozen or more Damned Dead seemed to explode within the rectangle of space in front of Kesairl. They came apart at the joints as if a great weight had been smashed upon them, and old blood turned the air into black-red mist.

Magyr crowed out in celebration and ran to join the younger prigon, crying, "You used the Falling Wall!"

His celebration turned into action. A score of Damned Dead were rushing to fill the gap left by their destroyed fellows, heading for Kesairl. Magyr pushed his wounded friend behind him and prepared to take the charge alone. Air began to rush around him, and Perin saw what he was going to do. The Flame Capture pulled the charging dead toward Magyr, hauling downed and upright fighters along the stone of the bridge, drawn like debris in floodwater, until he reversed the technique and performed the Flame Release. Once again, bodies tumbled into the blackness below, overcome by the shockwave.

Drongarrow took an arrow in the neck and went down on one knee. A damaged enemy, fighting on despite lacking its left arm and most of its side, hacked at his leg; but still the dead warrior hauled himself upright. He dispatched the attacker with cold efficiency and turned his skull-like glare on the regrouping rear force.

"So be it!" Drongarrow rasped as he ran past Perin, shambling because of his torn leg muscle, tearing the arrow out of his throat as he gathered speed.

He hurled himself into the oncoming ranks, alone, the last of the Bright Dead rushing to follow him. Two, three, five bodies fell against him in his last charge, and then he was lost in the tangle of struggling figures, and then lost for good. His men fought on for longer, but they were just seconds to be spent now.

There was no time.

I'm a gravedigger. I'm not a king. I'm—

Sudar, Forgos, Perin, and Neva regrouped, backs inwards, looking down each arm of the bridge. Kesairl limped to their side, his hands wreathed in flame. He looked exhausted, his breath coming in great gasps. Magyr was on his knees some paces away, calling on his own Falling Wall technique to forestall the enemy one more time.

Gods of Valo! Perin realised. *I'm not a king! I'm a gravedigger!* And suddenly he knew what to do. The waves of despair could hold off for now. Death was only a distraction. He knew what to do. There could be no fear, just thought and quick action.

"Magyr!" Perin yelled. "Buy me time!"

"What do you think I am doing?" the old prigon's voice retained some humour, despite his weariness. There was a crack to it that suggested fatal weakness drawing in. It meant nothing. Perin knew what to do. He nodded at Kesairl, who bravely returned the gesture and stamped to stand off, blocking the other way.

The two prigon and the four men were all that remained. Perin's whole world stood, hanging onto life and breath, halfway across the great bridge. Medrivar understood now. He would have to trust Perin.

"Forgos, Sudar. I'll need you to give me some seconds more."

They could not speak. They didn't need to. They stepped outwards at once. Perin reached out in both directions, his hands brushing Sudar and Forgos as they took position, desperate for a last connection with his friends, his brothers in arms. It was almost over.

He grabbed Neva in a fierce hug. "Listen to Medrivar!" He would have to trust the king to tell Neva what he, Perin, needed. Perin pressed his forehead against Neva's, hoping he would understand the images running through his mind.

Neva's blue eyes widened in realisation. He gripped Perin's arm.

"Can you do it?" Perin asked.

"Yes."

It was the third throne, Perin thought to himself as Neva translocated them off the bridge. The throne that nobody could sit on, holding and maintaining the balance of power, flowing in the bluevein throughout the Meddoszoru. The brightest point of blue in all the cavernous mountain.

It didn't just contain magic. If the two thrones were for *using* power, the third throne was for *creating* it.

The third throne served as the main source.

Perin and Neva appeared in the air, still embracing, a short distance above the inverted seat and far above the gaping black below. As gravity sucked Perin down, Neva let go and gasped out Perin's name. Perin reached out and grabbed for the throne as he fell. Neva fell past him, his magic spent, disappearing into the void.

Perin caught hold, letting Spade go, and clambered onto the upside-down base of the seat as if the bluevein were enervating him, holding onto the spindle of blue crystal that joined the throne to the bridge above. Battle raged on again above him, but he couldn't see who lived and who died. And it didn't matter.

He was not a king. He was a gravedigger. A gravedigger in the hill of the dead. With clarity, Perin could see Jesik Graves, could hear the oath he had sworn to his mentor.

"I'll *be a gravedigger forever, too, 'cos that's what you were."*

Gravediggers had one duty.

Bury the dead.

With the echo of some half-forgotten tune in his ears, Perin swung his short spade and smashed through the blue crystal that held the third throne in place.

It was more than just a blow struck with the strength of his arm. Perin put everything he had as a gravedigger, everything he had ever learned from Jesik, all the feelings he had ever had for the men he'd killed, the brothers he'd lost, into one command. One call on a magic that he *could* use, a sacred purpose that had led Medrivar to Erdhanger, to him.

Burial.

The Meddoszoru cracked from darkest root to highest crown. Bluevein shattered and rock split. The two thrones splintered. The mountain's stomach rolled, thundered. Thousands of tons of stone collapsed into the void.

Perin had a few seconds of falling into the dark before all the roofs came crashing down. A few seconds left to run images of his friends through his mind, sharing them with Medrivar, whispering goodbye.

Neva's face went last. Then the blackness around him became absolute.

THIRTY-NINE

PERIN WAS IMMEDIATELY aware of two things. One, he was still aware. Two, the blackness and weight around him had gone. He could see.

I am a spirit now—the thought came to him. *No, I always was. But my body is gone.*

He passed introspection over in favour of observation. The room around him seemed very familiar. For a moment, he couldn't place it. The roar and chaos of battle was still fading. The strain of having to fight, without hope or rescue, was fading, too. Then he saw.

It was the throne room, made large, made real. Not the one in the Meddoszoru. The one from his mind, the one that had belonged to Medrivar. There were windows, letting in light and air, polished wooden floors, cloth hangings. The small dais where Medrivar had often sat was there, but the throne was not.

"No, there are no seats of power here." The voice was real enough, loud enough, but somehow indistinct, as if Perin could not pin down the tone or timbre. He turned slowly.

The man standing in front of him was of ordinary height. His hair and eyes were of no particular colour. As he moved, Perin could see strange after-images of him left behind. His hands were held open in welcome.

"This is Medrivar's throne room," Perin blurted out.

"It is an audience chamber," the figure corrected him. "We wanted to give you an audience."

Perin tried to take note of facial features. It was impossible. Slowly, realisation dawned. He stared at the figure for some time before he said, "You're one of the gods."

"We're outside looking in." The man smiled. "You can call us whatever you like."

Nameless gods of Valo, Perin thought.

"We don't want to talk about us, Gravedigger."

Perin swallowed. "What do you want to talk about?"

"What you've done. What you've accomplished. The ending of Meddoszoru."

"It was a problem for you?"

"It was a contained problem. That's why it was sculpted. The Bright Dead gave us the means to hold back the Damned. Choice always provokes consequence. Without knowing it, the Bright Ones fought our battle for us. Keeping them all belowground, away from the true inheritors of Valo, now that was the trick. And keeping the ordinary spirits, the humans and the prigon out, that was harder."

"It didn't work."

"For thousands of years it did. Symmetry and balance are powerful forces. A long stalemate gave us time to plan."

"You planned it all? Medrivar finding me, everything that happened?"

"Don't be ridiculous." The man smiled kindly and sat down as a chair appeared for him. It was plain wood, unadorned. "We can't control your choices any more than we can control the choices of those such as Akrash Haal. But we can, to some extent, rely on them."

"Haal…is he like you?"

"Yes. Very good, by the way! He *is* like us *and* unlike us. On this or any level, choice makes of creatures what it will. Choice is power."

"We didn't have a choice! We were always going to die!" Perin felt angry for the loss of his body, angry for the loss of his friends. "Did we have to die because you wouldn't fight him?"

"You had to die because we could *not* fight him. He invaded your world. Unless we do the same, he is beyond us. But not beyond you."

"So now, what do you want?"

"We are on the outside looking in." The figure gestured, and one of the windows grew closer and larger. Perin could see a view through it, a view down a slope. Akrash Haal was there, slowing now, hands held parallel to the ground as if he was sensing what had happened in the Meddoszoru. "He is about to discover that there is no great power waiting for him here."

Perin watched Haal rage and stamp without much emotion. The fact that he was there at all suggested that the defence of Koban had fallen. What did it matter that Haal was inconvenienced?

"Would he have used the Dark Seat to spread his rule across Valo?" Perin asked for the sake of asking.

"That he could have done anyway. The Nation of Seven Cities is moving its armies as we speak. The Claimic troops are withdrawing from the frontier to meet the undead threat. The Westerners see an opening. Do you think the Seven Cities would be able to resist Akrash Haal's power?"

"No."

"No. If he wanted to rule Valo and depopulate it of all but corpses, he could. But Valo is not the territory he wants. It is not the battlefield he wants."

Perin stared. "You mean he wanted to come outside? Here?"

"It was here he came from. Before he and others chose to enter a world that had not been made for them. His mistake cost him centuries under the mountain you call Csus. Yes, he wants to fight us here. The Dark Seat could have allowed him to cross out, to come to us. He would have brought that mage body with him. That alone would have caused irreparable damage to this realm of existence."

"What do you want?" Perin repeated, staring at the image of Akrash Haal pacing up and down in indecision. "What can I do?"

"Your spirit was made for Valo. His was not. We want what he does, after a fashion—for he and others like him to rejoin us outside, where we can prove with our numbers and our power that he and the others should not have stolen from Valo.

"This body I show is an image for you to process, nothing more. If he brought a real body here, he would have a distinct advantage. Magic works here, too, though differently. We need him to be parted from that body. You helped unite him with it. It would be fitting that you separate him from it now."

"I'm dead." Perin pointed out the obvious flaw.

"You're not dead. 'Dead' only makes sense on the inside. Out here, you're as alive as you ever were. Your body, we admit, is dead. This is where, we confess, we are prepared to bend some rules." The nameless god grinned. "Your mass burial released enough power that we can afford to be very meddlesome indeed. We've had a good idea. We would like you and Medrivar to return to Valo. We'll give you bodies fit for the purpose. One each. Won't that be a luxury?"

Perin had only one question. It burned stronger even than his desire to destroy Akrash Haal, stronger than revenge. "Where are my friends?"

"Medrivar is here. One of us is explaining all this to him, even as we are to you. You can't see him at the moment because you don't need to."

"No, I asked, where are my friends? Apart from Medrivar?"

"Ah. Under the Meddoszoru. With your old body. Their spirits will cross out soon, but we don't need them for this."

"*I* need them!" Perin shouted. The nameless god looked taken aback. He raised his hands in an apology.

"We apologise for the insensitivity. But we really, really need you to destroy Akrash Haal's body, sending him to us weak and ready."

"If you're going to give me a new body, why not my friends too?"

The man looked thoughtful. "It's possible in time, we suppose. At the moment we're limited to two. You and Medrivar fit the purpose best. Look, you can claim reward after the deed is done, we promise. Make your demands then, not now."

Perin bit his lip. After the brink of death, after the end of hope, here was a chance to bargain for the lives of his friends. He nodded in agreement.

It was like a powerful translocation. Suddenly, Perin was cold. The snow around him steamed away and his body ached as if it had just suffered an impact. Even as he considered this, Perin felt the pain fade.

He was in a perfect copy of his old body, as far as he could tell. He wore some layers of linen, covered with a blue robe trimmed with gold. It was not clothing suited to the weather or to the environment or, for that matter, battle.

Medrivar was with him, climbing to his feet. The king was similarly clad, but Perin didn't notice. He had never stood beside the physical, regenerate Medrivar. The king's hair was thick and golden, his skin ruddy with health. "Majesty!" Perin managed.

"Not anymore." Medrivar grinned, looking at his own muscled arms and hands. "My kingship's over. As I understand it, I have one last thing to do. As a warrior."

"Together. We have one last thing to do together."

"Yes. Yes. It is good to see you! It is good to breathe!" He wasn't lying. Breath issued from between his lips like steam. Perin could see then that his companion's heart was beating.

"They've given you a living body!"

"It means I can die." Medrivar was almost weeping with happiness. "And I've forced a bargain on that account as well. But no matter. I'm not to die yet. Akrash Haal is about to be very surprised!"

Perin embraced the king briefly. "He's down the slope from here. But how are we supposed to hurt him? We aren't armed. I don't even have my spade!"

Medrivar smiled. "Then I think I am at an advantage here. The Nameless One told me how to fight." He extended an arm. Flexing his fingers, he closed his hand as if around the shaft of a spear. A spear appeared, as if his implicit command had called it into being. Medrivar whirled the spear around him once, then released it. It vanished the moment his hands let it drop.

"Different rules," Perin murmured.

"Different rules." Medrivar watched as Perin closed his own hand, trying to visualise his spade. For some reason, though, it was a Borderer's sword that appeared in his grip. Perin grinned foolishly, releasing and regrasping the weapon several times in quick succession.

"Medrivar...let's go avenge us."

Akrash Haal stared. The two coming down the slope seemed familiar somehow, though he was certain that he had never seen them before. They were walking towards him, easily, confidently. Unafraid. Something felt very, very wrong.

"*You* destroyed the Meddoszoru?" He stepped forward. He could see the pulsing of their lives from here. He had nothing to fear from two living men. But a doubt niggled in his chest. If they had destroyed the Meddoszoru...

"Yes," the younger one with dark hair replied. "That was us."

"Really, I think the honour was mostly yours," the golden-haired elder said to the youth.

"Well, you helped in your way." They appeared to be sharing some kind of joke.

It was very wrong. Now Akrash Haal recognised the boy's face.

"*Gravedigger!*" He extended a finger towards the boy. "No running this time!"

"No, no running," the boy replied easily. "I've got nowhere I need to be."

Haal stared. It was perplexing. Even the bravest he had faced had trembled, had had to force themselves not to buckle under the fear. This creature in front of him could not be the boy his stolen flesh remembered from the graveyard, after all.

"*You* cannot be *him*. You are *not* the Gravedigger..."

The boy shrugged. "Maybe I was in a past life." He closed his hand, and now it held a long, bright sword. Slowly, he raised his arm and levelled the blade straight at Haal.

The golden-haired man reached up and produced from nowhere a spear longer than he was. "I am Medrivar, King under the Meddoszoru! Or I was, before I breathed this air." There was an exultant glee in Medrivar's voice, as if victory was already assured. "Now I am alive. Trueborn. Akrash Haal, I pity you. You will be, and have always been, an invader in a land that is not yours."

"All lands will be mine!" Haal tried to brag. This was some ploy of his enemies that he had not expected. This was unfair. It was all very wrong.

Its wrongness stung him as the two men moved in on him, weapons raised. Haal continued to rage at the unfairness of it all when, by steel and the muscle and the power of his foes, his body was torn from him, piece by piece.

EPILOGUE

THE CLOUDS PASSED their shadows across the foothills, taking rain down to the valleys of Koban. In the West, men marched. Outside it all, Perin and Medrivar stood with the nameless god.

"Well done. Excellent. There is nowhere left for him to hide or hold now. The end of the Meddoszoru was the end of the power of undeath. He will cross over to us and be overwhelmed. Very well done." The god bowed deeply.

"We've not forgotten the requests you made, either of you. Medrivar, your desire was met by Perin's action in the mountain. The world was not made to sustain your Bright Dead, nor their enemies. Only the contrivance of the Meddoszoru gave them a means of continuing. They will cross to us as well. True death at last.

"Perin, you will see your friends again. Not all of them, I am afraid. Our power goes so far and no farther. Those that were killed when you brought the Meddoszoru down, you will see again. And I am going to give you something that you have not asked for.

"I am going to give you another life. We are on the outside looking in. You have been caught up in the Song after all. And you will get to sing it again."

Perin considered this. It was undeniable that he fiercely wanted to live as he had lived before. Dying had given him perspective. Death, true death, was a gift for the undead. But life was a gift he preferred. As much as he saw the purpose of ending, he could not esteem the purpose higher than what he had lost. Yet, before seizing the offer, he had a question that needed answering.

"What is the Song? Does it come from you, from here?"

The nameless god smiled. "Yes, from outside, looking in. We cannot force our will upon your world. We cannot play at controlling fate as men imagine.

The Song of Valo is a message, a guidance. It gives us access to those that know its tune and influence over them, and thus, a voice in Valo."

"So you did choose me. Us." Perin frowned. He wasn't sure how he felt now that it was confirmed.

The nameless god shrugged. "Yes, in a way. But don't concern yourself with songs and messages. The outside is not your burden; it is ours. Consider instead the gift we are offering you."

"I get to go back?"

"No. You get to go forward."

"What about Medrivar?" Perin asked, looking to his friend. The man who had once been a king smiled sadly, as if he knew already.

The nameless god answered solemnly. "Both of you will go into another room and sleep. Perin, you will wake up and go to some new work of your choosing, work that is needed. But not as a gravedigger. Not anymore. But Medrivar will not need to wake again."

"It is good." Medrivar breathed the sweet air of the audience chamber. "It is good. Don't fear for me, Perin. I've waited thousands of years for this."

Perin tried not to cry. It seemed foolish to shed tears, having died, having lost everything and everyone, having been brought back to life. It seemed foolish, but he could not keep the tears back.

The nameless god led them into a dry, light place resembling a cave. It had enough room for two stone beds, but was otherwise empty. "It looks harsh, but the years will fly by," the nameless god promised Perin.

Perin lay down. He found that he could reach across the gap and grasp Medrivar's hand. Already, sleep descended upon him in waves of comfort. The nameless god was gone.

Although there was plenty of light and air, Perin couldn't see any openings in the cave walls. It didn't matter. It wasn't real. Rooms within rooms.

"Don't grieve," Medrivar whispered. Sleep was beginning to claim him, too. "Don't mourn me for my sake, Perin. Dear one, you will see your friends again. But this is goodbye for us."

Perin nodded slowly. It was good. But yet...

"I don't want you to go." It wasn't a complaint. He didn't have the energy to explain that it wasn't a plea. It was just a fact. He did not want Medrivar to go away.

Somehow, Medrivar did understand. "Thank you, Perin."

And Perin slept.

Perin will return…

one thousand years later…

GLOSSARY AND PRONUNCIATION GUIDE

Pronunciation guide given where appropriate. Other words and names are spelled phonetically.

Claimfold—the human nation of Eastern Valo.

Claim—a jurisdictional region of the Claimfold, usually centred on a capital town.
Examples: Arpavale, Cserys, Hanger, Mezyro, Solorin, Temlan, Varo

Fold—a geographical area of the Claimfold and surrounding lands, often divided into Claims.
Examples: Csus, Helynvale, Joval, Koban, Narsun

Tacnimag—the council of human magi that rule the Claimfold.

Prigon—a powerfully built, intelligent non-human race. Horned and dark-hued, with a talent for magic. A nomadic people divided into family groupings, rotating through the Fold of Helynvale.
PRY-gon

Priga—the prigon language.

Drizen—a fierce, seemingly semi-intelligent non-human race, with partially hooved feet and facial tusks.

Torzsa—a prigon clan (plural: Torzsi) led by a single patriarch or matriarch who takes the name of the clan as their title.
Examples: Kelish, Abrun, Darmir
TORZ-sa

Torzsanag—a Priga term for an official gathering of the clans, a council of sorts.
TORZ-sa-nag

Kotuzska—an abundant mineral of Helynvale that undergoes a slow exothermic reaction in contact with water, releasing heat and light. Used as an alternative to firewood by the prigon people.
kot-UUZ-ka

Nagyevo—name of the capital city of the Claimfold and its surrounding Claim. Home to the Tacnimag Observatory.
NAG-ye-voh

Csus—the southeastern Fold centred around the great mountain of the same name.
cur-SOOS

Helynvale—the easternmost Fold of Valo, belonging to the prigon people.
HEL-in-vayl

Kigkarmzin and Kigzusta—'red serpent' and 'silver serpent', Neva's metalworked devices for storing magic energy, worn as adornments on his forearms.
kig-KARM-zin and kig-ZUU-stah

Meddoszoru—'hill of the dead'. The caverns beneath the mountain slopes north of Koban Fold.
med-dos-ZOR-oo

CHARACTER NAMES

Keresur—Tacnimag research mage. Distinguished by his red tattoos and his interest in the undead.
KE-res-EWR

Perin—teenaged gravedigger's apprentice.

Graves—gravedigger of Erdhanger in Csus, Perin's mentor.

Kesairl uto Abrun—prigon skirmisher, outcast from Torzsa Abrun, servant of Medrivar.
ker-SAIRL OO-toh AB-ruun

Medrivar—the spirit who leads the Bright Dead, wearing the reconstituted body of a long dead king.

Yana Hoer—runs Erdhanger butcher's shop with her husband.
YAH-na HOH-ur

Kelish—matriarch of the prigon clan of the same name.

Abrun—patriarch of the prigon clan of the same name, Kesairl's father.

Cama—custodial librarian of the Nagyevo City Library and a philosopher with an interest in the Western culture of the Nation of Seven Cities. Amateur cartographer (see map at beginning of book).
KAH-ma

Adamun — Lord Knight of Nagyevo, a primarily ceremonial position granted to high-ranking former military servants of the city.

Neva Yenesen — sixteen-year-old mage with unusual powers, in a junior position on the Tacnimag.
NAY-va YEN-is-in

Kard — officer in the Nagyevo Borderers, serving in Second South Response.

Törodè — leader of Second South Response.
tur-OH-day

Uno Sudar — laconic Borderer volunteer, nicknamed "The Quiet Spear" by Swordsman Kard.

Forgos — tall, shaven-headed Borderer volunteer, nicknamed "The Storm" by Swordsman Kard.

Gyorva Jolsen — slim, sardonic Borderer volunteer, nicknamed "The Mind" by Swordsman Kard.
GYOR-vah JOHL-sin

Harco Oksen — beefy, good-natured Borderer volunteer, nicknamed "Blond Warrior" by Swordsman Kard.
HAR-khoh OK-sin (kh sounds like ch in chutzpah)

Maka Nyacus — handsome, petulant Borderer volunteer, nicknamed "Twice Stubborn" by Swordsman Kard.
MAH-ka NY-a-kuus

Varostan — a mage at the head of the Tacnimag, titled "Master of the City".
VA-roh-stan

Tulbu — the mage in charge of the Observatory Guards.
TUUL-boo

Isdar — the mage in charge of investigating threats to the Tacnimag.
IZ-dah

Akrash Haal—the One and the Many. A powerful un-embodied spirit and leader of spirits.
AK-rash HARL

Darmir—patriarch of the prigon clan of the same name.

Kimr—patriarch of the prigon clan of the same name.
KIM-ur

Lyen— patriarch of the prigon clan of the same name.
LEE-en

Etzsar— matriarch of the prigon clan of the same name.
ETS-ar

Magyr uto Hegyr—elderly prigon battlemage from Torzsa Darmir.
MAG-eer OO-toh HEG-eer

Michael-Israel Jarvis is twenty-five and lives in Great Yarmouth in Norfolk, England. *Gravedigger* is his second novel, originally self-published in 2012, now republished through Booktrope Publishing.

He intends to live out his obsession for creating worlds and characters until he goes the way of Medrivar.

Michael-Israel got *Gravedigger* off the ground with early chapters written online at www.deviantArt.com. He is still committed to the deviantArt community, and grateful for the support of other writers and artists.

He is delighted to be part of the Booktrope family of authors, and looks forward to releasing many books in the years to come.

MORE GREAT READS FROM BOOKTROPE

Eyes of the Enemy **by Kelly Hess** (Young Adult Fantasy) In this magical fantasy adventure, twelve-year-old Beynn Firehand begins a quest into BlackMyst Forest to find help for his besieged village. He soon discovers his own magic abilities, but at what cost?

Forecast **by Elise Stephens** (Young Adult Fantasy) When teenager Calvin finds a portal that will grant him the power of prophecy, he must battle the legacies of the past and the shadows of the future to protect what is most important: his family.

A Kingdom's Possession **by Nicole Persun** (Young Adult Fantasy) A slave girl inhabited by a Goddess, loved by a Prince, hunted by a King. The beginning of an epic saga.

Magnus Opum **by Jonathan Gould** (Fantasy) Join Magnus Mandalora on an epic adventure of swords and baked goods.

Rise of the Flame **by K. N. Lee** (Fantasy) An introduction to six races, four realms, and one human girl who can bring them together in peace…or war.

Would you like to read more books like these?
Subscribe to **runawaygoodness.com**, get a free ebook for signing up, and never pay full price for an ebook again.

Lightning Source UK Ltd.
Milton Keynes UK
UKOW04f0420110116

266138UK00003B/75/P